THE PROMISE

The PROMISE

by Jim & Terri Kraus

TYNDALE HOUSE PUBLISHERS, INC. | WHEATON, ILLINOIS

Visit Tyndale's exciting Web site at www.tyndale.com

Designed by Justin Ahrens

Scripture quotations are taken from the *Holy Bible,* King James Version.

Library of Congress Cataloging-in-Publication Data

Kraus, Jim.
The promise : a novel / Jim &Terri Kraus.
p. cm. — (The circle of destiny ; 3)
ISBN 0-8423-1837-2
1. Women medical students—Fiction. 2. Women physicians—Fiction. I. Kraus, Terri, date. II. Title.
PS3561.R2876P76 2001
813′.54—dc21 00-047968

Printed in the United States of America

07 06 05 04 03 02 01
7 6 5 4 3 2 1

Prologue

Philadelphia
March 1841

Charles and Elizabeth Collins sat in the hard, almost brittle light of the drawing room. Neither had spoken for nearly an hour. Turning a page of his newspaper, Charles sniffed. The small sound filled the room. Elizabeth lowered her book and raised her eyebrows as if waiting for him to speak. He did not.

The tall clock in the entry chimed three times, the last note warbling off-key. From the kitchen beyond, Elizabeth heard the shuffling of Julia, their new parlor maid. It was teatime. Elizabeth set her book on her lap and smoothed her hand over the faded fabric of the settee, feeling the strained weaving, the pulls and snags. The wooden arm bore mute evidence of long years of service, its nicks and scratches marking time. What was once elegant had grown tired.

"All furniture looks shabby in the harsh daylight," Charles often remarked when he saw the pained look in his wife's eyes. "Even furniture in the best houses on Callowhill Square."

The front door opened, and the afternoon breeze poured into the foyer. The wind lifted several calling cards from the silver tray on the entry table there. The yellowed cards fluttered to the floor.

"Morgan? Is that you?" Elizabeth called out. "Please close the door. You've scattered the cards again."

"Please don't call me Morgan. It's Hannah. You promised."

A young woman entered the room, her blonde hair flustered from the breeze, her dark green eyes shimmering. She had several cards in her hand.

"Why, these folks haven't been here in years," she said as she examined the names. "Why are we keeping their cards?"

"I promised you no such thing," her mother replied, ignoring her question. "The name Morgan was good enough for your grandmother and great-grandmother. I see no reason to change things now. How would it look? What would people say if we suddenly began to call you by another name? Ridiculous, that's what. Or worse–faddish. I will call you Morgan as I have always done."

Hannah turned and rolled her eyes, remaining silent. She slumped into a worn leather chair.

The door to the kitchen opened, and a nervous Julia backed into the room. The cups and saucers on her silver tray chinked softly. The servant's eyes darted about. She looked down to the table by the settee, her eyes wide with question.

"Yes, Julia," Elizabeth snapped, "set it there . . . just like you've done before."

Hannah made no attempt to hide her scowl. "Mother, she's only been here two months. What do you expect?"

A large chip on the teapot caught Elizabeth's eye. Resting against the spout was a letter.

"It's for you, miss," Julia whispered. "I hope I didn't spill no tea on it."

Hannah grabbed the cream-colored envelope, tore it open, read it quickly, then leaped to her feet, startling everyone.

"They said yes!" Hannah cried. "They said yes. Harvard said yes!"

Her father sniffed again, louder this time, and lowered his paper, folding it precisely. "Tuition comes from your trust fund, you know." His words had a cold edge. "We don't have the resources to waste on such a frivolous activity."

His wife lifted her chin in defense. "Maybe she will meet a nice young man . . . from a good family. That would make her foolishness more palatable."

Hannah clasped the letter to her breast, looking so happy. Her mother frowned as if Hannah might, at any moment, spin about the room in joyful abandon.

But she did not move, save to offer the fading light her glorious, radiant smile.

Chapter One

From the Diary of Morgan Hannah Collins

New York City

September 1842

I have made so many promises to my mother that I scarce can recall them all. As I readied to leave for Harvard this fall, it was as if she had no recollection that this term will mark my second year at the university.

I wanted to announce on occasion, "Please, I am not a child, Mother."

But, of course, I did not. I simply sat upon my bed and nodded at the right moments as she opined about one thing after another, offering a string of recommendations, adding one suggestion after another. I know she means well, but I am a young woman now, and I am capable of making my way in this world on my own.

As I write these words I am sitting at a small table outside an ice cream parlor across the street from the train station in New York. Contrary to the previous hot spell, it is a delightful afternoon–almost crisp, and yet sunny. I was unable to book a direct rail trip so was forced to disembark in New York. I will have to wait for nearly two hours for a separate train headed for Boston.

Travel can be such a headache.

I would rather have stayed on board the train, but I could not, for it immediately departed back to Philadelphia.

So I am out and alone. I trust it is only my imagination, but I do feel that I am on public display–being a single woman and all. I imagine the passersby are sniffing that a woman without an escort is not proper and somehow uncivilized.

My mother expressed the very sentiment. She greatly disfavors the public advances pushed by certain women in recent years. In fact, once when shopping in Philadelphia, she issued yet another opinion on the sorry state of the modern woman.

"I do not understand what the world is becoming. Look there," she whispered, "but do not be obvious. That woman there. She should never be out in public by herself."

I noted a young woman a few years older than myself across the street. I actually think I knew her slightly, but I did not admit that to Mother.

"There she is," Mother continued, "walking down the street unescorted, with seeming nary a care in the world. Why, in my day, a woman alone like that . . . well, any passerby would be likely to think of her as one of 'those' women."

Dear Diary, I could not help myself on this one occasion. I turned to her, my face awash of innocence, and asked, "Mother, whatever do you mean . . . one of 'those' women? I am afraid I do not understand."

I thought I was being amusing–and it is much like the banter I and my friends engage in back at Harvard. And seriously, that woman had as much right to be on the sidewalk during the day as did any man.

But Philadelphia is not to be confused with the Harvard campus. And my mother does not have any slightest leaning to a more liberal inclination–as do many of my friends at Harvard.

My mother stopped abruptly, and her face tightened, wrinkles splashing at her eyes. "You know perfectly well what I mean, young lady, and I do not enjoy being sparred with–especially in that tone of voice."

"But, Mother," I protested, "I only meant . . ."

"Not another word. I will not be treated as one of your bohemian Harvard acquaintances. The very fact that a Collins woman is in Cambridge alone is enough to make me shudder. I will not have my daughter sink to their level of crude witticisms."

It was an old battle we two fought. That day I decided discretion was the better part of valor. I retreated, offering her an apology–and a promise never to let my noble sensibilities be sullied by my less-than-savory "acquaintances."

She accepted my promise with a gracious smile, yet I am sure her heart was not as forgiving.

I vowed again and again that day to preserve the peace between my mother and myself. I wonder at times like these, how such promises are viewed by God. After all, I knew full well that it was one destined to be broken.

And broken often.

New York City
September 1842

Morgan Hannah Collins, of the Philadelphia Collinses, dabbed daintily at her mouth with her napkin. She folded it, placed it on the table, and rose from her seat. After placing her diary inside her purse, she walked slowly to the train station. The large clock above the station's entrance sounded two chimes. Hannah, as she preferred to be called, did not hurry. Her Boston-bound train would not depart for another thirty minutes.

Hannah had no desire to miss this connection. The next train did not depart for hours and that entailed arriving in Boston after dark. Hannah considered herself a modern woman, to be sure, but she maintained her common sense.

Hannah swept through the station. She stared ahead as she walked, her eyes focused on her destination.

It was not that Hannah was a beauty, as beauty was oft described. Her eyes were not quite luminescent. Her lips were not truly voluptuous. Her cheekbones were not naturally highlighted. Although her long hair flowed down past her shoulders, ending in a soft turn, her frame and figure were not as rounded and full as might be considered ideal.

But if a master artist were to view her, dispassionately as any artist could be, he would come to the conclusion that Hannah possessed not a single feature that needed to be altered. As any artist knows, there is a point in any painting where to add one more brush stroke ruins the work. And Hannah's Creator had stopped at the perfect moment.

Each feature, if not just yet perfect, was only a breath away from perfection–and in its imperfection, her features together attained a higher degree of perfection than perfection itself. The sum of Hannah's parts far outweighed each individual component.

And what made her imperfection even more alluring was that she possessed only a fleeting awareness of her beauty. Frankly, talk of beauty and attractiveness bored Hannah, for it was her intellect and wit that she considered her most important element. However, she admitted freely that they were not traditionally sought-after female attributes.

When she arrived at the fourth coach on the Boston train, the young conductor held the door open for her, extending her his hand. She placed her gloved hand into his, stepped up into the carriage, and offered him a "thank you." He blushed.

She settled her pale green dress about her on the cracked leather seat. As the train started with a jolt, Hannah placed her hand on the armrest to steady herself. She was alone in the tiny compartment and, for a moment, wished she had someone to talk to during the long ride to Boston.

Cambridge, Massachusetts

Hannah was tempted to open the window, but the smoke and cinders from the engine colored the air and would sprinkle her garments with soot. She drew the shade, since watching scenery through the rippling glass often made her queasy. The train's movement was too severe to read, so she closed her eyes and let her thoughts run.

And after a moment, she smiled.

It was hard not to allow the pleasant memories of her first year at Harvard to fill her thoughts. And when they did, a smile followed.

Her initial battles with her parents were all but forgotten. They, of course, disapproved of her intentions. Harvard had only recently allowed women to attend, and those who did were not members of America's earliest and best families. They tended more to be the daughters of the newly rich and the adventurers. Hannah never admitted it to her parents, but it was these women with whom she most identified.

Hannah's parents did not.

But it was Hannah's trust fund, provided by her grandmother and written in such a manner that only she, and not her parents, had control. Those funds provided her the means. So attending Harvard truly was Hannah's own decision–much to her parents' chagrin.

She recalled the delicious whirl of new experiences that had begun the instant she stepped on Harvard's campus. It seemed impossible a full year had passed. When Hannah closed her eyes it felt as if only yesterday she had deposited her bags at the home of her aunt and uncle, Daniel and Constance Granger. Daniel was an importer of threads and fabrics. Constance was a brittle woman who passed her time with stitchery and church activities. The two were not really an aunt and uncle by blood, and Hannah's father always claimed they were only shirttail relatives, looking to improve their social standing. Because their two daughters were grown, married, and distant, their upstairs bedroom now lay empty.

Since the Granger house was only a short walk from the main square at Harvard, they had offered, a bit begrudgingly, accommodations to Hannah. "Better here," Constance had written, "than in some squalid and notorious house near campus."

It seemed as if no time had passed since Hannah first hurried to the campus, seeking out the administration building, to register for her classes.

She may have received curious stares that first day on campus. Women were not that common at Harvard or any institution of higher learning. But Hannah was used to stares and scarcely noticed any heads that turned as she walked past. After signing up for her first semester's classes–*A Compendium of Western History, English Literature,* and *Public Oratory*–she strolled among the brick and ivy-covered buildings, savoring every minute of freedom and challenge.

To Hannah, Harvard could be no more a magical place than it was that first day. The beginning tintings of fall tweaked at the sugar maples lining the streets. On the lush lawns students milled about, laughing, forming into earnest groups. Here and there a student sat under a tree with an open book propped between his knees, devouring the pages of words. Clouds pocked at the brilliant blue sky. From somewhere across campus a rumor of coffee scented the air. There was a tweedy scent waft of tobacco and a muskier scent of parchment. Engulfed by those sensations, Hannah had vowed never to become immune to their enchantment.

For hours she had roamed about, finding delights at every turn. She passed several coffee shops, a popular gathering-place called the Destiny Café, and even a storefront theatrical troupe. That week's offering was an abbreviated version of *Hamlet.* At the bookstore across from the administration building, she purchased her required texts and indulged herself by buying the September issue of *Graham's Lady's and Gentleman's Magazine* and a copy of a novel she'd been anxious to read, *The Deerslayer,* set in the frontier. She reluctantly returned to her aunt and uncle's home. At every corner she turned back, making sure the campus was not simply a wondrous illusion but a real place of mortar and bricks and slate.

Her aunt had been waiting for her by the door, a routine that would be repeated many times that first year.

"Morgan, where have you been? You have been gone for hours on end. We were so worried."

Seeing the obvious anxiety on her aunt's face, Hannah glanced over the woman's shoulder. She spied her uncle sitting in a proper chair, holding a newspaper at a proper angle and not looking up at her entrance.

"Oh, Aunt Constance," she exclaimed, hoping to control her excitement. *After all,* she thought to herself, *the Collinses are not ones who puff and gasp at the slightest whim.* "I've just been exploring. The campus is bigger than I thought. And since classes begin next week, I did not want to get lost my first day."

She looked down at the bundle of books she cradled in her arms. "And I have purchased my books as well."

As if noticing an uninvited furry creature, her aunt stepped back. "And you carried them home yourself? You could not have them delivered?"

Hannah smiled.

"And did you pay cash for these? You carried that much money on your person? You did not sign for them, did you? That practice is usury, and I am sure you know what the Scriptures say about usury."

Hannah was not sure what the Scriptures said about usury and, in fact, was not sure what the word meant, but she felt it wise to nod in agreement.

Her uncle never looked up from his paper, except to offer an affirming grunt at the word *usury.*

Classes and lectures that first semester had surprised Hannah. Not for their difficulty, but their ease. Hannah had often thought herself a clever woman but could never voice that assumption in public–at least not in the circle of her mother's hearing. Until now Hannah had seldom encountered any intellectual competition. The private schools she had attended never truly stressed knowledge and, more importantly, its application.

Hannah realized that women were not required to be clever. In fact, cleverness was seen as detrimental to some–at least when it came to the most desirable of female attributes.

But Hannah was clever. She excelled in her work. Some classes, such as her history class, to be specific, Hannah found to be of an excruciatingly boring nature–endless dates and names and places offered for memorization alone with no attempt at incorporating them into a larger, cohesive scenario. Hannah, who was quite good at recalling things, dutifully memorized them all and achieved a very good grade.

Public oratory was another matter. A student must not only find an idea worth researching but one worth defending and explaining in public. One after another, students stood in front of their peers and offered their speeches. Some were smooth and polished as if they had been bred to the art. Others, like Hannah, faced it with fear and trembling. But with a great deal of practice, she forced herself to appear glib and free of all stuttering nervousness.

On a lark, in her second semester, Hannah enrolled in a chemistry class.

"Are you certain you are in the right room, miss?" the professor asked as Hannah took a seat in the front row.

"If this is *Fundamentals of Chemistry,* then I am in the right location."

A baffled look appeared on the professor's face. "But, miss . . . ," he stammered, "you are what appears to be a . . . well, a woman."

A nervous, near-silent giggle fluttered throughout the room.

Hannah waited a full moment before responding. "Why, yes, I am." She actually batted her eyelashes at the professor.

In response, Professor Dallins took two steps back until he collided with the blackboard. "And this is chemistry," he continued, more flustered, "with charts and equations and experiments."

Hannah, at a loss for a cogent, polite reply, finally said, "Yes? I did read the course description." It was all she could muster.

The professor looked up. The rest of the class, all men, strained to hear this odd conversation. Professor Dallins scanned the rest of the class for some sort of support.

What he saw was a sea of blank, surprised faces. He gulped, then shrugged. "Well, then . . . Miss . . ."

"Collins. Miss Morgan Hannah Collins."

"Miss Collins, welcome to the class. If there is anything about which you need a special explanation, please see me after class. I do not wish to waste the time of any of the rest of the class on remedial lecturing to someone who is taking this course on a lark."

Hannah offered him a blistering smile in return.

And from that day forward, she was better prepared than any male student, often staying up all night to read the several books discussed in class.

She finished with the second highest grade–and the admiration of every other student.

At the midpoint of Hannah's first year, one conversation stood out in her mind. Hannah happened to be at the library. She was not really studying, but she had not wanted to return to her aunt and uncle's home just yet. So she leisurely thumbed through a text on Greece and studied the handsome engravings of the temples and palaces.

From behind she heard a rustling. Then Florence Galeswhite dropped an armful of books on the table opposite Hannah. Collapsing into a chair, Florence whispered, "I am befuddled."

Hannah smiled. The two shared an English class, and Florence struggled to keep up.

"About what?" Hannah asked.

"About everything. The final examinations are next week, and you're not even bothering with pretense."

"Pretense?"

"I know you don't have to study. But think about the less fortunate–like me. I find myself on very thin ice–and at any second, I may be plunged into the icy reality of failure. And here you are, calmly reading like nothing is happening."

"But I have kept up during the semester. I have reviewed some. There is no need to cram weeks' worth of learning into a few days' worth of work."

Florence dropped her head into her hands. "And she revels in her abilities–in front of me," she moaned.

Hannah giggled softly. Florence had a grand sense of the dramatic.

After busying herself sorting books and shuffling papers, Florence looked up and sighed.

Hannah leaned forward.

"Florence," she quietly whispered, "if this is such torture, why do you stay? Didn't you say that your father is a wealthy man? Couldn't you return home?"

Florence looked down for a long moment. "No. He had no sons–so I must pay the price for his lack of suitable heirs. He is wealthy and a self-made man, and he demands that those around him stay on pace with his work and thoughts. I suspect I could go home and find some nice boy to marry–but he would be so disappointed. He wants so much of me."

Hannah gazed into her eyes. "Has he ever said that to you directly? After all, despite what we hear around school, marriage is still a noble institution."

"No, he has never said as much to me. I'm sure I will marry someday. But first I am destined to graduate from here–come what may. I will make him proud of me. He has never asked, but I have made a promise to myself that I will do as he desires."

Hannah nodded, thinking wistfully, *How delightful if my parents truly wanted me to be here–and supported my desires!*

"And why are you here, Miss Collins?" Florence asked. "You could have your pick of men. Rich, handsome, privileged. Why are you here?"

Hannah listened to the question and could not think of a quick response.

Truly . . . why am I here? To my parents, I know it is an opportunity to find a rich young man. That would be fulfilling my promise. And if rich enough, then the Collins fortunes could be reversed. That is why they think I am here. But what of me? To prove my intellect a match for any other? To become wise? To find employment as a teacher . . . or nurse?

"Hannah," Florence's voice broke in, "are you still there?"

Hannah blinked her eyes.

"Well?"

"Well what?" Hannah asked.

Florence pursed her lips. "I asked why you are here. And you never answered."

Hannah blinked again. "I'm here . . . well, I'm here because I want to be here. That's why."

Hannah had never assumed there could be a greater epiphany in life than her initial decision to attend Harvard. Once that decision was made, her future would simply follow from that point, and all she would need to do is stay above water and watch for hidden rocks.

But her direction changed the last week of her first year.

She had taken lunch at the Destiny Café with another female student, Miss Margaret Ehrler of Stockbridge. Miss Ehrler was studying to be a linguist and already spoke several languages. They had been joined by a handful of acquaintances, all happy the term was nearing an end.

The talk was on summer travel and rest and relaxation from studying and thinking.

"Hannah, what will you do this summer? Head to Europe? I'm told London is the place to be."

Hannah smiled and shook her head. "No. I will be at home this summer. We may spend a time at my aunt's house in Cape May, but I will be home mostly, working on next year's studies."

Charles Spadon moaned. "Do not remind me of next year already. I was enjoying so much the prospect of this brief respite."

"And where will you head this summer?" Hannah asked him.

Charles moaned again as if he could not become much more despondent. "Nowhere. I am having only a week's break in New York with my family. Then it is back to Harvard."

"Back here? Why on earth would you return here?"

"My father says that if I want to enter their medical college, I must have additional studies in chemistry and anatomy. He has arranged for a tutor who will work with me all of July and August."

"A tragedy, Charles," came a reply.

"You should go to Philadelphia. Hannah could tutor you," responded another.

Then came a chorus of laughs and snickers. It was obvious Charles would greatly appreciate the chance to be close to Hannah.

Hannah's smile dazzled the young men around the table.

"Why not have Hannah simply take the same classes as you next year, Charles? Then you could copy from her. It worked this year, didn't it?"

Several students giggled in response, as if admitting there was a great deal of truth to the statement.

"Hannah? A doctor?" replied Charles. "Have you forgotten that she is a woman?"

Even to an outsider, it was clear Hannah bristled. "And I could not become a doctor, Charles? Are you saying I lack the cleverness to do so?" Her mouth was tight, and her eyes controlled.

Charles squirmed. "No . . . I mean that . . . well, you know."

"I do not know," came the icy reply. Everyone around the table watched in silent glee as Charles began to fidget and redden. "I should hope you will enlighten me."

"It is just that . . . well, I mean . . . a woman? As a doctor?" Charles sputtered. "How could that be? A woman could examine a man as to his illness? Poke and prod at the flesh of a stranger? And while that's a huge obstacle, I think no man would allow a woman to do what even a man might consider distasteful. And what of others? Think of what other people might say."

Hannah turned to Robert Lewis, a chemistry classmate. She placed her finger under his chin and turned his face to hers. She let her finger linger a heartbeat longer than necessary.

"I have a question that you must answer truthfully. Robert, will you promise to do it? On your honor as a gentleman and a Harvard man?"

Robert gulped, reddened, and nodded. A bead of sweat formed on his forehead.

"For argument's sake," Hannah said cooly, "let's envision both Charles and myself in Harvard's medical school. We both take all the proper courses. We both study on our own–much like we did in chemistry class this year. And let's just say we both graduate with degrees that allow us to become physicians."

Hannah glanced about. She had everyone's rapt attention.

"Are you understanding me, Robert?"

He nodded again, then licked his lips.

"And let us say that Charles and I have offices across the street from one another. And you, Robert, have grown ill–you've come down with a strange and exotic malady. It will require the greatest skill and knowledge that a doctor might possess to cure. If the doctor is wrong, you will die. If the doctor is skilled, you will be cured. But there is little margin of error."

Hannah again surveyed the crowd. She was enjoying herself.

"Which doctor will you visit? Me? Or Dr. Charles–both of whom you have seen in action in chemistry class. On which will you stake your life?"

Panic swept across Robert's face. He looked first to Charles, then to the anxious group surrounding them, then to Hannah. He lowered his eyes and dropped his head.

"You promised to be truthful," Hannah reminded. "Which of us would you see?"

Robert mumbled a few words.

"No one heard you, Robert. What did you say?"

Head now up, he avoided Charles' eyes, instead staring only at Hannah. "I would visit you, Hannah," he said softly, then he turned to Charles. "I'm sorry, Charles, but I saw how lost you were in chemistry. You nearly blew yourself up on that one occasion. Hannah is smart. She is really smart."

The crowd hooted and laughed.

Hannah smiled and folded her arms across her chest. "I rest my case."

And ever since that moment, the idea of actually doing what she jested about–becoming a doctor–had scarce left her thoughts. She admitted her desires to virtually no one, but she began to consider what she must do and planned out her second-year courses with that goal in mind.

Hannah could tell the train was nearing Boston without even looking up. The speed of the car slowed as they entered the congested city. The tracks groaned and cried louder here, as if the tightness of the buildings next to the tracks amplified the sounds.

She glanced up. Perhaps no more than twenty minutes remained until they arrived at the Boston station.

She smoothed the pages of her diary. A letter from her mother slipped out. It was dated a few days prior.

Hannah winced, wondering if her mother had read through her diary entries. She prayed that she had not. And her mother had acted cordial and friendly, as if nothing were out of the norm.

As the train rocked over an intersection, Hannah slit the envelope and slipped the letter out. Her mother's handwriting was like a dense thicket of words on the single sheet. Hannah brought the paper closer to her eyes.

From a Letter from Elizabeth Collins

Dear Morgan,

I could tell her a thousand times that I prefer Hannah now, but she does not listen, Hannah thought. *Oh well, I suppose there are worse things a mother could do.* She continued reading. . . .

I am writing this prior to your leaving us again. Father would have written but claims to be fatigued from his recent travels to Camden.

I shall not bore you with a cacophony of advice and suggestions–for if I do, I am sure you will dismiss them all as the ranting of a very old-fashioned and out-of-date woman.

I do not care to be dismissed, so I have only a few bits of advice. I pray that you will not only read them, but act on them as well. You know that your father and I want nothing but the best for you. You are our promise. And a promise always holds a golden future.

My dear daughter, please avoid all appearances of evil–or ribaldry. I note with trepidation that the young men of Harvard are versed in foolishness and downright hooliganism at times. We have allowed you to attend the university over our best instincts. Therefore, you must promise never to sully the Collins name and reputation. A woman's reputation–once damaged and bent–can never be repaired. Think of the future in every occasion and never let your reputation suffer for the promise of a transitory pleasure.

You must once again promise us this.

Hannah grew very nervous–perhaps her mother had indeed read her diary and was making a veiled reference to it now. She continued to read on.

While your father and I recognize your class evaluations and grades as befitting our family, I must caution you not to stand out by being too smart. Young men of today do not want a smart woman as a wife–they want a woman who will be accommodating and suit their purposes and goals.

You do have an obligation to this family, Morgan. You have your trust fund, which has provided a cushion against harsh reality. I am afraid your father and I do not have such a cushion.

I have passed your name and address along to a young man of the best family–Mr. Robert Keyes. He is in Boston training to take over his father's business. It has something to do with insuring the indebtedness of firms and stocks and such. (It is a jumble of financial matters that I know little of.)

The boy's aunt speaks highly of his morals and his future. He is a young man with great promise, she says, great promise indeed.

And he is, in her words, "so handsome it would make your teeth ache."

I cannot believe my mother would write or repeat something so . . . so passionate as that, Hannah thought, amazed, as she finished reading the letter.

Your life has a promise–a promise by the very nature of your last name. You must do your utmost to deliver on that promise–both for your sake as well as ours.

Regards,
Mother

Now, Hannah was certain her mother had not read a single word of the private pages. There were a few entries that reported on the scandalous behavior of her friends–behavior that verged on being both immoral and illegal. She was certain her mother would have fallen into apoplexy had she actually read the stories.

Hannah refolded the letter and slipped the envelope back into her diary. Without realizing it, she began to wonder how she and Robert Keyes would first meet.

Chapter Two

Cambridge, Massachusetts
September 1842

"HANNAH! Wait!"

Hannah turned to the voice and watched with amusement. Robert Lewis bounded across the yard, his tie flapping as he jumped over a picket fence, his hair scattering in all directions–much like a sheepdog at a full run.

She hid her smile as Robert reached her side, panting and adjusting his coat, and attempting to corral his hair with his free hand.

"You're back!" he gasped out.

She nodded. "And you are surprised? Why is that?"

His mouth opened and closed, but no words came. Hannah knew his face would color red in another second. It did.

"Well," he finally stammered, "I mean . . . a woman and all . . . and Harvard . . . and well . . . I just thought that perhaps . . ."

Hannah touched his wrist. "Robert, I will be at this school until I receive my diploma. I assure you that I am no dilettante." Her voice was soft and reassuring, as if speaking to a frightened child.

"I meant to say . . . that I am glad to see you again. I missed you over the summer," Robert said nervously.

"And you are sweet, Robert. Thank you. I missed being here as well."

A pained look nicked at Robert's face. He gulped and continued. "Are you going to class now? Do you have time for a short refreshment? There is a new restaurant on E Street. Some say it will provide the Destiny some well-needed competition."

"Well, Robert, it is sweet of you to ask. But if the clock on the tower is still accurate, then I have scant minutes until I need to be present in Medill Hall."

Robert turned his head. "Medill Hall . . . but that's the building for the study of medicine."

"Indeed."

"But . . . but . . ."

"Robert, walk with me. I cannot loiter here another minute."

It was clear Robert would have done nearly anything to stay at Hannah's side, so he immediately agreed.

"Would you like me to carry your textbooks?"

Hannah allowed a laugh. "Again, Robert, you are sweet, but I am fairly certain that my abilities extend to carrying a single book."

They walked in silence. A few students offered greetings as they passed. Both Hannah and Robert were no longer freshmen and no longer the butt of practical jokes and older classmates' ridicule. Although Hannah had never felt the sting of such good-natured cruelty, Robert had, and repeatedly.

"So you had an enjoyable summer, Robert?" Hannah asked as they strolled under the green canopy of trees.

"I did. I worked for my uncle."

"And who is your uncle?"

"Thomas Hart Benton. The senator. You know. From Missouri."

Hannah had never made an effort to keep up with politics, but she nodded as if she knew who he was.

"In his Washington office. I was his aide. Well . . . I was one of his aides."

"That sounds exciting."

Robert smiled. "It was. Perhaps I could . . . I mean . . . perhaps I could tell you about it . . . at dinner perhaps?"

Hannah turned to face Robert. He nearly tripped, attempting to stop.

"Dinner? That is sweet of you to ask. Perhaps we can do that. Soon. But this week is an absolute panic–with all my new classes. And next week shall no doubt prove as vexing. But ask me after that. Please do. I would like to hear all about your experiences." She patted him lightly on the wrist again. "I truly would."

Hannah spun about and hurried toward the entrance of Medill Hall, knowing that Robert stared after her, hoping she had not bruised his heart too badly, and yet somehow expecting that she had.

Her first class on the pathology of infectious diseases was not nearly as confusing or incomprehensible as she had feared. In fact, the textbook that was suggested was the same book she had read during the summer break in preparation for her studies.

She again endured the not-so-casual stares of nearly every other student–all males, of course. The professor, to his credit, merely called out her name.

"Morgan Collins," he barked.

"Present," she replied, making no effort to alter her clearly feminine voice.

The professor looked up and squinted. "You're a woman then, are you?" he asked, an English burr in his accent.

"I am."

He grunted in return. "Are you one of those sensitive flowers?"

Hannah was not sure at all what he meant but answered, "No, sir, I do not believe I am."

"Not prone to wilting, then. And you're not here on a dare?"

"No, sir. I'm here of my own volition."

"You know this is the study of diseases."

"Yes, sir."

"You won't turn ill? Pathology can be quite explicit."

"I won't."

He stared another moment, then continued down the list of new students.

Once that was accomplished, Professor Wilkins began a lecture, without touching a single note or referring to any paper, reciting from memory hundreds of diseases and conditions and briefly hinting at their symptoms. His list was done alphabetically. He began with "Abiosis–the state of being dead." As his hour in front of the class grew near to close, he took a deep breath and said, "Xeroderma–a condition of the skin in which it becomes hard, scaly, and dry."

He stopped, peered at the class, and then frowned at Hannah. Most of the rest of the students had stopped their futile note taking somewhere in the *B*s. Hannah attempted to keep up the entire class and succeeded for the most part.

"Miss Collins?"

She jumped in her seat.

"You have written down everything I said?"

"Well, sir, not everything. As much as I could."

Taking two slow steps, he hovered in front of her desk and glared at her stack of papers. Then he looked up and glowered hard at the rest of the class. "You gave up. She didn't." He walked back to his desk, muttering "a woman this time." He finished his lecture by saying, "You will be a very good doctor, Miss Collins. Tenacity will be rewarded. Class dismissed."

The table was empty, and for that Hannah was most grateful. Her last class had ended, and rather than return to her aunt and uncle's home, she most often sought out the musty silence of the library. She had her favorite table, at the northwest corner of the second floor, just under a window, tucked away by itself.

"But why don't you come home after class?" Aunt Constance flustered at her one day when Hannah found her way back only a short while before darkness settled on the town.

"I need to use the books in the library," Hannah explained, "and there are times when I need to seek the advice of a classmate."

Aunt Constance ruffled about, as though she believed Hannah's rationale was sound, though not very courteous.

If the truth be known, Hannah thought to herself, *I do not learn well with my aunt hovering about me, asking a hundred questions, appearing nervous with every flip of a page.*

The library was a much better location, and she had come to assume that one particular table as her own. She set her books and purse down and withdrew a pale envelope. Correspondence from her mother was unmistakable. She used the same sort of tinted envelope that Hannah remembered seeing as a child. The tight handwriting was always identical. Even the sealing wax was forever the same color.

She lifted the flap and extracted the letter. She scanned the first page–highlights of the best of Philadelphia society–a recap of parties and galas and the like. Hannah seldom paused over this news. Her parents attended few, if any, of these affairs, and her mother reported on them using secondhand sources–though her words gave the appearance of a firsthand knowledge. Invitations–at least the "right" invitations–came infrequently.

Hannah knew only the barest minimum of her family's fall from grace. Such topics were simply not broached. It had to do with a loss of money, for sure, but what else caused the tumble was a mystery.

And Hannah truly did not care. The few debutante affairs she had attended were dreadfully contrived and boring events, she thought. Hannah felt no loss in the lack of invitations.

Without ever mentioning it, and without ever offering a word of discussion, Hannah knew that her parents, especially her mother, assumed that one day the Collins family would retake its rightful position among the elite of Philadelphia.

And Hannah knew, with just as much certainty, that much of that expectation was now resting on her shoulders.

That was another reason not to dwell on the first page of her mother's letters.

Hannah skimmed over the news. . . .

another fine affair at the Legermans' this Tuesday past . . . a string quartet and a vocalist from Sweden, of all places . . . their daughter never looked lovelier . . .

She quickly turned the page.

A name midway down caught her eye—as if she had been accustomed to scanning documents for names the length and sound of Robert Keyes.

I have received correspondence from the mother of Robert Keyes. Apparently his father has been ill. Her sister, with whom I had a lovely luncheon recently, passed on your name to her. I am sure she described your obvious charms. Robert's mother wrote to me—a most elegant letter on exquisite stationery—if it would not be impudent of her son to seek you out in Cambridge, seeing as how he is residing just over the Charles River in Boston. Your Aunt and Uncle Granger have a fleeting acquaintance with the Keyes family—some shared membership in a trade association, I believe. Robert's mother asked if he might accompany you to a series of lectures at the First Congregational Church in Boston. I wrote back on your behalf stating your delight with such an arrangement. Dear Morgan, I know that we are not Congregationalists, but she assured me that these are lectures not on a spiritual plane but are presented by a fascinating man whose name now escapes me. Please accept his invitation with the Collins grace.

I trust that all is well in Cambridge.

Regards,

Mother

Hannah sat back and stared at the name again.

At least now I know how we will meet, she thought and found herself smiling.

The soft hushing grew in volume until Hannah was forced to lower the letter and look for the source of the noise. From behind a tall case of leather-bound volumes, Florence Galeswhite literally burst into the second-floor study area.

She spun about and unceremoniously dropped to the chair opposite Hannah.

"Honestly!" she exhaled loudly. "These corridors need to be larger or I need to ignore fashion and do away with all these petticoats."

Hannah smiled.

"Of course I know what you will say, Miss Collins. You do not have to berate me again for attempting to be stylish. A woman like you has no problems in attracting suitable young men. Women like me, on the other hand, have to work at the endeavor with more fervor."

"Nonsense," Hannah laughed. "You are a most attractive woman. I am sure that you are misrepresenting the truth."

"Me?" Florence asked with a feigned sense of outrage. "Misrepresent the truth?"

Holding back another, louder laugh, Hannah said, "Admit it–you simply enjoy shopping and buying."

Her hand to her throat, Florence held the pose for a moment, then collapsed. "You're right. I have been found out. But to be honest, I do not think any man I have met in Harvard knows the difference in the fashions of this year versus last. Men are simply baser animals and do not consider the finer things in life as necessary."

Hannah chuckled. "Then it is a good thing for me, for I am several years behind the current wave in fashion."

Florence was about to comment but appeared as if she could not devise an appropriate remark, either humorous or sympathetic.

"No need to be solicitous, Florence. I am certain that fashions would not interest me all that much, even if the extra funds were available." Hannah hoped her words rang true.

Florence leaned in close, as if she expected a dozen fellow students to eavesdrop on their conversation. "You will never guess who spoke to me today. Well, more than that, actually. He asked me to attend the upcoming violin recital with him," Florence whispered.

Hannah shook her head no. Florence spent a great deal of her time imagining various assignations with some of Harvard's best and brightest.

"A handsome lad, I must say," Florence added.

"Who?" Hannah asked.

"His father is a senator. Or is that his uncle? Or is it his cousin? Well, someone is a senator."

"Robert Lewis?" Hannah asked.

"You guessed," Florence said, a bit crestfallen.

Hannah did not hide her surprise. "Robert Lewis? He invited you?"

"And that is such a big surprise? You did say I was an attractive woman, remember? And you know Robert?" Florence asked, her eyes narrowed.

"Some. He is in a class or two of mine. Or was last year."

Hannah remained silent, and Florence tilted her head suspiciously.

"You're not waiting for him to find you, are you, Hannah? Don't tell me I won one of your beaux."

Hannah hurried her reply. "Of course not. I am just surprised. He seems like such a shy fellow, that's all."

As Hannah returned to her book, she wondered why part of her was a little hurt. The names *Robert Lewis* and *Robert Keyes* kept popping into her thoughts and mixing. The interludes were both disrupting and disconcerting.

From the Diary of Morgan Hannah Collins

OCTOBER 1842

I think I have just met the man I might deem to marry someday.

True to everyone's family honor and obeying all the rules and arcane regulations of society, Robert Keyes has entered my life. He sent a note to my aunt and uncle, both asking permission to call on me, as well as explaining the circumstances as to how he found my name and address. It must have been quite some note–I did not see it–for my aunt was in a state of nervous, near-giggling agitation until the day of his arrival.

Had my uncle been less parsimonious, I think dear Aunt

Constance would have purchased a new frock for me to wear. As it was, I made do with last year's model. I chose a rather severe and prim outfit, done in dark brown damask with velvet trim, knowing that such attire was less prone to being out of style than others.

Mr. Keyes was prompt, with a hired carriage waiting at the curb. He tapped at the door, and the first thing Aunt Constance saw upon opening it was a profusion of flowers. Such extravagance at this time in the season, I thought, though I am sure my dear aunt was ready to marry me off at that moment.

Introductions were made all around, and my uncle and Mr. Keyes exchanged pleasantries and discussed the state of business in the parlor while I saw to a few final details of my attire.

Dear Diary, it was so vastly amusing. I was adding a last-minute pin to my hair, which I wore more up than down that night. I hadn't intended on using the jewelry, but something about that young man nearly demanded the inclusion. Aunt Constance continued to flit about offering advice and consultation as to what my role in the evening might be. I have never seen her so animated and light. It was as if she were being escorted out, not me.

I descended the stairs from my room, my aunt only a step or two behind, and Robert was waiting for me at the door. Perhaps it was the light from the lantern in the hall or the candles on the half table in the entry, but Mr. Keyes is one wickedly handsome man with dark hair, a bold chin, and dark, liquid eyes. His lips were thinner than some but still attractive.

I am not sure I could recreate any specifics of the evening, save to recall it was a most marvelous time. The lecture was interesting–some fellow going on about a noble experiment just north of Boston where people will live communally and share all they have. I could tell Mr. Keyes was not enjoying it at all. Under his breath he would make comments. Some I heard; some I did not.

I found myself too busy catching sidelong glimpses of him to pay attention to much of the presentation.

After the lecture, we had supper at Anthony's, a wonderful,

intimate establishment overlooking the harbor. I think I had cod in a wine sauce. I think he had a lobster.

He talked about his profession on the carriage ride home. Like my mother's description, it has something to do with finance. I simply did not pay attention, focusing instead on the sound of his voice.

And when he bid me farewell that night, he offered his hand to me and wished me well. He did not try to become "more familiar" as I have heard Harvard men often do–even so early into a relationship.

But I held on to his hand for a very long time, almost hoping he would.

What is it about that man that affected me so?

And will he call on me again?

November 1842

"Gage, you are on time. How dear of you," Hannah said as she greeted him at the door.

"Are you inferring that I am a tardy fellow?" Gage said, his hand at his chest.

Hannah took his arm and headed to the carriage stand. "Not in the least. But I did tell you my appointment was an hour earlier than it is. And now we're on time."

Gage laughed–evidently both at Hannah's deviousness and her accurate assessment of his punctuality.

Gage Davis, the son of a wealthy New York financier, had somehow been "encouraged" to accompany Hannah to the annual review of her trust fund. Hannah imagined that her mother wrote to Gage's mother–they had met several times over the years–and Mrs. Collins parlayed those meetings into this current favor. Thus, Gage found himself joining Miss Collins on her trip to Boston for her financial meeting with her Uncle Winthrop, the administrator of the fund set up by Hannah's dour and successful grandmother.

Hannah liked the brash and energetic young man. They had met on occasion at the Destiny Café. One evening Gage had bemoaned the fact that his father was pressuring him to leave Harvard to tend to the family business–and Hannah had shared that she, too, had little support from her parents for her academic endeavors. From that evening, the two got along as kindred spirits, sharing meals on occasion or a late-evening stroll about campus.

Hannah often wondered why her mother did not mention Gage as a possible suitor. He was devilishly handsome and on his way to becoming very wealthy. Yet it was rumored–and most of such information was always shrouded in innuendo and gossip–that Gage's father was no more than a few decades removed from the vile longshoremen and stevedores in New York's Hell's Kitchen.

If that was true–and Hannah assumed it was–Gage had the money, but not the breeding, to be paired with a proper Collins woman.

And besides, Hannah thought, *he has never expressed the tiniest romantic interest in me. That would have something to do with it as well.*

"We'll take a private carriage into Boston, if that is favorable to you, Hannah," Gage said. "Taking one of those horrid Rockaway wagons, packed with old men and potatoes, is not how I want to spend the next hour."

"Gage, you are remarkably insensitive," Hannah said, pretending to be shocked. She was sure he was jesting.

"But it's true, is it not?"

She stopped and turned to him. "And what makes you think the old men and potatoes are willing to ride with *you?"*

Gage's stern exterior cracked, and he began to laugh. "You can see through people faster than anyone I have ever met, Hannah," he said. "Other people take me for a lunatic much longer."

"So a Rockaway would be fine?" Hannah asked.

Gage stopped a moment. "Good heavens, no. I do have limits, after all."

Hannah pushed at him playfully. "Oh, Gage."

"Hannah, please forgive my foolishness. There's a chill in the air, and the Rockaways are drafty. We'll make it a private carriage. It will be my treat. And you know I do not take refusals well."

She smiled. "Very well–a private carriage it shall be. But, Gage, I have a problem."

Gage's look reflected concern.

"What do I do with my bag of potatoes?"

He laughed loudly and long. For the next two blocks Hannah described her uncle and what she thought occurred every year at these reviews. Gage listened intently until they turned the corner at Ellis and Fountain Streets.

Gage brightened and called out, waving to a young man down the street, "Ahoy, there, Joshua, my fine man. What brings you out today?"

The young man turned to face the pair.

"Hannah, I would like to introduce you to my roommate–of a sort–Joshua Quittner from Shawnee, Ohio. He's acting as my guardian angel this year."

From the Diary of Morgan Hannah Collins

November 1842

I could hardly wait until I had a chance to put down the thoughts that raced through my mind this day. And even though tomorrow is Sunday and I need to be at church early, I must record the details of the past hours.

Gage met me–on time. It was only through my trickery that ensured it. He escorted me to Boston and the financial review of my trust. Gage was masterful in handling Uncle Winthrop. I am sure that even my mother dislikes that man–and perhaps with good reason. Gage was so sweet and smart–he listened for hours as to the facts and figures Uncle Winthrop presented, then sprang at him like a graceful, yet hungry tiger on a rabbit.

It appears as though an accounting irregularity had been occurring–for some years now–having to do with how funds and interest are posted to the trust fund. It seems the bank held the funds longer than required, and thus I lost interest over time. Gage calculated that

I was owed more than five thousand dollars, plus an increase in my yearly draw. And sputtering, Uncle Winthrop agreed.

Five thousand dollars! That is a king's ransom to me.

I will have more than enough for tuition, books, supplies, and even a new frock or two for each season–and still have a nest egg upon graduation. Gage is a miracle worker. I do not think I can thank him enough.

And if that was not excitement enough for the day, Gage, in a most casual and loose manner, introduced me to his "roommate." They do not share a room, but this young man, Joshua Quittner, has rented a tiny space in the house that Gage has occupied since last year.

Joshua, a rough young man from Ohio, stopped my breath in my lungs. I did not let on to Gage or to Joshua as to how I viewed him. As a modern woman, I have an obligation to dispel old-fashioned views on the flightiness of a woman's sensibilities, but land sakes, the boy was enough to make a weaker woman swoon. I am serious. A cascade of blond hair with a streak of red wisped in just the right way, giving an open invitation to smooth it back into place. He possesses the most remarkable broad shoulders, deep gray-green eyes, a mouth and chin that caught my stare, and hands that appear both gentle and strong at the same time.

Goodness, I am becoming flushed as I write. I must stop and catch my breath.

I will continue this story tomorrow–after church. Perhaps my racing heart will have slowed by then.

And I have an entire evening to report.

Cambridge, Massachusetts
November 1842

The congregation rose in unison. Hannah and her aunt and uncle sat in their normal pew, third back from the front, east side, out of the sun, and not really in direct view of the pastor.

Hannah enjoyed church most Sundays. It reminded her of her church in Philadelphia. But this Sunday her thoughts were elsewhere. She often sought out, in her copy of the Scriptures, the passages preached upon that day. However, today she had been content to simply hold the closed Bible in her lap.

"You seemed preoccupied," Aunt Constance remarked as they made their way down the side aisle after the service.

"Hmm, well, no, I don't think I was," Hannah replied.

The trio stopped for a moment as Uncle Daniel buttonholed Mr. Pickerson, jabbing piously at his chest, his words clipped and sharp, commenting vigorously on the church's proposed budget.

Aunt Constance whispered to Hannah, "They do this every year–argue about this item or that in the budget. They act as if it's their own money at stake–and very little of it is."

Hannah did not reply but stared quickly at her uncle, then back to her aunt. She had never heard Aunt Constance speak so candidly and so disparagingly about anyone.

"And all that money for the repair of the parsonage! In my day, the preacher would do his own repairs. These new preachers–none of them want to get their hands dirty with a little hard work," Mr. Pickerson hissed.

"And I heard that he asked for a pump to be installed in his kitchen. I don't see why a poor man of God should live better than me," Daniel Granger replied.

Hannah leaned away from the discussion. Pastor Phelps was a nice man, but he was neither young by any stretch of the imagination nor handy or skilled enough to handle any manner of repair. She did not understand why her uncle and others begrudged him and his family any comfort, much less a small luxury, at all.

Finally Aunt Constance took her husband's arm. "We must go now, dear. If you would like, invite Mr. Pickerson to dinner. You can continue your discussion there."

Both men took a step away from the other.

Mr. Pickerson sputtered and mumbled a few words that sounded much like a negative response to the secondhand invitation.

"He couldn't possibly come today, Constance. Could you, Pickerson?"

Mr. Pickerson shot back, "Too busy, too many obligations."

Aunt Constance smiled sweetly. "Some other day then."

As they reached the wooden sidewalk, Uncle Daniel turned to his wife. "Why on earth did you invite Pickerson to dinner? I was horrified he might actually accept. He's a crass old windbag."

She waited a minute, then replied, "But you two are always in a fuss about the church. I thought it would be a good way to settle things."

Uncle Daniel grumbled, "Do not attempt to invite him again, ever," and led the three of them toward their home.

As they ate dinner in silence Hannah wondered why the message of Christian brotherhood and acceptance only lasted as long as the echo of the final word of the pastor's message. Hannah considered herself to be perhaps not the most pious or obedient follower of God, but a proper one, with the acceptable amounts of deference, humility, and sinlessness.

Her family had attended the same church in Philadelphia for over a hundred years–the Collins family had unofficial claim to the fourth pew back on the north side. They approached church with a quiet nobility. Other than offering the pastor the traditional "wonderful sermon" at the end of the service, they rarely discussed their faith or anything spiritual. Hannah simply assumed that faith had been passed down to her from the long line of devout and faithful Collins families that graced God's church for so many years.

And she wondered how any man might be so driven to give up so much to serve God.

From the Diary of Morgan Hannah Collins
November 1842

I have returned to my diary. It is late Sunday evening, and Aunt and Uncle have retired early. I hear the rhythmic snoring of Uncle

Daniel. He can be a sweet man at times, but he is also so vexing, intolerant, and actually unchristian at others.

This afternoon, as the lights faded and the cold wind picked up, rattling branches against my window, I gathered in the chair by the window, drew a quilt about me, and stared out as the day ended.

The lantern's light flickers as the drafts pick through the room here, and I have taken this diary on my knees and the ink from the table beside me.

I suspect our conversations of last night piqued my thinking on many subjects.

Gage and I, after our meeting with Uncle Winthrop, returned to the Destiny for a light supper. We were met there by Joshua Quittner, who appeared to have been waiting for us for hours. And who else might appear but Jamison Pike, whom I met last year through Gage. (My defender, Gage, has a great habit of picking up friends like stray dogs–and, as a result, is well acquainted with so many interesting people.) I do not think I have mentioned Jamison before–because, I imagine, his cynicism and world-weariness so greatly perturb me. When we first met, I took an immediate dislike to his attitude–so unlike my own. Over the months, I have ameliorated that emotion somewhat. (And dare I say it–he is nearly the match for both Gage and Joshua in appearance. There is something smoldering behind his dark eyes that I am sure drives some women to distraction.)

Anyhow, the four of us talked late into the evening, much later than has ever been my custom. I knew that I would face the sternest of disapproving looks from Aunt Constance–and I knew she would remain awake for my return–but I could not leave the group early.

Our conversation soared and flowed, like we had been friends forever. This was what I sought out the university for–and it has richly rewarded me.

Not that I agreed with all or even the majority of what was discussed–but to be part of a give-and-take of ideas and great thoughts. I felt more alive that night than I have ever felt before.

The most interesting bit of our night together came near the end.

The Destiny was nearly empty, and we sat in a quiet pool of lantern light at a nicked table in the corner by the door.

I am not sure who asked, but someone sought out Gage's plan for his life–what he would do after Harvard.

Of course, Gage answered that he would seek out his fortune and fame.

Jamison stared at him and responded by saying fortune is no destination, for the end is always moving further away.

Even though I find Jamison disagreeable, I silently congratulated him on a most soul-nipping response.

Jamison said he was after travel, grand adventures, and perhaps even romance–he wanted to see the world while there were mysteries still left to explore. I rolled my eyes in response–and he looked hurt. Odd–I did not think the man capable of being hurt by a mere woman.

And our sweet, innocent, and alluring Joshua? He claims he will be a preacher in some backwater Ohio town. My first thought is, his talents will be wasted. But his words were so earnest that I believe we all envied his inner dedication and resolve.

I do take comfort in the fact that many Harvard men have aspirations–and many more will change them a dozen times in a dozen months. So Joshua may not wind up in Ohio. I would greatly enjoy getting to know him better–even if he is destined to be a man of God.

When the question came to me, I, for the first time, voiced my desire to become a doctor. Of course, they were all incredulous–claiming that no man would deign to be attended by a physician of the female species.

That may be true, and their reluctance to see it as a real dream encourages and inspires me all the more to see the dream to its conclusion. To see the looks on their faces when I am handed my diploma may be payment enough. I even mentioned Oberlin College, though I am not certain why. I think I have heard talk of its liberal leanings–they actually allowed a Negro boy to attend. If any college might offer medical training to women, it would be them.

As I spoke I watched Gage stare at me, as if he knew a Collins woman would never do what I claim to want. It was as if he said to me that I need to find a wealthy young man, marry him, have children, and settle down as a matron of society.

Does he not understand I am beyond that? Is he not aware I am a modern woman?

And sweet Joshua simply stared at me. How delicious was that, Dear Diary.

And he is to become a man of God? Well . . . we shall see, won't we?

Chapter Three

En route to Philadelphia
December 1842

HAD Hannah been able to choose, she would not have opted to return home at Christmas. She would have preferred to remain on campus and walk the empty, quiet streets and paths of Harvard. She would have preferred to spend the cold days in the library sitting and reading at the table by the fireplace. She would have preferred the splendid isolation of her aunt and uncle's home–who would be traveling this holiday season.

But she knew her desires would remain unfulfilled.

"Christmas is a time when we shall be together," her mother wrote in November, "and you shall spend your two-week holiday with us. We have several obligations to fulfill. There are many people who wish to see you, and I will not have them disappointed."

Hannah sighed as she read the stern note. She had hinted in a previous letter that she might find the winter break well suited to private, undirected study and reflection. And yet, even as she penned the words to paper, she realized there would be no way, short of a life-threatening illness, that she could avoid a return to Philadelphia.

So she packed a large, worn canvas bag, took a Rockaway carriage into Boston, and then, without smiling, boarded a train bound for Philadelphia.

As she stepped aboard and found an empty seat in the second-class car, the first flakes of winter began to swirl outside. The snow gradually increased in amount and velocity as the train headed south. Now, more than an hour outside of Boston, the wind began to rattle at the glass, and a biting draft clutched at her ankles.

A private salon on the train would be warmer, she groused to herself. *But if my parents saw me descend from such, I would not hear the end of the matter for days.*

Hannah pulled her feet up onto the seat and tucked a blanket around them and her legs, bundling the coat around her tighter. She did not like the looks of the blanket supplied by the railroad. Its previous users had not taken great care in keeping spills from the cloth–but Hannah could not ignore the cold. Stains she could simply choose not to see.

Even though my dear mother would argue that we of the Collins line are born and bred to the manor, she would not have me waste my trust funds on such an extravagance as a private compartment. And in addition, my parents no longer have the largess to afford a private compartment–even if they had desired it.

The snow clattered against the pane, and the wind and speed of the train set up a howling duet.

I wonder if Uncle Winthrop ever told my mother about the extra monies due me since Gage discovered the accounting error? I wonder if she knows. She has never said or written a word, Hannah thought as she turned away from the frozen scene outside the train and peered around the car.

Two seats in front of her sat a young man in a very fashionable suit and topcoat. He cupped his hands and blew into them, then caught her looking and grinned. Hannah smiled in return.

I have no business smiling at strange men, she chided herself, *but he appears to be respectable–and is quite well attired. And this is a public conveyance. What disastrous fate could befall me here?*

The young man touched the brim of his hat and nodded. He rummaged about a bit, as if gathering up possessions.

He's going to stand and come here. I know it. Why did I smile back? Hannah thought in a panic.

And after a moment, he did stand, reached down to the seat back to steady his steps, and made his way back to where Hannah sat. "Miss," he said, then seemed to grasp for words, "I . . . I . . . I saw you sitting alone. I know it is most presumptuous of me to ask, but is this seat taken?" He indicated the seat in front of her.

"No, I do not believe it is," Hannah said demurely.

The young man grinned and turned the seat back over so that he sat facing her and the rear of the train.

"Riding backwards never bothered me much," he said as he swept the seat of crumbs and dust. "Besides, with this snowstorm one really can't tell which direction we're headed, now, can one?"

Hannah examined the thick whiteness outside. "It does seem fierce."

The young man offered his hand. "I am Cyrus Field. Cyrus West Field, to be exact."

Hannah extended her hand, and he took it with a vigorous shake. "Hannah Collins. Morgan Hannah Collins, to be exact."

Cyrus laughed as she mimicked his introduction. He leaned forward. "The Philadelphia Collinses? Is your father Rance Collins?"

"No, I'm afraid not. But I know of the gentleman. Why do you ask?"

"He's one of the men I hope to meet on my trip. Are you sure you're not a relative? It might help open doors, and I look for all the open doors I can."

"No, I truly do not think we're kin. My mother claims he is a distant relative of some type, but we've never been able to make the connection. He owns some sort of foundry or wheel shop, doesn't he?"

"Just the largest foundry and ironworks in Pennsylvania! I hear tell he's growing all the time."

Forgetting the chill in the railcar for a minute, Hannah studied the young man. She liked his brash energy, even though he ignored all the proper rules of etiquette regarding introductions. Hannah knew that a young man did not simply introduce himself.

Mr. Field began a long, detailed monologue of how he had arrived late at the station, hurrying in from north of the city. Hannah nodded at the most appropriate moments, hoping she appeared to be listening.

"And is your final destination Philadelphia as well?" he asked. "I'll be in town for a fortnight. I might need to call on someone to ask of the best places to eat and stay."

Hannah blinked. Often she could control her first words, taming them to be proper and civil. Often she heard the voice of her mother before she spoke, admonishing her to be polite. Often she saw her mother's stern visage and was compelled to be prim and proper. But not on this cold day. She could not stop herself and blurted out, "If you're looking for the best, Mr. Field, then why travel in a second-class car?"

He looked confused. "Because, Miss Collins, those paying more for this journey arrive at their destination only a second before I do. I see no need to pay double for so little advantage."

"But aren't the private cars warmer? Less drafty?"

He shrugged. "Perhaps. But then you're stuck with whoever is sharing your cabin. Here there are a dozen people with whom I might speak. Why, if I foolishly purchased a private cabin, I would never have made your acquaintance. And that would be a sad thing, indeed."

Hannah tried not to blush. If her cheeks did redden, she hoped he would think it was the cold, not his forwardness, that caused the coloration.

"Yes, Mr. Field, Philadelphia is my final destination. My family home is there. My parents wanted me to return for the Christmas holiday."

"And so you work outside of Philadelphia?"

She smiled. "Not exactly. I am attending Harvard."

"Harvard? Why, that's grand! And you're studying some type of education? I did not realize that a woman had to attend a university to teach."

A frostiness not due to the car's interior came over Hannah. She imagined she saw a fleeting glimpse of her mother again, with a disapproving look, but ignored the entreaty to be ladylike.

"No, Mr. Field, I am not going to be a schoolmarm." Hannah's tone became icy.

Like an animal caught in a trap, Mr. Field began to squirm. He knew immediately he had committed a blunder. "I did not mean . . . I mean that . . . most women I know don't attend . . ."

She waved off his explanations with a curt hand gesture. "I am studying to be a physician." It was the first time she had ever voiced her dream in public and to a stranger. Inside, deep in her heart, she felt a flicker of great warmth. There was something inside her, she realized, that took no kindness with slights, whether real or imagined. And when the slight was cast upon her abilities, she rose up fiercely to defend her right.

Mr. Field sat up with a surprised look on his face–as if he had suddenly encountered a bear in a dark woods. "A physician? As in medical physician? A doctor? A medical doctor?" He grasped at the words, and they flew from him like leaves in a breeze.

"Are there other kinds?" Hannah asked evenly.

"No, I suppose not." There was a note of desperation in his words. "And they allow women to become physicians at Harvard now?"

She narrowed her eyes at him. "Allow women?"

"I mean . . ."

The trap had closed about his leg, and his fate was sealed.

"I know what you mean, Mr. Field. I deal with it every time I walk into a formerly all-male classroom. A man makes presumptions on what I can do and cannot do. I dislike being judged prior to ever proving myself. And what is it about a man's fragile view of the proper workings of the world? I do not understand why every male in America is so flummoxed and paralyzed with consternation over the fact that a woman might know something of the workings of the human body. All humans inhabit a body, the same as the ones inhabited by me and you, Mr. Field."

It was Mr. Field's turn to blush.

Hannah drew her lips tightly together and mentally crossed her arms. She waited while Mr. Field squirmed beneath her glare. Then, slowly, she let the tension escape from her jaw. Attempting a shallow smile, she said calmly, "Mr. Field, since you have been bold enough to ask of my career, what of yours? Why do you come to our fair city?"

He took a breath to compose himself. "I am in communications, Miss Collins. I am working on ways to vastly improve the manner in which we transmit information. And soon, if all goes as planned, I hope to be the man who links our continent with Europe–and the rest of the world."

"As with the telegraph?"

"You have heard of it?"

Hannah stared hard. "I am a woman, not a simpleton."

Mr. Field leaned back as if wounded again. "I just meant that . . ."

Hannah ignored him. Now she wished she *had* spent the extra money on the private compartment.

"And because you are a man, no one thinks it strange that you have dreams and goals and aspirations."

"No," he answered nervously, "that is not how things are."

"It is indeed, Mr. Field. If not, why would you think it odd that a woman has decided to become a physician? Why do men always look upon me as an oddity to be scrutinized?"

He held up his hands in surrender. "Miss Collins, I do not know why that might be. Perhaps we are simply squeamish about such things. But I pride myself on one skill–and that is being a good judge of character. I have known you for no more than an hour. And I think I can safely say that if you choose to become a doctor, then I imagine there will be no one to dissuade you."

Hannah kept her opinion to herself, but this time she did fold her hands across her chest. Mr. Field tried his best to appear composed and comfortable, though Hannah was certain he was neither. After several moments of stressed silence, he reached for his pocketwatch. "Well, then, it's two past."

Hannah decided he needed no reply.

"I think I'll walk down to the dining car." He rose, straightened his tie, and adjusted his scarf. "Would you care to join me, Miss Collins? A hot drink might be the ticket."

She waited before replying, "No, thank you, Mr. Field. I am sure my parents will expect me to have an appetite for dinner when we arrive."

"Well, then," Mr. Field said, "it has been nice to make your acquaintance. Best of luck with your medical studies. Perhaps we shall run into each other again."

"Perhaps," she said in a frosty tone.

She watched him as he walked back toward the end of the car and thought, *He is in a hurry to leave, that much I can tell from his quick steps.*

She stared off into space for a long time, then tightened the blanket about her feet again. Now that the flush of the discussion had faded, she felt the chill again.

Why is it that I always wind up sparring with gentlemen? I am not an unreasonable woman, am I? I simply want an education–and yet every time I mention that fact, men seem to stare as if I had sprouted a horn in the middle of my forehead. Are all men such puritanical, rigid thinkers? So far the only man who did not think me odd for wanting to be a doctor was Jamison–and he is one man who otherwise drives me to distraction. He said he had written about women like Elizabeth Stanton and Lucretia Mott, who are fighting for the rights of women. But he also warned me about the impenetrable walls that exist for women in medicine. It seemed he didn't want me to be disappointed if I couldn't fight my way through to become a doctor.

With her gloved hand she scraped away the heavy coating of frost on the window until she had cleared a small square. Peering out, she saw that the snow had tapered off to flakes, yet the gray sky looked cold and biting.

Hannah squinted. Up ahead she could see the faint silhouette of the bridge that spanned the river between New Jersey and Philadelphia. She would soon be home.

Philadelphia

"Has Robert Keyes called upon you again?"

A forkful of goose was nearing Hannah's mouth as her mother sweetly asked the question. Hannah had anticipated hearing it for the past week, and yet her mother had waited until now.

Hannah did not hesitate but filled her mouth with the food. She nodded as she slowly chewed the dry, stringy meat very well, giving her time to compose just the right reply.

"He has," she said and watched her mother's face brighten. Even her father, who had said scarcely more than ten words this day, smiled and turned to his daughter. Hannah took a sip of the weak Christmas wassail–a Collins tradition for more than a century, her mother claimed.

"And? He called upon you again? I would think it proper if you told us more. After all, I am not in Cambridge to monitor and supervise your comings and goings. A mother has a right to know of her daughter's gentlemen callers."

"I was about to tell you more," Hannah said, a curt edge to her words. Closing her eyes briefly, she added, "Since his first visit, I have been in contact with him twice more–once with a note he sent, and once when he accompanied me to a church recital."

Elizabeth Collins lit up like the flame of dried leaves. "He wrote–and came to see you again? Why on earth did you not send me a letter regarding this?"

Hannah had been most excited about his short note–a charming one-page letter that outlined his day and ended with a query as to the properness of his calling on her again. And after his second visit to Cambridge, Hannah had spent the rest of the week lost in pleasant reveries. He had spent only a few hours with her on a Sunday evening, attending a presentation by a less-than-professional string ensemble at the Harvard Club. He had been a perfect gentleman all evening, witty and solicitous, and Hannah was sad when he left early. He had made no advances but did take her hand in his when he bid her good-bye that evening.

But now, back in Philadelphia, in her parents' drafty old house, sitting in front of an overcooked goose, Hannah felt curiously reluctant to share any of those memories with her mother.

"Well?" Elizabeth Collins asked again.

Hannah tried not to wince at the shrill tone. "He asked if he could call. I wrote back and said he could. He accompanied me to a recital at the club. He talked of his family and business. It was a very nice evening."

"A nice evening? It sounds as if it were much more than that. It sounds as if he plans on calling upon you again."

Mother, how could you know something like that? I made no inference that he would call again. "Perhaps he will," Hannah finally replied. "I think he had a pleasant time."

Elizabeth was too well bred to throw her napkin down, but she clearly wanted to. Instead she folded it neatly and laid it by her plate, filled with half-eaten portions. "Honestly, Morgan . . ."

"Hannah."

"Well, then, Hannah, I am glad Mr. Keyes called on you again." She nodded toward Hannah's father, Charles. "Your father and I are very pleased. We, of course, would not want you to do anything untoward to encourage this fine young man, but I think a personal note every few weeks would mean a lot to him. After all, he is living on his own now, and I imagine that at times must grow lonely. A note from a friend would be greatly appreciated."

Hannah sighed and slumped a bit in her chair. "I will, Mother," she said, resigned to the fact that on the morrow she would write to him. If her mother suggested it, there would be little peace in the house until the task was done. "I will write to him at my earliest opportunity."

Elizabeth Collins smiled more sweetly and expansively than she had for Hannah's entire visit. "That would be grand, dear. Perhaps after dinner there might be time to compose a few lines."

Hannah sighed again. "Perhaps, Mother. Perhaps there will be."

Cambridge, Massachusetts
January 1843

A pile of books nearly obscured Hannah from view. The demands of school, only a few weeks into '43, were causing Hannah to redouble her work habits. It was not a pressure from the university or professors, but from within her own being. Hannah felt the need to be better than any other student in her classes. She did not always reach that goal–Harvard attracted some of the best and brightest minds in all of the Americas. But she always came close to the top–and always she bested the standings of the scattering of other female students.

There was some pride in those accomplishments, but it didn't distract Hannah from her goals.

She was buried in a thick tome on bodily functions, trying to decipher how certain internal organs worked in conjunction with one another. Some of it was clear and obvious. The stomach took in food, and that food fed the body. Other organs hidden away, tucked in behind, had much less clearly defined roles. Most textbooks only guessed at their function. Some could be removed with no ill harm to the patient. Others, once removed, would be a death knell.

From somewhere beyond the stack of books, she felt the stare of another. It was not obvious, nor blatant, but she felt observed . . . carefully observed. She glanced up, straightening in her chair.

That's odd. I don't see anyone. . . .

She went back to her book. After a few moments, the back of her neck prickled. She looked up again. From the corner of her eye, she caught a rustling glimpse of brown, nearly hidden by a large case of books on Greece.

She stared at the spot. *I need to study . . . and I don't need these distractions.* "All right, then. Who is it? If you're going to scrutinize me, then why not come out in the open and do it?"

Hannah waited impatiently. "Come on now. I know you're there." *Or am I just being too suspicious?*

"All right, you have me in your sights. I suspect I would be a dead man if you had a weapon." Jamison Pike shuffled into the open, holding an armful of books and papers. He walked to within five feet of the table where Hannah sat.

"You were spying on me?" she demanded.

"*Spying* is an ugly word. Let's just say I was–observing." Jamison was never at a loss for words.

"Observing? Isn't that just a nice word for spying?" Hannah asked.

Jamison came closer. "Oh no, Miss Collins, not in the least. Let me explain. Let us say that an ornithologist–someone who watches birds, if you will–is observing a rare bird in a rare setting. He watches to see how it behaves and what it might do next. Is he spying? I think not. The rare bird is simply cause for careful observation. And that, Miss Collins, is what I was doing."

Hannah was not sure whether to laugh or scold. "And you consider me a rare bird, Mr. Pike?"

"In this setting–in the narrow confines of Harvard, yes, indeed."

"How so?"

"You are a woman in Harvard. That alone is rare. And you have a sharp wit and intellect. That is rarer still. You have seemingly no fear of the male species. A rarer species yet. Verging on mythological proportions, I must say."

Hannah tried to show her annoyance but could not help smiling instead.

"And . . ." Jamison's voice faded to a whisper.

"And what, Mr. Pike? What else about me is birdlike?"

Jamison transferred his books to his left arm, then pushed his hair back from his forehead. "You are a most pleasing-looking species. To also be so beautiful is a rare trait."

Hannah turned her head. To hear that from Jamison Pike, the

cynical journalist, was so surprising that she felt her hand rise to her mouth.

At that moment, Jamison appeared to come to his cynical sense. His cheeks reddened, and he clutched his books. "And I . . . I have a class," he stammered, then turned and paced away in an instant.

Hannah watched as he hastened away. Her hand fell back to the desk. Her heart quickened, and a flush came to her cheeks. She leaned back, trying to make some sense of the encounter and her unexpected response.

Jamison Pike? But I don't even like him. She shook her head to clear her thoughts. *Am I just a giddy schoolgirl? Is that all I am?*

February 1843

"Florence, honestly, I don't have time for this. It's cold, and I have so much work to do."

Florence stomped her feet, her boots covered with snow. Miniature puddles formed on the wooden floor.

"Hannah, you're coming with me. It will only take an hour of your life."

Hannah stood in the front hall of her aunt and uncle's home. Florence Galeswhite, as unexpected as a visitor could be, had tapped at the door on the snowy winter evening. At first Aunt Constance was reluctant to allow her entry until Florence actually explained she was a classmate of Hannah's.

Now Hannah stood, looking first at Florence, then back to her aunt, who hovered in the dim light of the front parlor, wringing her hands.

"Hannah, she's in town for just this one night. And it's not a long, boring speech. It's merely a gathering of a few of us Harvard women at the Destiny. She said she wants to meet us. She says we are pioneers."

"Pioneers?"

"That's what she said." Florence's stubborn stance raised Hannah's curiosity.

"Who is this 'she'?"

"Lucretia Mott," Florence replied. "I've heard of her but don't know that much about her. But she's famous–or at least on her way to being famous. I hear five thousand people came to hear her in Pittsburgh–and most of them were women."

"Lucretia Mott?" Hannah asked, her curiosity piqued since she had heard about Lucretia's fight for women's rights.

"Come for just a bit, Hannah. Please?"

Hannah had never seen Florence so animated. Glancing back at her aunt, Hannah saw the expected frown of disapproval.

Florence seemed on the verge of jumping up and down. "She called us pioneers, Hannah. It's as if she believes in us!"

Hannah thought for only a moment, then reached for her coat. "Aunt Constance, I will be gone for an hour."

"But, Hannah, it is late already," her aunt protested.

"It's only half past five," Florence piped up, receiving a frosty glare in response.

"I will be back for dinner," Hannah said as she buttoned her coat and wrapped her thick red scarf about her face and throat.

Dinner was dry and cold by the time Hannah returned home that evening. It would not have mattered, for Hannah was too keyed up to eat. Such ideas and thoughts that swirled in her head! Each novel concept snatched away at a wealth of preconceptions and false ideas.

Lucretia Mott was anything but imposing with her small, mouselike figure and thin voice.

But once she began to talk, all time disappeared.

Hannah had been dumbfounded to learn Mott was from Philadelphia.

Soon Mott got the group of women laughing over her trials while forming the Philadelphia Female Anti-Slavery Society nearly ten years prior.

"Ten years ago!" Hannah had cried. "And where was I?"

The group broke out in laughter again when Florence reminded her, "Hannah–you were only ten years old! We were all ten years old."

Mott did not hold a long discourse but instead sought out from this small group of Harvard women the reasons for their attendance, the reasons they sought education.

At the end, Mott asked, "Then none of you are seeking liberation? None of you are breaking the shackles of repression?"

The group all looked uncomfortable in the silence that followed.

Mott continued, "Education is wonderful, Miss Collins. I am glad to hear you are pursuing the study of medicine. But for the rest of you–Harvard cannot simply be a method of locating your future husband. It has to be more than that. You can change the world if you choose. You must promise me that you will never simply accept things because they have been done a certain way since the dawn of time. You must promise me to question everything. When you find worth and value, then embrace the thing that provides it to you. It might be a way of thinking. It might be education. It might even be that husband. It might be bearing children. But make it a deliberate, conscious choice. Do not be content to follow what has been. Do you promise?"

And all there nearly cheered in their response to her challenge.

I can change the world, Hannah thought as she walked home alone. *I can.*

When she turned the corner to her aunt and uncle's house, she stopped. The heavy damask drapery that shielded the front parlor moved as Hannah neared the home. It was obvious Aunt Constance had lain in wait for her return.

That is the way it has always been, Hannah thought. *And how sad to know it will always be that way.*

As she turned the key in the lock, hearing the scuffling of footsteps up the front stairs, Hannah wondered what Miss Mott might have to say to Aunt Constance.

From the Diary of Morgan Hannah Collins

February 1843

If I did not have to record my thoughts in this diary at the insistence of my discourse professor, I would not. It is a commitment of time that I have found hard to keep. Writing and describing the week's events is a chore. And now Professor Baldwin has modified his rules and stated that we might instead describe a single event. I could not possibly keep track of everything–but last week a curious event did unfold.

And I am glad that the professor will never read this–he simply wants us to write–so write I will.

I had a prior commitment with Gage Davis. No matter that my family and his are separated by a large gulf, both geographic and economic. Bloodlines are bloodlines, and somewhere in this mix the Davis family feels that the Collins family is owed a favor.

Some stuffy recital, to be followed by dinner at the Harvard Club–all scheduled well in advance and at the prodding of our respective mothers, I suspect. Gage, who I am sure is loath to attend affairs such as these, has been forced to invite me to the affair. Yes, I know it makes little sense, but I could not refuse my mother, and Gage could not refuse his.

So I am powdered, tightened, waxed, and ready for the event. I arrive at the Commons and begin looking for Gage, even though I expect him to be late. Within a few seconds I hear footfalls on the pavement, coming closer to me, and turn with a smile.

To my very great surprise, it is not Gage Davis at all, but a blushing and stammering Joshua Quittner. He made up some ridiculous reason as to Gage's absence–having to do with emergency business reasons. I knew better, of course, but was most ladylike. I did not tell him I knew that Gage was with another woman until the end of the evening.

Just wait until I see that cad again!

But then again . . . the evening with Joshua was so very pleasant. The recital music was lively and kept us both awake. Joshua made me giggle when he said his definition of culture was "sleep-inducing." He made light of his lack of sophistication in such a disarming and, dare I say, sophisticated manner. It made his rural innocence all the more attractive.

And land sakes, is he handsome. He was dressed to the nines in a castoff from Gage. Even if it was a year out of style, Joshua made more of that castoff than any ten men could. There were a few women in attendance that night, and even though most were well past their prime–some approaching nearly forty years old–they all stared at Joshua and I am sure envied me for being his escort. Not that you could see their brazen stares, but I could feel them. Call it women's intuition.

And I am quite certain that Joshua–poor, innocent Joshua–hadn't a clue at all to the power he has over women.

CHAPTER FOUR

Cambridge Massachusetts
Summer 1843

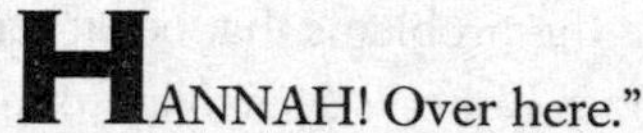

HANNAH! Over here.”

Hannah turned to find Robert Keyes’s voice. Through the crowd, she saw his face and outstretched arm, waving to her.

He is one imposing figure, Hannah thought.

“I apologize for not waiting outside,” he explained as he pulled out her chair, “but you said that meeting me here was more convenient for you, and I knew I would have to take the first open table. I do so hope you weren’t inconvenienced.”

“No, Robert,” Hannah replied, smiling as sweetly as she could. “You are much too dependable to have stood me up. I knew you would be here. And I know that Camden’s does not take reservations. So I did not worry for I knew you would be holding a table for us.”

Camden’s–a new, very boisterous restaurant downtown–was just a block from the trolley line.

A volley of notes had flown back and forth between Hannah and Robert, arranging this meeting. Robert’s business interests had brought him into Philadelphia for a week as he sought out new investors. His schedule allowed for two free evenings, and both evenings, he professed, were evenings he desired to spend with Hannah.

Hannah's mother was overjoyed. "He has all but announced himself as your suitor. You must offer him encouragement to make this relationship official," Elizabeth Collins had declared.

"Mother," Hannah had responded with exasperation, "I must finish my studies at Harvard. He is still in the midst of setting up his business. A wedding is the furthest thing from our minds."

Elizabeth Collins acted as if she heard not a single of her daughter's objections, for she fluttered about the house in genteel enthusiasm.

Hannah had been adamant in one thing–keeping Robert from visiting her home. She was certain that Robert knew all about the family's current reduced state of living, for such gossip flowed freely among society mavens. And she was certain as well that Robert would not think ill of her because of it. Quite the contrary, she felt, for he often expressed regret at the problems that befell some folks.

Hannah was not worried about Robert's sensitivity to their surroundings but what her mother might do. If Robert were to visit, Elizabeth Collins no doubt would have them wording wedding invitations and selecting china patterns in short order.

And that, she thought, *would simply not do.*

It was not that a wedding with Robert was so far-fetched; it was that neither of them had truly spoken of such matters. She did not want to pressure him into making a commitment before he was ready.

But he'll be ready someday, she wrote in her diary. *And that day might be soon.*

The waiter flustered about their table, naming special dishes, listing wines, and advising them on proper choices.

Robert was not curt with the server, but neither was he overly familiar–as was the case with many younger men who lacked a sense of common propriety when dealing with those who served them.

He sat up, snapped the menu closed, and in three short sentences ordered the meal for both himself and Hannah. Then he dismissed the young waiter with a wave of his hand.

"You look very beautiful tonight," he told Hannah after the waiter departed. "The color of your frock sets off your eyes well. You should use that color more often." Hannah saw his eyes travel over her form briefly, taking in the deep red of her dress.

"Thank you, Robert," she answered, pleased.

He then looked around, as if annoyed at the noise and bustle of the restaurant. Hannah was now certain he would have preferred one of the older, more established, and sedate eating places. She knew he would never have picked a place so suddenly popular.

"Well, then, how was your day?" he asked.

And Hannah spoke for several minutes about what she had done in the three days since they had last seen each other, the book that she purchased, the visits she made.

Robert said nothing but nodded occasionally and sipped his drink. When Hannah stopped, Robert leaned forward. "Well, then, I have had a most fascinating day. . . ." And he began a treatise on investments that consumed nearly a full half hour. What cut his discourse short was the appearance of their food.

They ate in relative silence, as was his custom.

After pushing the plate away, he snapped his fingers and asked if coffee might be brought as soon as possible. The waiter did not smile as he cleared off the dinner platters.

"Well, then," Robert said, "your mother and father–they are well, I take it?"

Hannah nodded. "Quite well indeed, Robert, and thank you for asking. And yours?"

"Well, Father is away on a trip this month to the Carolinas. He's boar hunting. Can you imagine that? Boar hunting! And meeting with the owners of several plantations down there. He is working on consolidating cotton purchases for several New England mills. To buy in bulk is to buy at reduced costs is what he says. And then to sell at better profits is what makes the deal."

Hannah spooned a thick dollop of cream into her coffee.

Robert looked down his nose. "So much cream spoils the taste of fine coffee, Hannah. You might as well drink hot milk."

She smiled, thinking he was jesting. "But it is the way I prefer–milk and coffee, or coffee and milk," she said, then realized by his expression that he was making no joke. Retracting her smile, she then said, "The next time I try it, it will be without cream."

He nodded with a hint of satisfaction. There was a note of silence in the restaurant and at their table.

"And your mother, Robert. How is she faring without your father?"

"Fine, I imagine," Robert answered, seeming surprised. "She gets along quite well on her own."

"Is she busy?"

"Busy? You mean, with the house and all?"

"No, I mean that . . . well, my mother is a member of several civic groups–and the Philadelphia Cultural Assembly as well. With meetings and planning and whatnot, much of her free time is consumed."

Robert appeared as if he had swallowed a lemon. "Good heavens, no. That would not be my ideal at all. My mother takes care of the house–and the children–though none are still at home. She oversees all the necessary details, which leaves precious little time for foolishness."

"What my mother does is not foolish," Hannah retorted and immediately winced at her sharpness.

Robert blinked once, waited a long uncomfortable moment, then replied, "No, I did not mean to imply that it was. It is just that my father has always held to the premise that a woman is most valuable when the home is run in a tidy fashion. That allows the man–the provider–to work and become successful while not worrying about the minutia of life."

Hannah tried her best not to show her strong disagreement. She could hear her mother's advice reverberating in her thoughts: *Listen and never argue. There is plenty of time to sort matters out after the wedding.*

So instead of responding with a curt word, she smiled and took another sip of her coffee with heavy cream. "But, Robert," she said, "what of my studies at Harvard? Surely you would not expect me to make no use of them in the future. That would be a waste of time and resources, wouldn't it?"

Robert offered a sly smile in return. "And you're asking about . . . our future?"

Hannah regretted the question, knowing it made her appear as if she were asking permission to attend college and also assuming the two would eventually marry. "No," she snapped back quickly, "it's just that I am a student and I do expect to make use of what I have learned–at least in some fashion. To expect that when I marry, I should forget all my education is . . . well, I think it would be unwise."

Robert nodded as if he agreed. "Well, then, Hannah, I believe the way we view things in not divergent in the least. I am sure my mother would have been a better mistress of the house had she had your opportunities. I am sure she would have found simple and more economical ways to attend to matters of the home and hearth. So no woman needs to abandon her education. She simply needs to put what she learns to the proper use."

Hannah curled her hands in her lap so tightly that she was afraid a nail might have drawn blood on her palm.

Just then Robert reached into his pocket. Pulling out a thick gold watch, he snapped the lid open. "My heavens," he exclaimed, "the hour is nearly gone. We must hurry if we are to be at the theater by quarter past."

He laid a few bills on the table, then hesitated and removed one, slipping it back into his pocket.

"Come, little Hannah, we would not want to miss the opening. I hear that the sets for this production are stunning. Shakespeare himself would be proud."

FROM THE DIARY OF MORGAN HANNAH COLLINS

THAT SAME NIGHT

I cannot recall ever being more frustrated and confused as I am this minute.

The evening with Robert went well–all things considered. Camden's was not the best choice I could have made, for it was clear that Robert did not care for its boisterous atmosphere.

The play was stunning. I have read *Macbeth,* so I was able to "keep abreast of the plot," as Robert inquired of me. The set and scenery were magnificent. A castle materialized from nowhere, it seemed, complete with turrets and drawbridge.

Yet as to Robert–he as much as admitted that he has no use for an educated woman and that I am wasting my time at Harvard. Does he really think all my efforts are being spent in order to run a house full of servants in a more efficient manner?

I believe he would like to think that.

And, of course, being the good girl my mother thinks I should be, I made no mention of my desire to attend medical school. Odd how I have told complete strangers of my plan–yet not a word to my parents or Robert.

And though I was so frustrated and near to angry with Robert, he took me home in a beautiful rented carriage. The night air was mild, yet he drew a shawl about my shoulders. As we climbed Derby Hill, he reached over and took my hand in his. I found myself drawing closer to him as the carriage swayed and bounced over the ruts.

Then at my doorstep, while the carriage awaited his return, he held my hands and . . . well, he drew me to him and I let him kiss me full on the lips.

(It was not the first time I have kissed a man, but it was the first intentional kiss in which I knew what to do and desired the event to last longer.)

I felt the gentle stubble of his beard against my cheek and his firm lips. I actually drew closer to him. Then he pulled back, leaving me in such a state of cupidity that I was angry over his intended departure.

He then paused and shook my hand, bade me good night, and promised a note would follow shortly.

He shook my hand? He will drop me a note? The man just kissed me in a most passionate way–does that not warrant more than a note and handshake?

Men! How will I ever understand what they mean?

New Jersey Shore
Summer 1843

Dorothy Collins, a stout young woman with red hair and a great swarm of freckles, took the reins of the decrepit wagon and slapped hard at the horse.

Hannah winced. "You're going to hurt the poor thing."

Dorothy roared with laughter. "Hector? Hurt? It takes a stout log to the side of his head just to get his attention. You are too far removed from the land, Hannah. A snap or two won't cause him any pain."

Hector, an ancient gray-and-black mule, always appeared tired and dusty. He provided the bulk of transportation at Bay Head.

Hannah and her parents had at last consented to spending two weeks at the home of the Newark Collinses–cousins who had made their money bringing in beef cows to New York's feedlots. Hannah's mother considered their business uncultured, verging on uncouth. But they did own a rambling house in Newark and a larger one yet perched on the shores of the Atlantic.

Every summer, scores of cousins, aunts, and uncles descended for weeks at a time. Hannah had been there only twice before and rarely met her cousins during the rest of the year. Weddings and funerals marked the times of family gatherings.

This summer, there were seven young, yet-to-be-married female Collinses in attendance. There was much giggling among them every evening as they strolled along the shore. And today, Dorothy had commandeered Hector and the wagon for a ride down the beach and called for her cousins to join her.

"It'll be fun," Dorothy called out as she pulled Hannah outdoors. "It's a great bluff. They say you can see New York City when the air is clear."

"I've already seen New York City," Hannah complained as her cousin Dorothy spirited her outside and into the wagon.

Wide-brimmed straw hats were distributed to each, and Dorothy navigated the carriage down the narrow main street of Bay Head. After only a few blocks the road gave way to a rutted strip of packed sand and crushed shells, then to simply hard-packed sand. Eventually, the road disappeared altogether and was lost to the deep sand. The women all leaped from the carriage and walked alongside as Hector struggled with the wagon in the deepening sand.

As the group strolled along, Hannah stared out at the ocean, a far breeze lifting her honey-colored hair from her face and neck. The days had been quite warm, and this one verged on becoming uncomfortably hot. Hannah unbuttoned her cuffs and rolled her sleeves up past her elbow.

"Be careful, now, Hannah," Dorothy laughed. "You don't want to be exciting any of the menfolk."

Hannah pretended to gasp and roll them back down. She felt good as their laughter carried on the breeze.

Hannah liked the warmth of the sun on her face, even though her mother claimed a pale complexion was the sign of good breeding. This day the ocean was a dusty blue, and the waves seemed almost playful as they rolled onto the gentle shoulder of the shore. Thickets of sea grass grew in greater abundance here, and each held a hillock of sand in place.

"It's just over that rise," Dorothy called, and the younger cousins–Helen, Rose, Sela, Honore, and Charlotte–all took off at a run, their hats flailing in the wind. Dorothy maneuvered the mule close to a tree and tied him there near a mound of grass.

"I do love it here," Hannah said. "There is something so magical about the water. It appears to be a different color every day."

Dorothy nodded.

The beach was protected by two fingers of sand, each well covered with thickets of sea grass. The fingers formed a shallow bowl, keeping the larger waves at bay.

"And the sound the water makes–sometimes the waves seem angry, and sometimes they are no louder than a cat's purr."

They reached a crest in the dunes.

"So where is New York City?" Hannah asked, staring to the north.

Dorothy squinted into the hazy sunshine, then swung her arm in a wide arc. "It's out there somewhere. Maybe. Perhaps. It was there a day ago."

Hannah laughed and tripped down to a small depression shaded by a group of stunted trees. She smoothed her skirt and sat down, drawing her knees up to her chest.

Dorothy, instead, threw herself on the sand, sprawling as wide and long as she could.

"You'll get all sandy!" Hannah exclaimed.

"And that will be a terminal situation, Dr. Collins?"

Hannah tucked her knees closer to her chin. "It might be."

Dorothy grabbed a handful of sand and tossed it at Hannah's feet. "So what my mother whispered to me is correct? You are actually studying medicine at Harvard?"

Hannah nodded. "But there are no guarantees. Harvard won't let me into their final medical program. But there is Oberlin College in Ohio. . . . And I hear a new college in Philadelphia is opening that is chartered to train only women in the medical arts."

Hannah and Dorothy watched the rest of their cousins race about the waves, gathering shells and kicking in the warm water, their skirts drawn up about their waists.

"I would have thought one of the Newark Collins women would be a pioneer. I always imagined we would do something bold like that," Dorothy said lightly.

"It's not so bold," answered Hannah. "And I haven't done it yet. I mean, I have a long way to go until it all happens."

Dorothy fanned herself with a large leaf. "And what does your Mr. Keyes say about all of this?"

"Does everyone know every detail of my life?" Hannah said, shocked. "I thought only a few knew of Robert."

"Such news is never held tightly in the hand. And you know what they say: I'm good at keeping secrets. It's the people I tell who aren't."

Hannah laughed. "You're right. It is hot here. Hand me one of those leaves."

Dorothy reached over, then stopped. "I have a much better idea."

She stood up and looked about. "You see no strangers within miles of here, right?"

Hannah stood and looked. "We are alone. As far as I can see, that is."

"Good."

Dorothy took her hat and tossed it to the side, then began to unbutton her frock and unlace her shoes while hopping on one foot. In a moment, she was down to her undergarments.

"I'm going bathing!" Dorothy shouted. "At least it is one thing the Newark Collinses can do first."

Hannah was tempted to grab hold of her cousin and pull her back into the shade, fearing that the heat might have caused her to lose her bearings.

"I am tired of wearing as much clothing at the seashore as I do at church on Sunday!" Dorothy shrieked. "Cousins, come join me! Be liberated and let us finally taste fully the joys of the water! Why should men have all the fun?"

With that, she ran toward the sea and flung herself headfirst into a gentle swell. She disappeared under the water for a split second, then popped back into the air, shouting and laughing, "Come on in, you cowards. It's delicious!"

The Collins women, in a ragged, giggling semicircle, watched in awe as Dorothy swam about in the sea. Then Rose giggled again and stepped forward. She tossed her hat to the sand and began to disrobe down to her final layer of clothing.

In a breath or two, the rest joined in. Soon there were a half dozen women frolicking in their unmentionables in the warm Atlantic surf.

"Come on, Hannah! Join us! You should feel this!"

Hannah looked around again. Dorothy was right. While bathing at the public beach, Hannah often felt as dressed as she did in winter. The cumbersome bathing attire restricted her movements to wading. No woman could swim, for the lightest current would pull the great folds of the bathing attire under the waters.

But this looked so very wonderful and free!

She checked around her one more time, then grabbed her hat.

And for an hour the entire group jumped and splashed and dove and swam in the shallow warm bay of a deserted beach at Bay Head.

On the way back to the Collinses' beach house, Hannah whispered over to Dorothy, "Do you think anyone will be able to tell what we did?"

Dorothy tried to smooth her hair, whipped into a frizzy mass by the wind and water. She rubbed at the rosy glow on Hannah's cheeks. "If we wait until dark, we might be able to sneak in the house unnoticed. But short of that, they'll know."

An anxious look creased Hannah's face. "If my mother finds out . . . she'll . . . well, I don't know, but she'll do something."

Waving off her concern, Dorothy replied, "What can she do? It's your trust fund."

Hannah sighed. "There really are no secrets, are there?"

Dorothy shook her head. "Not in the Collins family, there aren't."

From the Diary of Morgan Hannah Collins
That Same Night

I can never once remember feeling so free and unfettered as I did today in the surf. The delicious waves caressed us, moving us about, and we laughed like water nymphs.

Even better, there were no prying eyes–no one to warn that women did not act this way. There was not a single disapproving Collins glance.

I watched Dorothy as she threw herself for the first time into the great water. I know how she felt–loosening the binds and ties–and sailing off into a new and uncharted realm. It is how I often feel at Harvard.

"Come join me!" I want to shout, and there is no one to shout it to. And when I do celebrate my choices, there are people like my mother and even Robert who see no charm in my small victories, who see no nobility in the struggle.

Can they be convinced?

Perhaps not. And perhaps I fool myself into thinking a different outcome exists. Perhaps a wife and mother and keeper of the heart, home, and flame is sufficient. But what happens if I find that it isn't and I have given up the thrill and challenge of the water forever?

I am not certain that I can do that.

From the Diary of Morgan Hannah Collins

September 1843

I must remind myself never to share a confidence with a man again.

Classes had just resumed, and I was finding it so satisfying to see all the familiar faces and share stories of my summer adventures. I daresay the walls of the Destiny heard many, many stories.

Of course, Gage Davis was there. It appeared that he had a very businesslike summer. I pity him in some ways, never really enjoying the world–just its money.

And here is why women are viewed as the weaker sex. In a moment of unguarded candor, I mentioned to Gage about the Collins cousins' Dionysian adventure of bathing in the Atlantic waters. As I began to speak, I knew I had made an error in judgment, for I could see in Gage's face an unattractive combination of humor, lustful curiosity, and envy. He pressed for details, and I am sure I gave him far too many. Then he jested that he might tell Joshua of our antics.

I am not sure why, but the prospect of that pained me so much. Is it because I hold some part of my heart for the young preacher? Or is it that I do not want to be the one who corrupts his innocence?

Then later, Joshua did arrive and Gage, even though he hinted at being a cad, is not. I am sure he would not share our confidence.

The summer has been good to Joshua. He looks tan and even more fit this year. His jaw has taken on a more noble and demanding thrust. I have not forgotten how attractive he truly is. We spoke long into the night. Joshua does have a gift of describing the small details of life in such a way as to be both humorous and touching. His summer back in Ohio was filled with the most curious characters and the oddest activities. And while he spoke, he peppered his words with references to church and to God and to how even the least educated man or woman in Shawnee found solace and refuge in the arms of the Savior and in faith.

I found myself being both wistful and envious after his discourse. Here was a fellow student who had his life so carefully planned. He would be a preacher and minister to his fellows back home–seeing their passage from birth through death. How secure he was in that. And as he talked about his faith, it was as if he had something real and physical in his hands.

I, too, believe in God. I daresay no right-thinking person denies the Supreme Being–with the exception of people like Jamison or some heathen from a foreign land. But my belief is not the belief of Joshua. To him, God exists in all parts of life on a daily basis. God resides in his heart, as he has said many times.

I am often close to asking him how that reality occurred. How is it that he found this faith and I have not? But I think it far too personal a question to ask.

And besides, as I write these words, I admit that I am every bit as Christian as most people. I attend church. My parents attend church. We have a Bible, and I thumb through it on occasion. I do my best to live a good life. I think God will be pleased with me.

And then there is Joshua–the very attractive Joshua. Can it be true that a man so familiar with God might be used to cause a good Christian woman to stumble?

After our long conversation, I brazenly demanded that he walk me home, for it was much too late for a respectable woman to be out on the streets alone. It was a lovely warm night, with a full moon helping to light our way. The breeze was enough to just rustle the leaves.

I do not understand why, but I reached out and took his hand several blocks from my aunt and uncle's home.

Why did I seek out his flesh? I am not sure, but I think it was because I caught his profile lit by the golden moon. His strong jaw, his noble cheeks, his firm lips . . . I could go on, but I will restrain myself.

Robert is so far from me at the moment . . . and Joshua is here and is such a challenge.

I know that none of this makes sense, but then, what matters of the heart truly make sense? And perhaps this is just passion and not the heart–and if so–it makes even less sense.

We arrived at the front door of the house. My aunt, thankfully, must have been in bed, for there was no rustling of the curtain as we stood before the door.

He stood facing me, and now his features filled my eyes. I still held his hand.

Dear Diary, you must forgive me, for I am a weak woman.

I reached my other hand up and placed it on the nape of his neck and pulled him toward me. What a hussy I must appear! He did not resist, and in a heartbeat, he let his lips find mine. The kiss lasted only a breath–or maybe longer, for I was near to swooning. After a few seconds, or perhaps a dozen seconds or a minute, he leaned back . . . and nearly fell from the porch!

He bid me good night and stumbled down the walk as if intoxicated. I am glad I could stand for several minutes to regain my senses, for I am sure I was as loose kneed as he was.

And why did I kiss him?

(For a comparison to Robert? I must state that there is no comparison. It is comparing gold to gilding.)

I could not help myself. I am drawn to him. And yet as he walked away, I heard my thoughts shout out, *He will be but a church-poor preacher!*

Is that all I am really seeking–security? Wealth?

And why could not all the things I desire be wrapped in one man, rather than two or three?

Cambridge, Massachusetts
November 1843

"Who's up there?"

"Oh, Aunt Constance, it's me," Hannah called down.

"What are you doing home now? Is something the matter?"

Hannah then heard the familiar creak of the front steps. She knew what would happen next. The door to her bedroom edged open no more than an inch. She could see her aunt's eye in the narrow crack.

"Hannah? Are you all right?"

"Aunt Constance, please come in," Hannah replied. "I don't like talking through a door."

The door opened slowly, an inch or two at a time. Aunt Constance leaned in first, then stepped in, only a foot into the room. "You're packing?" she asked.

Hannah looked down at the large leather bag she was filling with her things. The bag was nicked, but it held a great many outfits. She did not want to carry more than two bags with her.

"I am, Aunt Constance."

"And where are you going? Does your mother know about this?"

Hannah held her long, exasperated sigh to herself. Instead she fastened a bright smile on her face and turned to the disapproving stare of her aunt. "Gage Davis . . . you know the family . . . "

Her aunt nodded.

"Well, he came upon several of us in the park today."

"The park? And not in school? Do you make a habit of going to the park instead of classes? Harvard is very dear, and I don't think it proper that you miss any class. Is there something here that I should know about?"

"No, Aunt Constance. It was all very innocent. I was finished with my classes today"–*and I hope I am not punished for my small lies*–"and Joshua Quittner, the seminary student, and Jamison Pike . . ."

"That ruffian writer fellow you talked about? The evil one?"

"Oh, Aunt Constance, he's not evil. Just cynical."

"Isn't that the same thing? I don't want you spending time with that feculent young man."

"He is not feculent," Hannah replied, not truly knowing the meaning of the word but imagining it was not positive. "He's just finding himself. Did you know that his father is a pastor in Pittsburgh?"

"Well, I imagine the theology in Pittsburgh is much less strict than it is at our church. He's not a nice young man. You should avoid him."

Hannah took a deep breath. *This is not going as I had hoped.*

"And so why are you packing?" her aunt asked thinly.

Hannah redoubled her smile, hoping it was charged with innocence. "Well, as I said, we were at the park, down at the river, just talking. . . ."

"You should not neglect your studies like that, Hannah."

"I am not," she replied, her words nearly petulant in tone. She took another quick breath and decided to plunge in full tilt. "And then Gage Davis arrived and invited us to his home in New York City for the thanksgiving celebrations that President Tyler suggested. He said we should all gather to celebrate the blessings of this year. And Gage said he would love to have us spend the week with him in New York City."

Aunt Constance appeared surprised. She was well aware of the Davis family and their wealth. For Hannah to spend time in that environment would be a good thing.

"And his parents want you there? All of you? Including that pernicious Mr. Pike?"

"Yes, and Mr. Pike is not pernicious."

Hannah now had a second word to look up.

"Well . . ."

"Aunt Constance, this will be a wonderful opportunity. Gage has promised that we can take in the opera and museums and all sorts of cultural events. And he said that the servants truly want to prepare a feast for the day."

"And you will be fully chaperoned?"

Hannah prayed Aunt Constance would not inquire by whom, since Gage's parents were out of the country on a trip to England and only servants and perhaps a spinster Davis aunt might be in attendance.

"Yes, I will be. And besides, Aunt Constance, you and my mother have done well. I am a most moral young woman. I go to church. I would let myself participate in nothing that might smack of impropriety."

Aunt Constance twisted her lips together in a sneer. "Well, then, if it's chaperoned . . . and it will provide a cultural experience . . . and it would not hurt to associate with some of society's more elite members, like Mr. Davis."

Hannah rushed over to her aunt and offered her a great hug, which Aunt Constance seemed to lean away from.

"Then will you help me pack, dear aunt? I have to be at the carriage stand in less than an hour, and I have no idea of what might be proper at the opera. Can you help? You have such a keen sense of style." *I suspect that a little flattery is not a sin, is it?* Hannah asked herself with a smile.

New York City
Thanksgiving 1843

Hannah, like Jamison and Joshua, was nearly overwhelmed at the scale and opulence of Gage's New York manse. It was not that they did not consider him wealthy–it was that they did not consider him wealthy enough.

The house, or what would best be described as a mansion, took up nearly a city block in a very elegant neighborhood of New York, not more than a five-minute carriage ride to the financial districts. To Hannah, the house, built of granite and carved limestone, seemed to hulk about the corner, seeking to possess the space by brute force. The lines of the facade were hard and edgy, lacking grace, but hinting at raw power instead.

The three friends had been reduced to mute silence as Gage showed them to their rooms, pointing out features of the house, calling for servants, asking if tea or coffee might be served en suite.

Wealth did not surprise Hannah, for some of her relatives were of older money and had used their fortunes well. Homes in Philadelphia were large and tastefully decorated. But nothing matched the Davis scale. Hannah wondered if her mother truly knew of the breadth of the Davis wealth–for Elizabeth Collins had never once mentioned Gage as a possible suitor for her daughter.

If she saw this house, he would replace Robert Keyes on her list in a heartbeat, Hannah thought with a bemused smile.

Her bedroom was larger than any four bedrooms in her own house and filled with an amazing thickness of furnishings. The intricately designed rug nearly swallowed her feet to her ankles. The bed was perched high and layered with perhaps five different coverings and a loud profusion of pillows. More than a little unnerving to Hannah was the young servant girl who had been assigned to unpack her belongings.

She sat at the edge of the bed as the girl, Irish by her looks, gently unfolded each garment and either set it to hangers or to a chest of drawers, each filled with a lilac sachet.

I should have taken more care in packing, she thought, *and I should have bought new things.*

As the servant neared completion, Hannah smiled.

If I am uncomfortable with all this, I wonder how our poor Joshua and Jamison are faring? It would take but seconds to unpack the pair of them.

"Would you like a pot of tea, Miss Collins?"

Hannah snapped from her reverie. "Uhh . . . I forgot your name. . . ."

"It's Mary, Miss Collins."

"Well then, Mary," Hannah said, regretting she had picked up Robert's annoying phrase, "I think I will wait. Perhaps later. But you could show me the bath and then direct me from there to the library. I think that is where Gage said he would wait for us."

"Yes, Miss Collins, indeed it was the library. And the bath is through this door. I have laid out a supply of fresh towels."

"Is there water in there?"

Mary looked puzzled. "Why yes, Miss Collins. There is always water in there."

It was Hannah's turn to look puzzled. She stepped through the door and saw the reason for the maid's confusion. At the sink, two pipes protruded from the wall.

"The left is cold, Miss Collins, and the right one is hot. The boiler has been stoked for hours, so it'll be most warm."

Hannah stood there dumbfounded. She had heard that a few New York hotels had the means of bringing water indoors but never imagined it could be managed in a private residence. There was even a private marble tub in the room.

"I'll draw you a bath, Miss Collins, if you would like."

Hannah hesitated. It sounded most attractive, but she knew Gage expected them to gather shortly.

"No, not now, Mary. Perhaps when we return, or on the morrow."

"As you wish. Will there be anything else?"

"No."

And she was left to marvel at an entire bathroom, nearly as large as her entire bedchamber in Philadelphia, filled with every imaginable bath toiletry and stacks of thick, fluffy towels and freshly pressed linens.

She took one more envious glance at the empty tub.

Baths at her Cambridge house were such complicated and unsettling affairs–with boiling water and bathing in the midst of the kitchen with a screen placed about the large tub for privacy–privacy that Hannah never truly felt.

This bathroom promised such complete and utter privacy as to be decadent.

A girl could quickly get used to such indulgences.

Yet as she washed her face and neck she was pricked with the thought that she was enjoying such a level of luxury that could scarce be imagined by most men and women anywhere on the globe.

Am I wrong to like this environment? Am I wrong to want much the same for myself?

She dried herself and began to comb and pin her hair. She set her hair off to both sides of her temples with a pair of ivory combs, each gilded with three tiny flashings of diamond. They had belonged to her grandmother and were a gift just prior to her leaving for Harvard. She selected a simple dark dress that buttoned to the waist and offered the most modest bodice of all the dresses she had brought.

The library is down this hall to the right . . . and then at the bottom of the steps . . . another right and down a short corridor? Or was that to the left?

Hannah walked slowly down the immensely wide hall, marked with a plethora of mirrors and paintings and chandeliers. The stairway curved back and forth twice.

Well, I do recognize the statue. We passed that on the way in, didn't we?

Then she realized she was lost and called out for Jamison and Joshua. When she heard their cheery voices, she knew she was on the right track. Finally she spotted them down a long hallway. "Have you ever seen anything like this in your lives?" she said once she reached them. "There must be a million dollars of bric-a-brac in this place."

"*Bric-a-brac?*" Joshua asked, puzzled.

"A rich man's word for expensive objects he wants to put on display to show how wealthy he is," Jamison said, laughing.

"But the Gage we know is nothing like this," Joshua said, sweeping his arm in a circle as they continued to walk.

Hannah reached the dark walnut doors of the library first. Twice her height, they were open a few inches. When she pushed hard against them, she nearly fell into the room. A full two stories, the room was packed from floor to ceiling with books–thousands and thousands of books. A balcony encircled the entire room, with an ornate thick iron railing protecting those who browsed through the titles. Two tight circular stairways ran to the balcony at each end of the room. A scattering of leather chairs and settees and lamps were dotted about, each with a stack of books tumbled at its feet, as if a horde of voracious readers had just left.

Jamison stopped short of the doorway. "And which king of Europe is without a library?" he asked, whistling.

"As I said, he's not ostentatious like this house," Joshua continued stubbornly.

From one of the balconies, Gage spoke. "Who is not ostentatious?"

Hannah jumped. "Gage, you frightened me! Don't go lurking in dark corners like that!"

He laughed. "This whole house is a series of dark corners. There will be no place for me to stand if I avoid them."

"Who has been reading?" Hannah said. "I thought the house was empty."

"No, I am sure most of this mess is because of my older brother, Walton. He has most likely forbid anyone to replace any of these books. He claims they find new spots every time and he'll have to spend hours searching for them again."

"A brother? I did not know you had a brother."

A dark look creased Gage's eyes. "We are not exceptionally close . . . to neither of our sorrow."

Hannah walked around the large room for several minutes, her hand trailing like the tail of a sad, slow kite, barely touching the chairs and books and cases.

Finally her burning question could wait no longer. "Doesn't this bother you?" Hannah blurted out, addressing Gage. "To have so much while so many have so little?" She pointed around the room. "Why, I daresay that an entire village could live within these walls."

With a scowl, Gage retorted, "And I see, Miss Hannah, that you have given up your fine dresses for sackcloth and have donated your tuition money to the poor."

A thick, angry silence flowed into the room.

Hannah, primed to exchange more words, pursed her lips.

Gage stepped to the staircase and clattered his way quickly down to the ground floor and his friends. "Please, let us not talk of wealth right now. Perhaps after a good dinner we can continue this discussion." He gave a polite laugh and then said, "Come, we'll be late. Our carriage awaits."

Just then footsteps sounded out in the grand foyer, and a thin-faced, pinched young man entered the library. Foreboding emanated from him.

"Ah, well now," Gage said slowly. "You all have the grand opportunity to finally meet my brother. Say hello to my friends, Walton."

Walton grumbled a few words of greeting, then tread lightly down the front hall.

As the four friends moved toward the waiting carriage, Hannah looked back at Walton, wondering if one of the two brothers had been adopted.

Their week in New York City passed as fast as a spring shower. Gage treated New York as if it were a small neighborhood. He appeared to know everyone, and so many people seemed to know him.

The four of them attended theater–in the Davises' private boxes, of course–and more museums than Hannah could count. They dined in elegant restaurants. These cultural high zeniths were often followed by the most crude affairs–dining in local taverns where a dozen tipsy sailors might serenade them in a myriad of foreign languages.

Hannah loved every minute. To be squired about by three handsome gentlemen was wondrous.

At the lowly taverns, patrons and serving wenches alike greeted Gage as if he had stepped out only moments before. At the elegant dining establishments, the headwaiter would nearly bow in deference to Gage (and his proffered, though discreet, tips).

The week was a heady mix of the cultured and the profane, Hannah thought. She had seldom encountered such a mélange of experiences–and scarce knew that so many worlds existed at the same time and occupied the same space.

From the Diary of Morgan Hannah Collins

November 1843

What a week we all enjoyed! Gage Davis is the most wonderful of hosts.

And I forced myself to apologize for my criticisms of his wealth. I believe I found a twinge of jealousy in my soul that tweaked at my tongue.

Why should he have all this–and not me? –is what my heart cried.

We did everything: from the opera to a waterfront tavern with a drunken solo by the largest man I have ever seen, decorated with tattoos and a ring through his ear.

My heavens, what a week of contrasts.

I had lunch with Joshua one day when Jamison and Gage were off somewhere–looking at a newspaper or some such thing. I spoke how much I will miss them all when we finally leave the cloistered walls of Harvard. I thought Joshua might weep, so I forced myself to keep the remainder of our conversation light and cheerful.

I do believe Joshua is in love with me. But I cannot let him think there is a chance for us.

After all, I think I have begun to know what my future holds–the promise of a life like Gage's. That life will be my life with Robert. That is the promise.

[illegible]

[illegible]

[illegible] and the re[illegible]

[illegible]

* * *

[illegible]

[illegible]

[illegible]

[illegible]

[illegible]

[illegible]

Chapter Five

Harvard University
January 1844

SO why haven't you ever introduced me?" Florence asked as she and Hannah hurried between buildings. The cold wind swirled about, and the air was pregnant with the threat of snow.

"Introduced you to whom?" Hannah replied, pulling her woolen scarf up around her ears.

"The handsome one."

Hannah knew exactly the man Florence meant. "The handsome one? Who might that be? I thought they were all handsome to you."

Florence responded with a sniff, and the two ducked into the Harvard Student Union. Neither had a class for the next hour, and the library was far to the opposite side of campus.

The two found a table near the fire and unbuttoned their coats. The large, ill-lit room was cluttered with chairs, tables, posters, and a handful of mismatched lanterns. To one side, behind a long bar, stood a half dozen waiters, standing in line to draw coffee from a polished brass urn.

Though she tried to maintain a hurt expression, Florence softened and began to laugh. "Hannah, you do know me too well. Perhaps I am a bit indiscriminant about such matters–but you know the young man I am talking about. He's got that great shock of blond hair and piercing eyes–and broad shoulders. The one who looks like he could pick me up in one arm and carry me off?"

Hannah knew. And if she had been truthful she would have found her reluctance to share his name with Florence to be hard to defend. Joshua was hers, she felt, even though he most likely would never be hers.

"Hannah? Do I have to bribe you? Do I have to tell your aunt and uncle what you did in the library last week?"

It was Hannah's turn to look shocked. "You saw? Where were you? We were hidden from view. No one saw."

Florence leaned close and placed a hand on Hannah's. "The walls have ears and eyes, sweet Hannah. And I was on the second floor behind a great stack of Greek classics. Nearly asleep, but there."

Hannah closed her eyes. *No one should have seen us!*

"Well, Jamison started it," Hannah said in her defense. "He was bored with his studies and said that women were not as brave as men."

Florence leaned in closer.

"Well, I think he says things like that just to aggravate me," Hannah continued. "And I had to prove him wrong."

"So he threw the first spitball?" Florence asked. "He was the first one to violate the library's rules?"

Hannah took a moment to reply. "No, I was. But he egged me on."

"And you thought your wall of books and papers would hide you?"

Hannah sat upright. "It did hide us. Mr. Henerly, the librarian, never saw the origination of any of our projectiles."

"Of course he did not. He is as blind as the proverbial bat. But then, Hannah, the two of you never saw me watching."

Hannah offered a sweet smile, then replied, "Florence, you wouldn't turn on another woman student, would you? We must stick together. We must protect our rights and privileges."

Florence giggled, soft and throaty. "Indeed, Miss Collins, I will support you as a woman–and I will take this information to the grave–as long as you do one thing."

Hannah knew what the request would be before it was given words. Florence's look of anticipation confirmed it. Hannah sighed. "His name is Joshua Quittner. He's from a small town in Ohio." Then, with practiced, sad deliberation, she added, "He's studying to be a man of God. He's going to be a preacher."

Florence leaned back as if struck. "A preacher? Him? He's far too handsome for that!"

"I'm afraid it is true. As a seminarian he must have taken all manner of vows to abstain from all forms of pleasures." Hannah hoped her words sounded true and that Florence might be dissuaded from her pursuit.

After a moment, Florence looked up, a sparkle in her eyes. "He's not a Catholic, is he? I mean, we don't train priests here at Harvard, do we?"

Hannah blinked. "No, he's not Catholic. And no, I think priests go to their own universities, don't they?"

Florence shrugged. "Then he'll be married someday, right? Our handsome Mr. Quittner, that is."

Hannah shrugged, trying to appear noncommittal. *I do not like this turn of conversation.*

"And if he'll be married, he'll be needing a wife," said Florence.

And with that, Florence uttered the name "Joshua Quittner" once more as if committing it to memory, adjusted her coat, and sat back with a smug, self-satisfied smile on her face.

"He preaches at local churches and you've never heard him?" Florence was incredulous. They had sipped strong tea for close to an hour and now each had to return to class–Florence to the history of Italian art and Hannah to a class in chemical compounds.

"Well, I have been busy, and Joshua has never truly invited me to attend any of the churches. I don't think he's ever invited anyone."

"But you could go. No one has to have a ticket to go to church, right? Unless they've changed the rules since I last attended, admission is free to all."

"It still is," Hannah replied as they cleared their books from the table. "I never really thought he wanted us–any of his friends, I mean–to attend one of his guest sermons. Perhaps he imagines we would find fault with his faith–or his delivery." She buttoned her coat and adjusted her scarf.

"A shy man," Florence replied. "I like that. I find it so very attractive."

Hannah gave her friend a playful nudge on the shoulder. "You find everything attractive."

Florence scowled, trying hard to hold her laughter. She was not successful. "You're right, Hannah. But with a man like Joshua, who could not find everything irresistible?"

Hannah offered no reply but silently offered her agreement.

The last pew was hidden in dark shadows. On cold mornings such as this, many churches were less well attended than on warm spring mornings. *This church must be colder than most,* Hannah thought. A draft swirled about the sanctuary, and Hannah kept her coat and muff on during most of the service. She might have been warmer had she ventured closer to the pulpit, nearer the woodstove off to the left. But she did not.

The church would hold five hundred, and half of the building was filled. Her home church in Philadelphia was nearly twice this size and a dozen times as grand. She wondered if the low attendance was because of the cold or the guest pastor.

Such is the problem of a winter climate, she thought. *And perhaps some of the less faithful stayed away. I would imagine that they must think that the senior pastor would not be able to chide them for their absence when he returned.*

Once she discovered that Joshua was to speak, she did not tell him, nor anyone else, that she would be attending.

I want to see Joshua in his element, without him offering any considerations as to my presence.

As he began his message, she berated herself for thinking she had that much power and influence on Joshua.

He is quite good, she thought as he marched through his outline. And for the first time in many years, perhaps the first time ever, she began to consider the import of the words, not simply the lateness of the hour, or what others might be wearing, or if she had an appointment scheduled for luncheon. Joshua, when behind a pulpit, changed his persona. He became confident and sure–so different from the shy young man she knew.

Joshua gestured, his voice rising and falling, cajoling and whispering–not unlike some of the best actors Hannah had seen tread the theatrical boards.

His dazzling good looks are not an obstacle in the least, Hannah mused. *But what does he mean that we should be about God's business on earth? Isn't that left to preachers and priests? Does Joshua really think that the people in the pews can do religious things? I would scarcely know where to start. I am a Christian–I have no doubt of that fact. But what Joshua calls church folk to do is much beyond what would be required of any average Christian girl. Then again, the beliefs of his denomination may be in opposition to my own. Perhaps I will ask my pastor when I return home to Philadelphia.*

As Joshua neared the end of his message–at least it seemed close to the end to Hannah–he stared out over the crowd. A shaft of sunlight found a clear pane in the stained glass and lit upon Hannah's upturned face. The warmth, though slight and winnowed, was a welcome touch.

It was at that moment that Joshua hesitated and appeared as if to stumble in his thoughts. Hannah felt his eyes on hers, but at that distance, she could not be certain he recognized her form. Then he stammered a few words, shuffled through his papers, and stammered again. He grabbed the side of the pulpit, almost as if he were seeking a steadying purchase in the dark wood.

Hannah was certain he was hiding his confusion. But then he

straightened up and intoned, "Let us pray." In unison, the congregation bowed their heads, some very eager to see the service ended, some slower as if they were savoring the intention of the message.

Hannah hid her smile. *I am a distraction to him! I was right in my assessment. He saw me and stumbled.*

After a short prayer, Joshua bid the congregation the peace of God. The organ, as if its reeds and pipes were cold as well, wheezed for the first several notes of the closing song.

Hannah rose, gathered her muff and scarf, and stood in the rear shadows, waiting for the messenger.

"It was a most potent message, Joshua," she said as she held on to his hand. Joshua stood at the rear of the church, greeting all those who filed out of the rear doors. A biting breeze kept conversations to a minimum. "I was captivated by your words today. I felt as if I was the only person in the pews. And by the end of the message, you had me–heart and soul."

Joshua looked both pained and terribly pleased.

"The last point you were making was interrupted by the clock, was it not? I heard the noon bells toll," she added.

Joshua quickly nodded.

And we both know the truth, now don't we, Mr. Quittner? Hannah thought behind her smile.

In addition to wanting to observe him speaking, Hannah had a second, less spiritual motive for attending church that day. Another obligation faced her–to attend a boring cultural affair, with a dinner and long speeches. She was loath to attend alone. And she could not be absent, for her mother would discover it and a huge price would be paid.

So she decided that Joshua would make a fine escort.

FROM THE DIARY OF MORGAN HANNAH COLLINS

JANUARY 1844

How I dislike most family commitments that may not be ignored. Such is what I am writing about now–though this one turned out much different than I ever might have imagined. This affair was in honor of my great-grandfather's contribution to a sister organization of my mother's in Philadelphia. My mother obtained a ticket for myself and a guest. I am sure she thought I would invite Mr. Keyes. And I would have, except he was already scheduled to attend as the guest of a potential partner. He claimed there would be no way he could break that arrangement.

The affair was a stuffy banquet and speech scheduled under the auspices of the New Amsterdam Cultural Organization.

At times, I feel the scheming female–and perhaps I am. But to attend with Joshua would be such a pleasure–especially after hearing him and seeing how powerful he was in his own element.

The evening turned out to be most pleasant–at least most of it was.

What was served at the banquet was inconsequential, but afterward I excused myself and dragged poor Joshua with me. I grew more brazen, and he and I retreated surreptitiously upstairs. We hid ourselves in a dark, private box–with the curtains drawn, of course.

We spent the entire evening, as the speeches droned on, whispering and giggling in the dark.

Joshua is a most intelligent fellow–and quite articulate once he recovered from his initial stupefaction. He has a biting sense of humor but often tempers it for fear of what I might think of his thoughts.

As we sat in the dark, I rested my legs on an empty chair, and the weight of my skirt and train pulled at the fabric. Perhaps a few inches of the bare flesh on my calf were exposed–and only for an instant.

In spite of the speeches and rumble of the crowd, I imagined I could hear Joshua's heartbeats nearly explode in his chest. His eyes grew wide as saucers, and I venture to say that he began to tremble.

What is it about us that so flummoxes men in so many ways? They stare and stammer at the slightest movement; they hem and haw and hide their eyes. Yet, for such sensitive creatures, they can be so remarkably insensitive.

Even Joshua has no idea that his words can often cut me to the quick.

And the climax of the evening lay in wait.

I had never mentioned Robert Keyes to Joshua. I think Gage may have known about him, for how much can be kept secret between his mother and mine? But the rest of my friends at the Destiny had no reason to know.

At the end of the evening, I saw Robert and made my way over to him, introducing him to a very suspicious Joshua. Later, much to my consternation, I foolishly mentioned that Mr. Keyes was a young man whom my mother would like me to consider as a suitor.

It was an innocent, spontaneous remark, yet I could see Joshua crumbling under its import. It is not as if he had any claims–or illusions to a claim–on my attentions.

Men. I shall never understand them.

Yet as I write these words, I struggle with my own feelings. I am a student–a woman who seeks to learn the science of medicine. I am a child of parents who are so very needy in so many ways. I know that they see in me their promise of a brighter and better future. And then, perhaps, buried under all of those truths is the fact that I am a woman with needs as well. I merely have to gaze at Joshua's stunning good looks and my knees grow weak and I feel a flush at my throat.

That is a truth–I am a woman with needs.

And then there is all the rest as well–I want a husband, of course, and children.

And yet, if I am attending Harvard to become a physician, do I abandon all of this to be that wife and mother?

How great a struggle am I to bear?

I hear the words of Miss Mott: *You can change the world.*

I know that is the truth, but how much of the world can I expect to change?

Cambridge, Massachusetts
April 1844

Hannah had no intention of ever seeking out such succor or rescue from Gage but knew she had little recourse.

Returning home one early spring afternoon, her aunt held out a thin envelope marked *Personal and Confidential* with a Harvard University return address. Aunt Constance fluttered about, thinking it was dire news of some sort.

Hannah slit the envelope and scanned the brief note. "I must take my leave again, Aunt Constance. An urgent matter, I am afraid."

"Urgent? It is not your parents, is it?"

Hannah forced a smile onto her face and shook her head no. "And Harvard would write me of my parents?" She tried her best not to sound condescending.

"I suppose not. Then . . . I know I should not intrude . . . but you are a guest in our home, and I would think we have grown to deserve your confidence. . . . That is all I meant in asking."

Hannah leaned closer and lightly kissed her aunt's cheek. "It is a trifling matter of required courses, Aunt Constance. It is not urgent, nor personal or confidential. I suspect all matters of this scope are marked thusly."

She grabbed her bag and wrapped a shawl about her shoulders. "I shall be back within the hour, I trust."

Hannah did not look back as she hurried down the flagstone walk of her aunt and uncle's home. She did not turn for she did not wish them to see her tears, which began to flow in copious amounts as soon as she reached the street.

"And they took your money for the class?" Gage asked, his anger obvious and growing as he scanned the letter. "They said nothing to you prior to payment concerning rules or prohibitions of the female gender in this class?" Gage tugged at his perfectly pressed jacket.

"No, they said nothing," Hannah said in a whisper. Joshua sat next to her, at a discrete distance, in the parlor of Gage's suite of rooms at 619 Follen Steet. Hannah had appeared, unannounced and totally unexpected, at the residence of Gage Davis and Joshua Quittner. She began to pour out her story.

"And now Dr. Schuyler has decided to close this door to women. He is saying the male students believe no woman of 'true delicacy' would consider attending the semester on dissection of the human anatomy and declared their unwillingness to mix with any woman who has 'unsexed' herself, thereby sacrificing her own modesty."

She took the letter from Gage and refolded it into the envelope. "If I think I will ever be a doctor, and I believe I am called in that direction–which I know you think foolish, Gage . . ."

Gage held up his hands in surrender.

". . . and if I head to that goal, I must avail myself of all the medical courses this university offers. And human anatomy–including the semester on dissection–must be included."

Joshua winced as if the thought of anyone, not just Hannah, cutting into a dead human body was unsettling.

"And you have been in class up until this point?"

Hannah sniffed and wiped her eyes with a dainty, lavender handkerchief. She saw Gage glance at the feminine item. "It was a gift from my mother," she said, sniffing as she slipped the handkerchief back in her sleeve, "and yes, all semester, I have been in class. All lectures to this point–and I am, I think, first in the academic standings."

"And it will be a real dead body?" Joshua asked.

Gage laughed. "No–it will be a dead body that is alive. Of course it will be dead!"

Joshua looked up as if that manner of question were expected from Gage. "It's just that . . . I mean, Hannah is a woman and all."

Hannah wailed softly. "Not you too, Joshua," she cried. "I am so tired of telling everyone it does not matter."

Joshua glanced at Gage, who offered no support. "I just meant that . . . well, a body is . . . I mean . . . do I have to say it?"

Gage held his smirk. "Unclothed? Was that the word?"

Joshua shrugged. "It is a consideration. The Bible warns against . . ."

Hannah stood, hands on her hips, quickly angry. "So if the cadaver is a female, then no man should gaze on her 'unclothed' form? Would that be the moral response?"

Gage stepped to the fireplace. "Joshua, you will not win this argument. If you win, you lose–if you understand my meaning."

Hannah glared at them both. Gage stoked the fire, and the sound of the crackling wood hid the painful silence.

Finally she spoke. "Gage, do you know anyone that can help? Is there anything that can be done? I need to finish this study. There may not be any second chances for me."

When his gaze tightened, Hannah felt certain Gage was remembering her comments about his excessive wealth. And now, here she was, coming to him in supplication.

There is no one else who might help, she thought.

Without smiling, Gage spoke softly. "I think there might be something I might offer." Silently, he found his topcoat. "I will return within the hour," he said, leaving.

Hannah and Joshua stared after him as he left. Neither spoke for several minutes.

"I didn't mean, Hannah . . . what I said before . . . about things being moral and all."

Hannah waved off his apology. "I know, Joshua. Yet it is what most men say without thinking–but then they never see harm in the reverse situation. That I find hard to understand."

Joshua could not come up with a cogent answer.

After a minute of silence, Hannah began to cry. It was soft at first, inaudible as a spring mist, but her pain built and so did her tears. She reached for her handkerchief again. As the tears coursed down her flawless ivory cheeks, she turned to Joshua with a frightened look in her eyes, as if she were afraid of being found out to be a fraud.

Joshua put his arm up and around her shoulder. Without a word, Hannah burrowed into his chest and let her sobs come without censure. Joshua did not move a muscle for a long moment, then gently stroked Hannah's silky hair.

Hannah cried for many minutes. Neither spoke. Neither moved.

A log crashed, threatening to roll off the grate onto the marble hearth. Joshua reluctantly disentangled himself from Hannah, took shovel and poker, and maneuvered the hot coals and wood back into the fire. He set another two logs upon the grate.

When he turned back to the sofa, Hannah was gone. He spun about, searching for her. She stood, one hand at her throat, still clutching her handkerchief, staring out the window that overlooked Follen Street.

Joshua looked torn, as if he did not know whether to sit or go to her side.

Just then she spoke.

"It's Gage. I see him. And he's smiling."

From the Diary of Morgan Hannah Collins

April 1844

I imagine that my request cost Gage thousands. I hope it did not, but I believe that it has.

He never made mention of what transpired that day, nor did I insist on a full accounting. He did return with a broad smile on his face and claimed that it was a simple misunderstanding.

Joshua appeared to believe him. But I, the more cynical or realistic of the two of us, knew that leopards do not change their spots so quickly. And in spite of the fact that I scorned Gage for his wealth, I have taken advantage of it, just as he once intimated that I would. He offered someone money or an endowment to let me finish my studies–I can be sure of that.

And as I waited that day, blubbering and weeping like an immature schoolgirl, Joshua held me as I cried. I have to admit that I like the feeling of his arms about me. He has the deepest calm and strength I have ever known. Robert has his own sort of power, but he lacks Joshua's depth of character and serenity.

And now I am in the midst of the dissection of a real human body–a dead one, of course. The professor in charge of the dissection, a prudish mouselike man with sideburns the size of a pork roast, appeared to barely constrain his outrage at my presence. The body was brought in–a bluish tint to its flesh. It was lying on a wooden gurney, draped in a sheet of stained muslin. We were told that all human fluids had been drawn off and replaced with a preservative to prevent putrefaction of the flesh.

The professor draped a small rectangle of cloth over the most "sensitive" areas of the form. I suspect that I will be asked to leave the room when the lesson gets to that place. But I will fight that battle when the time comes.

The stench would be enough to give anyone pause to reconsider their studies. But I swore that I would never be the weak-willed female that is so often made sport of by men–so regardless of the stench and gore, I forced myself to stand without a tremble or comment. I watched as the keen knife found the deadness of the flesh, taking notes as is my custom.

I am so proud of my fortitude.

Three of the "strong" men in the class fainted dead away as soon as the body was undraped–let alone cut with a scalpel. And several more found ways to add to the stench.

I doubt if I will be able to take any food for a month after these classes.

The dead man–an unknown citizen who had been found on the docks of Boston–appeared to have died from natural causes since we saw no marks upon him.

I am told that few schools, if any, offer such instruction. Most doctors learn about such things as an apprentice to an established surgeon, who cuts and operates while his students observe. Harvard is one of the few that actually instructs students in a scientific manner.

The dissection took two full weeks to accomplish, and I will, for the sake of modesty and civility, not describe all that I saw and learned.

But suffice it to say, I have seen what animates a man, and it is truly amazing. We all know, I suppose, what is involved in our mechanics, but very few have seen an actual heart or lungs or liver. And I am now among the privileged few. I am not sure that this process will serve me when I become a doctor–if ever–but I am stronger for the experience.

And as a woman, I feel doubly privileged.

Perhaps Miss Mott was correct. I can do this. I can.

And the world will be changed by what I–what we–do.

Hannah stepped into the Destiny and felt an imperceptible hush sweep across the room. Heads turned and numerous curious eyes found themselves on her form. She heard whispers of "doctor" and "woman" and "cadaver." Holding her head high, she made her way to the far table, as was her custom and the custom of her friends.

Jamison was there, scribbling on a sheet of paper with the nub of a pencil. He looked up, startled, when she was at his side. "Hannah," he said hurriedly, as he stood to draw out her chair, "I did not expect to see you this evening."

She sat down without speaking. She heard a chair or two slide and creak as several fellow students slid away, providing an additional few inches of space between themselves and her.

Jamison, as if confused, studied the room, then Hannah's face. "Have you contracted some sort of rare disease?"

She shook her head.

"Or committed some sort of unusual moral lapse? An interesting one that is particularly offensive?"

She shook her head again.

"Then it must be that you have done the unpardonable."

She refused to smile, though Jamison's screwed-up expression made it difficult. "And that is?" she all but whispered.

"You have learned the secrets of a man," he whispered. "You have seen how we work."

She at last let a smile find her lips.

"And it was not a pretty sight now, was it?"

Hannah could hold back no longer and let out a deep, throaty laugh.

Jamison luxuriated in Hannah's laughter, letting it wash over him like a refreshing shower. If Hannah had been more observant, she would have seen the gleam in Jamison's eyes and the glow that her merriment caused.

But she did not.

Chapter Six

Harvard University
September 1844

A light shower at dusk cleaned the dust from the air, and the cobblestone streets gleamed as if polished. The leaves had not yet begun to turn to crimson, with the exception of a few eager lindens and maples that lined the commons area like soldiers on parade.

Hannah took a deep breath. She held the air for a long moment in her lungs, then exhaled with a gentle sigh.

It feels so good to be back and among my friends, she thought as she made her way to the Destiny. She had returned to Harvard less than a week ago. When she left her relatives' home this evening, both her aunt and uncle offered practiced expressions of hurt and abandonment. During her first three years at school, Hannah would be stricken with sharp pangs of guilt each time she left–other than to go to classes–as if her aunt and uncle were miserable in her absence.

But more recently she began to realize that it was simply an effort to keep her home. On occasion she did stay home, thinking that they needed or wanted her there. But those evenings would pass in silence, neither of them truly finding comfort in her companionship.

Now she ignored their pained looks–or at least attempted to do so.

Hannah wore a new autumn frock for the evening, one she had purchased this summer while home in Philadelphia. She had not worn it for her mother. The saleswoman who sold it claimed it was in the style of the new "French-cut" dresses, all the rage on the Continent this year. Hannah came close to blushing when she first attempted to wear the garment. The sleeves were short, leaving most of her arms bare. The hemline did not reach the floor, and in the act of sitting or walking, the ankles and part of the calf might be seen. And the bodice was cut lower than she was used to. True, she could wear a chemise to cover more flesh, but tonight, with the mild air, she decided to wear it as sewn. After all, it still wasn't revealing. However, she knew what boundaries to cross and when–she wore a shawl as she left her aunt and uncle and bunched the dress in such a manner that made it less daring.

Once a block away, the shawl came off and Hannah readjusted herself into the garment. She peered about to determine if anyone was watching.

I am not even sure why I selected this dress, she thought as she strolled along in the dusky amber light. *But I do like the way it makes me feel.*

She fussed at the skirt and set the pleats just so.

I wonder who will be at the Destiny tonight?

The warm light spilled out into the street, and even from a distance away, she could hear the hum of a multitude of conversations. A knot of students gathered under the gaslight in front. She could smell the acrid smoke of a pipe–or maybe a cigar. One of the students leaned back and laughed.

How good it is to be back! she thought, content.

Jamison Pike sat at their table, the only one in attendance so far this night. He stood as she drew close. Hannah noted that he wore some sort of buckskin coat–so unlike the somber grays and blacks of his first two years. He needed a shave, and his hair appeared to be a week past the time for a trim.

"Hannah!" he called out. "How have you been? Have you had a good summer?"

She watched with some amusement as Jamison appeared to force his eyes to remain on her face and wander no lower.

"Yes, I have. It was not remarkable in any particular way–but enjoyable nonetheless."

Jamison smoothed the tabletop with his hands, a gesture he often resorted to when nervous.

Hannah continued. "We had plans to venture to the New Jersey shore again, but the weeks we had planned saw a large and violent storm sweep up the coast. It was said the waves crested near to the porch of my cousin's home. I suspect that bridges were damaged as well."

"So you stayed in Philadelphia then?" Jamison asked, his eyes going no lower than her shoulder.

"Indeed. But we visited some and people came to call, and there were recitals and a museum opening and church and the like. Plus all the studying that is required simply to keep abreast of schoolwork. And you, Jamison? An exciting summer in Pittsburgh?"

He snorted a reply. "*Exciting* and *Pittsburgh* are two words that are never used in the same sentence."

"Surely it is not as bleak as you make it out to be. It's on the river. Haven't rowing and sailing taken on as they have here? And there must be many travelers who stop for a night or so. That must add some interest."

"Perhaps," Jamison replied, "but that would require a man to spend his days and nights at the docks. And the docks are not the most seemly section of town."

The serving girl, Melinda, stopped at the table with a pad in her hand. Pulling out a chair, she sat next to Jamison. Hannah had often been surprised by her boldness, but no one else appeared to think her forwardness was worth comment. When she actually gave Jamison a hug, Hannah kept her jaw from dropping open.

"Welcome back, Jamison," Melinda said warmly. "I have missed you so over the summer. It is good to have you back where you belong." She hesitated, then added, "And welcome back to you, too, Miss Collins."

Hannah watched Melinda's eyes assess her new dress, and for a moment, they were creased hard with jealous disapproval.

"Thanks, Melinda," Jamison replied. "It is nice to be back."

"And what is it you want this evening, Jamison? What's your pleasure tonight?"

He could not help but smile in response. "Just a strong cup of coffee and some biscuits and jam if you've got them. I have only arrived today, and the journey was anything but pleasant."

"Of course. I'll brew a fresh pot for you," she purred, "and I think we've got some fresh biscuits in the oven." She stood and stepped away, then turned back. "Oh, Miss Collins, I forgot. Is there something that you desire–since I am going to the kitchen, that is."

Hannah tried not to glare back. "Just a pot of tea, if it wouldn't be too much trouble."

"No trouble at all," Melinda replied, her words edging to cold.

After she left, Hannah turned to Jamison. "Honestly!" she exclaimed. "Why the owner puts up with her is beyond me. Such impudence from a serving girl."

Shock was written on Jamison's face. "Impudence? Really?"

Hannah nodded. "And how forward could she have been–giving you a hug and all. If that isn't being forward, I don't know what is."

Jamison almost appeared pleased. "Melinda is a good egg," he replied. "She's had a tough life. The Destiny would be a much less friendly place without her." He smiled. "Much less friendly," he added.

Hannah narrowed her eyes. "And if a male waiter offered me the same greeting–that would meet your criteria of a 'friendly place'?"

Jamison laughed. "You're jealous, aren't you?"

"I am not," she said quickly. "I'm not. And of what? Why would I be jealous?"

Jamison shrugged. "Just sounds like jealousy to me." He offered a smug smile to seal his observation.

Hannah disliked the path this conversation had taken. *I don't even like him that much,* she thought. *Why would I be jealous if some trollop of a serving girl throws herself on him? If Jamison thinks it "friendly," then why should that be any concern of mine?*

She glared at him even as he smiled back at her.

"I'm not jealous, Jamison. You have no right to think that I am."

He arched his eyebrows in response.

"I'm not. If all the hussies at Harvard wish to embrace you–and God knows why they would want to do that–I would not be the least jealous."

Jamison tilted his head with a quizzical look.

"I'm not jealous," she insisted.

Melinda came to the table with a pot of coffee, a plate of biscuits still steaming from the oven, a crock of jam, and a dainty pot of tea and mismatched teacup and saucer.

"Here you are, Jamison," she said sweetly. "I hope this is to your liking." She set the teacup and pot in front of Hannah without a word. "You'll call me if I can get you anything else, won't you?"

He offered the grin of a small boy in return. "I will, Melinda. I will."

She smiled and slowly turned away. Hannah thought she saw Melinda wink at Jamison, but it might have simply been a reflection of the lamplight.

Jamison poured a cup of coffee, then studied Hannah. She could not hide her agitation. He tilted his head again and raised his eyebrows in that most infuriating manner.

"I am not jealous, Jamison Pike. I am not," she said firmly and perhaps too loudly, for the people seated at nearby tables all turned to the sound of her voice.

He ladled out a thick spoon of strawberry jam onto a warm biscuit. Taking a large bite, he chewed slowly. After a moment, he addressed Hannah. "Have you read *Hamlet?*"

She glared at him. "And you think I am totally uncultured, is that it? That I have no grasp of the classics?"

He did not appear surprised by her feistiness. "No, I simply wondered if you had read it."

"I have," she said with a haughty sniff.

"You remember what Hamlet's mother said to her son after the play–the play within the play, that is?"

Hannah glared again. "No."

"She said, 'The lady doth protest too much, methinks.' "

As she leaned forward to speak in a low tone, Jamison averted his eyes. "You are impossible, Jamison Pike. You truly are. I am not jealous of you, and I am not protesting too much. You simply infuriate me at times."

He took another bite and washed it down with a swallow of coffee. "Just doing my job, Miss Collins. Just doing my job."

From the Diary of Morgan Hannah Collins

September 1844

Jamison Pike is such a . . . I don't know what he is, and I will not allow barnyard epithets to be used in this diary. But he is one. And he knows it, too.

I don't know why the conversation took the turn it did, but I found myself in an hour-long argument debating if I was or was not jealous of Melinda's attention to him.

I daresay that Melinda's forwardness would cause many women of ill repute to blush–but Jamison seems to think it cute or simply part of the Destiny experience.

It isn't proper. That much I am sure of. Despite the fact that women are making strides to be more the equal of men, it is not right that a woman . . . that a serving girl . . . acts as brazen as a man might act.

After our conversation's contentious beginning, we both seemed to regret our actions and words and became civil to one another. He even offered to share his biscuits with me–and I took him up on the offer. Aunt Constance is a lovely woman but not adept in the kitchen.

After much conversation, Jamison admitted that his summer was pleasant and not the dire experience he made it out to be. He wrote a series of articles for the Pittsburgh paper–I forget the name of it–on travelers' impressions of the city. He said most of his time was spent near the docks, even though he originally claimed the area to be dangerous and vile.

So much of Jamison is a study in contradictions. He claims to care little for the world's pleasures and says he seeks only the truth. Then he admits to disliking deprivations. He tells me gentle falsehoods all the time.

Is it simply a practice of the male gender to keep us guessing all the time? I do not think I will ever understand them.

And his buckskin jacket? He claims that his new goal in life is to head west and seek adventure out there–among the savages and wilderness.

When I asked him if there will be a need for journalists out there, my question stopped him for a moment, but then he smiled. (And I do like him better when he allows himself to be happy.)

"There's a big audience for my adventures right here in Boston. I imagine that a tale well told will always have an eager listener willing to pay a cent or so to share in it."

And I believe he may be right. Perhaps he's another James Fenimore Cooper in the making.

October 1844

Harvard seemed unusually quiet the entire month of October. Even the Destiny, Hannah thought, grew muted and still, the loud boisterous exchanges now narrowed to quiet, intense conversations. There were few evenings where Hannah herself could afford the luxury of leaving her studies to be with her friends. The first three years felt simple in comparison. Her studies had taken no more than a few hours a week. Hannah knew she was a clever student and often received outstanding marks simply by paying attention in class and taking detailed notes. What she committed to paper usually stuck in her thoughts and was easily retrieved.

But her final year at the university, her senior year, when she thought her life would be more carefree and indolent, had become nearly the exact opposite. The courses, from their descriptions, were no more difficult. The professors appeared to be no more demanding. But Hannah perceived a doubling or trebling of her hours spent in study each week. She was in the fourth year of Latin–that was most taxing. Advanced chemistry classes and scientific principles were thick with instruction and chart after chart of memorization.

Despite the increased weight of studies, Hannah was no less committed to her goal–of being the first woman doctor in the state of Massachusetts. Yet, if asked, Hannah was often at a loss for words to describe exactly why her desire remained so strong.

Florence Galeswhite often sat near her in the library, marveling at her dedication, quizzing her on a huge list of chemical compounds, their effects on the body, and a list of ailments that could be addressed by each.

"You got them all correct," Florence said, "with the exception of the salts of antimony, which is used to correct ulcers and nervousness–not consumption as you stated."

Hannah slapped her hand to her forehead. "I shall never get them all," she wailed softly. "How do I expect to treat the sick if I can't remember what medicine to prescribe?"

Florence closed the massive medical book with finality. "That does it, Miss Collins. You must come with me. We will take a much-needed break."

"No, you go without me, Florence," Hannah replied, reaching for the book. "I must review one more time."

"Nonsense," Florence insisted. She rose, slipped her leather satchel under her arm, and grabbed Hannah's arm.

At first Hannah resisted, then realized that Florence had six inches and fifty pounds on her. She closed her eyes and allowed herself to be dragged out of the library and toward the main shopping street of Cambridge.

Hannah had not been down this street for months. Her paths existed between her home and Harvard, with only occasional trips made to the Destiny.

Cambridge Street ambled along the northern edge of the university. All manner of shops cluttered about the street, standing elbow to jowl, each merchant hustling his wares, competing for the attention of the customers.

Hannah, more accustomed to a refined and civil shopping experience in Philadelphia's more sedate, private salons, was often ill at ease in the hustle-bustle closeness of Cambridge Street.

"Come on, Hannah, let's have some fun," Florence called out as she pulled Hannah across the street. "Let's look at hats."

"But I do not need a hat," Hannah protested.

"Nonsense again," Florence replied. "There is never a time when a woman does not need a new hat. You must remember that, Hannah, once you get married. You always need a new hat."

Hannah laughed at her seriousness, hoping Florence truly knew how preposterous the advice was.

Why would I say I needed a new hat when I don't?

"And then we can look for shoes. There's a new cobbler just down on the next block who does the most divine work."

Hannah stopped and leaned out into the street. "A new cobbler?" *I do need a new pair of shoes to go with the dress my mother sent. I have absolutely nothing to wear with it.*

"Indeed. I saw the most outrageous red shoes with tiny little buttonhooks of silver. Perhaps they might fit you."

"Light red or dark red?" Hannah asked, wishing they could skip the hat shop and go directly to the cobbler.

"Dark red. Luscious. Smooth as silk. The color of a crimson rose."

In the rear booth of Wobert's Ice Cream Parlor, Hannah and Florence, surrounded by packages, nearly collapsed in laughter.

"It was an emergency," Hannah insisted. "Those shoes were an emergency."

"You would have died without them?" Florence asked.

"Exactly!" Hannah responded, and both began to laugh again.

Shopping had consumed the entire afternoon. It would be only an hour until lanterns would need to be used, and the two women sat, lit by the day's final golden light.

Empty ice cream glasses stood in front of them.

"Might as well travel the entire journey," Florence had said as she pulled Hannah into their last stop.

Between them, they had purchased hats, gloves, a frock, the red shoes, packets of potpourri, scarves, and a few intimate garments as well.

Hannah lifted her foot and admired the red shoes again–for the dozenth time in the last few minutes. "They are most exquisite shoes, aren't they, Florence?"

Florence grinned, spooning a thick dollop of cream into her coffee. "Sometimes a woman simply needs to escape the trials of academe," she said as she sipped. "And today was just such a day."

"They'll go well with my mother's gown. Perhaps I might wear it when Robert calls this weekend."

"Robert Keyes?"

Hannah nodded.

"And where is your gentleman friend taking you this time?"

"To Boston. There is a traveling show–at the Regal, I believe. The actors all come from England and will be performing some play by Shakespeare. I have heard it is most splendid."

"But didn't you say that Mr. Keyes has little interest in such frivolous things as plays?"

Hannah took the final scoop of ice cream, more cream than ice. "He isn't totally convinced at the necessity of such cultural events. But he gamely attends. One does meet a higher class of people at those affairs."

"Not the best reason to go," Florence added, "but a reason nonetheless."

"It's not that he is against it. He's a cultured man in his own way. He simply has very definite ideas of what should and should not be. I like that. Shows that he has spent time considering matters and has decided accordingly."

Florence shrugged. "I suppose."

Hannah bent to her left and stared at her shoes again.

"And what does he say of your becoming a doctor one day?"

Even as Florence asked the question, Hannah's glowing countenance changed. Her eyes and lips drew tight, as if a minor, yet irritating pain had entered her heart.

"He has told me . . . well, he has told me that he does not mind if I continue my studies at Harvard. He said that since I have already spent so much money on tuition, it would not be fiscally responsible to walk away before they grant me a diploma."

"And what about after?"

Florence leaned in close. On numerous occasions she had listened to Hannah tell of her dream of becoming a doctor, of helping others, of treating children and women who so often were ignored by other doctors.

It was obvious Hannah did not want to continue. But Florence ignored her sudden silence and pressed on. "And what about after? He would not stop you from going on to Oberlin or wherever, would he? He doesn't have that right, you know."

Hannah looked away for a long minute, then turned back to Florence. "He wouldn't stop me . . . at least he never said he would. The only thing he said about the matter . . . and we have not discussed it much . . . was that he thought becoming a physician for a woman was . . . unseemly."

"Unseemly? What does he mean by that?"

"He said that it may not be the right path for a woman of my breeding. He said that he indulged me in this up till now, but that any woman wanting to be Mrs. Keyes would not be interested in wasting her time on such foolishness."

Florence leaned back in obvious surprise. "You mean to tell me he asked you to marry him?"

Hannah sat up and waved her hand. "No . . . not at all. It wasn't like that. It was a general discussion with some of his friends. I wasn't even part of it. I overheard it, that's all. I was in the music room, and Robert and some gentlemen friends were in the study with brandy and cigars and all that. It was at the Reeds'–his aunt and uncle's house in Boston. You have heard me mention the Reeds, haven't you? And anyhow, Florence, you know how it is when some men talk with other men. They are filled with bravado and all manner of proclamations. Their stance is often much less firm when back with a woman. I am sure Robert was simply talking like a man that day."

Florence took her friend's hand. "You had best ask him directly, Hannah. If he thinks study and knowledge are just a temporary indulgence, then you had best tell him how you really feel. You must. It will only lead to problems later in life."

Hannah offered a smile that hinted at sadness, then nodded. "I will, Florence. I will."

The two stared at each other for a minute.

"But he is so handsome, isn't he, Florence?"

Florence laughed. "That he is, Hannah. That he is. But is he rich?"

Hannah waited a minute to respond. "He will be. He definitely will be."

December 1844

"You just missed them," Jamison declared.

"Missed who?" Hannah asked.

"Joshua and Gage. They were here all afternoon."

"Don't either of them have classes anymore?" Hannah asked. "I keep seeing them about campus, often in the midst of some heated dispute or another. What were they contending today?"

Jamison tilted back in his chair. "The same as always–the meaning of life."

Laughing, Hannah added, "Money or God, right?"

"Exactly."

Hannah settled into the well-worn leather chair. The student union attempted to maintain a certain number of upholstered chairs and padded benches for students, but the most comfortable had a method of disappearing. And every summer most would migrate back from rented rooms, and the hall would be filled again. To have a few good chairs this late in the season was surprising.

"Where did these chairs come from?" Hannah asked. "Florence and I were in yesterday, and I don't recall them here."

"A friend of Joshua's was tossed out of Harvard for cheating. That's the story I heard. He had them stashed in his room."

"A friend of Joshua's? Cheating? How could that be? Doesn't his goodness rub off on all those nearby?" she said, grinning.

"So where is your Valkyrie friend?" Jamison asked.

"Who? Who's a what?"

"Valkyrie. The tall blonde woman."

"She's a Valkyrie?"

It was apparent to all but Hannah that Jamison loved this polite sparring.

"Yes."

"Do you know what a Valkyrie is?"

Jamison rubbed his chin. "I'm not sure, but it sounds tall, blonde, and Swedish."

Hannah could not hold her laughter. "You're right about tall and blonde–but she's English."

"Close enough," Jamison concluded.

Hannah stared at him. "Well?"

"Well, what?"

"You asked about Florence."

"Who?"

Hannah threw her copy of the *Crimson Review* at him. Jamison ducked, laughing. After a moment, he sat up.

"You are simply impossible, Jamison Pike. I do not know why I put up with you. Honestly. A simple conversation with you can lead a person to distraction."

Instantly Jamison appeared contrite. Then a grin flickered on his face. "Is that outside Boston?"

"Is what outside Boston?" Hannah asked.

"Distraction," he answered. "You keep saying I could lead a person there, but I've never stepped foot in the place."

With that Hannah jumped from her chair, grabbed Jamison about the shoulders, and proceeded to shower a flurry of friendly blows to his arm. His face was turned from her, but his smile could be seen across the room.

FROM THE DIARY OF MORGAN HANNAH COLLINS

DECEMBER 1844

This will be a most brief entry. I am in the midst of final examinations in two courses and am attempting to pack for my Christmas journey to Philadelphia. I am praying the weather remains as mild as it has been. I so dislike traveling in snow and bitter cold.

Robert Keyes and I attended one holiday ball at the Kensington Club just across the river. The room dripped with pine boughs. Robert mentioned that the invitation had been most difficult to come by. It must have been, for he mentioned that fact innumerable times.

The guest list was most impressive–from the mayor of Boston to senators and philanthropists and all manner of notables. I even met a crowned prince from France. I did not inquire as to why there would be a prince in a country that practiced a democratic government, but I am told there are many displaced royals who attend these affairs as if it were their only occupation. There was much talk of the telegraph and the upcoming presidential election. Will it be Polk or Clay? Most say it will be a close race.

And who might I meet at this affair? The one person I would have never expected to attend: Jamison Pike, complete in a splendid morning coat and tails!

I suspect he had just stepped out of both a barbershop and a tailor for he looked downright handsome, though somewhat ill at ease.

He claimed he was attending as a reporter in the temporary employ of the *Boston Globe.* He showed me his press credentials, as I am certain my face showed my disbelief.

The rest of the evening passed in pleasant fashion, yet one incident does stand out. It was an hour past dinner, and everyone seemed to circulate about the room as if following an unseen, slow-moving current. Robert spent much time darting from one important conversation to another. He seems to be in much demand by many. As a result, I was often left alone–and not that I mind it–but I had chance to speak with many others as well.

It was during one of Robert's absences that I found myself next to Jamison, in an ill-lit alcove, resting on a bench that seemed to be built into the darkness. He sat next to me and inquired if I was having a good time. I said I was. I asked about his impressions of the event.

"Full of sound and fury, signifying little," he said. Then he extracted a tattered little book from his pocket. It was titled *An Emigrant's Guide to Oregon and California.* "This is the future of America," he said, nearly breathless.

"Isn't that thousands of miles away?" I asked.

He proceeded to tell me, in the span of an hour, all that the books mentioned about the frontier, the Indians, the grandeur of nature, and the dangers. He was as near to glowing as any fellow I have ever seen.

"We should be there, Hannah," he concluded. "You and I . . . we should be part of this grand adventure."

And then . . . I heard Robert call my name.

Such a dreamer, Jamison is.

Oregon.

Where is that, exactly?

CHAPTER SEVEN

Cambridge, Massachusetts
March 1845

ON the third floor of Harvard's administration building, an imposing brick and limestone copy of a Greek temple, a wide hall ran the entire length of the building. Since the hall was lined with tall windows, all facing to the south, the air warmed quickly on sunny winter days. One could sit in the sunshine, without coat or hat, and bask in the unexpected heat.

Today, the beginning warmth of the last few days of March had begun to seep into the hall. A scattering of chairs sat against the interior walls. On any given day, there might be ten or more students waiting their turn with professors and advisors. Harvard boasted that its professors took a close, personal interest in each student in their charge.

But students knew better. Most professors seemed not to know any student personally and desired any true relationship with a student as much as they desired sickness. According to university rules and dictates, every student was obligated to meet four times yearly with his or her academic advisor. These meetings, it was hoped, would forge lasting bonds and provide a mentoring relationship for those students who might not be keenly aware of their future goals.

All four meetings had to occur before the end of class each year or else a student would not receive final evaluations and grades. Two weeks before that date, the third-floor hallway would be crowded with hundreds of students keeping their appointments–some making all four for the very same day.

To avoid the rush, Hannah had decided that she would attempt to finish her appointments earlier.

Hannah reached the third floor and turned left. She was one of the few students who did, in fact, make regular appointments with her university-appointed advisor. Yet now, after having met with him more than a dozen times, she paused. She was not certain just what she felt–was it merely frustration or exhaustion, or something else more malevolent, more draining?

The well-worn floor creaked with every step. Professor Mocker, a scholar in ancient languages, had been her advisor since she began her life at Harvard. He was a short, round man with a halo of white hair encircling his face. He had never married, and it was rumored that he bought one suit and one shirt at the beginning of each year and wore it every day without ever washing, then discarded it the first of June.

The university handbook stated that a student could change his or her advisor with the written consent of the former as well as the new potential advisor, plus a letter of explanation regarding the cause of such a decision.

Very few students, if any, ever changed their appointed advisor. Hannah had been tempted on many occasions, but her umbrage wore off by the time she reached the first floor following each meeting. Now all she had left was this appointment and one other. And she was fairly certain she could endure two more hours with Professor Mocker–especially since it was late in the day and he would want to finish the appointment as soon as possible.

The door to his office was closed, indicating that he had another student with him. Hannah leaned close to the opaque glass panel. She could hear a soft murmur of conversation, pocked every so often with Professor Mocker's explosive and angry laugh. The first time she had heard it, she thought he was in the midst of a stroke or spell of some sort. Then she saw a disjointed smile on his face and realized that he was attempting to be humorous.

The first year, the fact that Hannah was a woman continually amazed Professor Mocker. He asked at length how it was that she found herself at Harvard and not at some school to learn how to become a schoolmarm or nurse. As she explained her reasons, she watched as he stared back at her with an uncomprehending expression.

She did not mention her desire to become a physician until she had already taken and passed nearly all of the required medical courses that were offered to undergraduates. And when she did, he blushed crimson, sputtered some incomprehensible fragments, and ushered her quickly out of the office. She had always suspected that he was the root of her initially being banned from the anatomy class. When Gage held sway with higher-up school officials, Hannah noted a certain air of angry resignation about the professor.

The door opened and banged against the wall, dimpling the plaster where it had been dimpled a thousand times before. Arthur Westhaven stepped out into the hall. Arthur and Hannah were not friends, but they had shared several classes. As he slipped into his coat, he rolled his eyes at her and jerked his head toward the inner office.

"What's his mood today?" she whispered.

Arthur whispered back, "Who cares? I have one more meeting with the ancient old man and all I have to do is stay awake."

She noticed his grin and tried not to laugh.

"Actually," he added, "he told me stories about how hard it was when he was young. We young whippersnappers have it so easy."

Hannah replied in a soft giggle, "Did he say he had to walk twenty miles to school every day?"

"And that he didn't have any shoes?"

"And that it snowed five feet every week every winter?"

"And that he studied for ten hours every night?"

"And that he had to get up an hour before he went to bed?"

Hannah placed her hand over her mouth to stop her laugh.

"And when he tells young people about it today, they just don't believe him," Arthur said, adopting Professor Mocker's indignant pose.

Hannah could not help snorting into her palm.

"Miss Collins!" Professor Mocker boomed.

"Good luck," Arthur said as he hurried down the hall.

Gathering up her coat and books, she whispered a loud, "Thank you," entered Mocker's office, and closed the door.

"A doctor, you say? Why in my day, we didn't have doctors and all this fancy medicine. But we survived. We managed. Takes a little common sense, that's all."

Hannah nodded dutifully.

"And what do your parents think of all this nonsense? I imagine them to be most unsettled."

"No, sir, they were not at all unsettled." She hoped lying to a professor would not be too serious of a sin.

"What? They actually think this is a proper choice for a young lady of your style and breeding? A woman doctor? Mucking about in people's insides? Horrid, if you ask me."

She blinked once. "Well, sir, they have always been . . . supportive of me."

"Makes no sense to me," he gruffed on. "When you first mentioned such an inane idea, I thought it was one of those woman things–a temporary aberration of logical thought. You are prone to those, are you not?"

"No, sir, I am not."

"Well, no matter. But then you foolishly kept after the idea. Normally I would think perseverance is a virtue, but not if the original idea is foolish. Now, as your advisor, I want you to stop this. There is no need for a woman physician. You may take my word on that."

Hannah nodded. *Haven't I heard much the same from my parents and Robert–even if they do couch their bias in more comforting words and phrases?*

"Then you agree? You'll stop this? You'll get your diploma and get married?"

She gazed out the window at the bare branches of an oak tree clattering in the breeze. "With all due respect, Professor Mocker, I cannot do as you wish."

He exploded. "I thought as much. You've been reading that nonsense that Stanton has been writing, haven't you? Blasted radical!"

She knew he meant Elizabeth Stanton.

"You know she refused to let the minister who married them use the word *obey,* don't you?" he continued. "Why her foolish husband agreed to such a condition, I don't know."

Hannah acted as if she knew nothing of Stanton, though the woman's activities had garnered wide coverage in most newspapers. Even Jamison had written a column on her decision, though he deftly avoided taking a personal stance on the matter.

"She did?" Hannah asked. "And the preacher agreed?"

Professor Mocker grunted and proceeded to turn toward his desk. "I think he was an Episcopalian, the liberal fools. And now with Polk in the White House, anything is possible."

Hannah waited while he busied himself thumbing through the same stacks of papers that had been on his desk for nearly four years. Five minutes later, he looked up and realized Hannah was still there.

"Oh, I thought you had left, Miss Collins."

"No, sir, I was waiting for you to sign the advisor's report. That we met and agreed on things."

"Did we?"

"I think we did, sir. We agreed on most."

He snatched the paper, scratched his initials on a blank line, and added the date. "Then we're done. Good day, Miss Collins."

Hannah gathered up her coat and hurried out, hoping he would not recall how their conversation truly ended. She turned the corner by the steps just as she heard her name shouted from behind. She gulped once, and as silently as she could, hurried down the steps, taking two at a time. She stopped only when she was well out of sight and did not stop her brisk pace until she was only feet from the front entrance of the Destiny.

Two hours later, in looking around at the yellowed walls, walls that had not once been cleaned or painted in her entire tenure at Harvard, Hannah felt a sharp pang of regret and loss. Even though graduation was nearly three months in the future, Hannah realized she had come to consider Cambridge as home. When she returned to Philadelphia for the summers and during Christmas holidays, it was as if she were now the stranger. No longer did she have that innate sense of place, a native's unspoken right. Few places there felt familiar or comfortable. When she first departed from Philadelphia, she could not imagine ever living anywhere else. Now she wondered if she might ever be able to return home.

The Destiny was home to a wonderful assortment of sounds and scents–all aimed, Hannah imagined, at making a stranger feel wanted. The nicked tables, some scarred with multiple engraved names of former patrons, and the mismatched chairs all assimilated into one cheerful group; the kitchen, with its storm of familiar foods, all conspired to induce the overwhelming thought: *I am home.*

Currently within the Destiny's walls, fifteen students and patrons lolled about, drinking coffee or ale, smoking pipes, and reading three-day-old newspapers. Earlier, when she had first entered, Hannah had smiled as she nodded to the owner, whose name she still did not know. She had made her way to her favorite table near the back, tucked close to the wall. As expected, it was empty. She had requested coffee and buttered toast with cinnamon, since she was not yet hungry for dinner.

Now she sat back, glanced about, and slipped a second chair close, lifting her legs onto it. She leaned back, folding her hands in her lap.

It has all gone so quickly. Four years have passed in the blink of an eye. I have learned a great deal, but am I ready for the future? I do not take anything Professor Mocker says to be predictive, but what he thinks the majority of men in America think. A woman doctor? That at once sounds so wonderful–and so absurd. Can I even think there is a glimmer of a chance that it all might come to pass?

She dumped three large spoonfuls of sugar into her third cup of coffee and then added a large dash of cream. Smiling, she recalled Robert's words. *At least I refuse to compromise on my coffee.*

She sipped and offered a silent sigh.

I know I am already a pioneer. A woman at Harvard is a rare animal, after all. Do I need to tread on new ground? I know what Stanton and Mott would say. Go! Do! Become! But is that what I want? I look at those women and wonder what they have given up to become what they are. I suppose everyone gives up something when any choice is made. Do I need to sacrifice the chance to be married and have children simply because I chose to be a pioneer?

And what about men? I like being around them too much to swear off them forever. I do believe Robert is a fine man and will make a wonderful husband. But will he insist on my abandoning my dream? Is that what the promise of marriage holds for me?

A wave of melancholy swept over her and she swallowed, feeling as near to tears as she had in months. She wiped her nose with a handkerchief and blinked hard.

Just then the door opened, and a fresh wind blew through the restaurant. The sunlight hid the newcomer from view. Hannah blinked again and shielded her eyes with her hand.

"Joshua," she called out, "over here."

Joshua looked wildly to both sides and then over his shoulder, as if assessing the chance of making an early escape.

"Come on, Joshua, I know you heard me. Come over here. I will not bite."

Joshua stepped over to the table and clumsily grabbed the chair farthest away from Hannah, as if he had forgotten how to sit.

She shook her head in soft amusement. "I have not seen you in a month of Sundays, Joshua," she said. "Where have you been hiding? You haven't been at the Destiny very often."

His cheeks were red. Hannah was not certain if it was the brisk wind or embarrassment.

"I . . . I've been here. I seem to get here late in the evening–well past the time that you must have gone home."

Hannah studied him, knowing then that Joshua had been purposeful in his avoidance of her. And she could tell by his expression that he knew she knew. Yet neither of them would address the reason for such a state between old friends.

Had Hannah asked for a reason, Joshua would have simply said, "Robert Keyes."

If Hannah had been asked, she would have offered the same response.

The two evaluated each other for a long minute.

"So, how have you been, Joshua?"

"Very well."

"Are your studies going well?"

"They are."

"Are you still preaching in the area?"

"Yes, on occasion." Joshua swallowed hard.

"Joshua, I do not expect a discourse," Hannah said, suddenly angry, "but I would expect you to follow the accepted standards of a conversation between friends. You might speak that way to a stranger, but why would you speak that way to me?"

It always puzzled Hannah, as she recalled conversations, how different she was with every man she counted as a friend. With Joshua, she could be assertive and nearly flirtatious. With Jamison, she would be argumentative and gaily contentious. With Gage, she felt as she imagined she would feel with an older brother. And with Robert, she became quiet, reserved, and most amenable.

"I am sorry, Hannah," he quickly said in apology. "I don't know . . . I mean, we haven't talked and . . ."

She laughed and dismissed his apology with her hand. "It is no matter, Joshua. Just treat me as you always have, and I will be content."

She reached over and clasped his hand. He looked back at her with wide eyes.

"So tell me–how are your sermons really going?"

"My sermons . . . are good."

"You must use up all your words when you preach and leave none for friends," Hannah said wryly. "Very well. If you will not converse, then I will."

Hannah described the latest events in her pursuit of a medical degree. It appeared there was a weekly confrontation or crisis with either a befuddled professor or an acutely embarrassed fellow student.

Joshua smiled broadly, as if he loved her stories.

"And then there is Robert. Have I told you about the curious matter with Robert and myself?"

Just then the clock tower began to toll, pealing seven times.

Joshua jumped up. "I am sorry, Hannah. I forgot that I am scheduled to see my advisor, and then I have another appointment. I'm behind as it is. I must beg your forgiveness and take my leave."

And within a breath, he was gone, the banging of the door an echo in the evening.

After Joshua left, Hannah sat, quiet and reflective. She knew he was uncomfortable in her presence now that he knew of Robert Keyes, but she could not understand why he was so acutely uncomfortable. *I would think that friendship is such a strong bond that he might overlook such matters.*

"Hannah!"

Her reverie was loudly interrupted. Gage nearly ran to the table. Taking her hand, he pressed it to his lips. "My dear Hannah," he bubbled as he pulled out a chair next to her, "this is such an unexpected pleasure. What brings you here tonight?"

Hannah gently extracted her hand. "Gage, I know it is very European of you, but kissing a lady's hand? Isn't that somewhat of an affectation?"

Gage laughed. "My whole life is often a huge affectation, my dear. Kissing a beautiful woman's hand is no more than a trifling aberration. And you haven't answered my question."

She sighed. "After meeting with Mocker–my advisor–I needed to feel comforted again. The Destiny provides that."

"And his advice?"

"To desist in my goal of becoming a doctor. To get married."

Gage leaned close. "Is that an invitation, my dear? Are you proposing to me?"

Hannah gave him a playful shove. "Mocker is old and crotchety–not insane."

Gage grabbed his chest. "I am wounded deeply. You must apologize at once."

She laughed and shoved him again. He straightened up and tugged at his sleeves.

"Have you seen Joshua?" he asked. "He was supposed to meet me here at seven."

Taken off guard, Hannah said, "He just left. He said he had an advisor's appointment and then something else."

"That was yesterday. We both went together," Gage said, puzzled.

"But he used it as an excuse to leave. I suspect that he didn't want to be with me," she replied with a note of sadness.

"Joshua? He lied to you? Another sign that Western civilization is in imminent danger of collapsing."

"So he did lie! He dislikes me that much?"

Gage grew serious, speaking very softly. "I think when you mentioned Robert, it hurt him more than he ever let on. He's a simple farm boy at heart–regardless of how intelligent he is. And I think he held out hope for more."

"But I never led him on," she replied.

Gage offered a wry smile in response.

"Well . . . maybe just a little," she admitted. "But he took it all so seriously."

"It is simply who Joshua is, Hannah. He is one serious fellow. He takes everything seriously."

"So I have lost him as a friend? You mean to say that a man and a woman cannot be friends? They cannot have a relationship without it becoming all convoluted with desire and all that?"

Gage leaned back, surprised. "My . . . a deep question."

"I'm serious, Gage. Can't a man and a woman be friends?"

He turned his head and thought for a moment. "No. Well, maybe some can. But not Joshua."

"Why?"

"I don't know. We're like children, you know."

"What? Like children how?"

"You haven't realized that fact? I'm surprised. But we are. All men are."

"How?"

"We want everything. We want what we don't have. When we get it, we often discard it and want something else. We pout when we don't get our own way. If someone has something we want, we either fight for it or simply ignore it altogether."

"That's the truth of men?"

"Well, all men except me. I am much more sophisticated than all that."

She shoved him again, and they both joined in laughter.

Hannah looked up as the bell tolled eight times and reached for her purse.

"I must think of going home," she said with regret.

"Stay awhile longer," Gage implored. "We have only begun to scratch the surface of the differences between men and women."

Gage offered his best little-boy, wistful grin. She put her purse back down on the chair next to her.

"Well, I have whiled away so much of today as it is, there is no reason to think I can redeem any of the time. I may as well waste it with you."

"Ah, madam, you charm me with your glowing recommendations of my ability as a companion."

Hannah loved being with Gage. He seldom took himself seriously and always sought out ways to bring a smile or laughter to the conversation.

She put her elbows on the table and leaned her chin into her upturned palms. "Graduation is only three months away. Are you sad, Gage?"

"Some. I will miss you and Joshua and the rest. But I am looking forward to starting my life as a real adult."

"Me too."

"And you've made your applications for further study, have you?"

Hannah nodded. "One of them is Oberlin College." She put her hand out. "And I know your opinion of the place even before I ask, so you needn't bother to disparage it now. There is a doctor who plans to start a medical school in Philadelphia–and will admit only women. There is another school in Virginia that has not yet said no, but neither have they said yes."

"Then your future looks promising."

Hannah's shoulders drooped. "I wish it were that simple."

"And it isn't?"

"Robert doesn't think my goal is suitable."

"Suitable?"

"It's beneath me. He said he would be embarrassed if his wife spent all day with sick people."

"Well, I know the type. And to be honest, Hannah, I understand how he feels."

"And you would prevent me from becoming a physician?"

"If we were married?"

"Yes."

"Are you proposing again?"

Hannah struck him this time, as hard as she could, on the arm. He winced and grabbed the bruise with great theatrics. "Are you drumming up business for yourself?" he cried out, laughing.

"Answer the question or I do the other arm," she said, making a fist and shaking it in his face.

"I surrender!"

"Answer the question."

"Well, I understand him–Robert. If my wife–if I ever marry–were a doctor and was at a party I daresay there would be some in the room who would be squeamish."

"Why?"

"Two reasons–one, that you have been around the sick all day, and two, you have knowledge of the workings of a man."

"And married women are totally ignorant?"

"It doesn't make sense, Hannah, but I have already told you men don't make sense. It is simply how it would be. There would be an awkward silence now and again once people knew. Me, I could easily ignore it–but then I am at a much different place than Robert. If he intends on advancing in society, he will be cautious and will do nothing that rocks the boat."

Hannah reached for her coffee cup. It was her sixth cup since she had entered the Destiny some hours before. Her hand trembled slightly as she did. "Then what must I do?" she asked as she brought the cup to her lips.

Gage shrugged. "I don't know. But I do know what Joshua would advise."

Hannah brightened. "You do? You have talked about it? What would he tell me to do?"

His eyes serious, Gage said slowly, "He would tell you to pray about it."

Hannah blinked. They were both silent.

"Yes, that is what he would tell me to do." She waited again for another minute before speaking. "What do you make of him, Gage? What about Joshua? Is faith the answer to everything?"

Gage nodded. "He says it is. He's been trying to convert me ever since we met."

"Convert you? But you're a Christian, Gage. You go to church."

He stood and spun the chair around and sat with his arms resting on the chair back. "That's not what Joshua would say."

"What do you mean? If you are not a Christian, then what am I?"

"Hannah, he would say that it is more than just external things, more than just what we do. It is what is in our heart that matters most."

"In our heart? I don't understand. A Christian is someone who goes to church, who gives to the church . . ."

At that Gage nodded enthusiastically.

". . . who does good things and lives a good life. I believe in God and I have a Bible. What more does he think I need?"

Gage held up his hands. "Don't get angry at me, Hannah. This is Joshua we are talking about. Not me, remember?"

"I remember. But what does he want you to do? Become a monk or preacher?"

Gage laughed. "Me, a preacher? No. We argued about this just the other day. He said I have to have it in my heart–Jesus, faith, and all that. If it is not in my heart, then I am simply an actor reading pleasant lines but not really believing in any of it."

"An actor?"

"It's what he called me."

"And does that make me an actor, then?"

Gage took her hand. "No, Hannah, you're not an actor."

She sighed, a smile on her face.

"You're an actress," Gage said with a laugh, holding up his arms to protect himself from the blows that were sure to follow.

And they did.

FROM THE DIARY OF MORGAN HANNAH COLLINS
APRIL 1845

Such a tumultuous few months. Such highs and lows and, well . . . all points in between those emotions.

I have heard from Mrs. Dix that if accreditation of the school for female doctors occurs, then she will take me in her first class. No word yet from Oberlin. Virginia University has said no.

Robert Keyes asked me to dine with him last week at his club in Boston. We had a most pleasant evening. I am certain he will ask for my hand once I graduate. After talking with Gage and realizing how simple men truly are, I can now see unmistakable signs that all point to that conclusion. When he addresses the future, he uses *we*. He is relatively at ease with taking my hand and offering me his arm in public. He has introduced me to others as his "very good friend, Miss Collins." He has no aversion to offering a good-night kiss to me when we depart.

All that is to say I am sure of his intentions.

He said that once he moves to New York City, we shall have to seriously think about the future. I expected him to continue on that point, but his cheeks reddened and he quickly changed the subject.

Yet, just as I am certain of that, I am certain that he will not encourage me to continue in my studies. His mother, his best example of a woman's life, has never sought out more stimulation than hearth and home can provide.

And I remain befuddled by it.

Florence, my dear friend, is aghast that I even think about abandoning my efforts so close to completion. She rails about and mentions Stanton and Mott as if the mere sound of their names would spur me on. "You must be a beacon to all women who would follow you," she says.

Of all the people I would fear disappointing, it would be her hurt that I most dread. Even I could bear the loss better than she, I imagine.

And my life at Harvard draws slowly to a close. If all courses end as I expect, of all the women who have attended Harvard, and I admit that the pool is not so deep, I will be the one with the highest graded average. If all students were compared to me, I would be in the top 5 percent. Florence says it is an achievement of the highest order.

I am not so sure myself.

I am furious with Joshua! I daresay he will never find my forgiveness.

A letter from home, with a troubling report on his father, arrived before the year's classes concluded. His grades and reputation are such that all professors allowed him early leave. And leave he did–without telling me and scarcely a good-bye to anyone in Cambridge. It appears that only Gage and Jamison knew, and they did not tell me until it was too late. I managed to dash off a note of farewell to him. The messenger swore that he would deliver it to Joshua even if he had to catch the next train west. He should–I tipped him substantially.

I wanted to at least offer a final embrace.

But perhaps it would have confused him. Perhaps he still holds out some hope.

Poor sweet Joshua. Had things been different, then perhaps . . . But I could not be the wife of a poor preacher in the woods of Ohio. I could not.

And I am sure that he considers me a simple actor . . . or actress.

How I envy his certainty, his sureness of the world. Had I been able to understand what he meant, perhaps all my worries and travails would be mitigated.

But that is not the truth.

And perhaps now it never shall be.

CHAPTER EIGHT

Harvard University
June 1845

"I cannot believe that four years have passed so quickly," Florence Galeswhite said as she danced about Hannah. The Harvard Student Union was filled with students, more students than Hannah had ever seen crowd into the room before. Conversations were punctuated with sharp peals of laughter and the occasional shouted greeting.

Classes had but one week left to run. Most of the students had just taken their final examination that morning. A few papers, a few class meetings, and any late assignments were all that remained. For most everyone this last week of school simply provided a convenient time to celebrate. The great majority of seniors approached this last week on campus with a focused zeal, some bordering on a panicky attempt at holding off the inevitable. For once graduation occurred, once seniors received their diplomas, they would soon be forced to face the rigors of the real world and the hard and uncompromising field of commerce and industry.

This week would be the last time these young men and women would be isolated and immune from the world and all its implications and concerns. Some members of the Harvard class of 1845 would slip back into a gentrified life of luxury and indolence, but for most, a lifetime of work awaited. The very rich might strive hard to preserve their wealth. The modestly rich would endeavor to increase it. The poor would struggle and claw to gain entry into the rarified world of money and class and society.

Hannah found a table by an open window and sat, happy to be breathing in the first truly warm air of summer. Florence scampered about, running from classmate to classmate, holding her yearbook in her hand, seeking out autographs and personal notes.

It was only the second year for such books and the first with actual photographs of all class members. Hannah had purchased one but did not bring it along. To gather signatures of others felt girlish and more than a bit immature to Hannah. But she enjoyed watching Florence approach the task with her typical enthusiasm.

Hannah's thoughts turned to her friends. Gage, born to wealth, would work hard at not just holding it, but increasing it. No doubt he would be wondrously successful. He had already demonstrated his business acumen even as a college student. Joshua, by seeking out the pastorate and God's work, effectively removed himself from the game. He would never be rich, and the lack of money and riches would never seem a loss. A servant of God, he once remarked, has no need for gold or riches.

Hannah spent little time pondering her own future. It was at once both set and unsettled, both predetermined and at the whim of fate. Despite the hours and days and weeks spent wondering and devising and plotting and planning, the future of more than a few days hence seemed as dark as a moonless night at sea. She owned no firmer, more solid view and refused to settle any issue facing her.

There will be time enough, she wrote in her diary, *time enough for all my decisions and revisions. I will determine the course of my life in due time.*

Jamison, of all her friends, remained an enigma. He had more spark and wit and nerve than most. On one occasion he might deride the pleasures of the wealthy, claiming them superficial and fleeting. On other occasions he might sit back in a luxurious leather chair, holding a brandy of great cost, and sigh that he was destined for such pleasures. Then at another time Jamison would decry all pleasures and claim that only adventure made life worth living. Hannah could never tell from a glance which Jamison occupied his frame–the hedonist, the aesthetic, or the adventurer.

Perhaps he is all three at all times, she mused. Perhaps he is more complex than any other friend of mine.

Florence waltzed past, a beaming and bemused young man at her arm.

"Hannah, you must join in the fun," she called out. "If you wait, there will be no time at all for gathering your mementos."

Hannah waved and laughed as Florence and her escort slipped back into the crowd.

"There will be time enough," she called back, not certain if Florence heard or if she truly expected her reply.

Time enough for decisions . . .

Hannah stared out at the main yard of the campus, where young men and women strolled past. Some were arm in arm with sweethearts. Their guests had come to Cambridge for the graduation festivities. Scattered about were larger family groups, mothers and fathers and young siblings in tow, trailing their proud son or daughter as they toured the campus.

Hannah's parents claimed that the trip to Cambridge would be too taxing. They asked if Constance and Daniel Granger could be their substitutes. Hannah, of course, said yes.

But on this day, as Hannah gazed out over the vast lawn of Harvard Commons, there did not seem to be a single person who strolled about as a single person. All were paired with others. All were part of larger groups.

She blinked her eyes. She would not permit a tear.

I keep telling myself that there will be time, and yet I have placed my biggest decision on the altar of time. Was I simply not willing to decide here and now? Am I so tied to my dreams? Am I willing to sacrifice so much for such a small promise?

A ray of sunlight slipped through an opening in the trees. Hannah closed her eyes at its brightness but felt its warmth. And she let the memory start again.

"Hannah, you have a visitor," Aunt Constance called up the stairs.

On the eve of her next-to-last final examination, Robert Keyes had called upon Hannah at the home of her aunt and uncle.

Aunt Constance fluttered about like a moth wounded by a flame, cheerfully offering tea or coffee or some manner of sustenance. All were carefully declined. Robert had a nervous digestion and partook of a very specific and evenly timed diet.

Hannah offered her aunt a semiwithering glance, and Aunt Constance winced as if struck with a dart. She nodded, then slowly withdrew from the room. Hannah had no doubt that she would remain within earshot. She looked about and stood, taking Robert's hand in hers.

"It is such a nice day, Robert. Shall we sit on the front porch? There was a most delicious breeze this morning."

Robert now appeared pained. "But there are all manner of bugs outside," he complained. "And you know that a woman should avoid the sun. It roughens the complexion."

Hannah would not be dissuaded. "The porch swing is out of the sun. And the breeze will keep all but the most determined insect away."

He looked around as if hoping Aunt Constance would return and help him plead his case. She did not.

"Very well, Hannah, but only for a short period. You know I am not enthusiastic about being outside."

"But, Robert," she said lightly, "this is not outside. This is simply the porch."

As they found seats on the swing, he replied, "Outside is outside and that is where this is." Immediately he slapped his neck. "I think I felt a spider. Do you see a spider on my back?"

Hannah leaned over to take a look. "No, nothing at all. Must have been the wind."

He continued to rub his neck. "If I feel swelling, then I am heading to the doctor posthaste."

"But, Robert," Hannah said, "I am as close to a doctor as you might need." He puckered his lips. "Well, then," he said, "I meant a real doctor . . . a man doctor, that is."

Hannah was not ready to do battle over his remark. He had made it clear before that he would only be treated by a doctor of the same gender, and no arguing or discussing would dissuade him. Hannah thought it wise to hold her tongue.

"If I see swelling, then by all means, have the matter attended to. There is a skilled male physician only two blocks west of here."

Robert actually turned and stared down the street as if he could ascertain the exact direction and location of this physician.

Wanting to change the direction of their conversation, Hannah took his hands. "Well, my university career is nearly at an end. And have you come to celebrate with me, Robert? I am puzzled by your visit. You have so seldom arrived midweek. There must be a unique reason for it."

Robert stared down at her hands in his. As always, he seemed pleased when she initiated any physical contact with him, no matter how small. But he seldom, if ever, would make that first move.

"There is a reason," Robert said, a nick of a stammer in his voice. He glanced nervously off down the street again, in the direction of the physician's office.

After a long moment, Hannah spoke. "And that is? I enjoy your company, Robert, but if I cannot tell my aunt of the reason for your visit, she will remain agitated for days and days."

Robert sat up straight as if that would be reason enough for a response.

Hannah placed her fingertips on his chest. "I am jesting, Robert.

Surely you can tell when I am merely adding levity to a serious situation?"

Robert nodded quickly. Hannah saw his eyes dart to her fingertips. She held them at his chest for a second longer than normal. She was certain he noticed it, too. Then she withdrew her hands into her lap.

"Well, Robert?" she said, sighing. "I am not getting younger, you know."

He cleared his throat. "Well, then."

She smiled at him and waited.

"Well, then," he repeated and she nodded. "It has come to mind . . . I mean, the fact that you and I have been in each other's company a great deal over these past months. It has been a pleasant time for me. I think that you and I have a great many commonalities. And as I reviewed these elements that we share–the mutual elements that is, I have considered that a merger of sorts might be a most appropriate venture at this moment."

Hannah blinked.

Robert attempted to smile. "And as I reviewed the pluses and minuses of this merger, I could only conclude that it would have great value to both of us. You come from a wonderful family in Philadelphia–a home to many of my recent activities. You are a very bright woman. That would be most helpful when it comes to settling matters of a home and family. You are very pretty." And with that Robert blushed crimson. It was apparent that offering such compliments on physical attributes went far beyond the point at which he felt comfort. "As I consider all the divergent and various factors, I find myself in a position that forces but one response."

Hannah closed her eyes tightly. *He's proposing!*

"And that response has been duly studied. Hannah, after all the time we have spent together, you know I am not a rash or impetuous fellow. I study and analyze. Then I move boldly."

She had not yet reopened her eyes. *He's proposing!*

Hannah at last opened her eyes. Robert did not exactly look at her but at her shoulder, or at a spot in the corner of the porch. He kept talking, yet Hannah had suddenly lost the power of hearing. His mouth moved, but she heard no words.

He's proposing! I have thought and wondered and planned for this moment for years it seems, and now that it is happening, I find myself lost and unable to experience it at all.

Robert continued to talk, looking as if he would have preferred to be holding a pointer in his hand and illuminating numbered items on a chart pinned to the wall.

He's proposing! Please do not let Aunt Constance hear! If she does, I will be married and bearing children before he leaves the porch this afternoon.

And now Robert stood and gestured about, ticking off things with each curled finger. Hannah would have liked to have heard what he said, but all was silent and still.

He's proposing!

He continued to talk.

Hannah leaned back, nodding at the appropriate moments, she hoped.

And in a blazing instant, she knew what she had to do. In an instant, all of her trepidation and fear and worries and vexations culminated into one overwhelming flash of awareness.

I cannot marry this man!

She felt her hand rise to her chest, so strong was the emotion.

If I marry him now, I will never forgive myself for abandoning my dream. I will sit inside–for we will never own a porch–and be master of what can be contained within the walls of a home. That cannot be enough.

Then she brought her hand to her throat.

But if not Robert, then who? And who else has the sterling prospects that Robert does? He is already on his way to being a captain of industry. He would support me in a grand style–and my parents would be so happy.

Her hand traveled to her mouth.

But shall I marry for my parents and my future? Or shall I marry for love? Could I not find it in my heart to love this man? He is kind and considerate and a churchgoer. What more do I think I deserve?

Robert walked to the railing and settled against it, still talking.

Hannah stared after him, still uncomprehending any of the words he was saying.

He's proposing to me! And all I can do is sputter and fret. I must come up with an answer.

At last, he stopped and faced her. A tentative smile was on his face. "Well?"

That I heard.

She looked around as a wild animal might if its leg was caught in the vice grip of a steel trap.

"Well, then?" Robert repeated, thinking she may not have understood his question.

I heard that, too!

He stepped to her side and sat down on the swing next to her. Even though her thoughts were spinning, she noted he was a few inches farther away than before.

I must answer him.

"Robert . . ." She managed only his name and then found no more words.

He nodded. "I am not proposing that this . . . merger take place immediately. I know that such things take months and months to prepare. Perhaps in the fall, or even the winter."

Hannah's eyes darted about. *Where is Aunt Constance now that I need her to interrupt?*

And then Robert began talking about planning and executing complex business matters as a parallel to a wedding.

I have to speak now! I have to! "Robert . . . this is all so sudden." *It will not dissuade him, but it will give me time.*

"It is? I thought . . . I mean, the manner in which our relationship has progressed . . . sudden? But you have kissed me on more than one occasion. Sudden? You do think it's too sudden? Should I have inquired of your father first? I should have, shouldn't I? Modern etiquette is so confusing. I thought that was but a charming relic of the past. Please forgive me, Hannah. I will seek him out posthaste."

Hannah held up her hand. "No, Robert. You do not need to seek out my father just yet. I can make decisions on my own. I can."

"Well, then, what are you saying? You have not said yes yet. Are you saying no?"

His responses jumped so much ground that Hannah felt winded trying to keep up.

"No . . . I am not saying no."

"Then it's yes? You have agreed to marry me?"

Hannah held up her hand again. "Robert, you must slow down."

His face fell. "I am sorry, Hannah. Things of the heart confuse me so. I tend to rush through them. I'm sorry."

She smiled and took his hand in hers. *He is a sweet man. A very sweet and sensitive man.* "I would love to tell you yes."

He winced as if cut. "But you can't?"

She squeezed his hand tightly, and he refocused on her face. "That is not the question," she said.

"It's not? But then I am confused. A proposal is generally met with a yes or no answer."

"Generally," she replied and squeezed his hand again. "I am in awe that you would consider me to be your wife. And I want to say yes and fall into your arms."

"Well, then," he asked, puzzled, "why don't you?"

She smiled, kissed her fingertips, and placed her fingers on his cheek. If she placed them anywhere else on his face he would blush again, and his concentration would fail. "I am not sure how to explain it. I struggle to understand it all myself."

"Well, then, just try."

She let her hands drop. "I know you will find it hard to understand this. But I have made a promise to myself that I will follow this goal of becoming a physician."

"But you are a woman. That means a wife and mother."

She did not argue but continued. "Robert, I know how you view my plans. I understand, and I am not seeking to change your thoughts."

"Then you will stop?"

She could not help but smile at his persistence. "No, Robert. I will not."

She watched his face and did not find a reaction. *Perhaps he did not understand me.* "I am committed to finish what I started four years ago. To become a doctor."

Robert furrowed his brow. "Well, then, is your answer to my question a no?"

He is not easily dissuaded, she thought, *and perhaps I do not want him dissuaded after all.* "No, it is not. But it cannot be a yes, either. At least not now."

"Well, then, when?"

Hannah sighed. "I am asking you for two years, Robert. Two short years. That is all the time I will need. I'll still be ready to bear children then. I won't be too old. And it will provide you time to fully focus on your business–without the incessant demands of a wife and home and all that."

He rubbed his chin with his hand.

"I do so care for you, Robert. I trust that you know that. I am so flattered that you think enough of me to propose like this."

"Well, then, your answer is still no, correct?"

This time she placed her hand against his cheek. She felt it warm to her touch. "It is not no. It is simply not yet. You must promise me that you will ask this question again two years hence."

He nodded, his eyes darting from her face to her hand against his cheek.

"You promise? Two years hence and you will again ask me to become your wife?"

He nodded again. "I promise. In two years."

She smiled and then embraced him.

He is such a kind man. She held him against her, then kissed him sweetly on the lips, despite that it was broad daylight.

His eyes darted to the street. It was empty.

Have I made the right decision? Her thoughts raced. And then she leaned forward and kissed him one more time.

Florence threw herself onto the chair and jostled the table. Hannah snapped back from her reverie.

"Where have you been?" Florence asked. "Every time I passed this spot, you were staring out the window as if in a trance."

"Well, something like that. Reflecting on four years, I guess."

Florence flipped the pages of the yearbook. Most were thick with signatures and notes. She looked up. "Someone was asking about you," she said. "Now who was it?"

Hannah blinked as if to clear her thoughts. "Who? You mean this day? Here?" *Did Robert slip back into Cambridge?*

Florence offered a sly smile. "No, it was not your Robert. I daresay he would not have let you alone all day if he were here."

"Then who was it?"

Florence flipped a few pages. Then she stabbed a small image on the page and spun the book around. There was no signature by the photograph.

All that was written under it was a name: Jamison Elliot Pike.

Hannah stared, then her head snapped upright and she surveyed the room in a sweep.

Florence closed the book with a slap. "He said to meet him this evening."

Hannah's heart began to beat faster than it had in weeks. "Where?"

Florence said softly, "He said you would know where."

Hannah drew her light shawl more closely around her shoulders and peered inside. The sky had grown dark, and the warm southern wind of the afternoon had been supplanted by one from the north with an edgy chill to it. Jamison was there. She did not see his face but could recognize the form, the angles, the attitude.

She had been certain she would find him there and was even more certain that he would have waited until dawn for her.

It was nearly ten in the evening. The Destiny would be open for one more hour.

Back at the Grangers', her bed lay rumpled and arranged with pillows placed full under the covers. A casual peek would indicate her presence. She could not have explained to Aunt Constance that she simply had to meet a young man so far into the night. And as she walked the quiet streets, she could not understand her reasons either.

I have said no to Robert, and here I am, no more than days afterward, deceiving my aunt and uncle, meeting a man whom I do not even like.

A shiver rattled up her spine.

But here I am. And there is Jamison.

She walked up the steps and heard the familiar groans and creaks. When she took the handle and the door opened, she smelled coffee and apple pie. She hesitated. Jamison had not turned to the door.

I could leave, and he would never know.

She waited.

But then I would not either.

Every step seemed to take a lifetime. She reached the table and stopped.

"Jamison?" she said, her voice as soft as fog.

He did not move for a heartbeat, then slowly stood and faced her. He did not speak, but his expression told Hannah everything. He would have waited all night.

"I didn't want this all to end and not have time to talk with you once more," he said evenly.

She nodded as he pushed her chair in.

"Coffee? Pie? Both are fresh."

She nodded again, though she had appetite for neither. Jamison gestured, and the waiter grunted a response.

"You'll be leaving at the end of the week?" she asked.

Now Jamison nodded.

"Where to? Someplace exotic?"

Jamison's laughter was pointed but not unpleasant. "Hardly. New York. The position is on Gage's paper–the one that his father owns a portion of."

"Is that where you want to work?" Hannah asked. "Do you want to be beholden to Gage?"

Jamison was not offended by her question. "No. I would have felt most obligated if his was my only offer. It wasn't. In fact, the editor bumped the salary offer twice until I said yes. I'm making more out of college than my father makes now. No, I'm not beholden. I got this job on my skill–not friendship."

"Then that's good," she said, sipping her coffee.

"I'll get to travel the world. I'll get to see exotic places. I'll have my dream. And I'll get to do what I love–write."

His smile was both serene and wistful. He looked deep into her eyes. Jamison had a way of looking that unnerved her. It was as if, she imagined, he could ascertain her very thoughts. He was silent for a long time. And when he did finally break the silence, his words were low, dark, and pained.

"Are you going to marry him?"

She held her gasp and managed to swallow her coffee without choking. "And who might you mean?"

Jamison neither smiled nor frowned. "You know who."

"I do?"

"You do."

"I am sure you are mistaken, Jamison."

"All right, then, I'll play the game. Keyes. Robert Keyes. He asked you to marry him."

"He did? You think I'm going to marry him?"

He shrugged. "I've heard."

She carefully placed her coffee cup on the table and nudged it another inch away. Then, without warning, she punched Jamison's shoulder. It was not a gentle brother-sister jab but a serious strike. Jamison nearly tumbled off his seat.

"Jamison Pike! Do you believe everything Florence tells you? You believe in every bit of gossip?"

Surprised, he grabbed his arm. "Then it's not true?"

She kept her fist clenched. "It is neither your concern nor hers."

"That is not an answer."

"It is the answer that you will have. It is the only answer that you deserve."

They evaluated each other, like prizefighters with fists raised. The light of three wobbly lanterns was the only illumination in the Destiny. Two young men sat at a table in the front of the room, engrossed in their own conversation.

Hannah held Jamison's stare and neither wavered.

It was clear to Hannah that she did not move first but that she did move. She watched as Jamison sat straight in his chair, leaned forward, and did not stop. Hannah felt herself respond, almost in like kind.

Jamison came closer and closer, as did Hannah. He reached up and put his hand on her shoulders; then it slipped around to the nape of her neck.

Her eyes flinched, but only for a heartbeat.

Then he drew her close and found her lips with his. She offered no hesitation nor resistance as the two drew closer and closer. When he placed his arms around her, she wrapped hers about him in a fierce, almost angry embrace. Their chairs tipped toward each other. She was certain her heart could be heard out on the street.

Hannah thought she knew what it was to be kissed, but it was clear to her now that her knowledge was that of a child. It was as if her bones themselves joined in the ache and passion of the moment.

She felt the gentle stubble of his whiskers, the power of his arms, and tasted the sweet hint of apple pie on his lips.

Their kiss lasted a full minute.

Then he released her, and she sat back. Her breath came in birdlike gasps. Her hand found her throat as if it would slow her rapid pulse.

His eyes were hard and focused. "Don't."

"Don't what?" she said, able to raise her voice no higher than a throaty whisper.

"Don't marry him."

And with that, he stood up. His chair fell over, clattering to the floor. He took a thin envelope from his pocket, laid it on the table, and walked away into the night.

Hannah,

I can ask you for nothing.

I have no right.

But you cannot give up on your dream. You must not.

You are the most able and brightest woman I have ever known. Do not let your light ever be extinguished. It would be a loss that I could not bear.

Jamison

Hannah sat alone in the Destiny until the staff was ready to lock the door for the evening. Then she gathered up her shawl, picked up the single page of paper, and also walked off into the darkness.

As she stepped up to the porch of her home at Harvard, she tried her best not to make any noise. She noticed a small sliver of white by the door. She reached down. The letter was addressed to her.

Aunt Constance must have forgotten to retrieve the mail that day. Hannah ripped the envelope and turned to catch the illumination from the gas streetlamp.

The letter bore the postmark of Boston Female Medical School.

We are pleased to offer you placement in our inaugural class. Please contact us at your earliest convenience.

She sighed, sat on the swing, and held both letters to her chest, rocking slowly in the delicious golden light of the moon.

CHAPTER NINE

Philadelphia
September 1845

HANNAH paced back and forth in the parlor of her home in Philadelphia. Her mother stood motionless, her back to the door, ignoring her daughter's agitation.

"I think it should be a little lower," Elizabeth called out. A tradesman in a rough blue coat and enormous scuffed boots stood on a short wooden ladder. He positioned the frame down an inch.

Elizabeth leaned back, studying the placement. "Morgan, stop pacing about like a wild animal in a cage and look at this. Is it the right spot?"

Hannah slowed. "It's fine, Mother. The last five positions have been fine."

Hannah's mother appeared to ignore her daughter's churlish tone. "I think that will be fine there, Mr. Patterson. You may hang it at that height."

The tradesman nodded and marked the wall with a pencil he had tucked behind his ear. "Yes, ma'am," he said, setting the frame against the wall and reaching for his hammer.

Hannah's pacing continued. She walked across the parlor to the window, then back again to the archway dividing the dining room from the front hall.

"Honestly, Morgan," her mother said, "it's time you stopped your obvious perturbation. It serves no one well, least of all me."

"I am not agitated," Hannah replied, though her tone made it obvious that she was. She waited a full moment. "I am not."

Just then the tradesman coughed, and the two women grew silent, as if having forgotten his presence in the midst of their tense discussion.

"This diploma for real?" he asked.

Elizabeth nodded.

"And it truly is from Harvard?"

She nodded again.

"It is my daughter's," Elizabeth Collins said, allowing a hint of pride to color her words. "One of the few women who have gone there. See that mark? That means the diploma was conferred with highest honors."

He nodded as he placed the heavy gold frame on the nail, nudging it to level with his forefinger. It was clear he was treating the framed object as an obviously sacred article. He turned and offered Hannah a smile. "You going to teach school, then?"

Hannah crossed her arms over her chest. "Pardon me?" she asked in reply.

"School. Children. Are you going to teach school?"

She started to scowl, then held back. "I am not."

He turned and cocked his head at an angle.

"I'm going to become a doctor," she announced.

His puzzled expression turned slowly into something deeper, as if he were first glimpsing one of nature's strange and explosive oddities–like a calf with two heads or an albino snake. "A doctor?" he finally replied. "Like prescribing medicine and all?"

No one answered.

"Well, don't that beat all. A fine lady like yourself being a doctor. My wife will crack a gut when she hears."

And just as soon as he uttered the words, he shrank back, knowing he had overstepped his bounds as a tradesman.

Hannah's expression chilled even further. "Honestly," she blurted out and spun on her heels, taking the stairs two at a time.

As she ran up toward her room, both her mother and the tradesman shared the same bemused and bewildered expression of embarrassment.

"You are not going to that horrid medical school in Boston, and that is that." Elizabeth Collins stood outside the door to Hannah's bedchamber and spoke with a harsh firmness. She had her hand on the doorknob but did not turn it. No one in the Collins home ever walked into another's room without an invitation.

Hannah remained silent.

"I have been in correspondence with Aunt Constance, who traveled well out of her way to investigate this so-called school," Elizabeth continued. "She said it is located in the most disreputable of neighborhoods and occupies the second floor of a most dubious building housing a tavern and an inn for transients. That is not a reputable school, Morgan, and I will not allow you to further tarnish the Collins name by attending it."

"It is not your money," Hannah called out from within the room. "I am over the legal age. I may spend my trust fund as I see fit."

"Morgan, I am most fatigued at having this conversation over and over again. Every time your father and I think the matter is settled, you insist on bringing the matter up again. We are reaching the end of our tether."

Suddenly the door swung open. Hannah's face was streaked with the trail of fresh tears. She held a handkerchief in her hand, and her hair was tousled as if she had been lying with her face down on her bed.

"I am at the end of my tether as well, Mother. I enjoy these arguments no more than you or Father. But I am resolute. I am going to be a doctor."

Both women glared at the other, neither of them retreating.

Hannah did her best to hold her lips still but could not. Her lower lip began to tremble with the anticipation of tears to follow. Hannah thoroughly disliked her emotions winning the best of her like this and struggled so very hard to keep them in check. But after months of indecision and worry, she felt worn and thin. She clenched her hands into fists.

It was not so much her mother's evaluation of the Boston school that bothered Hannah, but the subtle smugness of her mother's words. After all, Hannah had already been in correspondence with Jamison, who had spent that summer in Boston on behalf of his new employer. He had written back, sadly, with the same evaluation as Hannah's mother.

Dear Hannah,

I know you had such high hopes for this opportunity, but I have an obligation to tell you the truth. I investigated this so-called school and found it sadly lacking in all but the most rudimentary educational tools. It consists of a half dozen sparse rooms, with a shabby scattering of desks and chairs. I purported myself as the brother of a potential student and was given access to all. The fellow who runs it, a man by the name of Bowders, was indeed a skilled salesman. I could almost believe his grand sales scheme–but I could not overlook his lack of credentials and the absence of any skilled professors.

And why would he start a medical school over a tavern and what appears to be a rather low-class brothel? Be assured that I am not saying this with any firsthand knowledge–about the brothel and all that.

If you do attend, Hannah, you will receive no decent training. It would be better if you attended a qualified nursing academy. There you would at least have the benefit of a quality education.

I am most reluctant to tell you this, but as I said, I must speak the truth, for I care so much for your welfare. I will not have you defrauded nor deceived.

Always, your good friend,
Jamison

Hannah had received Jamison's letter nearly two weeks prior but had held on to her position, hoping that somehow, in some miraculous way, things would change and an alternative would be found.

"Morgan," her mother said, "you must be reasonable. A Collins woman would simply not attend that manner of disreputable school. Not there. Not in Boston."

"But, Mother," she replied, her words mingling with a sob, "it is what I want. I believe it is my destiny."

Elizabeth Collins was not in the habit of embracing her adult daughter, yet today she placed her arm about Hannah's shoulder. "You'll see, Morgan. This will all be for the best. You mustn't expect too much from life. You'll be disappointed if you set your sights too high."

"But it is what my heart wants."

Her mother offered an odd, soft laugh, as if she were hiding her own struggle. "You will see in time, Morgan, that the heart gets what the heart needs. And a woman can find contentment with little. I know."

Hannah sniffed loudly, feeling the familiar chill of cold and bitterness. To her mother's surprise, she simply wailed and embraced her. Elizabeth awkwardly patted her daughter's head. "You'll see in time, Morgan. You'll see."

Bay Head, New Jersey
September 1845

"But didn't you say there was a medical school in Philadelphia that was set up to train women doctors? I thought you were making plans to attend there?"

Dorothy Collins sat at the porch railing; her cousin Hannah was curled up on the wicker couch.

Hannah shrugged. "I wrote them, but I have not heard a word back."

Dorothy nearly shouted, "What! You sent one letter? And then gave up?"

Hannah examined her hands. She was visiting Bay Head as much to seek sympathy from her cousin as to escape the subtle gloating of her mother. "If they had an opening, I am sure they would have informed me." Hannah's voice was small and contrite.

Shaking her head, Dorothy crossed to Hannah and sat down. She looked out at the gray ocean. The air was warm, but the sky was dense with a thick blanket of dark clouds. The beach was nearly empty, the season all but past. The Bay Head house of the Newark Collinses had only three occupants for the last slice of summer–Dorothy, Aunt Mella, and Charlotte, Dorothy's younger sister.

"Hannah Collins, I am ashamed of you. When your letter arrived, its despondent tone indicated to me that your dream was all but shattered and that you had no alternatives to consider."

"But it is shattered," Hannah said flatly. "The Boston school is above a brothel. I can't go there. My mother is right."

Dorothy glared at her cousin. "Listen, Hannah, if you have come here for sympathy, you have come to the wrong location."

"I haven't," Hannah retorted.

"Nonsense. You have. Sympathy is a wonderful analgesic. It makes all the pain depart for a while. But I am not giving you any."

"I am not asking," Hannah replied, her eyes flashing.

"You were, and you cannot in truth deny it."

Hannah glared in response. It was obvious Dorothy was correct in her evaluation.

"You said Oberlin College might be accepting women in medical studies. Have you written them?"

Hannah shook her head no. "It's in Ohio," she complained.

"And?"

"Ohio. You would live in Ohio?"

Dorothy's hard expression slowly softened, and she began to laugh. "No, you're right. I can take hardship as well as the next fellow, but I would need to be close to civilization."

Hannah sniffed loudly.

"But, dear cousin," Dorothy said earnestly, "I've always looked up to you. All of us have. You can't quit now."

Stunned, Hannah replied, "You've looked up to me? Truly?"

"We truly did–and still do. You went to Harvard and graduated. How difficult was that? Especially with your mother the way she is."

"It wasn't all that much."

"It was, Hannah. It was. You may not know it, but you are an example."

For a long moment there was only the sound of waves rolling against the shore and the call of birds as they wheeled about in the sky.

"So what do I do?" Hannah asked. "From where I sit, I can see no acceptable alternatives. I feel like I am mired–I cannot go forward with my education and I cannot forget what I have learned. Where do I go? What shall I do with my life? Take second best and be a nurse? Or do I simply give up? Do I take Robert's hand? What do I do?"

Dorothy stood. The folds of her ivory linen dress caught the breeze and billowed about her legs. Wisps of red hair, not held in place by her ivory pin, fluttered about her face. She pushed a strand or two away and looked toward the empty sea. "Hannah, I do not know. But you had a dream. You had a place to go. You cannot simply turn your back on that. You must do what you have planned. To do less would be an act of cowardice so grave that forgiveness would be impossible. You must carry it through." Dorothy turned and folded her arms across her chest. "You must, Hannah. You must."

The afternoon turned quiet and hot. Both Dorothy and Hannah remained on the porch sipping sarsaparillas for most of the day but spoke only a few words, each seemingly lost in her own thoughts. Dinner had been quiet, the gentle scrapings of knife and fork on china the loudest sound in the room.

As the moon rose, Dorothy stood, took a white shawl from the hook by the door, and called over to Hannah. "I need to take a walk. Would you care to join me? We will not have many more chances. Let's take advantage of this precious time."

Hannah looked up from her copy of *Godey's Lady's Book*. "It's not too dark, is it?"

Dorothy offered a bemused smile. "The brave and pioneering Hannah is now afraid of the shore after dark?"

Hannah stood and peered out the windows. "No, I'm not frightened of the dark. And we will have more chances. You speak as if this will be a final meeting."

Once outside Dorothy lifted her skirts as she tromped over the rough clumps of sea grass. She hiked the waist of her skirt into her belt so the water and sand would not catch the fabric. "There may not be another time, Hannah. Things are changing in all our lives. You will be a doctor. Time will shift all things . . . in their time," Dorothy said.

"Or not," Hannah answered.

"You will soon be married. I understand Robert is ready."

"Perhaps I am not."

"But soon enough you will be, Hannah. You will get married, and then your life will change," Dorothy concluded. "With another family, with other obligations, well, dear cousin, we may not be together like this again."

Hannah reached over and took her cousin's arm in hers. "Don't talk that way. Family is permanent. We will see each other as we age."

"Perhaps," Dorothy replied quietly.

The moonlight played off the water, lighting their steps with silvery glints like a thousand tiny fires. They strolled north along the hard-packed sand, the water whispering at their feet. Only a few of the beach houses remained occupied. Most people had returned to their residences in Philadelphia, Newark, and New York.

"Hannah," Dorothy said, her voice not much louder than the water, "I need to tell you something. I think I have been unfair to you."

Hannah reached down and picked up a shell. "Unfair? How?"

"I encouraged you to follow your dream come what may. I said that you must carry on, regardless of opposition."

"While it may be hard to accomplish, Dorothy, what you said was not unfair."

Dorothy stopped and faced the water, gazing up toward the moon. "It is because I want you to do what I cannot."

Hannah stepped back, a thin film of water hushing at her feet. "Cannot? What can you not do?"

Dorothy turned away from Hannah. Her shoulders trembled, as if she was holding back a sob. Hannah laid her hand on Dorothy's arm.

"What is it, Dorothy? Is something wrong?" she asked softly.

Dorothy spun from Hannah's touch and ran a few steps away.

Hannah followed and asked, "What is it? Please, you can tell me."

"I am a terrible person, Hannah. I am. I called you a coward."

"You didn't."

"I did. I called you a coward for having doubts. My desire was to see you live your dream so I could share in it with you. I envied you so much, and I couldn't bear to see you give up on what I myself wanted so terribly."

Hannah took Dorothy's hands in her own. They were cold to the touch. The moonlight hid Dorothy's face in deep shadow. All Hannah could hear was the sound of the water and the hint of a sob.

"But, Dorothy, such a dream is not my personal province. You could share in it with me. You could attend school with me. You could."

Dorothy fell into Hannah's arms and wailed. "I can't. I will never be able to."

"You will," Hannah said softly. "You can. If I can, you can."

Dorothy stood back, her tears glistening in the pale light. "No. I can't. And I will never."

"But why?"

Dorothy took a large gulp of air. "Because I am getting married."

Hannah's eyes widened. "But that's wonderful."

"I'm with child," Dorothy said coldly and collapsed to her knees in the still-warm waters of the Atlantic.

With dragging, reluctant steps, Dorothy shuffled back to the beach house with Hannah's assistance. She did not say another word, except to sniffle and break out in a harsh sob every step or two.

Hannah had her arm about Dorothy's waist. If she had not, she was sure Dorothy would have collapsed again in the sand.

Hannah helped Dorothy onto the porch and immediately wrapped a thick woolen shawl about her legs and another on her shoulders. She hurried inside to set a kettle on the fire.

Minutes later Hannah carried out a hot pot of tea laced with honey and lemon and two cups and saucers. The tea steamed in the cooler night air. Dorothy managed a few weak sips. Hannah took the cup and placed it on the wicker tea table.

"What happened?" she asked, not knowing how it would be most proper to inquire.

Dorothy offered a harsh, brittle laugh in reply. "You know how it happens. You're going to be a doctor."

"That's not what I mean. Who is responsible? He's doing the honorable thing, right? You said you were getting married."

And in the darkness, lit only by a fading moon, Dorothy told her story.

Philip Warnett, a young man Hannah met last season, had taken an interest in Dorothy. This summer, Philip–older, more mature, and handsome–had delighted Dorothy with his attentions. It was a moonless night on a lonely stretch of shore that sealed Dorothy's fate.

"I had such dreams," Dorothy said. "And now I will be married with a child, and all has slipped from my fingers."

"It hasn't," Hannah replied. "Being married is not a defeat."

Dorothy shrugged. "And when I heard that sound of defeat in your voice, my heart hurt too much to remain silent."

"But being married is not the end of things. I am sure."

Dorothy wiped her nose with a handkerchief. "Maybe not, but I do not have any illusions. Philip is a fine young man, but I do not think he loves me."

Hannah twisted her hands. "But you will . . . you will grow to love one another. I am told that such often happens."

Dorothy replied with a sob. "I never want to hear those words again."

FROM THE DIARY OF MORGAN HANNAH COLLINS
SEPTEMBER 1845

I feel absolutely horrid. The entire train ride back home, I did nothing but fret and worry over poor Dorothy. It is true that she needs to be supported, but to be forced into a loveless arrangement seems harsh payment indeed.

Yet didn't Joshua preach at me that one reaps what one sows? Dorothy knew the risks, I am sure, and violated God's rules.

Even as I write those words, I feel the hypocrite. Yes, God has rules, but haven't I felt the flames of like passion? Haven't I felt near to wanting the same experience? I am grateful that the gentlemen in question were true gentlemen indeed. Perhaps this Philip is a smooth talker who found a woman willing to be misled.

I was so surprised by her anger at my trepidation. Yet her anger has fueled within me a new desire to find a way to make my dream a reality.

There must be a way. And I will endeavor to find it.

FROM THE DIARY OF MORGAN HANNAH COLLINS
JANUARY 1846

Robert was in Philadelphia for just a short time, investigating some foundry along the shipyards. We managed to get together for an evening at the Claris Restaurant, and he snapped at the waiters and sent his meal to the kitchen twice. I was caustic and mean-spirited all night. He saw me home and expected a kiss–which I consented to but did not enjoy in the least.

I have written Florence a long, long letter outlining all Robert's faults–primarily the fact that he does not share one iota of enthusiasm for my continuing education in medicine. He thinks it a temporary aberration that will cool and fade once I become a wife and mother.

And I think he assumes that I will become an acquiescent creature who is willing to brook any trouble.

I stew in private, for Robert does not enjoy sparring of any kind. A raised voice will simply not do and is indicative, he says, of poor breeding and poorer training. So I bite my tongue and listen and smile.

Yet, in the midst of it all, he can be a most decent and caring man. He is courteous to a fault, and his manners are most impeccable.

And, yes, I admit it–he is a most handsome man.

By his own admission, Robert is well on his way to becoming quite wealthy. He is not there yet, of course, and he works hard at the process. It is not that I am a simple woman and cannot understand the intricacies of the financial world; it is simply that I find it most tedious. I listen politely as he explains the working of his proposals and schemes one more time for me, and when he is finished, I am not more astute than when he started. I try my best to grasp it all, but it slips out of my head as soon as the words are uttered.

I think all the time of Dorothy. Her wedding will be a small family affair, she wrote. By the time arrangements could be made, she was showing. No Collins, even from Newark, would allow a daughter in "the family way" to be made spectacle of. And I am certain Dorothy would not want it either.

Mother quizzed me for hours on this situation. I said nothing. And I do not think she truly knows of it, but people do talk and this, I am sure, is a most delicious scandal for them.

I received a letter from Jamison, full of cheery notes and observations. He wrote while on his way to the Continent. He is such a rising star in the New York journalism world. At least that is what he told me.

He encouraged me once again to pursue my dreams. He has always been most considerate in that regard. He also mentioned two possible schools that teach advanced medicine that may be loosening up restrictions as to women students.

And as Dorothy said, I will also pursue the school right here in Philadelphia. I suspect that if I stayed at home and studied, even my mother would have to acquiesce to my decision.

Perhaps then I can have both the education and the man.

Perhaps I can have it all.

Chapter Ten

From a Letter to Florence Galeswhite
Philadelphia
September 1846

M*Y Dear Florence,*

I cannot believe that so much time has passed since I last drew pen to paper. I am in receipt of your last three missives and each time I pass my desk, sharp pangs of guilt attack me. There is no respite, and with this letter, I hope to end it.

I am excited about your new gentleman friend. He does appear to be a most considerate fellow, with the flowers and such a chivalrous approach to courtship. Do you think this might be your final beau? I remember at Harvard how often your head was turned. I do not write this to chastise you but simply to insist that you not enter into any arrangement without clear thought and a settled heart.

That much I know to be paramount to all relationships.

I scarce know where the time has gone; these past months have slipped by so rapidly. As I wrote prior, I will not be attending that school in Boston. Our friend Jamison did me a great favor by investigating it, and he found it most lacking.

In the interim, I have been in correspondence with every school on the

East Coast that offers medical training, and all have gone mute when they find out I am a member of the female gender. There are two schools operating in England, but the distance involved poses all sorts of problems.

Yet, even though I have not been enrolled in any formal school, I spend much of my days reading and studying through stacks of medical journals and books. If I do find a school to take me, then I will have that much an advance on my degree.

And my social life with all the family obligations seems to consume great amounts of my time. There was a recent wedding. My cousin Dorothy from Newark was married in February. It was a very small affair. I believe I was one of the only guests from outside the immediate family. There were many brave faces hiding tears that day. I must tell you about it–but not in the impersonal pages of a letter.

Mother remains as she has always been. Father has continued to shrink further into the shadows. I know that something must have occurred, something inimical, but there is no one who will tell me the particulars–for fear of damaging my emotions, I surmise. Yet strangers seem to know more than I. I was on a public tram the other day and heard the name Collins. I leaned over, and they mentioned my father's name and declared the whole incident a "deplorable tragedy of failure." And when I mentioned this to my mother, she brushed it off, saying that gossip is the news of fools. I dared not talk to my father. My mother described the most severe penalties for saying one word to him.

Is such secretiveness the part and parcel of married life? I should hope not. And let it be a warning to you, Florence, that if your new gentleman friend is to be a serious candidate, then you must insist on total honesty at all times. It is the only way to true happiness.

Oh, dear Florence . . . I was just visited by the postman, and he delivered such wondrous news. You remember me speaking of Oberlin College? They sent a response asking if I would like to visit their campus prior to asking for admittance into their "medical skills" program!

I know it is in Ohio, and I know how often I have disparaged that location . . . but even Ohio has become palatable to spending another month in the hushed confines of this house. And my dear cousin Dorothy has encouraged me in so many ways to consider this–and I do not want to let her down.

I must dash. There are a thousand things to do before I travel.

And since Oberlin is in Ohio, perhaps I might pay a visit on our friend Joshua Quittner. Do you think Joshua would appreciate a visit from me?

Shall I pass on your fond wishes as well?

Your friend,

Hannah

P.S. I will pass on a forwarding address, if there is one, to you as soon as I can.

Ohio! Who might have thought?

H.

"Oberlin College? I would not even consider such a school," said Robert haughtily. "I am sure that it offers an inferior education in a nearly rustic environment. The campus would be pocked with cows and rife with Indians, for all you know. Hannah, I only want what is best for you, but I forbid you to even consider this arrangement."

Hannah sat opposite him at Lee's, a small but elegant restaurant just off Logan Circle. Robert was in a dark suit and almost disappeared into the dark paneling behind him. The lamps only hinted at illumination. A full plate of chicken under a light mushroom and wine sauce lay untouched in front of Hannah.

"Forbid?"

"Well, then," Robert almost sputtered, "I know that *forbid* is a strong word, but you know of my intentions, of my reaction."

"No, I do not," Hannah said, keeping her anger hidden.

Robert speared a section of asparagus, and butter dribbled down his chin. He chewed thoroughly, swallowed, and only then reached for his napkin. "Hannah . . . what do your parents say about this? What does your mother say?"

He held his smile in check as he reached for his goblet. Robert had a manner of deflecting unpleasantness to others that often infuriated Hannah.

"She has not said anything about it." Hannah crossed her arms over her chest. It was obvious she would have preferred to stand and run out, but there were limits to what she would do in public.

Robert speared another piece of asparagus and sloshed it about in its bath of melted butter. "That means to me that you have not mentioned it yet."

"I have."

Robert pursed his lips and tilted his head just so. Hannah appeared on the verge of a scream.

"Well, then, she has changed a great deal since we last spoke," he replied. He waited for Hannah's response, but she remained silent. "She would let you march off to some rube village in Ohio to a college that lets colored boys study, filled with all manner of liberal practitioners–even advocating free love, for all you know. I daresay she would have something to say about it."

"They do not advocate free love. You are making that up," Hannah declared.

Robert forked the last green stalk. "Perhaps. I have heard things, though."

"Such as?" she asked.

He sat back in his chair and snapped his fingers for the waiter. He reached into his pocket and pulled out a cigar. "They are teaching the colored there. I know that much. That would be enough, if I had anything to say about it."

"But you don't," Hannah said quietly, then grew silent for the remainder of the dinner, only picking daintily at her dish and paying scant attention to the operatic recital at Carpenter's Hall that Robert had procured tickets to.

At the curb afterward, Robert opened the door of the hansom cab and helped Hannah enter. He looked in hard after her. "Shall I accompany you home, or shall I give the driver instructions?"

His question took her by surprise. Robert had never failed to accompany her to her door. Suddenly she became aware of her dreadful behavior, bordering on that of a harpy, this evening.

"No, Robert," she said softly, "please. I am sorry. Please come inside."

He had the grace not to smile in a self-congratulatory way, but for an instant Hannah thought he would have liked to.

Once he was inside the conveyance, she placed her hand on his forearm. He turned to her. As they passed the gas lamps, the cab would be bathed in a golden light for an instant, then would grow dark.

He might very well say good-bye, Hannah thought. *I do not want him to depart over such a matter. This is not worthy of a dissolution of our relationship. It truly is not.*

"Robert, I am sorry. I behaved abominably. You must forgive me. I can offer no reason for my rudeness. I have so many things on my mind."

Robert placed his hand over hers. Hannah knew there was a reason she no longer wore gloves on pleasant evenings. She liked the touch of his skin on hers.

Robert allowed himself to smile. "Hannah, you know how much I care for you. You know I only want what is best. Oberlin is not the best for you. If I had the right, I would demand that you disavow your intentions on attending that school. I do not want you to make a huge mistake. I am protecting you, Hannah. You must know that." He let his hand slip to her wrist and gently encircle it.

"I do, Robert. I do know that."

"And you know that the future for me is bright. And I want you to be part of it, Hannah. You and I make a fine, handsome couple."

He took her hand in his and intertwined his fingers with hers. She always felt so childlike when he did that, for his hand was so much larger than her delicate fingers. He faced her and, with one quick motion, slipped his hand about her waist and pulled her closer.

"You are the most beautiful woman I have ever met," he whispered to her. "I am not willing to share you with the farmers in Ohio. I am not."

And with that he drew her to him and pushed his lips to hers. He had done this on one occasion in the past, and Hannah waited a few heartbeats, then pushed him back. This time she did not and let his kiss linger for the span of two city blocks.

And at that point, the Collins home lay a dozen blocks more distant.

From a Letter to Robert Keyes
September 1846

Dear Robert,

How sweet of you to send the flowers. And how dear a message that was included. I did not show it to my mother for fear that she would interrogate me about the reason for your profuse endearments. I daresay I will not be able to ride along those streets ever again without offering a secret smile. It was such unexpected passion, my sweet. But it was also so very welcome. I do not know what came over you that night, but I hope to see that side of you more often.

But allow me now to address a serious subject–not that your passion is not most serious. You were right. I had not told my mother or father about Oberlin. And when I did, their response was so totally foreign that I found myself befuddled for days after.

My mother's words were, "You should go and investigate. You cannot expect to make a decision on the strength of a single page of paper. Go."

I am sure my jaw fell open when she said that.

Elizabeth Collins! Nearly ordering me to travel a thousand miles to the frontier to see about a college.

Can you believe it?

My mother actually encouraged me to go. After I considered her request for a day, I thought she was baiting me–hoping I would not travel so far and, even if I did, would find Ohio to be so horrid and rustic that I would come running home to the sophistication and civilization of Philadelphia. I am sure that she has tired of our perpetual disagreement over this issue and is giving me freedom (though I do not truly require her blessing) and counting on me to return home, defeated.

My mother could act in that fashion, I assure you.

Now comes the hardest part of this letter.

I am going to do as she suggested.

Please, Robert, do not hate me nor think ill of me, but I must not let this opportunity remain unexplored. I am making plans to travel to Ohio. I will depart in a few days, and I know I will not have the opportunity to tell you this news in person.

If I am to be true to my dream, I must do this. I must.

I trust that you will understand. We will have time for passion, but now I must pursue my promise.

Always, my dearest,
Hannah

From the Diary of Morgan Hannah Collins
Shawnee, Ohio
October 1846

Land sakes, I forgot just how handsome that boy was. He opened the door of his most humble parsonage, and I felt the breath leap out of my lungs. If anything, the deprivations, such as they are in Ohio, have further chiseled Joshua's fine appearance to perfection. He must be involved in more physical labor here than when he lived in Cambridge, for his shoulders appeared broader than before and his arms even more sculptured.

I have gone on, haven't I?

And this is a man of God.

And I am in a most serious relationship with Mr. Keyes.

(I will take a deep breath.)

I am sitting in Joshua's home, the church parsonage, actually, quite alone, as he has taken up residence with his parents for the interim while I am here. (A man of the cloth must be especially cautious of appearance and evil and all that.)

I was amused at Joshua's stumbling greeting. I took him most unawares, and it was an hour, I think, before he organized his thoughts in a coherent fashion.

Ohio and the town of Shawnee are indeed far removed from the glitter of New York. The streets are muddy and full of ruts. The town, such as it is, consists of a few ramshackle structures, all of which look as if a strong wind might topple them. There is a bar with rooms to let above–a most dubious enterprise, a store that offers foodstuffs and staples, a blacksmith, a small shacklike town hall, and a few other buildings, all leaning on each other.

I had no idea Joshua came from such deprivation and near squalor.

I must close now. I see him striding up the lane. He looks like a man with a purpose in mind.

En route to Oberlin, Ohio
October 1846

The carriage took another lurch to the left, and the three passengers bounced in their seats. Hannah clutched the window frame. It was almost too chilled to have the canvas window rolled up, but if it were lowered into place, no one would have a handhold to keep their seats.

The driver called out, "Sorry, folks! The rain we had last week battered these roads a tad."

Hannah peered out the window. The sun was hidden behind a thin cloud cover, but she imagined it to be near noon. They had been riding all morning without a stop, and she was looking forward to sitting on a chair that was not moving.

One of the other passengers was an older man who introduced himself and whose name Hannah promptly forgot. He said he was the representative of some rail company or other sort of concern. He smelled of garlic, and his hair glistened with a thick application of tonic. Hannah was glad that he chose a seat facing forward as she faced backward.

The other passenger was an older woman, perhaps thirty. Her name was Clair Dimitz, and she was headed to Cleveland to join her husband.

Conversation in a carriage could be no better than a few shouted remarks when the road went smooth, and all looked forward to stopping for the lunch break.

For the last several miles, the rear wheels issued a tight, metallic squeal.

"That doesn't sound good, does it?" the gentleman from the railroad shouted.

"No," Hannah shouted back. "What is it?"

"Sounds like the axle. Bet we stop in Zanesville a spell to fix it."

"Zanesville? Where is that?"

"Just ahead a few miles, I reckon. I hope you brought a good book with you. It might be a long spell."

The squeal grew louder, as if in response.

In an hour, the three disembarked, stretching and twisting, into the bright sun.

"This be our stop in Zanesville," the driver said. "'Fraid we have some problem with the back axle. There's a smithy right here, so I'm hopin' we get under way today."

"Sir," Hannah asked, "what happens if it is not repaired?"

He shrugged. "Then we be stayin' here till it is or till we get another coach."

Hannah squinted about. The road led north, and from where she stood, she could see a half dozen farms. She could also make out the smoke from a factory or foundry. "Is that Zanesville there?" she asked pointing north.

The gentleman from the railroad nodded. "Two miles. Maybe three."

"Why don't we go there if we are stranded here for the night? Surely there are better accommodations there."

The older gentleman laughed. "Miss, I can tell you ain't traveled much. This stop here, such as it is, is the best of a very bad lot."

She looked about. There was a large weather-beaten sign over the door of the inn and tavern. It read *Stough's. Est. 1823. All Manner of Rooms. Provisions. Horse Shoeing.*

"It is?" she asked quietly.

The gentleman laughed again. "They tell me even the president stayed here when he campaigned along this road. He came from Zanesville to get here, so you draw your own conclusions." He tipped his hat. "I think I need to wet my whistle, as they say. Would you ladies care to join me?"

Hannah arched her eyebrows in question at Clair Dimitz. "Well, I do not care to drink, but if they have decent food, I am hungry."

The gentleman from the railroad, a Mr. Davies, they found out, was much more interested in the liquid part of lunch and quickly found an apparently familiar spot at the bar. Clair and Hannah remained at an uneven table by the window.

The stew and bread were both hot and fresh and a bargain compared to prices in Philadelphia.

"Miss Collins," Clair asked, "would you mind a personal question?"

"Not at all, but please call me Hannah."

"What are you doing here? A woman of obvious breeding like yourself, out here among the dirt farmers and all? This picture just don't seem right somehow. Like you lost a bet or something."

Hannah glanced at the bare fields beyond.

I should tell someone.

Hannah nodded and began, slowly at first, to tell her story. It was clear that speaking to a stranger was a liberating experience. Hannah was cautious as she began but then found great release in sharing her true emotions and observations.

Hannah talked for nearly two hours, with only an occasional question from Mrs. Dimitz. It was obvious to Hannah that the woman was enthralled with her descriptions of Cambridge and New York and the galas and all.

As dusk closed in, the driver blustered back into the tavern. "It be the axle that went bad all right," he declared to the entire room. "But we're nearly done with the fixin'. We can leave at first light." He nodded in the ladies' direction. "You best be getting a room, then. I asked and they got the best room set aside for you. Quiet too. Won't be bothered by the noise later on."

❧

The moon rose over the flat landscape. Hannah watched as several buggies arrived at the tavern, each holding five or six riders. "I can see what the driver meant about the noise. Thirty people must have arrived in the last half hour alone."

"There aren't a lot of options out here. You either come here for entertainment or you stay home," Clair stated flatly.

Hannah closed the shutter and climbed into the high bed. When she turned back the heavy woven counterpane, she noticed that the linen sheets and woolen blankets actually appeared to have been laundered recently. Hannah thought she could sleep without too much trepidation.

It is no worse than the other places I have stayed on this trip. And it is not much worse than the parsonage in Shawnee.

In the dark, the women could hear the hoots and shouts begin from the tavern below. Yet the room was the farthest from the bar, so the noise was fainter.

"Hannah," Clair said quietly, "your story stopped as you left Philadelphia for this trip. I asked why you are here, in Ohio, in Zanesville, and you have not truly answered the query."

"I haven't? But I talked all afternoon."

"Yet you never mentioned why you are in Ohio."

"Really?"

"It's true."

"I came to Ohio to visit Oberlin College. I may attend there next year," Hannah blurted out.

Clair held her hand to her mouth and tried to stifle her laugh.

"What is amusing at that?" Hannah asked.

Clair waved her hand in reply, and Hannah could tell that she was embarrassed. "It's just that I don't see a woman of your type there. I've been through Oberlin, and it's a right small village."

"It is?"

"Smaller than Zanesville by a length. And not nearly as civilized."

"Truly?"

"Truly."

Both were silent for a long moment. The calls and coarse laughter from the bar below bounced up the steps and hinted at the patrons' boisterous activities.

"That's not the only reason I came."

Clair smiled. "I have known you for all of a few hours, Hannah, and yet I knew you had not explained all."

"I went to Shawnee to see a man."

"A man? Alone?"

"A fellow student at Harvard."

"The one from the seminary? The preacher? The good-looking one?"

"I mentioned him?" Hannah asked. "I didn't think I did."

"A dozen times," Clair responded.

Hannah giggled, then grew serious. "I so wanted to see him again. And Robert, I mentioned Robert, didn't I?"

"You did."

"Robert has all but demanded that I give up this foolishness and marry him."

"And that's why you visited Joshua?"

"Yes. No. I don't know."

"Do you want to marry Robert?"

Hannah stared off into the darkness above her head. "I think so. He's handsome and on his way to being rich. He comes from a good family."

"Then why did you visit this preacher boy?"

A bottle crashed, a few angry words were shouted, then the

sounds of a scuffle, and another shout, followed by a loud caterwauling of voices. It went on for a long minute until there came the slapping sound of a steak hitting a metal drum. Then there was applause and laughter.

Hannah was grateful for the pause. *Why did I visit him?*

"Why did you go there?"

"I . . . I think . . . I . . ."

"You wanted him to sweep you off your feet?"

Hannah sat up in bed. "That's not it. That is not what I wanted at all."

No one spoke.

"I didn't. Really I didn't." She started to cry. "I went to his church on Sunday. He was so handsome in his robe behind the pulpit. Everyone stopped staring at me when he spoke. He is such a fine preacher. He talked about God and how he has called us to a life of service. He said that we needed to know Christ and to allow him into our heart or else our service means nothing."

"That's true, Hannah."

"And then he insisted that to be called a follower of Christ, we must give our all to him and he will use us as he sees fit. He said that a person who does only good works has done nothing."

"I believe he spoke the truth."

Hannah let the tears flow. "When he was saying those words, it was like a beautiful vision settled on him. I realized that he had never once looked or sounded so alive when we were together. I realized that he would never have enough room in his heart and life for me."

"But, Hannah, that is not how it is."

"It doesn't matter, really. I could not live in Shawnee. It's so foreign to me. And I could never compete with his faith."

"Hannah, listen to me," Clair said. "That is not how faith is. God does not force out others to make room for himself."

"No, I will marry Robert. I will have a fine house in New York or Philadelphia, and I will serve others. I will become a doctor and do good works. That will please God, despite what Joshua said."

"Hannah," Clair said with finality, "you are not listening. That is not what God wants."

"I'll marry Robert, and I'll forget all about Joshua."

Hannah fell back to her pillow and closed her eyes tight.

"Hannah?" Clair asked. "Hannah?"

And from the bar below came a drunken chorus of shouts and laughter.

FROM THE DIARY OF HANNAH COLLINS KEYES

EN ROUTE TO PHILADELPHIA

OCTOBER 1846

Oberlin was a pleasant surprise. The campus and environs were most pleasant. The administration building was a small-scale replica of Harvard. Classrooms and dormitories and all the rest were of a fine quality.

But the town is very small, and one feels so isolated from the rest of the world there. Why, there wasn't a single millinery shop in the village!

All those I met were most friendly and assured me I could attend Oberlin and work on medical training. They would not assure me I could be granted a medical license just yet, but they imagined that in a year or two, by the time I finished my studies, all accreditation would be in place and I could make use of their diploma to be licensed.

There were many assurances but no guarantees.

I left promising that I would arrive at my decision after consultation with my parents. Yet I knew that I would not return the moment I first stepped foot on the campus.

I cannot recall ever being in such a tattered state of emotions.

First Robert demanded that I withdraw from pursuing my dream.

Then I saw Joshua and found myself out of his world, with no hope of reentering it.

Do I now return home to be married with no expectation of ever using my education in the future?

I am at a loss to know. There is an emptiness under my heart.

Returning home, I have scarce paid attention to scenery, fellow travelers, or my accommodations. I sit and stare out without seeing.

I never once imagined this to be the outcome of my life the day I first entered Harvard. What is it that I would need to change things? Cease being a woman? Cease worrying over the approval of my mother? Cease seeking to make a difference as a doctor?

I close my eyes and search for an answer, and no answer comes.

Philadelphia
November 1846

"I am so relieved that you have returned in good health and spirits," Robert exclaimed as he embraced Hannah. Both Hannah's mother and father had withdrawn from the parlor, leaving "you young people to talk."

Hannah at once hoped they would stay and wished them gone.

Now Robert edged closer to her on the sofa. He would not take further liberties, she was sure, based on the time of day–midafternoon–and the fact Hannah's mother might slip in at any moment, unannounced, with an offer of tea or coffee or a sweet lemonade, perhaps.

No, Hannah reasoned, Robert would be content to sit close, hold her hand, and talk.

"Your letter sounded as if you had a most urgent subject to discuss," he said.

Hannah twisted the lace handkerchief in her hands. "I do."

"Does it have to do with your decision not to attend Oberlin?"

"It does."

Robert tried to show a sympathetic smile, but it appeared more smug than sympathetic. "Well, then, I knew that a university in Ohio would not suit you. You have too much good taste for that. And you should never be removed from the civilization you have known. It would not serve you well."

Hannah did not reply immediately. "Perhaps you are right, Robert. Perhaps this was too much. I suspect that you and my parents are wiser than me."

Robert puffed up. "Not wiser, Hannah, for you are most intelligent for a woman. It is just that I see things as they are, not as they might be. A realist. In business, one needs to be a realist, for the idealist will be taken every time. A wolf and sheep, you know."

Hannah did not know. She tugged at her dark crimson dress, smoothing the satin. From behind them, the clock in the entryway chimed three times. It would soon be time for tea, although Robert preferred his coffee. Outside the wind rattled about the empty branches of the sycamore near the house. The sun had yet to break through this day, and the gray morning had dissolved into a gray afternoon.

Robert took Hannah's hand. "But before you speak further, Hannah, I think I shall need to say my piece."

"No . . . Robert. I mean, of course you can, but I should explain why I . . ."

"Well, then, there is no need for further explanations. You are back home. This is what is right."

She tried to return his smile but could not.

"Hannah," he said and cleared his throat, "I suspect we both knew this day would come . . ."

Is he telling me farewell? Hannah's heart lurched.

". . . but I have never actually said the words. I suspect that is an oversight, since I am such a busy man, and I have my mind on a thousand other matters at all times. But I should never be too busy for matters of the heart."

She closed her eyes and held them shut for much longer than needed.

He swallowed and turned his head to one side. A most solemn expression came over him. "Hannah," he said, "we have hinted at this for many months now. We have talked as though such a matter would resolve itself with no active participation by each other. It appears to me that such a merger would be of great benefit to both of us."

What is he speaking of? This "merger" business again?

"Hannah, I believe it is time that you and I . . . well . . . that you and I consummate our relationship into marriage. I propose to change your name to Mrs. Robert Keyes." And then he beamed at Hannah with a smile that looked rehearsed.

She found herself smiling in spite of his awkward proposal.

"Would you do me the honor?" he said quietly.

She examined her hands. He reached out and took them in his, swallowing them up with his fingers. She looked up. "Yes, Robert."

He exhaled and placed a hand over his heart. "You will make a fine wife, sweet Hannah. I am sure of that." He dropped her hands and embraced her, taking more liberties than Hannah felt appropriate.

She gently leaned back. "I have said yes, Robert, for I think you will make a fine husband as well. I will promise to be a most dutiful wife, and I will do all that I can to make you a fine home."

He nodded.

"But I want to ask for one promise from you," she continued. "Will you agree to one promise?"

His smile disappeared. "Does your answer truly depend on this? It matters that much to you?"

She lowered her eyes and nodded, then took his hand and drew him close to her. "Robert, since attending Harvard you know . . . and have known that I have been enamored with the promise of becoming a doctor. I am not even certain of the causes for this desire within myself. It has come upon me in a most sudden way, but in a most fierce way as well. It is not a passing fancy or an idle daydream. It is what I truly desire."

"But, Hannah . . ."

She placed a hand on his lips. "I will not attend Oberlin. But if we live here in Philadelphia or in New York, I will continue to seek out a way to make my goal a reality. If we marry, you must agree that I be afforded the opportunity to do so."

"But, Hannah . . ."

She swept her fingers along his cheek. "I will not be dissuaded."

They stared at each other for a long, silent moment. Finally he looked away, then nodded. "Hannah, if it means that much to you, then I will agree to that condition."

Her eyes showed her surprise. Then Robert took her in his arms again and drew her closer to him than she had ever been before.

From a Letter to Gant Keyes
November 1846

My Dearest Brother,

Hannah said yes!

Such a beautiful woman, and she said yes!

I am beside myself in joy. A more exquisite and passionate woman I could scarce describe. Her form and her lips and her face all conspire in delicious torment to excite and inflame me. And soon she will become my wife. I am the most fortunate man in the world.

She has promised me that she will be a dutiful and obedient woman, and in these unsettled days, such filial love is rare indeed.

I know I have often complained that she places too high an import on education, and that is still true. Why, even before she said yes, she made me agree that I would allow her to continue on her foolish quest to become a doctor. Of course, I agreed. I would not allow such a minor obstacle to prevent my taking her as my wife. I ache too much for her presence beside me to have allowed her condition to deny my needs.

And when the babies come–and that will happen very, very soon–her mood and outlook will change. She will see such a quest is as foolish as can be.

Be ready, my little brother, for I shall soon call upon you to stand beside me at the altar. You must promise, however, to keep your jealous looks in check.

For I, on this occasion, have been truly the lucky one in the family.

Your brother,

Robert

Chapter Eleven

Philadelphia
June 1847

THE sun skirted about the clouds yet left old St. Joseph's Church in shadow most of the afternoon. Rain threatened, and a few men, standing outside the Gothic-style edifice with their pipes, held their palms flat to the sky, feeling for drops.

Festoons of flowers tied to the massive stone pillars swayed in the chilled breeze, their ribbons flapping. With every shift in the wind, a handful of petals fell to well-worn slate steps.

The gentlemen outside waited for the familiar strains of the elegant organ music signifying the bride's arrival. The old church was filled to capacity with the best of Philadelphia's old society families. Even though the social standing of the Collins family had slipped considerably in recent years, to be invited to the wedding and banquet to follow was not to be discounted. A flock of feathered hats populated the church, and the gossamer filigree drifted and danced in the breeze that flitted in through nearly closed stained-glass windows.

Each pew was decorated with a profusion of white roses, lilies, and gardenias wrapped in delicate greenery and tied with a wide silk bow of pale ivory. At the heart of the bow was a cluster of pearls. A starched white silk runner coursed up the main aisle and was unsullied by any footstep, as all guests entered by the side aisles of the sanctuary.

The organist, a tiny older woman, nearly stood on her bench, searching for the first view of the bride. With only a hint of ethereal veil, she abruptly shortened a Bach organ prelude and launched into the Bridal March with nary a hint of transition. The booming chords echoed off the back wall as the entire congregation rose from the dark oak pews en masse, turning where they stood, and craned their necks to catch their first glimpse of Morgan Hannah Collins in her splendid wedding finery. Many in the audience had obstructed views due to the tall millinery creations in attendance and so jostled left and right or even, in some cases, stood on the actual pews to watch as she entered the sanctuary.

Her father was at her side in a dark gray morning coat with long tails and a high starched collar. He appeared most ill at ease, as if he had consumed one too many brandies that morning, fortifying himself for this task, as well as worrying about the huge costs involved in the day's festivities. A drop of sweat glistened at each temple, almost as if planned. Midway down the aisle, each drop fell to his lapels with the tiniest of splashes.

Hannah's face was hidden by the gauzy thickness of a handmade veil of Bruges lace, imported from a small town in Belgium. Her gown was of crushed imported French silk the color of a spring snow, with a tight bodice and wide skirt festooned with cascades of tiny pearls. Down the back, pearl buttons ran from her neck to her waist, ending at a huge bustle and bow and culminating in a long pearled train. Each hem of the soft gown was also decorated with the glint of pearls. Her simple bouquet was an abundant clutching of white roses.

She stopped at the entrance to the sanctuary. From the corner of her eye, she saw Robert and his brother at the right front, waiting for her to enter. His smile was curiously somber. His brother wore an eager expression. Robert's parents stood, watching her enter. Her mother stood to the other side, wearing a pale orchid gown imported a fortnight ago from Paris. A single diamond pendant hung at her bare throat. Hannah recognized it as her grandmother's.

The organist held her long bony fingers above the keyboard, unwilling to play further if Hannah did not come closer. She began the introductory notes again, as if encouraging the bride to begin her long walk.

Only when Hannah consciously considered moving her foot did it actually move, and then her gait was slow and quite methodical. If observers had been particularly keen in their observing, they would have said her steps were nearly reluctant.

Her vision telescoped the farther into the church she walked. At first, she saw everyone. But with each step her vision narrowed until she could see only individuals, then only their faces. Images blurred past as if she were falling. At last she could see only Robert and the minister. All else was a haze of indistinct watery colors.

Her hearing ceased as well. She saw lips moving and felt the organ's vibration, but no sound registered in her ears. She blinked and swallowed.

What happens when he addresses me? Do I know what I will say?

As if in a dream, Hannah stepped one foot in front of the other, all of the movements familiar, having rehearsed them twice on the day prior, but odd and disconnected at the same time.

Then suddenly Robert was at her side, and she looked over at him several times. He had the same somber smile on his face, as if it were now a permanent feature of his physical landscape. His eyes did not find hers but once, and then she thought she saw a hint of fear in them. Or perhaps it was the smugness of victory–she could not discern which.

The minister stood and talked for what seemed to be an interminable length of time. Then he called to them both. She knew, rather than heard, his instructions. When he addressed her, she remembered the correct answer to his question was "I do."

And those were the words her lips attempted to form. She had no idea if they sounded as they should or at what volume they were spoken. She noted no hint of surprise nor alarm in the face of the minister, a small precise man from Utica who often smelled of cabbage.

She assumed that her replies were as expected.

Then he stopped, and Robert turned to his brother. She stared straight ahead at the ornately carved cross. Robert turned back, and a glint of something flashed in his hand. He held it out to her, and for a moment, she could not discern his intention. Then she saw his eyes at her hand, and she raised it.

He took it and slipped a gold ring on her third finger. It at once felt both tight and heavy.

She looked down. She had seen it before, of course, in order to size it properly and had marveled at its fierce, yet delicate beauty. But today, it was as if she were seeing it for the first time. It caught only the dim light of a gray afternoon, filtered through a holy thickness of stained glass, and yet it sparkled and danced. She held out her hand and stared at it, hoping that others would not think it a vain thing for a bride to do.

Then the minister said, "And now I pronounce you man and wife. What God hath joined, let no man put asunder."

Hannah's world collapsed into silence again.

And then, with the barest hint of what lay in store, he added, "You may now kiss your bride."

Robert reached for the veil and lifted, then lifted again, as if struggling with a tough bit of sticky gossamer. Finally, the lace was removed from Hannah's face. She felt the layers tumble and lay hard against the back of her head. Robert came closer, his visage filling more and more of her narrow vision, until his face was the only thing she could see, his nose and lips and half-closed eyes looming over her. She felt his lips, dry as dust, on hers, for the barest of moments. She thought she should have closed her eyes, but by the time she could, it was over, and Robert had stood upright again.

"I now have the pleasure of presenting to you Mr. and Mrs. Robert Randolph Keyes."

Robert turned to face the church, and Hannah looked about. Then she realized that she, too, needed to turn and face them and did so. She still could not see farther than the steps a few feet away. They looked steep and treacherous, especially wearing the long gown.

Robert's extended arm nudged her side. She realized she should take his arm and did so, all the while staring at the floor, wondering how to step down without falling.

The organ boomed into life with the loudest bass note Hannah had ever heard, and she was nearly startled away from her grasp on Robert's arm. He took a step forward and she was obligated to follow; the music came crashing about them in a relieved crescendo as they walked down the aisle as husband and wife for the very first time.

From a Letter to Florence Galeswhite
June 1847

Dear Florence,

I am married!

I know you felt most dreadful in not being able to attend. I do forgive you since your travel to the Continent was planned well before my humble invitation reached your hands. How I wished I had you there with me that day! Perhaps you might have calmed me.

Since you could not attend, I will tell you all about it–at least what I can remember of it. A curious, numbing fog filled my thoughts and memories of that day. Perhaps it was best, for I was not nervous–just unaware. I had no opportunity to become flustered or embarrassed.

Of course, you know all about the gown, decorations, and invitations. I must have bored you with a hundred pages on such feminine trivialities, as Robert once labeled the preparations. Perhaps he is right, and all our worry means little in the overall scheme of things.

A friend once said (was it you?) that a man and woman married at the courthouse are just as married as those in a church. That is what we should have done but lacked the courage to do–not that Robert would have gone along.

The celebration after the wedding, I am told, lasted far into the night.

The Palmer House was a most elegant choice. I do not remember tasting the food that night, but others mentioned that it was lavish and most succulent.

Of course, as is customary, Robert and I did not stay long.

I blush as I think of our hasty exit, but Robert was in a most agitated state, insisting we leave at the stroke of nine. However, it was nearing ten before we managed to extract ourselves after tearful good-byes to parents and friends.

I will leave the remaining tale untold, but suffice it to say that I am indeed a married woman. I do not see what the big fuss is all about. You would think from the stories my mother and others have told me that I faced some Homeric or Herculean trial.

And despite the noisiness of a man's snoring next to me as I attempt to sleep, it is nice to have companionship on chilly nights.

A week later, I read through the nuptial vows that the minister included in our marriage certificate and papers. Included are a few instructions, that, had I heard at the church, I may have stumbled or hesitated to agree upon.

Love?

I can do that.

Cherish?

That is more of a man's instruction, but I will cherish Robert's virtues.

Obey?

That single word alone becomes problematic. If the man is kind and honorable, then this instruction is easy to uphold. Robert claims he is a Christian man and that as such he will follow God and treat me in the way the Good Book instructs.

And to him, the vow of the wife to obey her husband is important. And I did willingly make that vow.

Robert did, as I mentioned in an earlier letter, state that I could continue my pursuit of a medical degree. He has not disavowed that promise, nor would I ever expect him to back down on his word.

So in all other areas, I am to obey.

A few short years ago, I might have railed at such a vow. But now I am a married woman and I can see the wisdom inherent in such an admonition. A family cannot be a democracy as is the United States. If it were, every disputed decision would be a vote-to-vote deadlock.

No, Robert has wisdom and I will abide by his decisions. It is what the Bible has ordained, is it not?

And wouldn't Joshua agree to that?

I will write again soon. Robert will be home momentarily, and I must see if dinner has been prepared according to his specifications. He can be a dear but is the fussiest of diners.

Until my next letter,

Hannah

Philadelphia
October 1847

The door clicked open. Hannah, at her desk with a medical book and a packet of envelopes, lifted her head to listen. There was the sound of a cool leather heel on the marble.

"Robert, dearest–is that you?"

"Yes."

"I am in the drawing room. I will be out shortly," she called.

She dipped her pen into the inkwell and scratched out a final line to the letter. She dipped the quill once again and signed her name with a flourish. Signing *Mrs.* was easy, but learning how to draft the name *Keyes* in an artistic manner was harder. The letter *K* never looked quite finished, she thought.

In good time, I will learn, she told herself as she blew on the ink to dry it.

Just then the door opened, and a shaft of afternoon sunlight streamed in. Hannah blinked. The drawing room contained the most comfortable furnishings but, facing north, had the poorest, coldest light.

Robert claimed that owning a house involved all manner of headache; instead, he had leased the first and second floors of a fifteen-year-old mansion just off of Logan Circle in Philadelphia. He had ties, both business and social, to Boston but had found some successes in Philadelphia. Rather than build or buy, he had found this property, owned by a formerly rich fellow who now occupied only the third floor and attic with a separate entrance, and who was seldom in residence. They had a dozen rooms, all well sized, and their maid and manservant had rooms in the basement.

"And the way this city is growing, by the time a house is built in a fashionable neighborhood, the fashion has passed, and the values have departed. It makes more sense for now to lease, my dear, and that is what we shall do."

It mattered little to Hannah, and she busied herself finding furnishings and fabrics and monitoring the activities of the maid, whose prime occupation seemed to be staying out of Hannah's sight.

"And what are you writing there?" Robert asked. "Spending the day on a letter to Florence again?"

Hannah hesitated, then smiled in return. "That was only once, Robert. And, no, this is to a new school that I have heard of in Philadelphia."

Robert did not answer, he merely raised his eyebrows.

"It's a medical school, Robert."

He pursed his lips.

"For women."

Robert answered, "I thought we agreed that it would be foolishness to attempt school once children arrive."

Hannah closed her eyes, then took a deep breath. "No, Robert, we discussed this before the wedding." *And a dozen times since,* she thought. "And if I find a school in town that I can afford with my trust fund, then I will continue my studies. We understood that."

"Humph," he muttered and sat down on a large leather chair. He unfolded the newspaper and leaned toward the window to catch the light. After a long silence, he lowered the paper. "Well, then, I suspect you will not care if your children are raised by nannies and governesses?"

"Robert," she said as sweetly as she could, "if we are blessed with a child, then I will perhaps think differently. But we have not been so blessed."

He raised the paper again, his face now hidden. Hannah did not get angry, for she knew this was just his way. In a moment, he lowered it again.

"Is there something wrong?" she asked.

"Wrong? Yes, and I think you would know."

"I don't know," she said.

"You do."

"Robert, I truly do not. What could be wrong? You are a faithful husband. You have provided me with this wonderful home. You are considerate. What could be wrong?"

"That's not what I mean."

"Then what?" she asked, her words edging at testy.

"My mother gave birth to her first child ten months after her wedding. It has been months. I simply wonder if there is something wrong with you."

Hannah slowly lowered her book and placed it on the cushion beside her. She was not sure whether she felt more close to screaming in anger or crying in shame. Carefully she folded the paper and slipped it into the envelope. It was nearly a full two minutes before she spoke again. "Robert, I do not know how to answer you. I am not with child. That much I know."

"Well, then," he snapped, "I thought you wanted to be a doctor. I thought you would know what the problem is. I'm just very certain it has nothing to do with me."

Hannah held her lip from quivering. She stood up, opened her mouth, and no words came. Instead, she turned and ran from the room and up the stairs. After slamming the bedchamber door, she threw herself on the bed and let the tears come.

Darkness had come upon the city. Hannah did not raise her head for the longest time. She imagined that it was nearing nine in the evening when she finally sat up and wiped her face.

She heard a faint knock on the door.

"Yes?"

Robert leaned in. "I hope you're better now. Martha has left your dinner on the table. A pork roast with potatoes. Not wonderful, but fully edible."

"You ate?"

"It was late. You were in here. I was hungry."

She nodded.

"And I have an early day tomorrow. I have to see my mother off on an early train."

Hannah was reaching for her nightgown and robe when she spun about. "Your mother! Is she in town? When?"

Robert tossed his coat on a damask-covered boudoir chair in the corner and then sat upon it as he removed his shoes. "She came in yesterday on the morning train from Boston. I had lunch with her at Patricks Café."

Hannah clutched her nightgown to her throat. "Is she coming here? Why didn't you tell me? I could have met you downtown."

Robert kicked off his socks. One slipped under the bed. "It was only a short trip, Hannah. A visit to her solicitor. She said that she wanted to stay at the Palmer House. She said she didn't want to put you out at all."

Hannah stepped toward her husband. "But, Robert, she's your mother. We can't have her staying at a hotel. She should be with us."

"Well, that's what I said, but she insisted. And you know how she can be."

"Did your father come? Did she travel alone? I thought she always stayed home."

"She's alone. I don't know where my father was. She didn't say. And she travels some as her needs require."

Hannah stared and could not think of another question.

Robert added, "She suggested that maybe you should visit a doctor."

"Your mother said I should visit a doctor? Whatever for?"

Robert slipped into his nightshirt. "She wants a grandchild. And she has grown weary of waiting."

Hannah had not moved in the last few minutes. "But, Robert, it has only been a few months."

He slapped his pillow and turned down the lantern. "She was already showing by this time when she was married, she says. She wanted me to tell you that."

Hannah held her sob silent in her throat.

Dawn flecked the sky with the first hint of red as she finally found sleep.

Philadelphia
November 1847

Mrs. Keyes,

We received your letter and the Dean of Admissions brought your request to my attention. I must admit that we spent many hours in discussion concerning this matter.

Your credentials are most impressive. For anyone to graduate from Harvard in the top tenth percentile is quite an accomplishment, and for a woman to do that, it is even more noteworthy. We all took great interest in your choice of studies. It appeared from your transcript that you indeed participated in every available medical science course offered to undergraduates.

Again, your standing in those studies was most convincing. You bested nearly all your fellow male students. I can only imagine their great chagrin at such standings.

I am not a man who is impressed easily, but I was impressed with your long letter outlining your reasons for this decidedly unusual profession–at least for a woman, that is.

I even went so far as to call upon my old friend at Harvard, Mr. Mocker, your class advisor. Take no fear, for we all know he has an earned reputation as a curmudgeon. Yet, for all his bluster, he spoke most highly of you and your dedication to thought and ideas. He said that you are "unlike most women, whose heads are almost too small for intellect, but just big enough for love." He approved of your perseverance, yet scoffed at your desire to become a physician. But I would have grown concerned had he not.

All this to say, Mrs. Keyes, that we have thoroughly discussed your case. We have decided to admit you to our medical degree program that will begin this February. If you are still interested in attending, I urge you to contact me at your earliest opportunity.

Regards,

Dr. Willard C. Wilcott

Dean

Philadelphia Women's Medical College

Hannah read and reread the letter a dozen times before she ever left the entry hall. She carefully folded the letter and carried it to Robert's desk in his study on the south side of their apartment. The room overlooked a formal garden and fountain.

She seldom entered the room, for she knew how precise Robert was about his papers and possessions and would storm about if any paper or file was moved or, worse yet, lost. But his desk was large, and in the first drawer was a thickness of stationery embossed with their name and address.

She took out two sheets of paper and two envelopes. She wrote quickly with bold strokes. One letter was addressed to the school. The second letter was addressed to her Uncle Winthrop and advised him where her tuition money was to be sent.

Philadelphia
December 1847

Robert skulked about the house, not speaking for long periods. He entered the drawing room where Hannah sat with a small pyramid of books. Then he would stare, mutter, then exit without speaking.

On his fifth entrance into the room in the same manner, Hannah looked up and smiled. "What's wrong, my dear husband?"

He stopped as if struck. "You know," he hissed after glaring at her.

She had resigned herself to his piques of temper and had yet to respond in kind. She fashioned herself as a good Christian wife and met every snarl with a smile, every spoken coarseness with pleasant nature.

"I am sure I do not. Please sit down and tell me."

"No," he snapped and stomped out of the room again. He had been home for two full days, the heavy snow having impeded all traffic to and from the city. It would not pay to venture out, he reasoned, until the city or the sun managed to clear some of the snow from the main streets.

In another five minutes he was back. "You don't know what's wrong?"

She glanced up again from her studies. "I do not."

He narrowed his eyes. "It should be obvious."

She folded her hands on her lap. "Perhaps it is, sweet husband," she said softly and calmly. "But I may be slow to understand. Please tell me."

He walked closer. "You are serious about attending this school? You are certain and serious?"

She waited a heartbeat to respond. "I am. I hoped I had explained myself two weeks ago when I first shared the news."

He spun on his heels and walked to the door. He stopped, slapped his hand on the thick archway, and spun back. Hannah jumped at the sound of his palm against the wood. "I thought you would be home for me. Business is hard, and I am facing great risks every day in order to pay for all this. I borrow and lend and borrow and manage–all for you. I work hard at this."

"I know, Robert. I know you do. And I greatly appreciate all your hard work. And I will be home when you are home. I understand that my classes will be through by midafternoon. I will be home before five o'clock."

He began to pace. "And then you will be distracted, and I will be left alone when you have your nose stuck in a book."

"Robert, I have promised never to ignore your needs."

"Needs!" he spat out. "What do you know of my needs? What about what I face every day? There are great risks involved. Every day I come home with a great weight on my mind. I tumble and toss at night, worrying about all that might go wrong."

"I know you work hard, Robert. If I can help you in any manner, I will. You know I will."

He loosened the tie around his neck. Hannah watched with some surprise. Robert seldom appeared in less than full business attire, even at home.

"Do you realize the stress I am under? Do you realize how much I am sacrificing in order to gain the wealth we both want? There is much at stake."

Hannah felt a sudden sorrow for Robert. "But, Robert, you do not need to do all that for me. I would be content with less. I would."

"That's nonsense. It is my destiny. I will become more than my father. I will. I must." Robert's face grew red. A small vein in his forehead pulsed. "And now you make plans to go back to school to become a doctor? A female doctor? Who will go to a female doctor? No man worth his salt would, I know that! It is ludicrous."

She held her tongue. He was breathing hard. Finally she spoke softly. "It is what you promised, Robert. You promised me this opportunity."

His eyes widened, and his lips grew tight. "*I* promised! Why you ungrateful . . . and you promised me a child! And now you refuse to give my mother a grandchild! And *you* promised!" Leaping to her side, he grabbed her hand and yanked her to her feet. "I will have a child!"

"Robert!" she called out. "Please! You're hurting my wrist!"

"And you will obey me," he said, pulling her toward their bedchamber. "I will have that child! And I will have it now!"

He threw her into the darkened room and slammed the door with such force that a delicate English porcelain lamb fell from a whatnot shelf and shattered into a blizzard of shards.

CHAPTER TWELVE

Philadelphia
January 1848

A brittle silence filled the Keyes home over the holidays. Hannah attempted to make it festive with a perfectly shaped balsam tree decorated with lace fans, rosebuds, white glass balls, and silvery tinsel, but Robert was gone much of the time, even working until well after dark on Christmas Eve.

He and Hannah had exchanged gifts on Christmas morning after taking a sparse breakfast of tea and warmed biscuits and jam. Martha was gone for the day, visiting relatives in Camden, and Robert's manservant, Hershel, had begged for seven days off in order to visit an ailing relative in Pittsburgh. Robert grumped about the house for a week after relenting to his request.

With her trust fund, Hannah had purchased an elegant leather case for Robert, the color of a dried oak leaf, with pockets for a whole sheaf of papers and documents.

He handed her a small case that contained a fine gold chain.

They spoke only a few words all day, and their silence held for more than a fortnight.

Robert left the house at half past eight every morning and

returned promptly, unless involved in a business dinner, at seven o'clock in the evening. Hannah made sure that a satisfying meal was on the table when he walked through the door.

They sat and ate without conversation, passed each other in the hall without speaking, and save for a curt "good-bye" as he left the house, Robert hardly uttered another word.

He had never apologized for his brutality that night, and Hannah tried her best to stop the images from repeating themselves over and over in her mind. For a week she found it a challenge simply to look at her husband without feeling a sense of outrage and disgust. But she did her best to push those feelings aside and began to make pleasant conversation upon Robert's return every evening. He replied in terse, short sentences, often with more than a hint of anger. Hannah remained kind and accommodating, as she knew a good wife should behave. And every day Robert grew a few degrees more civil.

By late January, life at the Keyes home slowly lurched back to normal.

Hannah located all the required texts for her first year of classes and spent every available minute studying or taking notes when Robert was out or sleeping. She knew that the sight of a stack of medical books would drive him to distraction, so she took out only one volume at a time and secreted the rest behind her dresses in her closet.

One evening at dinner, on the last day of the month, as a cold winter wind snapped and growled, Robert drained his third large goblet of wine. He pushed the remains of his meal aside and stared at Hannah as she nibbled her food.

"Well, then, I take it that your school begins next week?" he asked.

Surprised, she responded, "Why, yes, Robert. It does begin next week. My first day of classes occurs on Wednesday. There is orientation on Monday, and we are encouraged to meet the faculty on Tuesday."

He ran his finger about his empty wineglass and looked over to the wine rack. "Well, then, I suspect you are going ahead with this most foolish idea."

Without hesitating, Hannah replied, "Yes, Robert, I am."

He nodded, then rose and selected another bottle of wine. He fussed for a few moments with the cork and the corkscrew, complaining under his breath about the help's inattention to details. He returned with the open bottle, poured a handsome amount in his glass, and took a long swallow. "Well, then, I expected as much. I mean that, from your statements, I did not think you might be easily dissuaded."

"No, I am not going to be easily dissuaded," Hannah said, still holding her fork, but motionless.

Robert sighed very deeply and glanced out the window in the dining room. It was all darkness, save for a flickering gas lamp nearly a block away. Snowflakes swirled slowly about. "Then it is settled."

"I imagine that it is, Robert."

He took another large drink and drained the remains of his wine. He leaned forward. "Listen, Hannah . . . ," he began, then pursed his lips as if pained.

Hannah did not move or speak.

"I have been thinking. . . ."

She lowered her hand to the table and lay her fork upon the plate.

"About that night . . ."

She did not respond.

"I want to . . ."

She blinked.

"I suspect I should apologize."

She waited a minute, then simply said, "Yes."

He cleared his throat and refilled his wineglass for the fifth time. "I was carried away. That is what happened. I let my passions inflame my sensibilities. You don't know how much my mother wants a grandchild. I could not help myself."

Hannah remained still, for she had not yet heard an apology.

"Such a thing will never happen again."

She nodded.

"Will you forgive me? I was angry and upset, Hannah, and your comeliness and feminine charms so inflamed me that I could no longer control myself. I am but a weak man about such things. I look at you and the longer I look, the less control I have."

When he stopped speaking, it was evident to Hannah that he had explained all he was going to and this would be the full extent of his apology.

He has made an effort, she thought, *and perhaps he is truly contrite. And I am sure my expected response is to offer my forgiveness. For his offense was not in kind but of style.* But she still searched his eyes for more. "Very well, Robert. If I can take your words tonight to be your word as a gentleman, then yes, Robert, I forgive you."

He breathed out a great sigh of relief.

"I have grown so weary of this silence," she said.

"And I am weary of living alone in this house," he said, then paused. "Perhaps it might be time . . . if you are so disposed, to celebrate our renewed relationship?"

She hoped she held her wince in check. "Perhaps," she finally replied.

Later that evening, Robert, in his silk dressing gown, sat in the boudoir chair in their bedchamber and read the morning's newspaper. He flapped through several pages, folding and creasing the paper just so. It was a ritual that at first amused Hannah, but now the endless turning and folding and flipping was a constant, yet minor, aggravation to her. She sat at her dressing table and tried not to notice.

"By the way . . . ," he said without looking up.

She turned to him. "Yes?"

"I received a letter this week from my mother."

Hannah's stomach tightened. "Is she well? How is your father?"

"She did not mention him."

Hannah stood with her comb and brush in hand, waiting to probe further, knowing there must be more to the correspondence. She determined she would wait.

Robert flapped the paper over again. He peered up at Hannah over his nose.

"She will be here the day after tomorrow. She wants to spend the weekend with us. She knows how hurt you were last time when she stayed at the Palmer House. She wrote that she wants to make the oversight up to you."

The brush fell from Hannah's hand and bounced off her foot, but she made no cry. Robert did not notice.

"The day after tomorrow? Thursday?" she asked.

Robert appeared puzzled. "Yes. Thursday. Is there a problem?"

He knew about this for a week I am sure, she thought angrily but also realized it would do no good to argue about such matters. To Robert, such a visit was good news. "No, Robert. There is no problem." She waited an appropriate time and then asked, "And how long will she stay?"

Robert did not look up from the paper. "Until Tuesday, she said. She'll take the train back on Tuesday."

Hannah nodded to the face of the newspaper, then bent to retrieve her hairbrush. *Tuesday! I wonder if the orientation is all that important–for I will not leave Robert's mother alone in this house.*

"Why, this is perfectly lovely," Mrs. Keyes said as she swept through her son's home. "And you have done so much with so little. An outstanding effort, Hannah. I am sure my son realizes how well you have done, considering."

Hannah hoped her face and eyes did not look as drawn and as tired as she felt. Martha had cleaned the entire residence, and Hannah had followed her, cleaning again what she had cleaned. Every surface, she felt, had to be without mote or streak.

"And which is my bedchamber?" Mrs. Keyes asked.

Every time Hannah was in the company of her mother-in-law, she felt an odd dislocation. Robert described his mother as the perfect maternal example, who remained at home, tending to babies, gardens, cleaning, and cooking, always giving of herself, and sacrificing everything to ensure a thick blanket of domestic tranquility was wrapped about the Keyes home.

But when Hannah had first met Robert's mother, she was not able to speak for the longest moment, her surprise was so great. Mrs. Keyes was a tall, slender woman who always wore the most elegant and tailored outfits. Perhaps they were not as stylish as some, but each was cut and shaped with the finest fabrics and decorations. Had Robert been born a girl, he would now look like his mother: a thin nose and thin lips, with a strong jaw and hair the color of the night. But her eyes were sharper and more finely drawn than her son's and lacked their warmth and depth.

She talked softly and slowly, and to Hannah, it seemed as if she carefully weighed every word that was spoken and knew without a doubt the true import of each and the deeper meaning behind it.

"Well, you will have our bedchamber, of course," Hannah said. "It is the largest and most comfortable."

The older woman stopped short. "I will do no such thing."

Hannah grew hot with panic.

"I will not turn my son out into a small, uncomfortable bed. He needs his rest. You stay with him. I will have whatever bedchamber you deign acceptable."

"No, we insist. You must take ours."

Robert, a full five steps behind them, seemed to shrink further and further into the shadows with each response.

"I will not hear of it," Mrs. Keyes said firmly. "Robert! What room would she have me take?"

He scampered to his mother's side and pointed to the room across the hall from their own. "This one, Mother. It is a nice room. This will be our nursery . . . when the time comes."

Mrs. Keyes offered Hannah a knowing smile. "This room will be perfect." Then she whispered suggestively to Hannah, "I trust that the walls are thick."

"So tell me, my daughter-in-law. Robert says you are involved in some sort of medical training. What is this about?"

Over her shoulder Hannah could see Robert blanch. At that instant Hannah was certain Mrs. Keyes knew little of the truth of the matter. And Hannah also knew this was not the perfect time to explain the entire story. So she merely said, "It is simply a continuation of my studies at Harvard. I have taken an interest in medical matters. I know it is odd, but I find some of it fascinating."

Mrs. Keyes sipped from her cup, then held it out in front of her face, holding it to the light as if looking for a crack or flaw.

"Is there a chip in it?" Hannah asked quickly. "Let me fetch a new one."

Mrs. Keyes held up her other hand. "Please, Hannah, sit down. This will be fine. You mustn't trouble yourself with such trivial matters. And after all, I am family."

With a great deliberateness, she turned the cup about and then sipped from the other side. She placed the cup back in the saucer and smiled. "So–if it is medical studies, I am curious."

"About what, Mrs. Keyes?"

Mrs. Keyes smiled. "You are to call me Mother Keyes, if you would, dear. 'Mrs. Keyes' sounds so harsh. Using it would make it appear as if I am here for some manner of evaluation. And that is not the case. I am here to visit my son and his bride." She sipped again and placed the cup and saucer on the table, still half full, and pushed it away, indicating she was through. "I am curious, though–if you are studying the intimacies of the human anatomy, why is it that you still remain barren? Is it that you do not want to provide me a grandchild?"

It was not that Hannah did not expect the question, for she did. But even though expected, she had not thought of it being asked in this context and thus could not immediately word an appropriate, rational response. She thought she might burst into tears but knew Mother Keyes would not find that response believable.

Hannah knew, from her studies, that any number of reasons could be attributed to such a condition. But none of that mattered.

"After all, dear," Mrs. Keyes continued with her soft drawl, "by the time I was wed as long as you and my son, I was nearing my time of delivery."

Hannah bit her lip. *How do I answer that? What do I say?*

In the background, on the couch beyond the table, Robert sat, his elbows on his knees, his eyes focused on the knotted Turkish rug by the fireplace.

"Well, dear?" Mrs. Keyes said. "I am certain the fault does not lie with my son. The Keyes men have always been . . . as they say . . . potent."

Robert closed his eyes. Hannah's cheeks were red and hot.

"If I might make a tiny suggestion . . . perhaps you should simply relax, dear," Mrs. Keyes said as she patted Hannah's knee. "A child will not arrive in a house that is filled with rushing about and tension." She cocked her head at Robert, then glanced penetratingly at her daughter-in-law.

That glance stabbed Hannah's heart. She blinked, then felt her lip begin to tremble. "I . . . I . . ."

But she could say no more and ran from the room, tears blinding her as she completed the stairs and reached for the bedchamber door.

❧

When Robert and his mother stepped out the door Tuesday morning, Hannah began to draw her normal breath again. And, rather than the short, quiet steps she had taken about the house, her strides began to lengthen as well. She was able to stand and hold her shoulders back. The tight-grained knot of tension between her shoulders began to edge away.

She had made arrangements to be away from school until the first classes began on Wednesday and had intended on spending this afternoon reviewing what she had missed and taking notes on what questions she had found.

She did neither. Instead she sat in the quiet of her husband's study and closed her eyes to the bright winter sun, feeling the warmth on her skin. She had brought a pot of tea and the newspaper. Without looking, she sipped the strongly brewed drink. Mother Keyes had not let her touch a drop of tea during her stay, claiming that it interfered with the inner workings of a woman, making the system nervous and unreceptive.

Now, Hannah luxuriated as the warmth of the rich beverage filled her belly. She stretched out and raised her feet, placing them on Robert's desk. She had taken her shoes off, of course, and tucked her long skirt around her knees and calves.

For nearly an hour she dozed. What awoke her was the lilting call of the coal vendor, who sang out in a beautiful Irish tenor voice. She sipped the now cool tea. *I think I now understand Robert a bit better. To deal with Mother Keyes is a most difficult task. I am sure he was on edge the entire visit as well.*

She sat up and wiped a smudge of dust on the edge of the desk.

Robert is often so tense and jumpy. I see where that might come from. I am sure I would be much different than I am now if my parents had been like her.

She folded her hands on the desk and stared out into the empty garden. The small fountain and statue were wrapped with stout canvas and circled with rope for the season. *I may never forgive him for his brutality on the night when tensions grew so that he lashed out in that most hurtful and degrading way . . . but perhaps I understand his thoughts with more sympathy. Perhaps I have done something untoward that further inflames him, and perhaps I can halt that tendency in me. Perhaps there is a civil manner in which we might discuss this further.*

She watched as a crow landed on the statue, its harsh caw grating the silence. *No . . . I am sure we will not. It is his mother, after all. He appears set in his way. No, he will not change. It is up to me to accommodate him. I am to obey.*

She looked up into the thin blue of the winter sky. *Isn't that what a wife is to do? Be accommodating? Be available? Be what your husband wants?*

Her lip began to quiver again and she blinked hard, holding off her tears. *If that is what is to be, then I must pray for strength and guidance.*

She lowered her head and sat in silence for nearly an hour. Then, realizing it was nearing the time when Robert would return home, she stood and brushed at her dress, tugging at her sleeves and setting the bodice just so. It was then she noticed the newspaper. She had brought it in with her but ignored it until now. She picked it up and glanced at the headlines. She stopped at a small story on the bottom of the first page. A name jumped out at her from the type and struck at her heart.

> INTREPID REPORTER ON A PERILOUS JOURNEY
> WILL TRAVEL BY BOAT, HORSE, COACH, TRAIN, AND ON FOOT HEADING INTO INDIAN COUNTRY
> FOLLOWING THE STEPS OF THE GREAT EXPLORERS
>
> News reporter Jamison Pike has left a fortnight ago, armed with only a paper and pencil, seeking to cross America and its frontiers. He has forsaken all the comforts of civilization, and he has promised that he will provide ample reports so that anyone with a bold heart and courage may follow his path to the west and the great Pacific coast.

Hannah sat with her hand on the paper, her forefinger at the name of Jamison Pike. Without thinking, she smoothed her fingers across his name. At first it disappeared under her hand, and then a smudged trail remained. She turned her hand over; it was grayed with the hint of ink.

She closed her eyes. *Oh, Jamison . . . where are you now?*

Philadelphia
March 1848

Hannah closed the door behind her and leaned against it. She exhaled and closed her eyes.

"Ma'am? Mrs. Keyes? Is that you?" Martha called out from the kitchen.

"Yes, Martha. I am later than I thought. Is dinner nearly done?"

Martha hurried out to the entryway, her hair in a hundred directions and palm prints of flour on her frock and apron. "No, ma'am . . . I'm sorry, but I didn't get started on time and then I think I forgot the yeast in the bread and I don't know . . . Hershel was gone all afternoon and I tried to clean and I forgot the roast and I . . ." She bent her head, and a sob rolled up from her throat.

Hannah walked over to her and patted her on the shoulder. "It's all right, Martha. Such things happen. Is there any food that we might salvage before Mr. Keyes returns?"

Martha shook her head no. "I don't think so," she said in a trembling voice.

There was a sharp tapping at the front door. Martha took a step toward the foyer.

"Martha, you clean the kitchen," Hannah said calmly. "I'll see who it is."

A messenger boy, no more than ten years old, stood outside with a pale envelope in his hands. Hannah took great pity on the boy, and as she took the letter, handed him a fifty-cent piece. The boy's face lit up as if given a rare gift. "Thank you, ma'am. Thank you so much," he said as he sprinted away.

The note was from Robert.

Dear Hannah,

I am staying the night at the club. There is a dinner I must attend, and afterward I am hoping to have drinks with Mr. Frederick MacBride–the German industrialist I mentioned to you.

I will be home tomorrow afternoon.

Love,

Robert

Hannah had no recollection of the name, but Robert mentioned many names of business associates over the course of a week. She tossed her coat on the bench in the hallway and made her way to the kitchen. Martha had been right. It appeared as if a cat and dog each carrying a bag of flour had been involved in a most spirited dance.

Martha held a very charred piece of meat.

"It doesn't look as if we can save it, does it, Martha?"

"No, ma'am."

"Well, we are in luck this evening. Mr. Keyes is overnighting at the club. We're on our own."

Martha appeared most relieved.

"If you would, please clean up this disaster," Hannah said, "then perhaps make me a pot of strong tea and some toast. Could you do that, Martha?"

Martha nodded eagerly.

"I will be in Robert's study."

Hannah dropped a stack of books on the desk, pushed back a strand of hair behind her ear, unbuttoned her cuffs, and pushed her sleeves up. She extracted one hefty tome and began to work through it slowly, taking notes on a single sheet of paper. She paused every moment or so and dipped the quill in ink. The soft scratchings were the loudest sound in the room.

Martha brought in her tea and toast, and Hannah sipped and nibbled as she worked.

It was nearing midnight when she finally stopped. She stood and braced her hands behind her neck and stretched. There was a popping sound, and she twisted and turned. There was a stack of a dozen pages, each filled with her now tight, methodical writing. Some words were underlined, some had Latin phrases in parentheses, some had arrows drawn from one word or definition to another.

She took a final drink of her tea and walked to the window. The lantern on the desk flickered, making the glass nearly translucent. As she came closer, she began to see shapes and shadows in the garden. The first greenings had occurred, and against the moon, she could see the tufts of buds erupting from the magnolia.

"If that new life could happen to me," she said softly, "then perhaps Robert would truly find peace."

She stared at the darkness until the clock struck one. *I should be bone weary, but I am strangely energized,* she thought. She sat back down. Taking out a fresh sheet of blank paper, she dipped the quill into the ink and began to write.

From a Letter to Jamison Pike
March 23, 1848

Dear Jamison,

I demurred at penning this letter for the longest time. I saw your name in the paper as you set out on your journey and felt then a great compulsion to contact you. I realize that I must send this to the newspaper and hope they will forward it. Perhaps you will not see this for months and months. If that is the case, so be it.

I am making good on my promise, Jamison.

Do you remember what you told me? It seems like ages ago now. You told me that I must not let my light be extinguished. I took it then, as I hope you meant it, that I must continue on my dream of becoming a doctor.

I recall those wondrous late nights at the Destiny as we talked and laughed and told each other stories.

You truly wanted the best for me, didn't you?

I am now a married woman, but I should think that you would know of that by now. I married Robert Keyes last year and we are happy. He is involved in all manner of financial dealings–most of which I cannot keep straight. He enjoys what he does and says it is only a matter of time until he equals our dear friend Gage Davis in accumulated wealth.

That is not so important to me now.

I am enrolled at the Philadelphia Women's Medical College. And they have agreed that upon successful completion of my work I will be a doctor.

I was most surprised. I expected that the studies would come as easily to me now as they did at Harvard. Or were you and I the only students that did so little work for such outstanding marks?

But this academy is a most serious affair. I am not considered an oddity as I was at Harvard. But then I am still a bit odd in that I am married.

Most women here are single and can focus completely on their studies. A number of my fellow students have asked me how my husband has endured my decision and how tolerant he must be.

I wonder how the real truth of his opinions might be received.

Robert is a fine man and a good provider, but he has never been generous with his "allowances and permissions." We have argued, sometimes with great bitterness, over my steadfast decision to follow this dream.

My professors are of the least prejudicial and judgmental I have ever met. It is so refreshing to be in a place where my intelligence is valued and furthered–even though I am a woman. At Harvard my answers and observations were nearly always held in question until proven correct. I had won a few faculty over to my side as it was–because of my good looks, my acumen, or my keen grasp of medical intimacies–or perhaps a combination of all three. Some older faculty saw me as a daughter, others as a lady with hints of another, even older profession. I know I am as smart and clever as the keenest fellow in any class–and I believe that amused some of those old doctors.

Nevertheless, I think even they were frustrated by my fellow students' irrational behavior. They would roll their eyes as I was questioned for the dozenth time, yet I stoutly refused to rise to their bait and become angry or flustered or, even worse, teary. I smiled and repeated my answers and defended myself–all the while I wanted to roll up my notebook and begin striking the worst, most obnoxious offenders with it. But here it is quite the opposite.

Sweet Jamison, I am not sure of why I am so set on this course. Like others, I have been swayed by the preaching of Mott and Stanton. But now that I am a married woman in the real world, some of their rhetoric stands curiously in question. It is one thing to rail against injustices from the outside; it is a whole different matter to endure them and to attempt to formulate a method in which you can endure them without losing what joy and grace you have to begin with.

I am failing to explain myself in this letter. I am not sure why I am rambling on so long.

But . . . I have not talked to a friend for so long . . . a friend who was willing to give me unconditional support–as you and Gage and Joshua had done. I could never have realized how much I savored those times. I suspect a man with a full stomach can never imagine the pangs of hunger.

I have gone on too long. And I'm sure I am boring you with my maudlin tales.

How is your journey? Have you encountered any savages yet? Your newspaper claimed that the land beyond the Mississippi is so defiled with bands of infidels as to be downright suicidal to cross. I am sure they were writing that to inflame passions and to encourage sales–I trust I am right in that assessment. I was horrified to hear the story of the group of pioneers led by the Donner brothers. How their shortcut through the Wasatch Mountains led them to be trapped by snow when reaching the Sierra Nevada. Is it true that the survivors had to resort to cannibalism to remain alive until a search party found them? You always told me that what you read in the paper is written by fools like yourself and never to be fully believed.

But I trust you, Jamison. Please write to me when you receive this.

Your friend,

Hannah

When she was finished, she signed her name quickly, folded the pages, slipped them into an envelope, and sealed it thoroughly. She slid the envelope into a text and inserted the book into the middle of the stack.

And afterward, she sat back again and took a deep breath. She lowered the light on the lantern to the barest flicker of illumination. Then she leaned forward, put her head in her hands, and began to sob.

CHAPTER THIRTEEN

Philadelphia
September 1848

THE campus of the Philadelphia Women's Medical College, such as it was, occupied a half dozen small buildings south of Rittenhouse Square. As Hannah took notes in Advanced Anatomy, she could sit up tall and see the top pediments of the four-story Barclay Hotel several blocks to the north. And she imagined at times that she could see the entire distance to Logan Circle, another seven blocks away.

The location of the school served Hannah well. On pleasant days, when the weather was temperate, she could walk from her home to her first lecture in under an hour. On days when the weather grew harsh or inclement, a public tram ran north and south, requiring her to dash only a block in each direction.

Since the school was relatively new, and a separate medical training facility was still a most novel and untested concept, Hannah seldom told others about it. To do so would then require a full explanation–not only why a woman was enrolled, but why a fellow would not simply study alongside an older physician. That is how most doctors of the day received their education, and Hannah was absolutely positive that no doctor she knew would have ever consented to apprentice a female.

The faculty at the college was of the highest order, with physicians that had served in the Royal Court in London and one with the Prussian Royal Family. Hannah disliked that particular professor, for he spoke with a thick German accent that made note taking nearly impossible.

Dr. Willard Wilcott, the founder, was a familiar sight on campus, strolling about in his frayed white coat streaked with flecks of blood. He seemed to be able to ignore all but the grossest remains on his coat and seldom had it laundered. When he did, ghosts of the blood remained. At the end of the semester, his coat had a near uniform burgundy tint to it–as if he had dipped it into a barrel of red wine.

Whenever he saw Hannah on campus he would call her over and chat, asking her how her studies progressed and how she was holding up under the obvious pressure. She enjoyed these conversations and came to understand that he believed her goal to become a doctor was worthy and correct for her.

The college did not follow a traditional two-semester year but instead operated nearly all year, with only a few weeks' break between courses. Such a plan allowed students to finish the strenuous studies within two years, but it also meant they would all swelter through the summer weather, often studying dissected organs and flesh that was nearing malodorous putrefaction.

The delights of summer at the shore would be a fond memory for Hannah, who yearned for a clearing sea breeze every hot day as she approached the campus. *Just to feel the warm, wet sand oozing between my toes would be such bliss,* she often thought as she made her way to class.

This day broke hot, with a thickness of humidity cloying in the air. Hannah would have walked but knew she would be sweating profusely by the time she arrived. Instead, she jumped on a tram and enjoyed the faint breeze as it headed south.

"Hannah," Dr. Wilcott called out as Hannah alighted from the tram, "how nice to see you. You are such a refreshing sight from all the somber-faced young women who skulk about this campus."

"I am glad to see you also, Dr. Wilcott. And you are well?"

"Indeed. On my way to dissect a liver and kidney. Care to join me? Or do you have a class this morning? We could have breakfast as I work."

Hannah thought for a moment. She had left the house with only a cup of tea, and breakfast did sound enticing. She enjoyed watching Dr. Wilcott work as well.

"I do have class with Dr. Lange this morning. But not for another hour."

"The Perfect Prussian?"

Hannah giggled.

"My dear, we all know our nicknames," the doctor said with a smile. "It does no good to feign innocence."

Hannah drew herself up in mock dignity. "I have heard that appellation as it refers to Dr. Lange, but I have never once uttered it–not out loud, anyway."

Dr. Wilcott laughed. "So you will join Wobbling Wilcott for a liver and kidney breakfast then?"

"I will be delighted," Hannah said with honest enthusiasm.

❧

Dr. Wilcott had a cup of coffee in one hand, a scalpel in the other, and a thick piece of bread and marmalade on a plate just inches away from the metal tray that held a rather large liver and a smaller kidney. He took a drink, set the coffee down, then grabbed the bread, chewed off a large piece, and began to saw away at the liver, slicing it down the middle, then quartering it.

Hannah sat watching as she sipped her tea. She pulled up a tall stool and rested her plate on her knees. She was fascinated with Dr. Wilcott's dissection techniques and enjoyed his running commentary as he sliced through the flesh.

He held up a sliver of the organ to the light and wiggled it. He looked as if he were a boy teasing a dog with a slice of bologna. "You see here," he said pointing to the edge of the section with his coffee cup. "You see how that is so discolored?" He poked at it once.

"And why is that?" asked Hannah.

Dr. Wilcott appeared deep in thought for a moment. Then he shrugged and offered a booming laugh. "I have no idea, Hannah. I truly do not."

She laughed with him. After a minute or two she asked, "What did this fellow die from?"

Dr. Wilcott shrugged again. "I'm not sure." He picked up a tag lying on the table. "Says they found the body by the docks. White male. Fifty, maybe. I would bet a heavy drinker. Maybe that's what caused the discoloration."

Hannah nodded and took a final bite out of her biscuit.

Dr. Wilcott put his cup down and tossed the liver slice back into the tray. He leaned forward. "You like it here, Hannah?"

Hannah was taken aback by the abrupt shift in conversation. "Why . . . yes, I do, Dr. Wilcott."

"Good," he replied and prodded at the kidney with the scalpel. He began to slice into the small burgundy-colored organ. Halfway through, he paused and looked up. "You will complete your course here, won't you?"

Hannah blinked. "Why, yes, Dr. Wilcott. I plan on doing so."

He snorted and bent back to the kidney. Without glancing up again, he continued. "That's good. You may not know this, but at the moment, you are the highest-rated student in this academy."

She blushed with pride, for she had not known it. Rankings were released only once a year and would not be made public for another month.

"I ask if you're going to stay because you will make an outstanding doctor. We need compassionate people, and most men don't care a whit about their patients–if you want to know the truth. It's the way we men are. But a woman–well, that's something altogether different. You listen. You understand. You know when to hold a hand. I don't. None of my fellow doctors do either."

He stopped and sliced one last time. The kidney neatly separated. "You won't do something foolish like have a child, will you? That would change everything."

Hannah became silent.

"You want to have a child?" he asked gently.

She did not raise her eyes and did not answer.

"Your husband wants a son, is that it?"

There were tears on Hannah's cheeks. Dr. Wilcott looked at once compassionate and terribly uncomfortable. "Hasn't happened yet, I take it?"

She shook her head no. She whispered, "Do you know why? Is it my fault?"

His doctoral expression came back. He paused and pursed his lips. He swallowed once. "Everything of a female manner working as it should?"

She nodded.

"No unusual pain?"

"No."

"Have the attempts–" his face reddened to a beet color– "have the attempts been regular?"

She blushed scarlet as well and then whispered, "Yes."

He wiped his hand on his coat and then stroked his chin. "Could be anything. Could be nothing. That's one area we don't know much about. Some women find it easy. Some don't."

"Is it my fault?" she asked, her voice going faint as a petal falling to the grass.

"Wouldn't be able to say. It takes two, as they say. . . ." Tears continued to roll down her cheek. He wiped his hand off one more time, then placed it on her shoulder. "Sometimes it's just God's way. Sometimes he says yes, and sometimes he says no. Maybe he's saying no for a reason."

Her face was marked with a most pained expression.

"I don't know for certain, Hannah," he said with surprising

tenderness. "I'm just a fool doctor and not a preacher. Maybe you should ask God."

He then took her hand in his and squeezed it. She sobbed again and nodded.

Hannah did not mention her standing in the college to Robert, even after it was published. In fact, she seldom ever discussed her activities at the college with him. She did at first, but when she began to tell him of a dissection on a diseased lung, he went white, then green, and ran from the room. When he came back, he forbid her to ever speak like that again in his house.

Robert had found great success in Philadelphia, borrowing and lending and borrowing and lending. There was talk of great westward expansion, and industries such as shipbuilding and rail works sprang up almost overnight. And every one of these facilities required capital. If a venture posed great risks, many more well-known banks would not deign to participate. But if great profits were promised, money would find a way. Robert acted as liaison–sometimes silent, sometimes not–between banks and the new industrialists.

Several of his schemes paid very well, and by summer he felt secure enough to buy a piece of property only two blocks east of Logan Circle. It was a quarter of a block and contained a few ramshackle dwellings. He immediately ordered them demolished and ground cleared for the new Keyes residence.

"I know I said that a home is a headache," he explained to Hannah, "but I cannot be seen living in rented rooms. A man of my stature needs to have a home of his own. And while it will not be as grand as some, it will be most substantial."

He spent much of June with architects and builders, working on plans and devising schedules. What he promised would be a modest family home soon turned large and opulent–and even more so as his fortunes continued to increase.

❦

Robert unrolled the plans and grabbed books and paperweights to hold the edges flat. The plans covered his entire desk.

"What do you think?" he asked Hannah with obvious excitement. "Do you like it?"

Hannah walked to the desk and looked first in one direction and then another. The drawings and details filled the page. She squinted. "It looks like a temple," she offered in a soft voice.

"Indeed! That's what it is supposed to look like! The temple in Athens . . . or was it Rome? Well, then, never mind. It looks like a temple then and that's what it should be."

She peered closer. "Do we want to live in a temple?"

Robert stared at her as if she had spoken in a foreign tongue. "It's not a temple. It just looks like one. Inside it will be a regular house."

"But it does look like a temple, then."

"Hannah," Robert said with a sigh, "I can see that you simply don't understand. Of course the house looks like a temple. It is supposed to. That's what people will see from the outside, and that's what will be most impressive. A temple does that. Makes people wonder who might live there and be in awe."

Hannah put her hand to her throat. All she could think of was Gage Davis's family home in New York City. "And that is what we want? To live in a temple?"

He picked up the plans, scattering the books and paperweights, and began to roll them up, exasperated. "I can see this is of no use. It is not a temple. It is a house. It looks like one from the outside, for that is what the style is today. Inside you will find bedchambers and kitchens and all the rest–we're talking about an inside privy as well. So we will not live in a temple; it will just look as if we do."

He tucked the plans under his arm and walked out of his study, leaving Hannah most perplexed. "But it looks like a temple," she said softly again, even though there was no one to hear her, other than herself.

❧

At dinner that evening, Hannah knew she had to repair the conversation.

"Robert, I am sorry about this afternoon. You were so excited, and I am slow to understand. I could not grasp the importance of things. Perhaps if you explained it one more time . . . slower, so I can follow." Hannah bit her tongue mentally as she said the words. But she knew that a touch of deference went a long way to make Robert a more cheerful husband.

Robert again explained his needs–for a house that only looked like a temple so that passersby would be duly impressed.

It still made little sense to Hannah, but she was not sufficiently interested in the project to fight a battle over it. She was certain it would be a large, imposing house. As long as she found the necessities of life included, she would be content.

After Robert had spoken for nearly a half hour on the need for such an imposing facade, she simply smiled and nodded. "Now I understand." She waited a moment and then took a bite of roast beef. "It will have a kitchen?"

Robert smiled and nodded. "Of a good size."

"And it will have a bedchamber?"

"Many," Robert said with a more leering smile.

Hannah quickly asked another question to distract him. "And you say it will have an indoor privy?"

Robert began to beam. "It is the latest in technology, they say. Copper pipes and water closets and all manner of humanly devised comforts. It will be a marvel. Of marble."

She smiled. "A marble marvel."

"Yes!" he exclaimed.

"And it will make you happy?"

Robert appeared puzzled. "Happy? Well, then, I suppose it will." He furrowed his brow, then brightened. "But it will also show me as a financial force in this city–and that is far more important than being happy."

Philadelphia
October 1848

The Philadelphia Women's Medical College would not begin its fall lectures for another week. Hannah surveyed her assignments and realized that she would not have to spend much time in preparation. Most of the material was a near duplicate of studies she had done at Harvard. These would be more intense and more comprehensive but would cover no new ground or information.

She looked forward to a full week with little to do.

"You should visit your parents," Robert advised as he munched on breakfast. "You haven't seen them for many months."

Hannah did not look enthusiastic. "Perhaps I should invite them here for dinner. We could show them the progress on the house."

Robert gulped his coffee. "No."

"No?"

"No. I will be busy most evenings this week. It will be better if you visit them."

Hannah was tempted to argue but did not. Once Robert had decided, it remained decided. *Best to smile and obey,* she told herself.

That Tuesday, Hannah saw Robert off at the door, then gathered up her things and went out to the waiting hired carriage. She did not smile the entire trip.

Her mother appeared glad that she visited.

"Where is Father?" Hannah asked.

For a moment her mother looked extremely uncomfortable, as if asked a most rude and embarrassing question. She took a long time to answer. "He is not here today."

"Will he be back before I have to leave?"

She again waited to answer. "No." And then her mother took hold of her arm and escorted her into the drawing room. "I have tea done up. And scones, too. Would you like a scone? I know the English insist on having them with afternoon tea, but I seem to prefer them in the morning."

It was unlike her mother to prattle on so, but she did, and Hannah made no attempt at interrupting.

After a long dissertation on scones, breakfast, and the futility of finding quality servants, Elizabeth Collins at last stopped, took a deep breath, and relaxed in her chair. "So tell me, how is Robert?"

Hannah told her of his recent accomplishments and the new house that had been started.

"New house? How wonderful. You never mentioned it. Is it large?"

"Quite large, Mother."

"How many floors?"

"Three."

"And it is quite expansive?"

Hannah knew what she was asking and quickly lost the desire to toy. "Yes, Mother. It will be very large. And there is an entire wing that will be empty. I suspect that it would be large enough for you and Father, should you decide this house is too much a burden to you."

Elizabeth attempted to exude both shock and gratitude, although both emotions were quite foreign to her. "My dear Morgan. How sweet of you. But I do not think we could impose."

"Nonsense, Mother. That's why it is being built as large as it is."

"But, Morgan, it is too much to ask."

"It is not."

Her mother waited a full minute until she broke the silence and asked, "When did you say it would be ready again? I mean . . . we would need time to consider moving . . . and pack if necessary."

Hannah spent the rest of the morning with her mother. Robert had expected her to spend the night there as well, but Hannah knew that, by lunch, she had smiled as often as she could.

After lunch, she explained to her mother that a sudden headache had seized her and that the only medication that proved effective had been left at home.

"We can send a messenger," Elizabeth protested.

"An unnecessary expense," Hannah replied, "and I will feel best if I lay in my own bed. Truly, Mother, I will be fine. And I am sure you have better things to do this afternoon than tiptoe around the house so as not to disturb me."

She shrugged and then embraced Hannah. "I am so glad that soon we will be together again–all the time. Tell Robert that we asked after him."

"I will, Mother."

And with that she was back in her carriage.

"Back to Logan Circle, Mrs. Keyes?" the driver asked.

Hannah waited until the house had become small in the distance. "No . . . take me to . . . to Filbert and Fifteenth."

The driver nodded. "To the market district."

Hannah smiled and did not reply.

She had the driver wait down the block. She knew she was running a risk of being discovered and her subterfuge found out. Yet to be free and unfettered for an entire afternoon proved to be so deliciously tantalizing that no amount of apprehension could ruin the day for Hannah.

She slipped into one dress shop after another, buying nothing but realizing that her wardrobe was hopelessly out-of-date, nearing on provincial.

Perhaps when I graduate, I can splurge some of my trust fund on a new and smart outfit or two. Now it would be ruined by chemicals or hidden by my white frock.

But she greatly enjoyed the process.

At the end of Filbert, there was a cluster of booksellers. She frequented Toby and Sons, an elegantly frayed store with stacks of books tilting to the ceiling and where the air would be tinted the color of ancient paper, filled with the scent of print and words and leather. On more than one occasion she paid the high prices they demanded–for they found several out of print medical texts where all others had failed. She opened the door, and the bell gaily announced her arrival.

"Mrs. Keyes, how nice to see you," the elder Toby called out.

"Mr. Toby, likewise."

"And you are looking elegant as always. How far till you become a doctor and I can make a private appointment to see you without raising any suspicions?" he jested. Then he coughed and doubled over.

"Are you all right, Mr. Toby?"

He waved his hand. "It's just the dust in here. Outside I'm fine. But I can't sell books in the rain."

She smiled and nodded.

"So when will it be?"

Puzzled, Hannah asked, "When what?"

Mr. Toby shook his head. "You try to be flirtatious with these young women, and they don't even stop walking."

Hannah began to blush.

"When will you be that doctor? I think I need an examination . . . if you know what I mean."

Hannah tilted her head. "Mr. Toby, I won't be a doctor until next June. And then you will be how old? Ninety?"

He clutched his chest in mock pain. "I am wounded to the quick, Mrs. Keyes. Wounded indeed."

She laughed and tapped the high counter. "Do you have the new edition of *Gray's Anatomy?* I heard the color plates are much improved."

He scratched his cheek. "I actually believe my son ordered one of those. But where would he have put it?"

"In the medical section?"

Mr. Toby laughed. "Much too obvious. Look around while I search. You're a good customer. Anything you want, I give you 5 percent off. As a favor from a doctor of letters to a real doctor."

And with that he went scuttling off into the dark regions of the back room. Hannah stepped slowly through the stacks, craning her head sideways to read the titles, pulling out a book every now and again, flipping through pages, reading a paragraph, slipping it back on the sagging shelves. She picked up a copy of the recently published

Evangeline by Longfellow that she'd heard so much about. The door chime called out several times as she wandered about the store.

At the far end of the stack, she came upon a table piled high with books. There was a most lurid cover on the book, a garish painting of a band of Indians giving chase to a hapless lone traveler on horseback. A volley of arrows filled the air, and the horse reared back in mute panic.

Hannah scowled. *Such horrid trash,* she thought, yet she felt obligated to pick up a copy and examine it. She fanned through the pages, then closed it in her hand. For a moment, her eyes did not register a conscious thought.

A Western Odyssey, she read. Then three words swam into focus.

By Jamison Pike.

If she had been prone to swooning she would have done so at the moment.

He wrote a book!

She looked hard at the cover again.

He wrote this book!

She could not stop staring at the name and then the lurid cover.

Did that man resemble Joshua?

The door chime called out again.

She stood there, her eyes focused and hardly blinking.

Then a voice came up from behind her, at once familiar and at once so very, very strange.

She spun about.

"Would you like that autographed?"

It was Jamison Pike.

She swooned, and this time it was for certain.

"Hannah? Are you all right? Shall we call for a physician?"

She blinked her eyes. Standing above her were Jamison Pike and Mr. Toby.

"Where am I?" she asked, placing her hand to her forehead. There was a cool cloth on her skin.

"You fainted. Mr. Toby has a couch in his back room. I carried you there."

She attempted to sit and felt the room swim again. She clutched his arm.

"No, no, no," Jamison insisted. "Lie down. Don't rush. It will be fine."

She held one hand to her forehead, and the other grasped Jamison's forearm tightly.

She began to whisper.

"What?" Jamison leaned forward to hear. "What did you say?"

Hannah grabbed his shoulder, painfully hard, and said with a quiet fury, "What on earth are you doing here?"

And then she swooned again.

"My publisher sent me on this trip. I sign a book or two. I talk to reporters. I give a lecture. Then I move on. They say it will help sell books. And I'm lending a hand with a news service called the Associated Press. They claim it will help reporters in the field get their stories in faster. But I'll believe it when I see it."

Hannah had recovered, but Jamison insisted he accompany her to take a beverage and a sandwich. There was a coffee shop two doors down.

"But what were you doing at Toby's? I rarely go there, and when I do, you show up. How did that happen?" Hannah appeared as if she were truly indignant.

Jamison could only shrug. "Serendipity, I imagine."

She scowled at him as only old and dear friends might allow. "I do not believe it."

Jamison tried to wash the sheepish expression from his face. "It is the truth, Hannah. And you know, as a reporter and now as a book author, I have taken a vow."

"A vow?"

"To be honest in all that I say and do," he said with great solemnity.

She glared at him until his somber expression failed and he began to chuckle. Then she reached back and struck him, hard on the shoulder with her fist, almost as much to make sure he truly existed as to punish him.

Hannah glanced out at the sun, which had slipped well to the west. "I should be getting home."

Jamison looked as a boy might when a puppy is about to bolt from his grasp. "Have supper with me. I leave on the eight o'clock train. Please."

She hesitated. A cauldron of emotions simmered in her–emotions she would not acknowledge. "I shouldn't. I am a married woman and all."

Jamison was unfazed. He consulted the clock at the rear of the store. "It is now after five. I must leave for the station in less than three hours. What can happen, save two old friends catching up on each other's lives?"

"Well, then, I suppose it might be all right. Robert does not expect me for dinner this evening," she said, relenting. "But if we are to dine together, it must be at a very public place, like Latham's. And the station is only six or so blocks distant."

"Very well, then, Latham's it is," he answered, then stood and extended his arm.

"Is this place expensive?"

Hannah appeared concerned. "Oh, I am sorry. It is. I should have asked. I did not . . ."

Jamison began to laugh. "No, no–it should be expensive. The publisher is paying for the trip, and I have never eaten as well or as often as I have for the last month. The more expensive the better."

During the elegant dinner, Hannah sat enraptured by Jamison's tales and exploits. The book came from his travels out to California and back. He claimed that while most incidents were nearly accurate, he did admit to some careful embellishments. Jamison was a natural-born storyteller, and Hannah began to dread the tolling of the large clock.

When it rang for half past seven, Jamison smiled–a most wistful smile. "I must go now. My bags are waiting at the station. If I miss this train, I miss an important lecture in Reading. And that will make my publisher unhappy. Since he is paying for all of this . . ."

Hannah nodded. "No, I know that you must go."

Her eyes met his.

He stood and extended his hand. "It has been so very nice being with you, Hannah. I like talking to you. This evening was just like those late nights at the Destiny, wasn't it?"

"Yes. It was. It truly was."

It was obvious Jamison did not want to leave any more than Hannah wanted him to go. "I really must be going," he said softly.

"I know," she said.

He did not move.

"Did you ever get my letter?" she asked.

Jamison brightened. "I did. I did. It met me in California. It was wonderful. I read it a thousand times. It was a good thing to have memorized it for I lost it–and everything else–when our ship sank off the coast of Vera Cruz."

"I'm glad it found you, then."

"Me too."

Finally Hannah could stand it no longer and rose and took Jamison in her arms and hugged him with a fierceness she no longer thought she possessed.

After a long moment Jamison let his grip soften. "I must go."

Hannah let her arms drop. "Will you write to me?" she asked.

"I will. I will write to you of Reading and all points west." He smiled.

She laughed.

He turned on his heels, walked away, and did not look back once.

She was glad, or he would have seen her face slowly crumble and dissolve in a wash of bitter tears.

It was nearing ten in the evening when the carriage slowed outside Hannah's front door. She had waited at Latham's for another hour after Jamison left, sitting in front of a cold cup of coffee that servers kept asking to remove.

It was so wonderful to see him again. It was so wonderful to laugh and to hear such stories. It was so wonderful to smile again. Jamison is such a calm and sweet man. I hope that he keeps his promise and writes to me. He did promise, and he does keep his promises, does he not? she asked herself.

Finally she had called for her carriage and paid scant attention to the short ride home. She slipped the driver a bill and a most generous tip. He waited at the curb until she unlocked the front door and entered.

She was very quiet, not wanting to wake Robert. She sniffed the air. There was a heavy scent of lilac. She placed her bag on the table, climbed the stairs, and edged down the hall to her bedchamber. Her heart began to pound. Her hands grew cold. She heard the sound of a most feminine laugh, followed by Robert's explosive braying. Then the woman laughed again. At their door she stopped. The scent of lilac was now overpowering.

The door was open the thickness of a man's finger. She looked in. A single candle flickered on the night table. There was no mistaking that what she saw was anything other than what it was.

She turned and ran, slamming the front door, and did not stop until she reached the green open space of Logan Circle.

CHAPTER FOURTEEN

Philadelphia
October 1848

HANNAH returned home at noon the next day.

It had not been an easy night. After running to Logan Circle, she realized that it was too cold to spend the night outdoors, and there were stories told of a most criminal element that inhabited the park after dark.

With tears stinging her cheeks, Hannah walked south two more blocks and entered the tavern Angus McCord's. She passed the establishment every day on her way to the college, and while she had never entered, she noted the small sign hung by the door that offered *Rooms for the Discriminating Traveler.*

If the man at the bar appeared suspicious, Hannah did not notice or care. She slapped a bill on the bar and asked for a key to the best room in the house.

In the dark of that tiny room, she stared out at the street and sobbed until dawn.

Hannah had no idea who the woman in her bedchamber was, nor did she care to know. She felt hurt and betrayed and angry–and more than a little ashamed.

What have I done to cause him to do this? she asked herself and found no answer.

As she watched the sun creep up and bring color back to the street, Hannah's emotions and thoughts simply ceased to be. What had hurt so much, that small spot below her heart, now became a dark void. She let her thoughts go back to Robert, and it was as if his face no longer brought pleasure, or pain, to her.

Is this how I must live? she asked herself in the thin light of dawn.

She waited until well after ten o'clock that morning to leave the rented room. She splashed water on her face and tidied up as best as possible, then slipped out, blinking in the harsh October sun. She slowly walked north, heading to her home, praying it would be empty.

It was.

Robert must have left at his normal time, for she knew he had an important meeting scheduled at the Barclay Hotel at nine.

The scent of lilac still hung heavy and cloying in the air. Hannah peered in at her bedchamber, as if unwilling to once again cross that threshold. The bedcoverings were in disarray, and it hurt to look at them.

Martha will be in soon enough, she thought, *for I am not touching them.*

She gathered up her clothing and carried it to the bedchamber across the hall–the one that was reserved for the nursery. She made a dozen trips. By then all evidence of her presence had vanished from the master bedchamber.

Martha busied herself cleaning, and Hannah did not say a word. Yet, from the averted look in Martha's eyes, Hannah surmised that she knew all. Hannah kept her lip from trembling and hurried out into the kitchen for tea, then retreated into the office. Martha cleaned there but once a week, and Hannah would be safe from having to answer that look.

She placed the tea on the desk, and a sob heaved in her chest. She lowered her head into her hands, and the tears began once more.

Hannah could not be sure how long she cried again. She sat up, then took a single sheet of paper from the desk and began to write.

October 6, 1848

Dear Florence,

Things are going well in Philadelphia. But how I wish I had you here to talk with. I so miss our times of intimate conversation.

My training goes well. I take some small pride in being listed as the college's most proficient and top-graded student. I will hasten to add that the class is much smaller than the class at Harvard. There are only some twenty students, yet being the first of twenty is a good position to occupy regardless.

Progress on our new home goes well. Pillars are in place, walls are nearly done. What is most amazing is that we will have a privy right inside the house, with a bathtub that draws water from a heated cistern in the basement. Such luxury does not even grace the halls of the royal residences in Europe.

At least that is what Robert claims.

And as she wrote Robert's name, she caught herself gasping for breath. She closed her eyes, for they had soon swelled again with tears.

After a minute she wiped them with the sleeve of her dress, long ago giving up on the dainty, but useless lady's handkerchief.

She extracted another sheet of paper and dipped her pen. She began a list on the right side of the paper.

Robert is a good provider.
He is considerate and well mannered.
Once a union is ordained by God, it is ordained forever.
It is a woman's role to obey.
I must forgive as commanded in the Bible.
I have no place to go.
I cannot embarrass my family with such a disgrace.
My empty womb has pushed Robert away.
I have no place to go.

She let the quill fall from her hands and stared out the window at the cold sky. No tears came, just a hardness in her throat and a tightening of the muscles around her heart.

She took the single page and crumpled it in her hands. She looked at the letter to Florence, half written, and picked that up and crumpled it as well.

She stood, wiped her cheeks, and walked out of the study, ready to face her new world.

Philadelphia
October 1850

"Florence! Over here!"

Hannah jumped up and waved her hand. She was nearly lost in a sea of passengers and travelers who crowded the Reading train station. Florence Galeswhite, now Florence McComber, had finally managed to arrange a two-day visit. Though she and her new husband lived only a short distance away in New York City, matching schedules had proved fruitless until this day.

Hannah did not even want to consider the years that had passed since they last met. The last few years had in some ways felt like a dream to Hannah. Most days she felt as if she were but a visitor to her own life–as if someone were doing all the things she needed to do. It was a most curious way to watch life and time pass. But today she would not think of anything unpleasant and would simply enjoy the company of an old friend.

Florence looked up and beamed. "I see you! Hannah!"

The two old friends embraced and nearly danced about on the crowded rail platform, oblivious to the stares and smiles of others.

"Where are your bags?"

"This is all I have," Florence said, holding a hefty Gladstone in her hand. "I have learned to pack light in this day of such instant travel."

Hannah took her arm and tried to share the burden. "I wish I had your discipline, Florence. Even for an overnight stay I require two bags and then some."

The two chatted and giggled as the carriage carried them from the station, down Arch Street, and up Sixteenth. They turned at Logan Circle and down Race Street to Hannah's home.

"My goodness," Florence exclaimed, "there's the river. Can you see it from your home?"

Hannah shook her head no. "I thought we might, but the new homes farther west have altered the view. I can get a glimpse of it from the attic–if I jump up and down."

Florence laughed and said, "So where is your home? Is it far to walk?"

Puzzled, Hannah said, "We live here."

Now Florence appeared puzzled. "Here? I thought this was a church!"

Hannah laughed. "It's what everyone says. Robert wanted it to look like the temple on the Acropolis in Athens–and what he wants, he gets."

Florence craned her neck about. "You live here?"

Hannah nodded and took her arm, pulling her closer to the entry steps. "We do. Once inside you'll forget all about the outside. It is just like a regular house."

Florence stopped again and stared hard at her old friend. "Hannah, just how rich are you?"

They sat in the drawing room after dinner with coffee and sweets.

"I am so sorry that Robert is out of town," Florence said. "I would have liked to get better acquainted with him. Especially after seeing this house. If he is as grand as what he built, then I am sure I would be most impressed."

"He wanted to be here," Hannah replied as she passed a plate of petit fours to Florence. "But it was an emergency meeting of some sort in Pittsburgh. Something to do with freight rates for coal or steel or coke or some sort of commodity. Robert has ties into so many industries; it's hard to keep it all straight."

"It must be so exciting for you," Florence said. "Galas and travel and all sorts of society functions."

If she only knew how little of that Robert consents to–and the little we do is so stultifying boring. "It has its moments," Hannah replied cheerfully, pouring cream into her cup.

"And this grand house. I cannot imagine how wonderful it must be to have all this space. In the city, space is such a premium."

If she only knew how tomblike this house is at times. Robert stays to his quarters, and I stay to mine. We pass and nod and do little else. "It is nice to have room to entertain and have guests stop by."

Florence smiled and examined the massive sitting room, hung with a dozen stern-faced portraits.

And wouldn't you be surprised to know we never entertain? You are the first guest, other than our parents, who has spent the night here.

"You must be so proud. I can see on your face how wonderful it all is."

And can you tell how proficient an actress I have become as well? "I am. But I am even happier that you are here with me. How I wish you could stay until next week. It would be so wonderful to have you at my graduation."

Florence appeared to be genuinely remorseful. "I am dismayed that I cannot. I despaired at having to leave my precious Malcomb for two nights. I cannot fathom leaving him for longer. His nanny and governess are wonderful and treat him even better than I at times, but they are not his mother."

Hannah nodded as if she understood and hoped she hid the pain she felt. Every time she encountered such a situation–a mother or father boasting about offspring–Hannah would smile profusely and hope to change the subject. Her failure to conceive was a pain she felt every morning and every afternoon and every evening. It rarely left her thoughts.

"Did I tell you that I heard Lucretia Mott and Elizabeth Cady Stanton speak in Seneca Falls in July?" Florence asked.

"No. How did you manage that?"

"They held a convention of sorts for women, to draw up a document called the *Declaration of Sentiments.* Since it wasn't very far, I was able to arrange a short trip there. Fascinating meetings."

"Really?" Hannah asked.

"They're pushing for women's rights and privileges–the rights of regular citizens. What they really want is the right to vote."

"Truly? And they think that's possible?"

"Yes, I do, Hannah. After all, New York has granted property rights the same for women as men. Other states will follow. You'll see."

"And they think these meetings are helping?"

Florence replied, "I truly think they are. People are talking. Things are happening."

Hannah poured more coffee.

A silence followed; then Florence cleared her throat and spoke. "So tell me, Hannah–what is it like to know all the intricacies of the human body? What's it like to have no mysteries left to the imagination?"

Hannah could tell from her tone what she meant. "Florence, you have not changed a bit since Harvard. And now that you're a married woman and all. You should be ashamed."

Florence blushed a bit, but not much. "Oh, I am ashamed, Hannah–but not enough to keep me from asking." Florence stared at Hannah, trying to be serious and contrite, then dissolved in a gale of laughter.

"You haven't changed a bit."

"So you really want me to attend your graduation as a buffer between you, your parents, and Robert's parents?"

Hannah sat on the bed and munched on a scone, dribbling crumbs all over. She brushed them off. "Robert's mother. I have only met his father twice, once at the wedding and once when he toured the completed house. He said very little that day. It was as if he were sad to have been bested by his son."

"But his mother?" Florence asked as she dipped her scone in the pot of strawberry preserves, leaving a little puddle of crumbs in the sweet confection.

"She is another story altogether. Had I known more of her before we married, I would have understood Robert so much better."

"Men," Florence exclaimed with a laugh. "They are at once both deep and shallow. There is no full understanding of them."

"That is the truth, isn't it?"

"It is with Stewart, I know," Florence said. "If he has a hot meal in the evening and a friendly wife under the covers, he is a happy man. There is no more that he wants."

Hannah blushed as she giggled, then stopped short as she caught Florence eyeing the bedchamber again. It was obvious Robert did not share the room. There were no traces of anything masculine, nor any of his clothing or accessories.

Hannah was certain Florence was observant and just too polite to pose the question. "This arrangement works best for us," she said softly. "I study until very late at night, and he has a very busy schedule."

Florence dropped her scone onto her plate and slid closer. "Hannah, I was not thinking of that at all. I have no right to know, and you are not obligated to explain. It is this way in many homes, I am sure."

Hannah felt a need to explain, a sudden rush to the truth, a desire to unburden herself. But she looked at Florence, who appeared most uncomfortable, and realized that if she told the whole story, it would take hours and simply place a burden on Florence that she had no right to share. So instead Hannah offered her most sincere smile. "Florence, Robert and I get along together very well. And I think you know what I mean when I say that." She tried her best to edge her words with playfulness.

Florence smiled in reply.

"It is just that our sleeping habits are so different. Other than that, our marriage is . . . well, it is ideal. And we are sure that not having a child yet is no matter of concern. Some women, I understand, remain childless for a time. Even those in their thirties have no cause for alarm."

Florence reached for her hand. "It will happen in time. I am sure of it."

Hannah squeezed back. "Thank you for being so . . . so much like an old friend who just understands. I am happy. I am."

"Then I am so happy for you, my old friend. You deserve to be happy."

They embraced.

"And I deserve another scone. You must get me this recipe."

Florence left the same day Robert's mother arrived. His father once again begged off, claiming some sort of urgent business arrangement. Hannah wondered if Robert, in his failings, had simply modeled his behavior after his father. If it was true, she would see herself as less of a failure. But she realized she would never know the truth.

Hannah was grateful that her mother and father would also be attending the graduation and spending the week at their new home. When Elizabeth Collins was in residence, it deflected Robert's mother's intrusions and complaints veiled in sugary tones. Both of the older women seemed then to be more preoccupied with circling about each other, testing and prodding at sensitive subjects, like two wary adversaries.

Hannah disliked the tension that their game produced but welcomed the fact that she was a noncombatant in the struggle.

Graduation ceremonies were held in the civic auditorium of the City Hall, a grand palace of gilding and statuary. Since only twenty students would receive diplomas, the crowd easily fit into the small auditorium.

Hannah had struggled and worked as hard as she knew how, but her ranking had slipped from first to second. She was bested by a thin young woman from Missouri who spoke with an amazingly thick accent. It was joked that the Precise Prussian gave her high marks because neither could understand the other, and neither would admit ignorance.

Hannah may have laughed at the observation, but she knew the woman from Missouri deserved the honor. Being second highest was not a dishonor, she knew, but she had secretly hoped to graduate as number one.

It would not have made a difference to either set of parents. They offered only the slightest of congratulations and spent most of the time commenting on the temperature, the weather, and the lack of decent food–regardless of where they were or at which establishment they ate. Hannah was exhausted by the time they left and had given little thought to what she would now do–once the reality of her dream had come true.

Her promise had been fulfilled, and yet she had no idea of what might occur next.

January 1851

"Dr. Wilcott! What are you doing here? How delightful to see you."

Flustered, Hannah stood with the door half open.

"I was visiting a patient of mine. I do see the odd patient on the side. Supplements my meager teaching salary," he said, laughing. "And he is truly an odd patient."

Nodding, Hannah opened the door the whole way. "Come in. May I offer you tea? Or coffee?"

"Coffee would be grand. It is chilly outside, and I must have stared at the numbers on this house for five minutes before I came to the door. It looks like a temple."

Hannah smiled. "I have heard that before. And I am glad you had the courage to knock on God's door."

Dr. Wilcott barked out a laugh.

They sat in the drawing room, a room designed to hold thirty. With only two occupants, it felt nearly cavernous.

"The coffee is good. Your staff knows how to impress a visitor."

"I know you well enough now, Dr. Wilcott, that you would not have stopped without a reason."

"You think I am so cold and calculating that I cannot simply drop in on a former student?"

Hannah laughed. "Yes, that is what I think."

Dr. Wilcott shook his head. "I have become transparent in my old age, haven't I?" Then he looked sharply at Hannah. "I asked you once if you were going to finish your studies. You said you were, and you kept your promise."

"Yes, I remember that. You wanted to make sure I was not a dilettante wasting your time and taking up valuable class space."

"Yes, that is what I wanted your promise on." Dr. Wilcott's expression changed from genial doctor to something sterner, more harsh, and unforgiving. He wiped his lips with the back of his sleeve. "You're a doctor now, Mrs. Keyes. A good one. So I shall henceforth call you Dr. Keyes. But you have made no effort yet to put your knowledge to practice."

Hannah did not answer. It was now January, and Dr. Wilcott was correct. She had done nothing with her education since receiving her diploma.

"It is not such a simple matter to explain," she said softly. "Robert . . . my husband . . . he doesn't think it seemly for a woman–a woman who happens to be his wife–to be a doctor. He was fine in allowing me to attend the college, but now . . . well, I am not sure what to do. Maybe I should just stay home."

Dr. Wilcott slapped the table, upsetting his coffee and splashing his knees. "That's nonsense! I will not have it. You will not waste your promise. Running a house–even a servant can do that. You are a medical doctor!"

Hannah refused to cry in front of him.

"You are a fine physician, and I insist you carry out your promise!" he repeated.

She sniffed. A single tear formed and rolled down her cheek. "I don't know what to do," she whispered, her voice hoarse.

"I do. That is why I came. I know what you must do."

"Dr. Wilcott speaks highly of you."

Hannah nodded. She held a thin leather case in front of her, almost as if it were a shield. She tried her best not to gawk about in this office. It was large and lined with walnut and books stacked floor to ceiling. On one wall, almost as an afterthought, were framed pictures of the doctor with a variety of personages–including two U.S. presidents and most of the Royal Family in front of Buckingham Palace.

His desk was littered with books and journals and an odd assortment of medical devices. The flame of a silver lantern, etched and filigreed with tiny scrolls and decorations, fluttered at one corner. The office matched the man.

Dr. Copley was a massive fellow, standing over six feet tall and nearly as wide as he was tall. Bushy sideburns rounded his face, and from a distance, one would be hard-pressed to tell the doctor from a bear.

"That is very kind of him," Hannah stuttered.

"And he says you need to practice. Says you're gifted. Says I should give you a spot here."

She nodded, her head still in a whirl.

Only two days ago, she wept in front of Dr. Wilcott. And now she was in the office of perhaps the best-known doctor in all of Philadelphia.

"I'm told that I have no manners with patients. That they get better because they are frightened of me." He glared at Hannah. "Do you have any idea why that might be?" he bellowed.

Hannah refused to cower, as she would have at home. "Yes, sir, I do. At this very moment I am very frightened."

He stared hard for several seconds, then leaned back and laughed so loud that his assistant cracked open the door to find the reason for the outburst.

Dr. Copley motioned the assistant in. "Lawrence, come in. I want you to meet my new partner, Dr. Morgan Keyes. I know it is customary for a new doctor to spend time in internship, but it appears there is little more that I can teach her."

Lawrence, a very thin man with a square face, stepped in and when he saw Hannah, obviously a woman, he stumbled to his knees.

"I bet they all do that when they learn that this Morgan is really a Hannah," Dr. Copley said wryly.

Hannah looked at Lawrence, sprawled out on the floor, then back to Dr. Copley. Her expression shot from compassion to confusion to outright terror.

Dr. Copley reached over his desk and extended his hand. "Hannah, I am not one to dawdle. Do you want to join my practice?"

Hannah made sure her jaw was not open. She swallowed once. "Yes, Dr. Copley. I do."

Most doctors of the day lacked all but the basic rudimentary knowledge of medicine–and were often self taught or apprenticed to an older doctor who was most likely self taught as well. Hannah's professors at Harvard bemoaned the fact that any fool could hang out a shingle, call himself a doctor, and begin to treat patients. There were scant regulations regarding licenses and education, a fact that many in the field of medical education were lobbying hard to change. More than a few were no better than animal doctors, and many worse than butchers.

A few doctors, like Dr. Copley, advertised their education, pedigree, and training, and garnered great respect–as well as numerous patients–as a result.

There would be no other doctor that Robert would have consented as worthy for Hannah. But Dr. Copley was as well known as the mayor and most likely more powerful in Philadelphia. Not only did he come from one of the best–and wealthiest–families in the Delaware Valley, he had parlayed his money and his insider knowledge and amassed a not-so-small fortune in land and investments. He was courted by politicians and seen by royalty.

"He asked you to join his practice?" Robert exclaimed when he found out. "*The* Dr. Copley? The famous one?"

Hannah held her gloating for private. She rejoiced in the fact that she would now actually get to practice what she had learned and was amazed at Robert's sudden change of heart.

"If you work with him, I will have entrée into the very best of the very best," Robert gleefully exclaimed. "This is absolutely perfect. You are a true gem, Hannah. A true and wonderful gem."

And when Robert said those words, Hannah felt a tiny thaw in her heart. She knew Robert might simply use her to get to others, but it was the first compliment she had heard from his lips in years. It was warming and comforting and good. She turned the words over and over in her thoughts.

Maybe he is truly changing. Maybe we can find a way to be civil and then . . . who knows . . . maybe we can truly be man and wife again. How I yearn for such companionship.

"This is your office," Lawrence explained as he showed Hannah the full layout of Dr. Copley's office structure. It was housed in a former embassy near City Hall. Dr. Copley kept the top floor as one of his residences, and the other two floors were examining rooms, operating theaters, and a very well-equipped pharmacy and laboratory.

"This is all so wonderful," she said as she ran her fingers over the recently painted name on her door. *Dr. Morgan Keyes.*

"But don't you think we should have put my real name on the door?"

Lawrence rolled his eyes. "I told him the very same thing, Hannah, but he would not hear a word of it." He bent closer to Hannah and whispered, "I am sure the real reason is that he wanted the pleasure of seeing near-naked men flee down the hall when you enter the room. I must admit the prospect is most amusing and enticing."

Hannah looked dismayed.

"Don't worry," he added, "word will travel soon enough. The

game will not last long." He held the door open for her. "You are a good doctor, aren't you? Dr. Copley is a good man, and I don't want this to hurt him at all."

Hannah then realized how protective the doctor's staff really was. "Yes, Lawrence. I am a very good doctor."

Before he left, he turned. "And one day a week, the doctor wants you to help in some clinic that his church has set up–near the tenements by the river."

"A clinic?"

"Yes. Dr. Copley is a very devout man. He takes service seriously–despite looking like a bear. You don't have a problem with that, do you?"

Hannah set her bag on her desk. "No, Lawrence not at all. I just didn't know. I imagine I will be delighted."

He pursed his lips. "We'll see. The clientele at the clinic leaves much to be desired, if you ask me. The neediest of Philadelphia, to be sure. But if Dr. Copley says to do it, we all do it."

From a Letter to Jamison Pike
May 1851

Dear Jamison,

Thank you so much for the wonderful card you sent at Easter. I hear such mail is all the rage in England. I will keep the engraving displayed long after the holidays have passed.

I cannot begin to tell you how totally thrilled I am to wake every morning and rush off to work. I would not have thought such excitement possible. Every day is different and challenging and filled with rewards.

I have discovered how much I do not know about medicine. Yes, I can give most things names, but this profession is learned, not studied, acquired, or degreed.

When I am correct in a diagnosis and I help prolong a life or alleviate pain, I am so wonderfully happy.

But often as not, there is little to be done, and I can only hold them and cry with them.

Dr. Copley is most appreciative of my abilities. He claims I have a much better sense–because I am a woman–as to ailments and causes. Imagine–the first time being female has served me well and I am lauded for it.

One of the reasons for this letter, my dear old friend, is to inquire after your professional services. As I wrote last, Dr. Copley–who is, by the way, a very God-fearing man–and who knows more Scripture than I think did Joshua–helps operate a clinic in the very worst section of town. His church is the sponsor, but I believe nearly all the funds come from my employer. He does this so no one will point to him and praise him for his benevolence. I now spend two days every week there. The people are so desperate and often so very, very ill.

Yet that is not the reason I write.

In my work, I often will treat the women and children–for they do seem to have a more willing rapport with me–as opposed to a gruff, unthinking male. (Not all men are like you, you are aware, are you not?)

It is the children who break my heart. Some children five and six years of age are being injured and maimed every day as they work in factories, side by side with grown men.

I find it reprehensible that owners of such factories do this, but it is a painful truth.

Here is my proposition.

Come to Philadelphia. Come on a Tuesday or Thursday–the days I work at the clinic. Let me show you what is happening. Talk to these children. See for yourself.

And then I want you to write about it in your paper.

Will you agree to that for me?

And afterward, I want to treat you to the most lavish dinner you could imagine. For it was you, after all, who encouraged me the most–not to give up, not to let my light be dimmed. Your high opinion of my abilities kept me going through some very dark moments.

I owe you that much. Please write and tell me you will come.

As always,

Hannah

CHAPTER FIFTEEN

Philadelphia
July 1851

THE small waiting room was nearly standing room only when Hannah first arrived at the clinic. On the days she drew duty, she made a point of arriving at least an hour earlier than required. And once her habit had been established, patients soon learned that if they arrived before the first scheduled appointments were taken at nine, Dr. Keyes would ignore the patient list and examine them.

As she entered, they all grew silent, turning and stretching to catch her eye. She stopped in the middle of the room. Every eye was on her. From the corner came the squalling of a baby in pain.

Hannah's shoulders slumped. "Do any of you have appointments?" she called out.

A few raised their hands or called out, "I do."

"Then the rest of you are trying to see me?"

A ragged chorus of "yes" rose up.

She took a deep breath as she opened the door to her office and examining room. "Well, I'll do what I can."

She looked out on the crowd. Tiny infants were wrapped deep in blankets, clutched tight to their mothers' breasts. A handful of children with clean faces and ragged clothes watched in earnest, trying to see her before they must report to work. A few older men shuffled about, hope all but lost in their eyes.

"If you would, line up out here in the hall. Please, those who truly are sick, let them get to the front of the line. If you have a baby with a fever–I want to see them first."

And with that she stepped into her office, put on her white coat, and called out, "I'll take the first in line, please."

It was a young mother, on her own, with an infant no bigger than a house cat.

"The wee one refuses to take my milk."

"How old is the child?" Hannah said as she peeled back the blankets.

The mother, with gaunt, hollow eyes, softly said, "Only a week."

Hannah felt the child with her palm. "Has she fed at all? Has she taken anything?"

The mother started to cry. "It doesn't work. It's not working . . . you know. There's no milk to give."

Hannah looked up from the child. "When have you eaten last?"

The mother, no more than a child herself, looked away.

"When have you eaten last?" Hannah sternly asked.

The new mother snapped back around and sniffed. "A few days . . . I don't have much."

With a gentler voice, Hannah asked, "What's your name?"

The girl smiled. "Hannah."

"That's my name," Hannah replied. "And your baby?"

"I'm calling her Becca. Her father said to call her Hazel after his mother, but I thought that name sounded like a tree or something."

Hannah smiled. "He's not with you? The father, I mean. He's not here?"

The frightened young Hannah glanced away.

Hannah closed her eyes. She had heard it all before, a hundred times. He said he loved me. He said he would marry me. He said he would leave his wife. He said he would send me money once he got work.

"Where are you living now?"

The girl would not turn to face her. "I found a place. By the rail yard. It's safe and out of the wind."

Hannah wrapped the baby back up. "She needs food. If your body won't do it, then buy goat's milk. The druggist on Filbert sells a glass bottle to feed her. She needs food. She needs it now."

The patient nodded, as if she would do what the doctor instructed. But then her lip began to quiver, and tears rolled down her cheeks. "I can't do that, Doctor. I don't got any money. I can't go begging . . . or worse. I can't."

I have heard it all before–a hundred times a hundred.

Without pausing, Hannah reached into her pocket and slipped out a gold piece. The young woman's eyes widened like saucers.

"Buy the milk and a bottle and a place to stay. Feed her as often as she'll take it. You get some meat and milk to eat yourself."

The young mother took the gold piece and stared at it as if it were a most wondrous object.

"That won't last for long. Do you know the area around Bainbridge and Front Street?"

"By the docks?"

Hannah nodded. "At the corner, there is a house that the Friends run. Tell them Dr. Keyes sent you. They'll put you up for a while and see that both of you are properly fed. Do you understand? Do you know where that is?"

The young Hannah nodded as she rose with her baby in her arms.

"You get that milk this morning. Your baby won't live unless she gets some milk in her immediately. Do you understand?"

She nodded and backed out of the room. "You are an angel, Dr. Keyes. Bless you."

Hannah waited until the door snapped shut, then lowered her head into her hands.

I have been part of the same story a hundred times a hundred. Will it ever end?

"Dr. Hannah!"

The sun had fallen to behind the building to the west when Hannah's office door burst open.

She looked up and blinked.

A large woman barreled into the room and in a step was at the desk, embracing Hannah in a fierce, robust hug.

"You don't remember me, do ya?"

Hannah stared at the woman. She had a whirlwind of red hair and only a few teeth remaining. Her clothes were clean but threadbare.

"I'm sorry. . . ."

"No matter," the stranger said in a loud, happy voice. "Most folks don't recognize me."

"Please sit down," Hannah offered.

"Got no time for it. Just came in to say thanks."

"For what?"

"You fixed me up, Doctor Hannah. 'Bout a year ago I came in–drunk prob'ly–and filled with all sorts o' pain. Couldn't move my leg too well. And you fixed me up and now I'm better and I wanted to tell you that I'm gettin married and movin' where it's warmer. But I couldn't leave 'til I thanked you."

Hannah had no recollection of this woman–absolutely none at all. "I cured you?"

"Told me to stop drinkin', start eatin', and gave me some pills to take. And now I'm cured."

"Well, then, I am most happy for you."

"C. J. Van Wagner."

Hannah brightened. "Now I remember you! I recall your first name as being unusual."

"That's me–unusual. But I was a lot scrawnier then. Now I feel like a new person. And I had to say thanks. If it weren't for your help, well, I guess I'd be dead now."

As the woman blustered out of the office, Hannah smiled and thought, *Sometimes I make a difference.*

Lawrence tapped at the door and creaked it open. His reedy smile filled the room.

"Hannah," he said softly, "I'm about ready to leave. And I'm the last one. You best come with me. It's after dark, and then even I get nervous walking these streets."

Hannah turned about and nodded.

"Were you reading it again?" he asked.

"I guess I was. I suspect I read most of it once a day," Hannah answered.

Lawrence walked over to the framed newspaper article that hung on the wall behind Hannah's desk.

> THE FORGOTTEN INNOCENTS
> CHILDREN AS YOUNG AS SIX MAIMED BY MACHINERY
> INDUSTRY USES YOUNG FLESH AS A COMMODITY
> PAID LESS AND RISK MORE
> BY JAMISON PIKE

"That Mr. Pike was one handsome fellow," Lawrence said as he locked the door to the clinic. "Has he been back in Philadelphia since he wrote that series?"

Hannah bundled her coat up against the cold. "No, I haven't seen him for months."

"He did a fine job with his story."

"He did. I nearly weep each time I read it."

"So you weep every day, then?" Lawrence said lightly.

Hannah laughed. "No, but I could."

"It was a fine piece. Too bad not more has changed here."

Hannah and Lawrence turned the corner onto Lombard. There was a carriage stand two blocks west.

"But it did help. We had some generous donations. And some of the politicians promised they would look into the matter."

Lawrence sighed. "And you believed they could help?"

Hannah shrugged. "It has to start somewhere."

Lawrence extended his hand and helped Hannah into the carriage. It would take both of them within blocks of their homes.

"Well, the next time your Mr. Pike comes to visit, I have a few other ideas for articles. You tell him he has to talk with me."

Hannah placed her hand on his forearm. "I will tell him, Lawrence. The next time I see him, I will tell him."

It was so nice when Jamison was here. We had dinner and laughed. It felt so much like the Destiny that I had to blink to prove it wasn't. And the way he writes–like a composer in front of an orchestra. It was so beautiful and so sad. He did make a difference. Even today, there are people who are agitating that the laws be changed. Children shouldn't be forced to work. And when it happens, Jamison will have played a part.

The carriage jostled over a rut in the road.

And why hasn't he written me? It has been months since he and I have shared a letter.

February 1852

The foyer of the house, two stories tall and filled with artwork and crystal, was silent, cold, and dark. Hannah slipped off her coat and hung it on the rack behind the door. She laid her doctor's bag on the floor next to it, a routine she practiced every night. She listened and heard nothing.

By the time she reached the kitchen, she heard the low hushed voices and a sound that came close to a sob or wail.

She hurried in and stopped dead short. The kitchen was littered with broken plates and pottery. What looked like a roast dinner lay puddled in a far corner. Drawers were pulled open and cutlery strewn about like leaves in the fall.

Martha knelt in the middle of the room, just by the servant's dining table. Hannah rushed to her side, kneeling and taking her hand in her own.

"Martha! What happened? Are you hurt?"

Martha looked up, a terrified expression on her face. "I'm not hurt! I'm not hurt!"

Hannah knew that when people panicked, a gentle embrace was often a calmative. She draped her arm about the woman's shoulder. Martha continued to sob and gasp for breath.

After several minutes, Hannah asked again, "Martha, can you tell me what happened? Who did this?"

Martha cowered lower, ducked her head, and mumbled.

"What? What did you say?" Hannah asked.

Martha wiped her eyes with the palm of her hand. "Mr. Keyes did."

Hannah sat back, sure that she had misunderstood. "What about Mr. Keyes? Did he surprise the intruders? What happened?"

"No," Martha bawled out, "he's the one that did this. Mr. Keyes . . . he just went crazy. And I didn't do nothin'. You got to believe me, Mrs. Keyes. I didn't do nothin'."

Hannah stood, pulled Martha up with her, and examined the devastation in the room. Martha had grease on her face and apron. Her hair was loose and tossed.

"Mr. Keyes did this?" Hannah's heart tightened. "I don't understand."

Martha grabbed Hannah's hands. "I didn't do nothin'. I didn't. Everybody else was gone, and Mr. Keyes came in. I was bastin' the roast, and he asked when he might expect dinner and I know he likes his dinner prompt, but I knows that you are always a bit late on Thursdays and this bein' Thursday, I said it would be another few minutes 'cause then I knew you would be here and get to eat everything nice and hot. Well, as soon as I said that, Mr. Keyes starts a-yellin' and a-tossin' things about and dumpin' over drawers and bustin' plates, and then he shoved the roast right off the counter, and then he just screamed the most awful names at me and stormed out."

Hannah could hardly believe her ears; her expression must have matched her emotions.

"It be the truth, Mrs. Keyes. Honest. I wouldn't be makin' this up out of air. It was like somethin' came over him. Like a demon took him over or somethin' like that–some evil spirit. I ain't never seen anything like it."

Martha was obviously horribly upset, for she began to slide into a backwoods English–a habit Hannah had worked years on preventing.

"Where is Mr. Keyes now, Martha?"

She shrugged. "I for certain weren't about to follow. But he headed that way," she said, pointing toward the front of the house. "I didn't hear no door slam, so I don't know."

Hannah stepped in that direction.

"You won't let him come back here, will you, ma'am? Say you won't let him back here."

Hannah could never once, in her wildest imagination, have pictured herself in these circumstances. If what Martha said was true, then something must have happened–something horrible and drastic and evil.

She lifted the hem of her skirt and climbed the curving stairway that led to the second floor and their private rooms. Hannah's pulse quickened. Ever since she had first moved into the nursery, she and Robert had ceased to share a bedchamber. It was not that their marriage was without intimacies, for Robert was a normal fellow with normal male urges. Hannah tried to forgive him for his dalliance and prayed it was a singular occurrence.

She had never mentioned her discovery to him, and of course, he had not said a single word about it either. She never expected anything more of him.

"It is simply the way of the world and the way of a man," her mother once said of a neighbor caught in the same predicament as Hannah. "Her husband is just a man like any other with a weakness, and she'll just have to forgive him. After all, where would that woman go?"

As the months passed, the hurt in Hannah's heart lessened, and she found herself looking at Robert with a very hesitant affection rather than scorn and anger. In time, she was able to put those terrible images out of her mind, and they resumed what she considered an ordinary marriage of contentment, even though distant at times. When things were pleasant, Robert was gentle and kind and accommodating, and he so greatly resembled the man Hannah had married.

But when he boiled to anger quickly, everyone stayed clear. It happened infrequently, but it happened.

As Hannah climbed the last step, she realized his rage had never escalated to this level. She could never have imagined that he would terrify the servants and do such wanton destruction. There had to be another explanation.

Her clinical mind seemed to take over in these sorts of moments, and her feminine, more intuitive self receded. As she diagnosed, she found that an equal serving of both personalities allowed her to be most proficient.

But this night, she had no idea which self would be needed.

She hesitated outside his door.

The hallway was nearly as long as the house, and a long carpet–the color of blood, Hannah thought with some dispassion–ran the entire length of the corridor and muted her steps. A gas lamp hissed, illuminating the darkness with a flickering. She leaned to the door and held her ear against the thick walnut wood.

There were no sounds.

She tapped.

There was no answer.

She opened the door and peered in.

All was in order. There was not a single pillow tossed, no clothing strewn about–all was in its place. She noted that his room smelled of Bay Rum hair tonic–the kind Robert always used.

"Robert?" she called.

Silence was her answer.

She turned and continued down the hall. She had noticed a sliver of light from her door. Usually she left it tightly closed but thought that perhaps one of the upstairs maids might have attended to it and left the door ajar.

Without hesitating, she entered her room and then stopped, frozen. It was as if a huge carnivore had descended on the room, tearing the contents limb from limb, strewing about bits and pieces of clothing and jewelry and beauty notions. The bed had been stripped of its linens, and an entire dresser had been toppled to its side. The air was filled with the scent of too much spilled perfume and toilet water. Hannah stepped into the room, and the door suddenly slammed behind her.

Robert must have remained hidden behind the door until Hannah had come fully inside.

"Robert!" she called out. "You have frightened the life out of me! What are you doing here in the dark? What has happened to my room?"

Robert smoothed his hair, then wiped his mouth. "Your room? I thought that all this was mine. And indeed it is. I have paid for all of this. Not you. It has never been you."

His voice had an edgy, scratchy quality that clutched and tore at Hannah. Her heart beat faster and faster. She found herself stepping backwards.

"Robert, please calm down. I don't know what has happened, but we can talk about it. We have always been able to talk about things."

Robert kicked an empty bottle, sending it spinning into the wall. "Oh yes, we can talk. We can settle things. And then you can go back and laugh at me. Like you always do."

Hannah stepped back one more step. Her eyes darted about. She had very little room left to retreat. "I have never laughed at you, Robert. Never. You are a kind and decent man."

He tilted his head and laughed, cold and brittle. "And that's why the cook holds dinner for you and not me? You're not laughing at that? I'm hungry, and we wait for you? You don't see any humor in that?"

Hannah held up her hand. She was beginning to become

genuinely frightened. "Robert, I never told Martha to hold the meal for me. She would have served you if you asked."

He bent forward. "But don't you see? I shouldn't have to do the asking. It should be done as I wish. I want dinner on the table when I return home, and it isn't. And it is because of you, the great Dr. Keyes."

Hannah squared her shoulders. "Robert, that is plain foolishness and you . . ."

She was unable to finish her sentence, for Robert jumped close to her and, with a full extension of his arm, swung it about, striking her as hard as he could with the back of his hand. She saw stars as his hand struck, and her head snapped to the side. She felt blood on her cheek.

He looked down at his wounded and bleeding hand. The skin of his knuckles must have found her teeth.

"Now see what you've done!" he screamed. She had no time to avoid the blow, even if she had anticipated it. He reared back and struck her as hard again with his left hand. This time she toppled backwards, against the wall and to the floor.

He stood over her, panting. Her dress was at her knees. She held her hand to her mouth. Her bodice was askew. He stared hard at the exposed flesh of her leg and thigh, the trembling rise of her chest. She felt his vision as if it bored into her skin.

"See what you made me do! See what you have caused!" he screamed and lunged at her again.

Hannah closed her eyes and clenched her fists, letting no sound come from her lips as he threw her on the bed. She knew her screams would never be heard as far as the kitchen.

She let Robert's blinding fury storm over her like a thunderhead, hoping somehow that someone would protect her.

The next morning, Hannah woke, barely able to move. Her mouth was swollen and her lip crusted with dried blood. She knew her eye had puffed up, and she found it hard even to blink. She had simply collapsed on her bed afterward and fallen near to unconsciousness.

She stumbled to the mirror and looked. Her face was red and bruised; it appeared as if she had suffered a beating.

I did! she told herself.

She bent to the water bowl and splashed her face, wincing with every touch. Gingerly she patted her skin dry.

With aching arms she stripped off her dress, threw it over a chair, and grabbed a plain frock in her armoire. It took her a long time to dress and manage the buttons. As she looked for her shoes, she heard the doorknob slowly turn.

Martha! No one must see me like this!

She pulled the drapes, darkening the room. "Who's there! Don't come in!" she called out.

The door swung open to reveal Robert standing in the hall, wearing a long velvet robe. The knuckles on both his hands bore a white strip of gauze bandage.

Hannah shrank back into the corner. She held her arm in front of her face.

"Oh, Hannah, I am so sorry. I didn't mean to hurt you. I had hoped it was all simply a horrifying dream." His voice near tears, he fell to his knees in front of her, wrapping his arms about her legs.

"I am so sorry! I didn't mean to hurt you. Please forgive me! It is the stress I face. That did it. It took hold of me. I never would have done this. I don't even recall it occurring. It wasn't me. It was someone else. Not me."

And then he started to weep, calling out the name of God every moment or so and blubbering, "I don't deserve you. I don't know what came over me."

His tears and consternation were so intense that Hannah helped him crawl to her bed to lie down. His litany of excuses and explanations lasted nearly an hour and was only subdued when Hannah agreed to extend forgiveness to him.

She did not truly mean it, and they both knew it, but Hannah rationalized her action as the only way to move forward.

❧

She stayed in her room for three days. Robert brought food of all varieties and even helped clean and straighten what he had torn asunder.

This indeed is a first. He has never cleaned or picked up anything in this house before, Hannah thought.

And with every visit, he continued to profess his great sorrow and his lack of a rational explanation for his behavior–other than saying it was because of the intense pressure he was under. Every time he stepped into her room, he begged her to forgive him, saying that he did not deserve her loyalty and that he was now contrite and would never do such a horrid thing to her again.

Hannah listened and nodded and granted him forgiveness several times, but Robert continued to ask, as if he did not believe her words.

At the end of three days, Hannah knew her bruises had healed sufficiently to be covered with powder and cosmetics–at least well enough to venture out.

As Hannah left for work that day, Martha saw her in the kitchen, then averted her eyes and ducked into the pantry as if she had pressing business to attend to.

Hannah drank her tea in the solitude of the kitchen, once again spotless and bright.

❧

March 1852

It was six weeks after Robert's explosion. Hannah made her way down the stairs. The house was quiet, and the massive clock in the hall had just chimed three times. There had been no repetition of that awful night in February with Robert, but Hannah's sleep had become erratic, and she hastened to the kitchen to find milk or tea or something to nibble on.

She pulled up a stool to the tall working counter and tore off a piece of bread and sliced off a sliver of yellow cheese.

Then she felt it–like a comforting twist in her belly.

It was warm and presented to her the most full and complete sensation.

She placed her hand over her stomach.

"It can't be," she wailed quietly. "It cannot be a child!"

A stark silence filled the room like an avalanche. Hannah's vision narrowed, and all she could see was the plate of bread and cheese in front of her. She noticed the dribble of crumbs on the counter and the odd way the cheese broke. She smelled the milk and the yeasty bread. It was as if, in the absolute silence, the room had begun to amplify itself, so that it nearly overwhelmed her.

She pushed the food away, held her head in her hands, and breathed in deeply. Then she began to weep and did not stop until dawn approached.

Chapter Sixteen

Philadelphia
March 1852

HANNAH trudged up the stairs to her home in the darkness. Each step seemed a mile in duration.

Her condition was still a secret to all but herself. The signs were unmistakable and irrefutable.

How could this tiny life that I already love so much occur from such a violent act? she cried to herself.

She struggled with each step, and by the time she withdrew her key, she felt as if ready to collapse. She stepped into the hall. Hershel hurried to her and took her coat and bag.

"You have a visitor, Mrs. Keyes," he said in his clipped manner. "Someone from the Pennsylvania Bank and Trust."

Hannah weakly protested, "But I am sure he wants Mr. Keyes. And he should have been home hours ago."

"No, ma'am. He distinctly asked for you. I inquired twice as to whether he might be mistaken. He insisted he had business with you."

"But I have no accounts at the Pennsylvania Bank and Trust. Can't you see if he could come back tomorrow?"

"Ma'am, I would, but he has been waiting for over three hours. He said he wasn't leaving until he talked to you. I've already served him two pots of coffee."

Hannah's shoulders drooped in resignation. "Do I have to see him?" she asked.

Hershel shrugged. "Ma'am, I wouldn't rightly know. But he looked upset–as upset as a banker ever gets."

She sighed again. She patted her hair, adjusted her sleeves, and walked into the expansive drawing room with its brace of mustard-colored sofas. The tall man perched on one of them popped to his feet and pulled his black case under his arm.

"Mrs. Keyes? I'm Thomas Manch of the Pennsylvania Bank and Trust. I'm in charge of the delinquent loans."

"Loans?"

"And I am afraid your loan is most delinquent. I apologize for my abrupt manner, but I have found that it is the best way. If I hint at such things, the client simply remains confused. Yes, delinquent. Quite delinquent."

"Delinquent?" Hannah said, startled. "I am afraid you must have me confused with my husband, Robert. I have no loans. And Robert, I assure you, is current with every account. He is not involved in any business that permits or encourages any delinquency."

Mr. Manch shook his head slowly. Hannah thought she heard him mutter, "tsk, tsk, tsk," under his breath as he walked toward her, withdrawing a paper from his case.

"No, Mrs. Keyes, it will do you no good to deflect such things. Owning up to your responsibilities is the best way, I always say."

Hannah quickly grew angry. "I don't know you, Mr. Manch, but I do not appreciate your tone. I am sure Robert will straighten all this out as soon as he arrives home. Would you care to wait?"

Mr. Manch rolled his eyes. "We have been looking for your husband for weeks, Mrs. Keyes. He makes appointments, never to appear at the appointed time. For us to actually make a call at a client's home is most unusual for us. I cannot recall the last time I left the bank on bank business. As I said, this is highly unusual."

Hannah could not quite comprehend what the banker had just said. "You've been looking for him–my husband?"

"Yes, ma'am. For some time."

She looked around the room as if some great charade were being played out. The room, however, was occupied by her and the banker alone.

"But what do you want with me? I have no dealings with your bank."

"Oh, but you do indeed. A substantial loan."

Hannah's face told of her disbelief. Mr. Manch procured a second paper from his case and handed it to her. She scanned the document, then glanced up at him with a pleading look in her eyes.

"Yes, it is hard to read," he admitted. "It is a promissory note. For a quarter of a million dollars."

"What?"

"A lot of money, Mrs. Keyes. And you will notice the signature at the bottom."

She looked. The signature was *M. Hannah Keyes.* "I didn't sign this."

"It is your name. It was notarized. And the bank gave your husband the money. We would like it back now. After all, your trust fund did not nearly cover the principal."

"Trust fund?"

"It was used as collateral for the loan. Now we want the rest."

"My trust fund?"

"Yes. And you did not have but a quarter of the money that was required for repayment."

"You took my trust fund without my consent?"

"Oh yes. We had to. There were no repayments made for some time. It's all stated in the contract. Very legal and aboveboard."

"You took all of it?" Hannah suddenly felt light-headed, and the child in her twisted in an odd way. "But that was my money."

"When you were married, it became your husband's money. And we would like the rest of our money back. When do you think it might be expected?"

Late that night, Hannah heard the creak of the wood floor in the hall. She had not slept a wink. Jumping out of her bed, she grabbed her thick flannel robe as she dashed out.

She saw Robert hurrying to shut the door to his bedchamber.

"Robert!" Hannah shouted. "You wait!"

He stopped and lowered his head an inch without yet turning around.

With that small gesture, Hannah suddenly became aware of the horrible truth.

"You spent my trust fund," she said, hoping anger didn't color her words.

Robert did not say a word but nodded.

"Are you going to pay them back? Mr. Manch was here. He wants his money."

Robert looked up into Hannah's eyes. For the first time, Hannah saw fear.

He shrugged.

And then turned and walked into his room.

Hannah blinked in surprise and, for a moment, did not know what to do next. She waited in the hall for a long moment, then walked to his door, turned the handle, and stepped into the room of her own volition–for the first time in months.

Robert sat on the corner of the bed, weeping into his hands, his shoulders lurching. "It's all gone. It's all gone."

Hannah felt a most curious mixture of fear, pity, and relief.

And in that dim light, in the glistening, flickering light of evening and candle, Hannah saw the image of her father again, sitting on the bed, at the precipice of being broken and defeated and lost.

Over the next two hours, Robert, through his sobs, told her the entire story. His business was based on borrowing and lending again at a higher rate. He investigated the smaller companies, those with a bright promise but limited capital. They would be all too eager to accept loans at higher interest rates. As long as the economy prospered, Robert and other financiers like him would prosper. But if the economy slipped or faltered in the least, the small companies would suffer first, then those whom they owed money to would suffer, and then finally, the large banks that were at the head of the chain would feel the pinch.

Hannah placed her hand on Robert's shoulder and smoothed the fabric of his shirt. "How much have you lost?" she asked in a tender voice.

He sobbed. "All of it."

She blinked. "All of it? How much is that?"

Tears streamed down his face. "The money is gone. The house has a dozen liens attached to it. Your trust fund is gone. It's all gone. All of it. Nearly two million dollars."

Each word thumped against Hannah's heart. But with each word and each thump, she felt a growing sense of giddy freedom, as if the constraints and complexities and pressures of the house and everything else all conspired to hold them both in bondage and pain, and at last those bonds were being undone.

"It is all gone? Will we have to sell the house to pay our debts?" she asked.

He nodded and wiped his eyes with his palm. "We can stay for another month or two. The banks owe me that much for all the profit I have given them."

"A month or two," Hannah repeated, staring at Robert. And as she voiced those words, the child within her kicked for the first time and strained at its enclosure.

She put her hand over that place but did not move and wondered when it might be the proper time to tell Robert of her condition.

Hannah looked up from her desk at the clinic. It was nearing dark, and Lawrence had just stopped to fill the lantern and trim the wick.

"No one does this," he said as he worked, "and then they all curse at the bad light. Well, I for one do not want to work in dim light. Especially not since I bought this new day coat. Stunning in the daylight. Dingy in the dark."

Hannah laughed and thanked him as he continued the rounds of Dr. Copley's medical practice. She worked on the last of the forms and notes she needed to complete.

There was a tap at the door, and Dr. Copley breezed in. She could tell he was upset because his forehead was furrowed into deep ruts. He sank into the largest chair, slumping as if very, very tired. Yet his eyes were darting and alive.

"I'm worried," he said.

"About?" Hannah replied.

"How many patients have you had today complaining of a hardness of breath and a sensation of chills, then fever?"

Hannah thought for a moment, then flipped through her appointment book. "Six," she said. "Is that a problem?"

Dr. Copley ran his hand through his hair. "I don't know. But I do know that I saw more than a dozen who had similar complaints. And one last week–remember Mr. Calgani? The Italian grocer fellow?"

Hannah nodded.

"Well, I just was informed that he died last night."

Hannah placed her hand at her throat. "He did? But he was such a robust man."

"He was. Until he caught what everybody seems to be catching."

Hannah blinked.

"It's some sort of influenza, I think."

"I thought we had passed the season without any incidents," Hannah said. "I have never heard of a case this late in the year."

Dr. Copley shrugged. "Always a first time." He explored his breast pocket looking for a cigar. He never lit them but chewed the ends. Not finding one, he stared at Hannah. "I'm worried about what I have seen today. If the situation worsens, we will have a calamity on our hands, Hannah."

"I will inform you the next time I see a patient complaining of those symptoms," she said, knowing now he was truly concerned.

As he left, he called out over his shoulder, "Don't you get sick now."

A sensation tickled her throat, and she immediately placed a hand over her belly, as if protecting the life that grew there.

She knew it would be only a matter of weeks before she could no longer hide that truth behind blousy dresses and layered frocks.

April 1852

The waiting room boiled over with sharp, hacking coughing. A normal day might see ten or so patients waiting at any one time, but this day brought nearly forty people, all crowded together, waiting to seek their particular relief.

Lawrence slid into Hannah's office. "It's another mob out there, Hannah," he said. His words were calm, but his face was gray with worry.

"Lawrence, it will be fine. I'll work faster. We'll see them all."

She wiped her hands on her white coat. "You can send in the next patient."

It was Mrs. Lipsomner, the wife of the owner of a very successful cooperage.

"Dr. Keyes, thank you for seeing me. I think I am dying."

Hannah had seen her often, and she was always on the brink of death. Hannah examined her for fever and listened to her breathing. "You have no fever and your lungs are clear, Mrs. Lipsomner. I think you may have overreacted."

The older woman appeared as if attacked. "Overreacted? I have done no such thing. People are dying out there, and I want protection."

Hannah touched the woman's hand. "It is not that bad, Mrs. Lipsomner. It isn't."

The woman snatched her hand away. "It is. You just don't know. I have lost three servants already."

"Lost? You mean they left?"

Her laugh was caustic. "Left? No. They died. All of this influenza. I came to you to ask if I was well enough to travel. Mr. Lipsomner is taking the entire family to Maine. He says it's healthier there by the sea. Something to do with the cooler air. Made no sense to me, but then little he says does. His mind is made up, and we are leaving tomorrow. I can travel, can't I?"

"Three of your servants died?"

She nodded. "In a single week."

Hannah sat there, stunned by what appeared to be happening.

"Biblical proportions," Dr. Copley said. Hannah was too numb to respond in any manner. "I can't imagine why God would be punishing us, but it appears we are in the middle of some sort of judgment."

"But God doesn't do that," Hannah said softly. "Does he?"

"I spoke to a friend at City Hall," Lawrence said, "and he claimed the morgue was full, and they were dumping all the bodies into trenches over in Westchester County. Hundreds and hundreds of them, he said."

Dr. Copley stood up and took a well-worn Bible off his desk. "I think we should all spend a moment in prayer," he said solemnly.

And as they prayed, Hannah could think of nothing more than the precious pressure in her belly and the growing pain in her throat.

"Mrs. Keyes," Hershel said as he took her coat, "you best get upstairs to Mr. Keyes's room."

"What happened? Is he hurt?" Hannah said as she took to the steps.

"No," Hershel called after her, "but he's in bed with the chills and that awful cough."

The bedchamber smelled of lemon and camphor.

"Robert," Hannah said as she stroked his sweat-matted hair, "the lemon won't hurt, but the camphor won't help."

He coughed, and his shoulders shook. "My mother swore by it. And I'm using it."

Hannah could tell by a mere touch that Robert had been gripped by the fever. As he breathed, it was as if the air were passing through water.

"How long have you felt ill?" she asked.

"Since yesterday."

"You should have told me."

He shrugged. "Didn't want to worry you."

In the weeks since his admission of bankruptcy, Robert had been as contrite as any holy penitent, and twice as meek.

He began to cough again, and the coughing was both liquid and sharp.

"I'll fetch some tea and whiskey," Hannah said. "That might make you feel better. And some crushed iron root and menthol. That should help break the cough."

Robert nodded and began hacking again as she hurried out of the room.

A single day had passed. It was now barely dawn. Hannah stumbled from the bedchamber with dark eyes.

Hershel met her on the steps. "You need a cup of tea, Mrs. Keyes. I'll fetch you one."

She paid no attention to him and kept walking, taking each stair with an agonizingly slow, deliberate step.

"Does Mr. Keyes need anything, ma'am?" Hershel asked softly.

Hannah stopped and turned back to him. "No." And then she turned around and spoke to the empty space in front of her. "He's dead."

Hershel spun about. "What?" he cried out. "What did you say?"

Hannah kept descending the stairs with such slowness. "He's dead, Hershel."

He ran down the steps and stood in front of her.

She looked startled for an instant, as if she did not realize she was talking to him only a minute before.

"He's dead, Hershel. I was talking to him and put a cold compress on his forehead. I gave him a bit of the iron root and he said he felt better. Then I sat in that big chair in his room and listened to him breathe and it sounded so horrible but he said he felt fine and then I dozed off and when I opened my eyes, he was so very, very still and the room was so very, very quiet. I ran over to him and . . . he was gone. There was nothing there."

Her eyes were filled with fear as she stared at Hershel. Then she fell into his arms, weeping.

"I am with child, Hershel. I never got to tell him that I am with child. His child."

Because of the crush of the recent dead, space in any reputable funeral home was at an absolute premium. Hannah sent notes to a half dozen that she had acquaintance of and all sent back regrets–they were simply too full to accommodate another person. She imagined that some turned away all business, not wanting to expose themselves or their families to this virulent form of death.

Williams and Sons sent a messenger that they could accommodate Mr. Keyes and party in the afternoon, two days hence. Hannah blinked as she read the note. She handed the messenger boy a dollar and told him to reply with her thanks and that two days hence would be sufficient.

She quickly penned three notes–one to her parents, one to Robert's parents, and one to Jamison. Anyone outside that small circle would have to hear about it from another source. She gave Hershel the three envelopes and three gold pieces.

"I know that this is twice the needed amount, but I am sure that even messenger service will be scarce. I want these delivered as rapidly as possible. If his parents get this by the morning, they will be able to attend. They need to know."

Hershel bowed, took the envelopes and coins, and ran from the house, holding a cloth soaked in vinegar over his mouth. It was a widely used nostrum for keeping the illness at bay. Hannah knew it proved nearly ineffective.

For the next day, Hannah wandered about the house, as if walking through a most unpleasant dream. She would stop to touch certain objects, to see if they were indeed real and to say farewell once their reality was determined. Once Robert was buried, the house would fall to the bankers. Hannah imagined them waiting outside the door, waiting until she returned from the cemetery to ask for her key and instruct her to leave by sundown.

Perhaps a miracle will occur, she told herself.

A haze of rain fell throughout the day, and the sun was but a faint memory. Hannah, dressed in black, stood at the edge of the fresh dirt.

A small rivulet of mud cascaded past her foot. She watched as the water tumbled into the open hole. She imagined that she might hear the water as it struck the mahogany box, but the words of the minister drowned it out. She did not move until all was silent. Then she looked up.

Everyone stared at her–her mother and father, Robert's parents, the servants, the minister, six of Robert's business associates, even a banker to whom Robert owed a great amount. Two grave diggers stood at the rear of the group; both appeared to be nearly exhausted. They had their hats in their hands. The rain began to fall in a greater amount, and Hannah felt it against her face. Then she remembered. She held in her hand a single rose and tossed it into the grave.

The minister nodded and simply said, "Amen."

And with that, everyone turned toward the line of carriages on the winding cemetery road.

Hannah did not move.

Finally, the driver of the funeral carriage descended from his perch and walked over to her. It did not appear as if he saw her immobility as unusual. He placed a hand on her arm and gently pressed. She stepped in that direction and did not stop until he helped her into the carriage.

She rode alone.

Her mother-in-law had made her feelings known in the note she immediately sent back to Hannah. It read in part:

You are responsible for my dear Robert's death!

You have mucked about with all manner of sickness and disease and have brought this home upon your own household. How dare you! You are worse than the most callous murderer. You have killed our beloved son.

They stayed at the Palmer House rather than at their son's home. Hannah's mother-in-law spoke not a single word to her but glared at her during the ceremony and service.

Hannah's mother offered no great comfort either.

"But where will we live?" she wailed when she arrived at Robert and Hannah's home. "Our house is mortgaged with liens. We were to live here. And now that promise is dashed!"

Hannah moved through the two days slowly, as if swimming in a most viscous liquid. Sounds became muted, and sight turned to a water-colored haze. She responded to those around her with an indistinct voice, not sure of what she was saying.

Dr. Copley visited the evening Robert was buried.

He wrapped his big arm about Hannah's shoulder and drew her close, whispering that all would be worked out according to God's plan and that she should trust in Providence for her support.

She nodded and thanked him but felt cold and empty and near to death as night fell.

Hannah remained at home the rest of the week. Lawrence stopped by for a brief visit with food and an enormous bouquet of flowers.

"Are things as bad as they were?" Hannah asked as she nibbled the fresh fruit pastries he had brought.

"Not quite so," he said, crossing his legs and adjusting the crease of his trousers. "The waiting room is always full, but there is no longer a line out the door. Dr. Copley said he recalled another such epidemic when he was young. Within three weeks it had passed, he said, but a lot of the sick never recovered."

Hannah nodded, her eyes red from crying and lack of sleep.

He patted her knee. "You need to come back to work. Dr. Copley is a bear when you are not around. An absolute bear. Yesterday he barked for an hour over a chart he could not find. Turns out that he was sitting on it the whole time."

Hannah giggled, the first time in a week. "Thank you, Lawrence."

He beamed at her.

"Thank you for the pastries and flowers and for being such a dear friend. You made me smile."

He looked away, blushing. Then he stood and brushed the crumbs from his lap. "I simply must go. If I am late again this week, I am sure the good doctor will demand payment from me, rather than the other way around."

Hannah rose to see him off.

As she neared the entrance hall, a sharp cutting pain started in her belly. She ignored it for a step or two, hoping it was a simple muscle spasm. By the time she reached the door, she felt as if the floor swayed and canted. She grabbed out to Lawrence to steady her walk.

"Dr. Keyes, are you all right?" His voice rose nearly an octave in his fright as she doubled over.

She did not answer but clutched his sleeve, then collapsed to the floor, and the world went dark and silent.

Cold touched Hannah's forehead and temples. She did not yet open her eyes.

There was a scent of alcohol and blood in the air. She felt the cool skin of leather beneath her head and shoulders. There was a blanket covering her, and the wool scratched her skin. She moved her fingers a hair's distance. Then her toes.

At least I can move . . . but where am I?

She opened her eyes the barest amount. Wherever she lay was dark and still. In the corner behind her, there was the fluttering of a lantern. She turned her head a degree to the side. Lawrence sat there, apparently asleep, covered by his new coat.

She licked her lips. Her throat was as parched as the desert. "Lawrence?" she called out.

He did not move.

"Lawrence," she croaked louder.

He jumped up, spilling his coat to the floor, his arms flailing. "You're awake!" he nearly shouted. "You're awake!" He ran from the room, banging the door open, shouting, "Dr. Copley! Hannah is awake!"

She shut her eyes and felt nothing.

In a moment Dr. Copley entered the room and moved a chair next to the low operating table on which Hannah lay. He stroked her forehead, and she blinked.

"How do you feel?" he asked softly, most unlike his usual bluster and bark.

She attempted to shrug. "I don't feel anything."

Dr. Copley nodded. "I gave you some laudanum. You won't feel anything for a few hours."

She attempted to raise her head but was stopped by a wave of dizziness.

"Stay down," Dr. Copley said as he gently pressed her back to prone.

She attempted to nod, but even that brought on dizziness.

The old doctor picked up her hand in his and held it tenderly, as a father would hold a daughter's hand. He leaned in closer to her. "Hannah, why did you not tell me you were with child? Why did you continue to work?"

She opened her eyes and looked up at his face. It was then that she knew. The pain in his eyes told her all she needed to know. "It's gone, isn't it?"

He drew a sharp breath and nodded. "You should have told me. Poor Lawrence nearly died of fright when you collapsed. He carried you for blocks until he could flag down a carriage." He squeezed her hand. "You lost too much blood. I could do nothing to prevent it."

"What was it?" Hannah asked in a small, hurt voice.

"It was a little girl, Hannah. It would have been a girl."

Then Dr. Copley did something that was so unlike his hard exterior. Lawrence, who was standing in the doorway, holding back his own emotions, had never seen him this way. He bent to Hannah's shoulder and placed his head next to hers and began to cry. He embraced her as a father and held her tightly in his powerful arms as he wept. Hannah simply closed her eyes and allowed him to hold her, much like a child holding a doll.

After a moment, he let her down again. He sniffed, wiped his eyes, and sat back and sniffed again. It was apparent he was as uncomfortable as he was inexperienced in letting his emotions bubble to the surface in this manner.

"Close your eyes, Hannah, and let sleep free you for now."

She did as he instructed.

"But before you sleep, Hannah, I have to do one more thing."

She waited.

"I have to pray for you. You know I am a believer, and I don't make much of it here. But this day–of all days–may I?"

She managed a nod.

"Our great Lord," he began, his voice not more than a whisper, no longer full of command and order, but the feathery voice of a child coming before a father, "I am a man of few words. For most tragedies I have always held the absolute belief that your hand was in on every event, every situation–and if we could not see, we, in our humanness, did not have the vision. But today I must admit my failing as a believer–for I see and have no vision. I am angry at what you have done to my friend Hannah. Could you not find some other way to draw her to you? Did you have to destroy everything in her life so that she would turn to you? I do not understand this, Lord. You are sovereign. I accept it as your will, but I do not understand. I commit this child, who drew not a single breath, into your loving arms. Cradle her as close to you as her mother would have done. And for Hannah–bring her heart peace. Heal her body, dear God."

He sniffed one last time. Hannah's breathing had slowed and became deep.

Then he whispered, "And use this to bring her to you, my Father. Please, Lord, bring her to you."

And from the doorway, Lawrence sobbed and ran down the hall, to the door and outside, and into the darkness of the night.

CHAPTER SEVENTEEN

Philadelphia
June 1852

SPRING had come late, as if it hesitated to show warmth to the barren ground. The cold winds from the west and north had continued nearly through the end of April. Even the first week of May was cold, and a storm brought a driving, freezing rain. What few buds had shown were knocked and damaged by the wind.

Hannah hardly noticed. After Robert's death and the loss of her unborn child, she remained as a sleepwalker. She appeared alive only at work, when her personal side disappeared and her professional side took over.

The influenza had visited the city like a tornado. Illness and death decimated some areas and left others nearly untouched. Boston was hard hit, as were Providence in Rhode Island and Richmond to the south. Other cities scarcely noticed.

As spring and then summer arrived, the citizens slowly emerged after the long winter and took a collective deep breath of clean air. Nearly ten thousand had perished, and the rebirth of the land about them was the first positive, cheerful sign they had seen for months and months.

Even though Hannah every day walked past a profusion of flowers in Logan Circle, she stared straight ahead, never seeing the colors or smelling the fragrance. If she passed a mother with a child in a perambulator she would grow tense and angry and cross the street to avoid coming too close.

The sound of a baby's cry or laughter was as a knife in her belly.

And yet, her practice at Dr. Copley's thrived, and so many of her patients were young mothers and children. She felt detached as she doctored, and the reality of another mother's child would not cause her pain.

Dr. Copley tapped at the clinic's door late one June evening.

"Hannah, it is time that you go home. You are working too hard."

She offered a wan smile. "I will."

He stared for a moment. "Hannah, are you all right? Do you feel all right?"

She finished her writing. "Yes. I feel fine."

"Are you sure?"

With a practiced smile, she replied, "I am fine, Dr. Copley. I know you are worried about me, and I find that touching. But I am fine. A little tired perhaps."

He came in and sat on the chair at her desk. "Are you keeping the house? Are you worried about that? You can always stay with my family. You know that."

She nodded. "And it is so sweet of you to extend the offer."

"And there are a few small rooms in the attic in this building. We could plaster the walls and paint–make a little apartment for you."

She replaced the quill in its stand. "Dr. Copley, I appreciate that offer as well."

"It's genuine. All you have to do is ask."

"I know. But I will be fine."

"Are you sure?"

She nodded, hoping she gave the definite impression that the discussion was over.

"Well," he said as he rose from the chair, "you will let me know if there is anything else I can do, won't you?"

She nodded again, offering a brave, positive smile.

"And remember we are praying for you–praying that God will help you through this difficult time."

"And I appreciate that. I really do."

He tapped at the door frame as he left the office. "Anything you need, Hannah. You tell me."

She nodded as he left, but then her smile disappeared. It was replaced with a look just shy of angry.

July 1852

Hannah left the office at midafternoon and hurried across Race Street and toward the recently constructed train station. It was the last bank yet to be visited.

She had spent every evening for nearly a month poring over Robert's records and files. To her dismay, she discovered Robert acted at being a precise businessman better than he actually lived it. He had no complete ledger system; payments and loans were often jotted down on scraps of paper, sometimes even on a cloth napkin where a meeting might have been taking place. He had no comprehensive system to indicate how much of his assets–their assets–were in circulation. He had no process to determine risk nor to arrive at possible repayment scenarios. It was as if every scrap of paper, every contract, every promissory note was simply noted and tossed into a large box or drawer.

Not fully understanding all the complexities of business and finance to begin with, Hannah often felt as if she were reading documents written in a foreign language. She knew people said that of doctors and their own language as well.

Now she would need to know another tongue.

Ultimately, she did make some sense of it all and managed to locate all of Robert's outstanding creditors and debtors. To everyone who owed her husband money, she wrote letters requesting payment. To everyone to whom Robert owed money, she wrote requesting patience and understanding.

To her astonishment some banks simply forgave the debts. These were often smaller amounts, and the officers there must have assumed the debt to be uncollectable. Others, to her amazement, showed no concern over her predicament, suggesting, or in some cases insisting, that the house be sold promptly and that all the furnishings be sold and liquidated as well–in order to fulfill the agreed-upon payment schedule.

And Hannah, now armed with a full portfolio of all assets and liabilities, marched down the street to the Commerce Bank and Trust of Philadelphia. From what she could determine, Robert had borrowed a hundred thousand dollars, re-lent it to a shipbuilding firm in Norfolk and a large wheelwright concern in Lancaster, and had yet to receive any repayment from either.

"But, Mrs. Keyes, surely you understand that this loan is in serious default. No attempt to repay any principal, let alone interest, has occurred within the last six months."

Hannah sat in Mr. John Lochra's office. She wore her most modest dress, buttoned up to everywhere, and tied her hair back into a severe bun. She wore no makeup or jewelry and attempted to look as prim and unpretentious as possible.

"That I understand, Mr. Lochra. I know full well the severity of an obligation that has not been met. But you also understand that Mr. Keyes is dead. He has been dead for several months."

She hoped her expression would convey both her loss and her desire to make good.

Mr. Lochra, a man as thin as paper, rocked in his chair, building his fingers into a pyramid of flesh, and did not smile or offer any hint of mercy. "That may be, Mrs. Keyes, but your signature appears on this contract."

"A signature not of my hand."

"So you say, Mrs. Keyes, yet I have no way of ascertaining the truth of your claim. You know, we here at the Commerce Bank and Trust of Pennsylvania have had the unfortunate experience with other clients who claimed they never signed a document. It was all an elaborate scheme on their part to deceive us and not repay the proper amount."

Hannah sat up straight. "I can assure you that I am not deceiving you at all, Mr. Lochra."

"So you say again, Mrs. Keyes. But there is one thing you could do that would settle this matter."

She took a deep breath. "And that is, Mr. Lochra?"

"You could repay the loan," he replied, hissing each word as if he were a serpent. "We want our money, Mrs. Keyes. You have a lovely home."

He stared at her. She felt like a mouse under the gaze of a coiled rattlesnake.

"Sell it," he said with finality. "Sell it, or we will take steps to take it from you."

Her bottom lip quivered only the slightest amount.

Mr. Lochra leaned forward on his elbows, sliding closer to her face. "Do it now, Mrs. Keyes. I am not a patient man. I expect the first installment to be substantial."

She stared back blankly.

"Sell the house," he said once again, "or we will do it for you."

Hannah sat on the edge of her seat as the carriage clattered up to the house.

"This is a temple or a church," the driver said. "I thought you said it was your home."

Hannah didn't bother to defend the residence again. She counted out the amount in coins, then added a most modest tip. "Well, whatever it is," she said as she stepped down, "it's for sale. Would you care to buy it?"

The driver whistled and jumped back to his seat. "No, ma'am. Much too rich for my blood." He snicked at the reins, and the carriage headed off.

Hannah closed her purse and stared up the long cascade of front steps and the row of pillars that appeared to be standing guard. She looked about the neighborhood, realizing there was little benefit to being the largest and most opulent house in the area. She sighed deeply, grabbed her dress to lift the hem from her feet, and began to make her way up the steps.

She paused at the entry door and glanced behind her. The clouds to the west still glazed red and gold. Across the street stood three modest homes, all versions of a Federal upright, all of red brick. Down the street to the west, if Hannah craned, she could catch a glimpse of the river. Downtown started three blocks to the east.

It does boast a wonderful location, she thought. Placing the key in the door, Hannah hesitated. She touched the door knocker, a massive brass seashell that was engraved with a great *K*. From the corner of her eye, she could see the copper coach lights, each flickering with a gas flame. The porch was strewn with gaily potted flowers amidst the wicker furniture.

It's a fine house. Someone will fall in love with it.

Opening the door, she felt the great silence that now inhabited the residence.

Several servants had left, fearing what might happen. Martha remained, as did Hershel and six other house servants.

I will tell them tonight. It is no good to prolong the agony.

And afterward, it was only Martha who cried, and then only for a little bit. It was not that she had been worried about her future–a good cook and serving girl could always find work. It was that Martha was in tears for Mrs. Keyes.

"But, ma'am, what will you do?" she cried. "You can't be waiting on yourself and doing your own cooking and cleaning now, can you?"

Hannah placed her hand on the woman's shoulder. "It might amaze you, Martha, but I can. I am well versed in domestic arts."

Martha did not reply, but her expression spoke enough of her disbelief as to make no words necessary.

"I am," Hannah repeated. "I truly am."

"Our hallmark is being discreet," said William Steele, head held high. "We have been in business for more than one hundred years, Mrs. Keyes, and one does not service the elite of society by being a gossip."

Hannah and Mr. Steele sat in the kitchen of the vast, silent house. She turned up the lantern. "Would you like some tea, Mr. Steele?"

"That would be so nice . . . but no, Mrs. Keyes. I know the servants are gone, and I will not have a woman of your grace serving me."

She jumped up faster than she needed. "And that, Mr. Steele, is poppycock. I may have grace, but I am not a cripple."

He stood as she did. "I did not mean to infer . . ."

Hannah managed a tight laugh. "Please, Mr. Steele, sit down. Let me put a kettle on for both of us. I know you meant no disrespect."

"Indeed I did not," he said, flustered.

With a few strokes, the small hand pump pulled fresh water from the cistern, and Hannah filled a copper kettle. In a moment she had the fire glowing and set out the cups and saucers, honey and lemon.

"I know it may be impolite to ask, but I am past that now. How often do these sales occur, Mr. Steele?"

Mr. Steele, a proper, refined gentleman with a gray beard and a thin head of hair, pursed his lips. "Very often. Today, fortunes are made and lost in such a short period. Not like in my father's day. No, wealth so often slips through a man's fingers like a whisper."

Hannah poured the hot water into the teakettle and looked around, realizing that soon all of what she gazed upon would be gone. "How long until your staff inventories and catalogs all the contents?"

Mr. Steele blew on his cup. "A week."

"And then how long until all is disposed of . . . I mean sold."

"Perhaps a month at most. Three weeks. You have exquisite taste, Mrs. Keyes. Most everything you have will find a quick buyer."

"That's a good thing. And the amount to be generated?"

Mr. Steele coughed politely. "I cannot hazard an estimate. If I am high, you are happy, but if my estimation does not come to fruition, then you will hold me responsible."

Hannah sipped her tea. The cup she held did have a tiny crack in the rim. She felt the nick with the tip of her tongue. "I will do no such thing. I want to know . . . for it determines a great deal of what I do in the future. An approximate figure is all I ask." Hannah did not want to plead, but she would. If the sum was substantial, she would rest with more calm. "Please, Mr. Steele."

Her eyes caught his. He almost scowled, then scrawled a few figures on his paper. He scrawled a few more. He moved his lips as he added the figures. "Perhaps a hundred thousand dollars. Perhaps half again as much. It truly depends on the evaluation of the three large oil paintings in the drawing room."

Hannah tried hard not to appear either impressed or dejected. She simply nodded and said, "Thank you, Mr. Steele. I appreciate all that you have done."

Within the month, the house was nearly empty, as Mr. Steele had promised. Steele and Sons had done their job well. What could be removed and sold–such as the paintings and silverware–went to several jewelers and art galleries. Larger furnishings remained there, and Mr. Steele and his associates brought potential buyers to the house.

Hannah had reserved her bed, her night tables, her chest of drawers, her armoire, and a few small crates of tableware and kitchen utensils. She also held back a settee and a pair of chairs, a corner table, several lamps, and two rugs. Along with her clothing, that was all that remained of her marriage to Robert.

One of the buyers Mr. Steele brought through took a great liking to the peculiar house and discreetly inquired if Mrs. Keyes might meet him to discuss a price and other particulars.

Hannah sold the house after thirty minutes and at a greater price than she had hoped. It was obvious that the young purchaser–a shipper/importer by the name of Alan Fitch–had taken pity on the young and attractive widow.

He was a single gentleman, he said, and was looking for a home base. He also inquired if Hannah might at some time, following the proper months of mourning, be interested in partaking of a dinner with him.

As he wrote out the check, she stared at the successive five zeros added onto the amount. After all this, she might manage to pay off all of Robert's debts in no more than a few years–given her current earnings.

She looked up at Mr. Fitch. He was well dressed, awfully good-looking, she thought, and obviously younger than she by at least five or six years. And he exuded the air of invincibility. It was the same confident air that had first attracted her to Robert.

In spite of the fact that she was so recently widowed, she found herself blushing and then agreeing to his request. "But not until much later," she added. "Perhaps by next spring."

Mr. Fitch frowned. "This fall, Mrs. Keyes. I will call on you when autumn descends on this lovely town."

She did not dispute his request.

"And the rent is how much again? And I want the rate for a month, not merely a week. I am not a transient. I am asking that you factor in the rate for a long-term tenant."

The landlord inspected the small trio of rooms. There was a drawing room, a bedchamber, and a kitchen with an old cast-iron stove.

The nearest water was a well in the back of the building.

The privy was in the farthest corner of the lot.

He looked at Hannah again. "I'll give you a price, ma'am," he said, scratching his head, "but before I do, I need to inquire as to why you are here. An obvious gentlewoman like yourself has no business in this neck of town."

Hannah ran her finger along the windowsill in the main drawing room. Her finger left a long trail on the dirty wood. She had thought it was painted a dark color, but it was instead discolored by a thickness of grime.

"I am here because I can afford to be here." She explained no more. "At least I hope I can afford it."

"The rent be eight dollars a month."

"Eight dollars? That is a steep price for such . . . a well-tended apartment."

"But it's a private place," the landlord insisted, "and in the evening, you'll not have rowdies and the undesirable element about like you would in lots of other locations. A pretty woman like yourself would be the point of much speculation, ma'am." He wiped his chin. "No offense intended, ma'am."

She walked into the kitchen.

The stove is horribly old but serviceable. There is a greengrocer at the end of the block and a butcher and a baker two streets up. And he is most correct in that the building will have but one occupant at night and that will be me. And the clinic is but three blocks away, and the tram stop to Dr. Copley's is only one street over.

"If the price is seven dollars, I will sign for a year."

"A year?"

"I have the money in hand." Hannah held up her purse as if offering evidence.

"Then the place is yours. And I'll toss in a cord of wood, if you'd like. And a load of coal as well."

Hannah offered him the sweetest smile.

"Oh, what the blazes. Two cords and two loads."

"I would be so grateful."

From a Letter from Elizabeth Collins
July 1852

Dearest Morgan,

I trust that this will find you. I am sending this to you in care of Dr.

Copley. I know Mr. Steele has been "involved" in your current situation. No one keeps such a secret for long.

Your father has all but forbidden me to write you. He is devastated. We both had assumed we would have a place to spend the rest of our days.

That promise has turned out to be a falsehood–a brutal disappointment.

We had begun to make arrangements to sell our home. Because of certain "entanglements," we will receive but a pittance of the sale. It will not be sufficient to find another dwelling.

We are forced to spend the rest of the summer at Bay Head. I hate the ocean and all the horrid Newark relatives. But there is nowhere else to go.

We may be forced to take temporary shelter in Bay Head the entire winter. Can you fathom the disgrace involved? The horror of it all.

The Bay Head house is drafty and cold even in the summer. I cannot imagine what a winter will be like.

And this is how far your parents have fallen. Do you like what you see?

I thought the promise of a Harvard education would assure such an ignominious future would never occur. I suspect I was wrong.

Mother

From a Letter from Jamison Pike
Arrived July 1852

My Dear Hannah,

You must forgive me for my lack of correspondence. I could claim busyness, but then I have used that excuse in the past as well and I know how truly false it is.

The real reason for my lack of communication is deeper than that. I did not tell you the last time we spoke. I could not bear to.

I am going away for a very long journey–perhaps a year's duration. The newspaper and my publisher are funding my travels to all manner of exotic locales. I will report on what discoveries I make and what adventures I find along the way–and send them back to the New York World. *At the end, a full book will be prepared from my dispatches.*

I left in early April and did not pen this letter until nearly off the coast of Brazil. I am sure that with the trade back and forth between nations, this letter will get to you quickly–within a month or two, I would hope.

I will not be able to receive letters from you, for I have no set itinerary. I will be in China and Japan and Russia and India and perhaps the African continent as well. I may even get back to California and visit Gage and Joshua. How they have changed and grown older! (Unlike you and I, of course.) I will miss being able to know what you are doing. I trust that all will go well and that Robert will soon be the tycoon of his dreams.

I hope that the clinic is fine. If you are ever in need of further publicity, please call Benjamin Grossman at the New York World. *He has been ordered (by me) to serve you in any manner possible.*

I treasure our shared memories. How I wish I knew–back at the Destiny–how truly special those days were. I would have paid closer attention, I believe. I would have done many things differently.

And one thing most differently of all.

Pass my regards on to Lawrence and Robert.

I will send you further correspondence as I can.

Always,

Jamison

CHAPTER EIGHTEEN

Philadelphia
February 1855

"WHO is it?" Hannah called out as she touched the doorknob.

She heard laughter, then smiled and swung the door open.

"I was trying to think of something clever to say, and I did, but all I could do was laugh," he said.

She stepped aside. "Please come in. You are late. I hope nothing untoward happened?"

"No, nothing at all." He had kept his hand behind his back as he entered; then he swept it around. "And for you, sweet Hannah, a pleasant bouquet of flowers. By this time every winter I so yearn for a dash of color. But no, all about me is gray and brown and then more gray. I spotted these at the grocer's on the corner and could not resist. Now you have a bit of spring on this wonderfully bleak and depressing day."

Delighted, Hannah exclaimed, "Thank you so much. They are just so beautiful. But much too expensive. I will have to share the cost with you."

"Hannah, if you dare reach for your purse I will be ever so

offended and will leave immediately. Take the gift for what it is and do not sully the thought by offering to pay. Honestly, you take all the joy of gift giving away."

She laughed again. It was obvious that she enjoyed his company and that he brightened her day.

"All right, Lawrence," she said, exhaling, "I will keep my money–and my flowers. And I thank you so much." She went to him and kissed him on his cheek.

"Now don't climb all over me," he protested, blushing. "It's just a bouquet of flowers. I'm glad I didn't include some chocolate fancies as well. Who knows what you might have done?"

Playfully, she pushed his shoulder. "You do protest too much, methinks."

"Methinks?"

"Shakespeare. *Hamlet.*"

"Really?"

"You don't know it?" Hannah said as she placed the flowers in a pottery vase.

He puttered about in the kitchen, sniffing the aromas. "Well, not everyone in the world managed to go to Harvard, if that's what you mean."

She laughed again. "I didn't study it at Harvard. It's a play. I've seen it several times. It's very good. One of his best tragedies."

Lawrence flopped into one of Hannah's reclaimed chairs. "That's why I don't know it–it's a tragedy. I have enough of that in my life without seeing some fatigued play about someone else's problems."

She placed the flowers on the table. "Very pretty. Thank you again, Lawrence."

He shrugged. "I thought I should bring some brightness to this drab part of town. And why you continue to live here is beyond me. You can afford to move to a better section of the city. Even my less reputable friends look at me as if I am deranged when I tell them I am coming to see you for dinner. They say, 'Why doesn't she move uptown?' And I have no good answer for them."

Hannah stirred one of the pots on the stove with a thick wooden spoon. "And you need to answer them?"

"Well," he replied, "that is the polite thing to do, isn't it? Answer questions, I mean. Or is being mute something you also learned at Harvard?" He drew out the name *Harvard* with a long exhale.

Hannah loved Lawrence's company. He made her laugh and was sharp and witty. "Yes, I did, as a matter of fact. They teach all sorts of radical things," Hannah said.

He stared at his hand. "Of course, it was a very long time ago since you attended. I would guess that many rules have changed since then. After all, it has been nearly half a decade."

She spun about, gesturing with her spoon. "Now, Lawrence, you are treading on thin ice. You may make fun of my obvious sophistication and grace and education–but when you venture into commenting on a lady's age, that is most dangerous territory."

He stared back at her. "Will you refuse me food if I do not cease?"

"Yes," she answered firmly.

"Then by all means, you are the youngest graduate of Harvard that I have ever known."

She nodded. "That is the proper response. Now help set the table, and we can begin to dine."

"Does Dr. Copley always rap on the doorjamb when he leaves?" Hannah asked as they were close to finishing the Brunswick stew she had cooked.

"He does," Lawrence said gleefully. "Every time. He taps at the jamb."

"Why is that? Superstition? Checking the carpentry work?"

Lawrence shrugged. "Habit, perhaps. He has done it for as long as I have known him."

"And what of Dr. Pordett? Has he ever cleaned his boots? I swear that they carry more mud and dirt on them than I could shovel in an hour."

Lawrence began to laugh. He loved examining the foibles and

quirks of Dr. Copley's staff. "And Dr. Benett? Do you think he could mumble any more effectively? I would think not more than one patient in ten leaves knowing what in the world he had told them."

"And what of Mrs. Yount?" Hannah put in. "Does she really think we enjoy being near asphyxiated by that magnolia toilet water she wears in such profusion?"

"And Dr. Copley," Lawrence volunteered, "does he offer prayer for every wayward soul in his employ?"

Hannah was taking the dishes to the wet sink and spun about. "What?" she asked.

"Dr. Copley and his prayers."

"He says he prays for you?"

"Of course he does. He thinks I am a wastrel and a lost cause. I am dry tinder for his heavenly flame."

Hannah appeared pained, for she had believed that she alone was the target of his prayers.

"Oh come now, Hannah," Lawrence kidded, not realizing her hurt. "You must have known that he goes about praying for everyone all the time. I think that's what they do in his church. They sing a few turgid hymns, take the collections, then pray for all of us lost souls."

Hannah put the kettle over the hot griddle on the stove. "And what does he pray for you, Lawrence?" she asked, thinking Dr. Copley's words must be a simple routine.

"Oh, the usual . . . that I find God. That I turn away from my vices–the pleasant carousings, my affinity for games of chance, the odd encounter. He wants everyone to have a neat and tidy life. Just like his. But I don't."

Hannah measured out the tea. "And that doesn't bother you?"

"No. Should it?"

"When he says he prays for me, I always feel a little guilty," Hannah admitted.

Spooning out three huge tablespoons of honey into his teacup, Lawrence looked surprised. "Guilty? Why on earth would you feel guilty? After all the horrid things that you've endured? Guilty? You alone have no reason to ever feel guilty–with what the fates have heaped upon you." He fussed with his sleeve. "So what is it that you feel guilty about?" he asked, perhaps hoping she may truly have something to confess.

She filled the teapot with hot water. "I'm not sure. Just guilty in the most general manner. Maybe because all his prayers don't seem to have done much good. I'm still a widow. I am still in debt. And I live here," she said with a sweep of her hand.

"And you are cursed with friends like me," Lawrence added with a cackle.

"Exactly. He prays for you and he prays for me and we are both no better off than when he started. Doesn't that strike you as a foolish waste of time?"

He leaned back, and the chair squealed in protest. "I suppose. But for his prayers to work on me, I would have to agree to many, many changes. And I won't do that. But you, Hannah, I daresay his prayers have worked on you."

She bristled. "They have not."

Lawrence snatched a fig cookie and popped it into his mouth, chewing it with great gusto. "Yes, they have."

She put her palms on the table and leaned forward. "And tell me how you have come to that conclusion."

He took a second cookie and held this one, gesturing with it as he spoke. "You are still a widow, yes, but there was that handsome Mr. Fitch that you apparently insulted away. He would have been a catch, and I can tell from the look in a man's eyes if they are ready, believe you me. He was ready, had you allowed him to proceed."

She twisted her mouth. "Mr. Fitch was practically young enough, I discovered, to have been my son."

"If you had had children when you were ten!" He laughed and continued. "You chose to turn him out. And yes, you are in debt, but from what you have been telling me, all is nearly paid back. That is a remarkable accomplishment."

He ate his cookie and took yet one more.

"Lawrence," she said, "you said his prayers have worked. But I still live here–in what you claim is the worst section of town."

He stood and patted his belly. "That is true, Hannah. But you have made these walls beautiful and this space very special. There is good food and laughter and I daresay contentment here. That did not exist a few years ago."

"And this is because of prayer?"

"It might be."

"And then why aren't you changed?" Hannah asked.

He chuckled as he took their teacups into the drawing room. "I am lost. I know that I am lost, and I simply must say that I enjoy being lost. And an enthusiastic sinner is the most lost cause of all. Even Dr. Copley has admitted that to me. He calls me his special concern. I like that. It makes me feel needed."

They talked late into the evening, and Lawrence fell sound asleep in the chair. Hannah rose, took a woolen blanket from her closet, and draped it over him. She turned the wick in the lantern off and slipped into her bedchamber and closed the door. It did not have a lock, and even if it did, Hannah would not have bothered.

The echo of Lawrence's words concerning the effectiveness of Dr. Copley's prayers kept her awake until dawn.

If she had leaned over an inch, she could have seen her reflection in the polished surface of Mr. Manch's desk. He was no longer just a common loan officer as he was when they first met. According to the size and shine of his desk, it would be apparent to all that he was now an important executive in the bank.

With his promotion he could have passed her account to a junior officer, even made her deal with a simple teller. But he had enjoyed her resolute determination to make good on her husband's debts. Every month, on the fifteenth, she would march solemnly into the bank with cash in hand. She would insist on a handwritten receipt and would then ask Mr. Manch to officially note the bank's master file in her presence. He found this request to be most charming and allowed her to watch as he initialed the amount, subtracted that sum from the total, and posted a new, lower balance. Then he would rise, extend his arm, and escort her from the vault where all such records were stored.

For the past three years it had been routine.

If anyone had asked, Mr. Manch would have said, in strictest confidence, of course, that the fifteenth of each month was his favorite. He had never married, and he looked forward to that one day when he could spend a few minutes with a very intelligent, very pretty, very honorable woman–one who treated money and debts with a near sacred reverence.

This day Hannah sat up with a smile and pulled from her purse a thick packet of bills.

"More today than usual?" Mr. Manch asked.

Hannah nodded. "I withdrew some money I have been setting aside."

Mr. Manch appeared wounded. "But you must not dip into savings, Mrs. Keyes."

She looked up sharply.

"I mean, Hannah. Savings are not ever to be used in a frivolous manner. What if some sort of emergency should befall you? What would you do with no savings in hand? No, Mrs. . . . Hannah. I cannot let you do this."

She did not respond to his entreaties and continued to count off the ten-dollar bills. "Five hundred dollars," she finally said, her voice confident and proud.

Mr. Manch took the stack and slowly recounted. "That is correct."

Hannah stood quickly. "Now, let us mark the record," she said and turned toward the vault.

"Hannah, please wait."

She turned, impatient.

"Sit please," he said. "I have the book here with me."

He pulled the thick gray ledger from his desk drawer and thumbed through the pages, rich with numbers. He stopped at the page marked *Robert Keyes/Hannah Keyes.* He looked at her with a wistful expression, then reached for his pen and scratched out an entry and entered his initials. He did not do this with his usual flourish.

Spinning the book around, he said, "I am certain that you know the import of these five hundred dollars."

Hannah nodded. "I do, Mr. Manch. I do."

He had written on the last line, *Paid in Full, T.S. Manch.*

She beamed at him. "This loan has been the last of Robert's loans to be repaid. I am now out of debt."

Mr. Manch posted a brave smile of congratulations. She gathered her bag and readied to leave.

"Please, Hannah, wait . . ."

She turned in the chair. "Yes?"

"I have enjoyed your visits," he mumbled. "Will I . . . will I see you again?"

In that moment she knew she should be gentle with this man, even though she planned on never entering the inside of this bank–or any bank–for the rest of her life.

"Well, perhaps you will, Mr. Manch. Perhaps I will decide to place my accounts in your bank. If I move closer to town, now that I have additional funds, I may well do that."

Mr. Manch rose, offering Hannah the most hopeful and pleading smile that she had ever seen. She extended her hand, and he held it for a full moment longer than Hannah thought comfortable.

That evening, Hannah bundled herself in her thick winter coat and walked down her street to a coffee shop and sweets store. She had passed this establishment hundreds of times in the past three years, and each time, the aroma would beckon her, like a siren luring a sailor toward dangerous and hidden rocks on the shore. And every time she breathed that richly perfumed air, she would debate with herself.

Do I go in, or do I pass by? Can I continue?

Until this evening, she had never entered the store. There were two reasons for her continued abstinence.

The primary reason was money. Counting every penny and nickel, Hannah had not treated herself to a pure indulgence for years. She could brew coffee at home, she reasoned, and purchase a sweet from the grocer at a lower cost.

But the second reason was fear. She feared that entering into that rich environment would carry her senses back years and miles to the Destiny again and that dislocation would injure her soul and the scant amount of contentment and happiness she had managed to squirrel away these past hard years.

And every time she passed, fighting the urge to stop, and being victorious, she always allowed herself one morsel as consolation.

When I am finally free of all debt, then I will treat myself to the largest, richest, most decadent sweet they have and a cup of the richest, darkest, and most potent coffee brewed by man.

And this evening was that time.

She entered, and the bell above the door chimed. She breathed in, and the coffee and chocolate entered her senses with the heavy, sudden impact of a speeding freight train. She nearly swooned from the richness.

To her left was a set of cases, each filled with fine chocolates and cakes and all manner of marzipan confections. To her right was a bar, with gleaming brass fittings and urns with scrolled silver and spouts for all types of coffee making.

She despaired of ever knowing in which direction to turn first.

In the end, she carried a large plate with a wedge of chocolate cake, three chocolate-covered fruits, and a small mound of marzipan delicacies in one hand, and a huge mug of steaming coffee from Turkey, rich and swirling with honey and thick cream in the other.

What she spent this night nearly equaled what she spent on a week's worth of groceries.

She located a booth near the rear of the store and slid in.

In a half hour it was all gone and she leaned back, a chocolate smile on her face.

She found her equilibrium affected by such opulent tastes. Staggering out into the chilled night air, she felt full and satisfied and, for a moment, somewhat at peace.

Her delicate peace disappeared as she heard the bell from St. Olaf's toll at midnight.

It was neither sickness nor distress that brought her awake. It was another emotion altogether.

I have paid the debts! I should be asleep with the slumber of the innocents, for I have no longer this weight above my head.

But she tossed and turned until the first red streaks of dawn colored the clouds above the dockyards to the east.

The weight of obligation was gone. But now, for the first time since Robert's death, she became aware of her heart. There was no pain, she knew, but instead a creeping, encircling emptiness.

As she peered out at the dawn, she despaired of ever feeling right again.

She washed, dressed, and slipped out into the chill. She walked west, down a dozen blocks and more, and did not stop until she reached the banks of the Schuylkill River.

Full from the late winter thaw, the river hissed and slipped and poured along the banks. She watched as the water swirled past her. She thought back to a conversation long ago, held on the banks of another river–the Charles in Cambridge.

They had taken turns at guessing the future. She had been as wrong as the rest but never once had thought her future would be devoid of joy. She never envisioned a time when anger would be as close to her heart as happiness.

She watched the water until the chill crept into her bones. Then she allowed herself a second indulgence in as many days. She hailed a carriage and gave the driver Dr. Copley's office address, then sat back and closed her eyes for the ride.

❧

Hannah's last patient, a rather portly man complaining of pains in his extremities, clearly did not take Hannah's advice to heart.

"You must take a bland diet, Mr. Weaver," Hannah said as she wrote out a prescription. "The rich foods that you say you eat can often inflame the joints."

He snorted. "I worked hard all my life to get where I can afford the finer things–and by blue blazes–I am going to eat the best. Pain or no pain!"

He squeezed out of the chair, adjusted his jacket, and hurried out.

"But, Mr. Weaver," she called out to him.

She sighed. So many patients heard what she said but so often never took it to heart. It was clear Mr. Weaver was one of those who wanted a doctor to give him license to do as he always had done.

A second later, Lawrence tapped at the door. "Are you free?" he asked.

She brightened. "Of course I am. And I will not even charge you for this visit."

He laughed softly at her more than well-used witticism. He closed the door tightly. He lifted the paperweight on Hannah's desk, feeling its weight in his hands. Because he was seldom silent, Hannah imagined he was troubled.

Finally he looked up. She thought there might be a tear in his eye.

"I am leaving Philadelphia," he said as his throat tightened his words to a croak.

"Leaving? But why, Lawrence?" Hannah quickly and obviously became most distraught. The threat of losing perhaps her best friend was greatly troubling.

Rather than answer, he lowered his head into his hands and sobbed. "I have to leave. It is either that or I face arrest. And I would simply perish in prison."

"Arrest? Prison? What on earth has happened? Tell me, Lawrence. Please."

When he looked up, his eyes were cold and vacant and without hope. "Hannah, you are my best friend in all of Philadelphia–but there is so much that you do not know of me. And I will not share it with you. You would hate me if you knew."

"I wouldn't. I promise I would not," Hannah pleaded, leaning close to him.

"You *would* hate me," he said. "That would be worse than prison."

Hannah did not speak but took his hand in hers and held it tightly.

He sniffed loudly. "There is a large sum of money . . . and a woman . . . and a man. . . . It is all so sordid that I cannot go on in your presence. I cannot. And I will not." Sitting up straight, he wiped his eyes with a colorful handkerchief. His expression grew somber and serious. "Hannah, remember that dinner a few months ago when we talked about Dr. Copley and his praying for us?"

She nodded.

"Do you recall that I said that his prayers seemed to work for you, but I was the lost cause?"

"Yes."

"I told myself that I had to do this one noble act before I left. You have to promise me something."

Hannah appeared worried. "I'll try."

"I said that I was beyond hope. And perhaps I am, Hannah."

"No one is beyond hope, Lawrence. No one."

"I daresay some of us are. But that fact has nothing to do with your promise."

"Then tell me, Lawrence. What is it?"

"I may be beyond his prayers–but you are not. Because of my sins, I am forced to leave my home and my good friends–all that I hold dear. And my soul feels empty and cold and dark. If such is to be my lot for the rest of my days, then I truly despair, for there I will have no more hope, nor joy, nor laughter. It is as bleak as a cold day on the ocean."

"But, Lawrence, doesn't Dr. Copley say that no one is beyond God?"

He bowed his head. "He has said as much, but I do not believe him. I am."

"You are not."

"If you only knew. I am."

"But, Lawrence . . ."

"You must promise to listen to his prayers. You must promise to heed his words. Of all the men I have ever known, Dr. Copley is the kindest, most generous, and compassionate man–and it is because he believes."

"But you can change, Lawrence."

His laughter was caustic and angry. "No. I can't. But you can. You must. I will not rest unless you say that your soul will find happiness. I know I have no reason to feel this way, but you are a true friend to me, Hannah. I cannot let you waste your future by being stubborn and not allowing . . . not allowing grace to enter into your life. You must, Hannah. You must promise me that."

His eyes were filled with such plaintive longing that Hannah had to say, "I will try to do as you ask."

"You must promise!" he said sharply.

"I promise," she said with quiet earnestness.

Lawrence sniffed and stood. Hannah realized that when he left, she would never see him again.

"Where will you go, Lawrence? Will you write?"

He shrugged. "California, I think. And I will write only if I find peace." He turned back as he entered the hall. "So please, Hannah, don't expect a letter. And remember that you were my best friend."

Hannah stared at the empty space for an hour until she forced herself to move.

April 1855

Hannah ran her fingers down the printed page of the Bible. The words swam together, lost in a sea of angry letters. She had flipped through the pages, stopping every few chapters, reading a verse or two but never truly comprehending what the words meant.

She held the open book on her lap, then drew it into an embrace and stared out her small window. A single tear coursed down her cheek.

Everything I have ever loved is gone. I do not understand why this has happened. I am not a bad person and have done good things all my life. What more does God want from me?

She thumbed through the pages. She recalled Joshua railing at the practice of divining God's instructions by letting the Scriptures fall open haphazardly.

"It's no better than a holy lottery," he fussed. "If people want an answer, let them look and search. God is not a sideshow fortune-teller who dispenses kernels of wisdom upon demand."

Her smile was wistful as she recalled Joshua's verve and conviction. She wished he were near this evening, for she had no idea of where to start looking.

In truth, she did not know what it was she was looking for. She was simply trying to fulfill–or at least begin to fulfill–her promise to Lawrence.

When Dr. Copley had heard of his sudden departure, he simply shook his head in sadness and walked away, not adding one more word of explanation to Hannah.

And now she sat alone with the Bible in her arms and despaired at ever finding an answer . . . or even a direction.

She laid the book down, flipped a few pages, and offered a one-word prayer: *Please.*

And then she began to read from the book of James. *What doth it profit, my brethren, though a man say he hath faith, and have not works? can faith save him?*

"But I have works," Hannah said aloud. "All my life I have done good things for others."

If a brother or sister be naked, and destitute of daily food, and one of you say unto them, Depart in peace, be ye warmed and filled; notwithstanding ye give them not those things which are needful to the body; what doth it profit?

"I have never done that. I have always given to the poor."

Even so faith, if it hath not works, is dead, being alone.

"Well, I have done good works and I remain unrewarded," Hannah said, insistent. "What more does God want?"

Yea, a man may say, Thou hast faith, and I have works: shew me thy faith without thy works, and I will shew thee my faith by my works. Thou believest that there is one God; thou doest well: the devils also believe, and tremble. But wilt thou know, O vain man, that faith without works is dead?

Ye see then how that by works a man is justified, and not by faith only.

For as the body without the spirit is dead, so faith without works is dead also.

"But . . . I have works. That's what these words mean, does it not? To have works is what God wants from us."

She stared at the words for a long time and, suddenly, like a lantern being lit in a darkened cavern, the meaning grew clear and distinct.

Hannah was trained in the scientific approach. One plus one was two. Element A reacted with element B and produced C.

And as she stared at these words, she realized that she had but a single side of the equation. She had works. And through those works, she had attempted to find her path to God and peace with him. But she had never once took along the faith that those good works would prove. It was as if she held up a fine suit of clothes and expected that attire alone would produce a living entity.

It did not nor ever would.

"It is faith that I do not have," she whispered to herself. "It is faith that Joshua preached, and I assumed that faith simply accompanied my works."

She closed the book and stared out at the darkness.

"But how is it that I find this faith?"

"You simply accept Christ's gift of life. You acknowledge that he died for you. You acknowledge him as your Savior–and the only path that will lead you to heaven," Dr. Copley told her bluntly.

Hannah tried her best not to scowl. "But, Dr. Copley, it has to be more than that," she protested. "I just believe and then faith is there?"

He shrugged. "It appears simple, yet it is not. But belief brings faith and faith brings works and works strengthens faith."

Hannah blinked. "Then I am confused."

Dr. Copley took her hand. "Don't be. Do not fight this with logic and scientific method. The two are not always compatible. You must do this from the heart first. You must give your heart up. You must be as a child to come to God."

She scowled again. "But it seems so simple. There must be more than this."

"No. It is a simple act. But as simple as it is, it is profound and will change your life forever."

She thought for a minute. "Then what do I do? How does this faith start?"

The old doctor smiled. "Pray with me. Can you do that?"

"I believe I can do that."

"Dear Lord in heaven," he began, and she dutifully repeated the words, "I am a poor sinner, and without you I have no hope of life. I desire to be your servant. I accept your substitution for me and know that sacrifice cancels my eternal damnation. Grow me up as your child. I give you my life. Lead me in your paths. Amen."

"Amen," she said, then opened her eyes. "And that is all I must do?"

"You have given him your life. Now you must do whatever he asks you to accomplish. Do his work, Hannah, and your heart will be at peace."

"And how will I know that it is his work?"

Dr. Copley's face lit up. "You will know, Hannah. You will know."

That evening, as she lay in her bed, she looked up at the dark skies and prayed.

Lord, I do not know how this is to be done. I have accepted the gift you have given me, but it seems shallow, as if I simply repeated the words. How does this work? Will you tell me what must be done? Will you show me what path to take? Will you heal this emptiness in my heart? Please, Lord, show me the path–if that is how faith works. Amen.

And she slept more soundly than she had in years.

Two letters rested on her desk when she arrived at Dr. Copley's the next morning. She thought it might be a posting from Florence, or her married cousin in New York, now with a second child on the way.

One bore a smeared foreign postmark. She could not wait to tear it open.

Gibraltar
January 1855

My Dear Hannah,

This trip has assumed monumental proportions and consumed more years than I had anticipated. I am now in the small country at the mouth of the Mediterranean Sea called Gibraltar. I am in the employ of the London Observer. *It seems as if the English take great pleasure in having one of their former colonists report on events with a fresh vision.*

The book is nearly complete, and I am sending the last chapters to New York in a fortnight or so.

Forgive me for not staying in close correspondence with you, but to send you missives with no hope of ever hearing a reply was simply too painful to me. I apologize for my boldness, and I know that these words are inappropriate for a man to be writing to a married woman–but I must.

I think of you often and I yearn for the days we spent–callow and carefree at the Destiny. Do you ever think we might see each other again?

Perhaps you might visit the Continent? Do not all wealthy folks make that a pilgrimage at one time? I would so like to have dinner with you and Robert.

I will write again.

Jamison

The second bore a postmark from the new state of California.

Monterey, California
March 21, 1855

Dear Hannah,

I have a most interesting proposition for you.

But before I outline what I have in mind, let me pose one question. What do you think of California?

I am again a man of means–though the story of my downfall and rebirth is so complex and convoluted it would take a skilled storyteller a complete book to do it justice. I am not a storyteller, nor do I have that much paper.

I have considered writing this letter ever since I heard of Robert's passing. (I trust you have received my condolence card–it went by way of the clipper ship Esmerelda, *which they say made it to New York but failed to return to California.) You are a doctor, and a very talented one from what I have heard.*

I am building a hospital.

I need equipment and a staff.

Enclosed is a bank draft for twenty-five thousand dollars for supplies and staff. If you accept my offer, spend it wisely.

Also enclosed is a draft for ten thousand dollars for the clinic that you support. We have received a copy of Jamison's story, and I was most moved. Spend it all on improving the lot of those poor children.

And have you heard from our wandering reporter? He wrote saying that he could not leave the Continent until he put something out of his heart. Do you have any idea of what that might mean?

As always,
Gage

Hannah let the letter fall onto the desk.

She looked heavenward and whispered, "This is one sign too many. One sign too many."

CHAPTER NINETEEN

Philadelphia
May 1855

"YOU want fifty beds? Delivered to where?" the man asked.

"Monterey, California."

"Never heard of it."

"Monterey?"

He opened both palms upward in a gesture of surrender. "Lady, I ain't heard of either Monterey or California. And I ain't deliverin' nothin' till I get cash and a map."

Hannah did not appear concerned or frustrated. In fact, the response of Mr. Lloyd Howell, of Howell and Sons Medical Supply, was as typical of a response as Hannah had encountered all month. She no longer became agitated or upset. She simply sat down and wrote out a bank draft for half the amount.

"I will pay another quarter when the beds ship, and the final quarter when they arrive in either San Francisco, California, or at Monterey Harbor." She capped her new fountain pen and placed it gently into her bag. "I normally offer a bonus of 15 percent additional for a successful delivery, but since you inflated the costs of these beds a full 10 percent when I walked through the door, I shall not include that sum in these negotiations."

Mr. Howell sputtered a bit, then wiped his lips on the back of his hand.

"And it is because I am a woman, Mr. Howell, that you inflated your price."

"Ma'am, you have it all wrong. I ain't done no inflatin'."

She pulled the drawstrings of her bag. "Mr. Howell, I am a doctor. I have worked for several years with Dr. Copley. He has purchased a number of these beds just this year at a sum that was 10 percent less than what you quoted me just now. Therefore, you have lost that bonus amount."

"But, ma'am, I don't think that's quite fair. I didn't know about that bonus when you stepped inside."

She laughed in spite of his obvious admission of guilt. "It makes no matter now, Mr. Howell." She stood to leave. "I will expect those beds to be shipped within a fortnight. That can be arranged?"

Mr. Howell shrugged and then grumbled, "Yes, ma'am. I guess it can."

Cambridge, Massachusetts
May 1855

"California? Why on earth would you travel there?"

Hannah calmly replaced her teacup to its saucer. She had written to her parents, asking for an audience. Ever since they sold their house and began living for months at a time with relatives, they seldom initiated contact with their daughter. Weddings and funerals were the few family gatherings where Hannah had words with her parents. Her father had spoken but a dozen sentences to her. Her mother did her best to maintain a chilled relationship with an accompanying air of civility and forced graciousness.

The three of them sat in the parlor of the Grangers–her aunt and uncle–in Cambridge. It had been years since Hannah set foot on this piece of geography, and her emotions had brought her to a level of painful nostalgia that she had not expected.

But now her fondness for the past evaporated in the glare of her parents' scorn.

"California?" her father sputtered. "Nothing more than ne'er-do-wells and rascals all set to make a quick dollar." He folded his hands over his stomach.

He has gained weight since I saw him last, Hannah thought, *and his tremors have increased.*

"That is what I have heard as well," Hannah's mother agreed. "Nothing but men on their way to procure a fortune at any cost . . . and women willing to do anything to take it from them." She sniffed as she set her teacup on the table in the drawing room. "No proper lady would ever travel there." She eyed her daughter with suspicion. "You are still a Collins, you know. You do have a duty to maintain the family tradition."

Hannah blinked and successfully kept her teacup from wavering in her hands. She wanted to stand and throw the teacup against the wall and shout and gesture wildly. *The Collins name! Tradition! Father lost the house because of improprieties and a poor choice of a mistress! And all these years I thought it was because of something I did!*

But Hannah said nothing. She had heard the whispered truth, such as it was, of her father's misdeeds, late one night after her cousin Hazel's engagement celebration. It was her cousin Dorothy who, after consuming several brandy cordials too many, sat with her and slurred out the sordid story of bribes and mistresses and scandals.

Hannah said nothing then and said nothing this day either.

Since finding her way to faith, she worked so very hard at forgiving them both.

It is too hard, she thought as she watched her mother look down her nose at the very mention of California. *It is just so hard to be a Christian around them. But still . . . I will not do battle . . . for that is not the way of a child of God . . . even if what they do makes me feel angry and hurts my heart.*

Hannah tried to smile but was sure that it looked false and forced.

"Mother, I am sure that not every person in California is out to steal a fortune. In fact, it appears now that the gold has peaked, people are forced to return to the professions they once left. That is what Gage has discovered."

Her father looked as if he had swallowed some ill-tasting fish. "Gage Davis? Nothing more than a common criminal. Run out of New York City in disgrace. Nearly bankrupted the fine Davis family. That you should work for him, of all people. He is but one step removed from prison."

Hannah stared. This had been the longest discourse she had heard from her father in years. Perhaps this was the start of a new dialogue–and then done so only to discuss Hannah's poor life choices.

She sighed softly. She had decided before the dawn of this day that she would not raise her voice nor descend into sarcasm.

"I would not know, Father. But I have heard that he may be running for the office of governor of the state."

He scoffed. "Then the whole state is indeed nothing better than a land of criminals. Any locale that would elect a criminal . . . well, who knows what strange folks may eventually get elected there? It would not surprise me if they considered a thespian as a potential candidate, so foolish are those people there."

Hannah did not respond or show any emotion. "Well, they have a hospital nearly complete, and I have an invitation to run it," she said softly. "That does not sound either criminal or strange."

Her mother shook her head slowly. "I thought you would finally give up on this foolishness. After Robert passed on, we both thought you would see the light and stay away from medicine. All you see is death and illness. We were certain that such sights would warp your judgment. And when you began to practice with that Dr. Copley, who suffers from an inflated sense of himself–well, we had hoped his excesses would bring you to your senses. But so far, nothing has done that. Now it is California! When will all this end, Morgan? When will you stop this and become a normal woman and daughter?"

Hannah tightened her fingers about the cup, willing her hand to remain still and not tremble with anger. She continued to describe her own activities and leave her mother's comments alone.

"And I have bought most of the supplies required. I shall be leaving within two months, if the weather remains fair."

She did not answer her mother's question. She could not and obey the Scriptures at the same time.

Neither of her parents spoke. They exchanged a series of odd looks between them, as if her lack of anger had upset their logic and line of reason and her actions were so unexpected as to be puzzling.

"And you will sail there by yourself," her mother finally asked, "on a ship with lonely and bored sailors? Do you think that prudent? Do you think a Collins woman should put herself in such a compromising situation?"

Hannah simply looked up.

"I mean, Morgan, let us both be realistic. You are a widow. And everyone knows that a once married woman now deprived of . . . companionship . . . will seek out such comfort from nearly any source. All those sailors . . . staring at you . . . walking close to you . . . all during the voyage. In such intimate quarters."

Hannah remained silent. She knew her mother was now deliberately attempting to inflame her emotions and sensibilities with such comments. And at the same time, it was obvious Elizabeth Collins was fearful that the mechanism for finding and stoking her daughter's ire was gone.

"I shall be sailing on the *Vancouver,*" Hannah said, her voice tight, bearing witness to her effort at remaining calm. "And I am told that the ship is new and will be carrying, besides myself and my equipment, a full complement of well-bred passengers. I think I will be safe on this voyage."

The bell in the tower at Harvard Commons tolled five times. Hannah stood. "I am sorry, Mother and Father. I must beg your forgiveness. I have . . . well, I have many details to see to. I am sure you understand." She drew her shawl around her shoulders, slipped her bag under her arm, and stepped to the door. "Will you be up to another visit this evening?" Hannah asked. "I may be somewhat late."

Only now did her parents rise.

"If it is past seven in the evening, then, no," her mother said. "I am afraid we will be retiring early this evening. We are both feeling most fatigued."

Hannah slipped out into the crisp spring air. "Then I will wish both of you a good night," she said pleasantly.

She smiled and turned away, hurrying down the walk.

Hannah did have many details to attend to. But this evening was not filled with any appointments. Medical supplies had been purchased. Crates and crates lay in a locked warehouse on the docks of lower Manhattan waiting for the arrival of the clipper ship *Vancouver.*

She knew she must leave the Granger's home and her parents' company immediately. It was either leave or face committing several sins in their presence. Rather than test her faith and convictions, she had decided, even before taking the trip to Cambridge, that she would retreat before she would do battle.

The air was chilled, and the night promised even a further drop in temperature. Hannah buttoned her coat closer to her neck and dug her hands deeply into her pockets. She had forgotten to bring her hat and gloves, yet the cold air was refreshing and cleansing.

She walked south three blocks and three blocks east and then stopped. She could see the bell tower in Harvard Commons. Her heart lurched.

It had been so many years since she had stepped on the grounds of the college.

It was not that she had had no chances prior to this day. She had traveled to Boston on many occasions and could have slipped over for a visit–but had never done so.

I want to remember it in my thoughts–as it was back then. To see it again might tarnish that golden image.

But on this day, she did not hesitate and continued walking.

When I leave here, she thought, *I will never return to the east. I will never see these locales again.*

Hannah had not admitted that supposition to anyone, but she knew it was true.

Not much has changed, she told herself as she walked slowly across the commons, taking in every inch of the architecture. She sniffed the air. It was the same as she remembered–a hint of paper and grass and an odd musty aroma–as if the very environment was laden with the scent of books.

She closed her eyes and breathed. She thought she smelled a hint of coffee as well and turned to face the direction of the Destiny Café.

A young student came up to her. "Excuse me," he said, "may I help you? Are you looking for something?"

Hannah shook her head. She realized that the sight of her, breathing deep and not moving, must have looked odd. "No, thank you. I am fine."

The young man, his dark hair cut short to his face, smiled. "Well, ma'am, if you're sure, then."

Ma'am? Ma'am? Do I truly look that old and haggard?

She smiled to herself. "I suspect I do," she whispered. She began to walk east again and did not stop until face-to-face with the Destiny.

"Do I dare enter?"

Hannah stood outside the café and whispered. She recalled the window as larger and the steps wider. In reality, she saw the place as an almost run-down eatery, badly in need of new awnings and paint.

She stood aside as a group of four students, laughing and jostling, made their way down the steps and headed briskly toward campus. An aroma of tobacco smoke and coffee followed them. Hannah thought it a most heady scent, and it drew her closer.

The steps creaked in the same place as she had recalled, and the nicked door squealed as it had always squealed so many years ago. With the door half open, she stopped and peered in.

The interior was bathed in the golden amber of a dozen lanterns and gaslights. There was the sound of laughter and dishes and the brittle edge of a loud discussion. A fog of smoke and steam hung in the air.

She paused with her hand on the door and closed her eyes. It was as if the last ten years had not even occurred–such was the power of impressions that the scents and sights held.

Oh, to relive those days!

But still she hesitated and did not enter.

Finally, after a long moment, she pulled the door shut and stepped back down and onto the sidewalk.

If I go in, I will miss them all that much more. And I will never find what I am looking for.

She began to walk toward campus. There was a carriage stand not far from the restaurant. She would be back in Boston by seven. She stopped seeing as she walked and let her memories guide her.

I would be looking for a way to return back to the promise of my youth, she told herself. *And that would simply hurt my heart. No, it is better that I remember it all as it was and not be disillusioned by what it has become.*

Hannah awoke from her reverie as she waited by the carriage stand.

"Where to, ma'am?" the driver called.

Hannah blinked several times. "The Hamilton in Boston. Do you know it?"

The driver nodded. "Sure do, ma'am. Any baggage?"

She smiled as she stepped into the open carriage and draped a robe over her legs. "No, just what I'm carrying with me."

And with that the carriage clattered off to the south and to the river.

Boston
May 1855

Hannah decided against a second, even more protracted meeting with her parents. Yet she did stay in Boston for an additional two days. She had to deal with a sheaf of shipping logs and set an appointment to meet with two recent graduates from the Harvard Medical School. A hospital required staff, and Hannah wanted to bring the best.

The meeting began as most such meetings did–with a fair amount of incredulity on the part of the two young doctors.

They were led to her private dining table in the rear of the restaurant at the Hamilton. The two hardly looked old enough to have graduated from grammar school, let alone medical school, Hannah thought. They offered their names and extended their hands to her, followed with the most befuddled expressions.

Dr. Ian Ballantine, a thin young man with the reddest hair Hannah had ever seen, was the first to ask the question. "When will Dr. Keyes be arriving? The letter said to be prompt, and I do not want to disappoint him."

The second young doctor, Miles Neuman, nodded. "It's not often that recent graduates are given such an offer. All expenses paid to California with a free practice at a new hospital. Ian's right–we can't afford to irritate this old rich doctor."

He looked to Hannah. "Since you're his assistant, any tips on what he's looking for? A firm hand? An acquiescent sort of fellow? A jovial one? If you key us in–well, I daresay we could spot you a few dollars or so. What do you think?"

And then he winked at Hannah, as if attempting to settle the deal. Hannah held her tongue.

"We really want to see California," Dr. Ballantine added. "We hear the weather is temperate all the year and that there is still a lot of gold being found. Wouldn't mind to get in on some of that, you know."

Both men laughed and slapped each other's shoulders in a most playful manner.

Then Hannah rose and extended her hand to each of them in turn. "I am Dr. Morgan Hannah Keyes," she said slowly. "And I am heartened by your desire to travel to California."

It was a full quarter of a minute until either of them spoke.

"You are jesting, of course. You cannot be Dr. Keyes."

Hannah smiled. "And why not?"

"We were told Dr. Keyes was a brilliant doctor."

"And?"

"And . . . well, you're a woman."

Hannah did not scowl nor frown. She had expected the response and was no longer angered or incensed. "And?"

"But . . . but . . . ," Dr. Ballantine sputtered. "You're a woman. Women can't become doctors, can they?" He glanced desperately at Dr. Neuman. "I didn't think they could. Did you?"

"Gentlemen, I assure you that I am indeed Dr. Keyes. You can ask Dr. Copley if you are unsure of my qualifications. He was the one who recommended you to me."

"Dr. Copley? You're the Dr. Keyes who worked with him?" Dr. Neuman asked incredulously.

"I am indeed," Hannah said with a degree of smugness.

She waited until both men wiped their brows. Beads of nervous sweat had appeared in a heartbeat.

"Gentlemen, your response is most common–and expected. I can accept your shortsightedness without rancor. If you are willing to forget that I am a woman and only think of me as a doctor, then I am willing to forget that you both behaved with ill manners this evening."

Both men nodded, looking as contrite as they were able.

And after an extensive three-hour interview–as rigorous as any examination that either of them had taken–Hannah hired them both, for they were indeed as qualified as Dr. Copley had said.

New York City

On her way back from Boston, Hannah made one last visit to New York. There were two stops in the city that she had to make. One was at a firm that was devising a new model of stethoscopes that would be shipped to Monterey as soon as completed. And the other was to the newspaper office where Jamison once worked.

She carried with her a letter written to Jamison. It was actually the seventh draft of the same letter. With each previous copy, Hannah grew frustrated that she could not convey her true feelings and tossed the pages into the fire. Then sighing, she had begun again, refining and revising. Even after so many attempts, she was still not settled in her message. The draft that she carried in her bag was no more certain and direct than the first draft–but she could not write one more word.

He will have to figure out what I mean by my jumbled words and thoughts. It is not my fault that I have no precise understanding of what he means to me.

As she entered the building, she smiled.

I once imagined that as one gets older and more mature, all these matters of the heart become simpler.

She scanned the directory for the name that Jamison had mentioned as his assistant.

But I have come to discover that it remains complicated. Will it ever be simple?

She read the name: *Benjamin Grossman–Third Floor.* There was not another woman on the entire floor. The pulsating hum of conversation ceased, as quickly as a brick falls to earth, as Hannah stepped into the open office from the stairs. She scanned the room, and nearly every face turned to look back at her. Some men, obviously grizzled and veteran reporters, stopped to stare, some with food or drink that was paused midway between their desk and their mouth.

Hannah saw no nameplates, so she addressed the man at the first desk. "Benjamin Grossman, please."

The man spun about and pointed toward the corner. Every head turned to the same direction. Hannah looked and saw a desperate-looking gentleman in a state of full emergency blush.

"Thank you," she said sweetly and stepped toward his desk. By the time she sat down in the offered chair, conversation slowly began to refill the stark silence of surprise.

"Does a lady always do this?" Hannah asked. "Numb the room mute, that is."

Mr. Grossman nodded. "We don't get many ladies up here. And when we do, they're usually one of . . . well, one of those women."

It was Hannah's turn to blush. "I hope no one thought of me as such a person."

Mr. Grossman said apologetically, "No . . . I didn't mean that you were . . . I mean we could all tell you weren't . . . I mean . . ."

Hannah smiled. "Mr. Grossman, please sit down. I am not offended by your candor in the least."

He breathed a sigh of relief. "Then what can I do for you, Miss . . . ?"

He called me miss and that counts for something. "I am Hannah Keyes. I am a friend of Jamison Pike."

Mr. Grossman stared at Hannah. "Hannah Keyes?"

"Yes," Hannah added, "Jamison and I met at Harvard and have kept in touch. . . ."

"You're the former Hannah Collins?! You're Hannah Collins?"

Hannah did not know how to respond. "Well, yes, I am."

Mr. Grossman leaned back in his chair as if he had practiced the maneuver a thousand times. His bottom shirt button was undone, and Hannah tried not to stare.

"Well, I'll be . . ."

Hannah tightened her expression. "Is there something wrong?"

He tilted forward with a crash, and Hannah leaned back for fear that he would tumble into her.

"No, nothing is wrong. You just are not how I pictured you at all."

"Excuse me?"

He pushed a pile of papers from the corner of his desk as if suddenly trying to tidy up. "No, I don't mean anything by that. It's just that I thought I knew what you looked like, that's all."

"And why would that be?"

"Well, old Pike talked about you all the time."

Now Hannah herself leaned back. "What? Jamison talked about me? All the time?"

Mr. Grossman reddened a bit, as if he had given away a secret.

"Well, not all the time, Miss Keyes. But once a day, I bet. At least that."

Hannah tried not to let her jaw drop open from surprise. She truly wanted to know what he could have found out about her but was too embarrassed to ask.

"Well, then, what . . ."

Because she was flustered, it took Hannah a minute to remember why she had come. She reached into her bag. "I have a letter for Jamison. I was not sure where he might be. The last correspondence I received said he was in Gibraltar and did not know when he might return. He said to come to you if I needed anything. I am on my way to California and wanted to send off a letter before I left. And that is why I am here."

She held the envelope out to Mr. Grossman as proof of her story and her intentions.

Mr. Grossman's expression turned from incredulity to absolute befuddlement. "But why would you do that?" he asked, finally locating his composure.

"Do what?"

"Send a letter."

Hannah grew confused. "I . . . I simply wanted to send this to Mr. Pike. I was not sure of where he was, and he did say that you would be the person who might be able to track him down. I don't want to send this overseas if he has moved on."

Mr. Grossman wiped his lips and face with a meaty palm. "But, Miss Keyes, you don't have to be sending this anywhere. Jamison is in New York. Or he was. He'll be back within the month, I'm told."

Hannah tilted her head. "I don't understand. Is he not stationed in Gibraltar? He said he might be there for years."

Shrugging, Mr. Grossman opened his palms in surrender. "He's never been stationed there, Miss Keyes. He went to England a year ago to do some lectures and write a few pieces. He did stop in Gibraltar. But he was never going to stay there."

Hannah narrowed her eyes. Her hand slipped on a pile of old

newspapers on the corner of his desk. "You mean Jamison has been in America?"

"Since last year."

"But he said . . ." Her voice went silent.

Mr. Grossman's eyes widened a bit. "I ain't the one privy to any special information, and I don't truly understand any of this, Miss Keyes. It's obvious to me that somehow, something ain't been communicated just right. And I think I know who might be at fault, Miss Keyes."

She found herself sniffing. "It is Mrs. Keyes. I'm widowed."

"Yes, whatever . . ."

"But why would he lie to me? Why wouldn't he tell me that he was back?"

Mr. Grossman shrugged again. "Like I said, Mrs. Keyes, I never married so I wouldn't be sure. But I know if he told you that he wasn't here, he had a good reason for it. Jamison is a fine man, and he wouldn't do anything to hurt someone as nice as you. At least the way he talks about you, I can't imagine that he would have done anything intentional in that direction."

Hannah leaned forward. She could smell a hint of old whiskey on the bachelor newsman. "He talks about me all the time, you said."

He nodded.

"It is all . . . pleasant talk?"

"Oh yes, always. Pike's not the type that would kiss and tell." And then he blushed even more furiously than before. "I didn't mean nothing . . . I mean that anything between you and him . . . I mean not that I thought . . ."

She held her hand up, bidding him to stop. "And he has never been stationed out of the country?"

Through his blush, Mr. Grossman nodded. "He's taken some long trips, but he always has come back."

Hannah sat back hard against the wooden, slatted chair. She felt the back squeal and heard a minor splintering. From across the room, there came a roil of laughter and shouts.

"And he's in New York now?" she asked.

Mr. Grossman now looked as if he had figured out that he had just broken some gentlemanly confidence with Jamison. "Well . . . yes, he was. But then he left for a story in Charleston a few weeks ago. Maybe he's back. But then . . . maybe he stayed on longer."

Hannah hardly heard the answer. The letter, which was still in her hand, felt awkward now, and surprisingly heavy. "May I borrow a pencil, Mr. Grossman?"

He scrabbled for a sharpened one and handed it to her. His hand was actually shaking a bit.

She thought for a moment, then wrote:

Jamison! What falsehoods have you told me? Gibraltar? As a friend, I demand more honesty. If you can, come to Philadelphia before I sail on June 15. If you miss me, I expect a letter and a full explanation.

If not, I will no longer consider you my friend.

H.

She handed the pencil to Mr. Grossman. Then she handed him the letter. "If any of this is erased or changed, I will hold you personally responsible, Mr. Grossman. Is that understood?"

He gulped once and nodded.

CHAPTER TWENTY

Philadelphia
June 1855

M*Y little Hannah,*

No doubt you will be on your way as you read this missive. I feel that is the proper way, for I know that sentimentality and tears would overtake me if I dared to address this in person. Of all the persons I have been involved with in my practice–and I hesitate to name both that number and the number of years that I must examine–well, you are the one I will hold closest to my heart.

Perhaps this dearness is because I have been privileged to watch your journey–and perhaps because I was one of the chosen few to help direct you to the truth.

When you came to my practice seeking work, I was astonished that you were a woman. You signed your application "Morgan" and knew it would be seen as a man's. And there you were, in front of my desk, with your eager smile and earnest spirit. How could I say no to that? I knew within a moment of meeting you that you would charm every patient who came in my door–and I was right about that.

But still, it was your journey to the light that I shall most remember.

When you came to me, you had everything life has to offer–but you had nothing. You had riches, a large home, a glittering future–all the things that the world offers us, tantalizes us with. But all these things can leave us empty and broken.

That was you, Hannah. As you have found, money and power promise so much and offer so little. I will not speak ill of the dead, but your husband did not live as the Scriptures instruct. And when that tragic day came, and you were left widowed and alone, I watched you handle all the adversities that life threw at you. Yet your skill and successes led you to believe that all manner of problems could be handled by yourself alone, with no help from anyone.

How I wished I could have simply handed you the secret of joy and faith then–but the time was not right.

And then all your struggles to pay off the debts and your estrangement from your family–how I wept for you as you struggled–and how I prayed for you. Yes, I know that there were some in my employ that thought me an odd duck for praying like that–and who even resented my prayers–but I must do as God commands.

When you finally admitted that you were lost, that is when God found you.

And how overjoyed I was to learn of your faith.

What has been most gratifying is to watch you grow and mature as Christ would have us all grow and mature. I know it is wrong to take pride in this, but I will think of your name and smile, for I know I was part of your journey to God.

And now you are leaving me.

How I wish I were a young man, for I might aspire to this journey as well.

California!

It sounds exciting and filled with all the golden promises of tomorrow.

And for you, Hannah, as a physician–to have the chance to be the head of a hospital–why, you must be very proud.

I have advice for you, as all us old men have advice for those younger.

Some will be foolish, some sage. It is your job to determine which is which.

Read your Scriptures daily if possible. Let God lead your path, and all will be as he planned.

Follow your instincts. Above all things, Hannah, I know you are the most intuitive physician I have known. You must follow those instincts, for I know that they will seldom lead you astray.

And finally, you must follow your heart. You are a young woman, Hannah. And a woman needs a man beside her. It is not that I think you are less capable. But you need someone to share your life, Hannah. Again, let your heart lead you.

I am making a muddle of this. I have thought of you as my daughter. I will continue to pray for you and will hold you fondly in my heart for the rest of my days.

Yours,
Doc Copley

Hannah read the letter twice. The words were just as he spoke, filled with bluster and heart and touched with God's grace.

She watched the waves slide past the bow of the ship. The coast of New Jersey was but purple edging to the west. She sighed once, very deeply, and realized that she would miss him so very, very much.

The Caribbean Sea
June 1855

The *Vancouver* cut through the waves like an aquatic animal. As a clipper ship, it had few peers. Even though there were now steam-powered vessels making the circuit, few could match the grace and speed of the *Vancouver.* With all canvas unfurled and snatching up great gulps of wind, the ship surged, as if a very part of the wind that scoured the surface of the water.

Most of the passengers huddled in their tight quarters, unwilling to venture out into the elements. Every moment at sea, for the first leg of their journey, the air warmed and grew more humid and luxuriously fragrant. Hannah could not tolerate the claustrophobic confines of her cabin and spent most of daylight above deck. She seldom ventured farther than the quarterdeck near the middle of the ship. When the winds were high, great flumes of water would break over the bow, and she would be blessed with a rainbow of salt spray. The ship would ride up the face of the wave, then dive into the next valley of water.

Others around her suffered greatly from the rolling and turning and twisting motion, but Hannah took to the sea as if she had been born to it. Yet until this voyage her only experiences on the water were a few riverboats and several idyllic afternoons with Gage Davis in his fancy boat on Boston's placid Back Bay.

The other passengers were cordial but treated Hannah with diffidence. As she introduced herself as a doctor, a widow, and journeying alone to California, she watched with amusement as they recoiled in three stages, each time leaning farther back, as if each revelation from Hannah was more and more frightening.

Even the hardscrabble sailors treated her as a great curiosity.

One calm day, just south of the Florida Keys, Hannah reclined on a chair on the quarterdeck. There were no other passengers to be found. Now that the rough seas had passed, some complained of the effects of the harsh sun. A few hardier souls might venture out at dusk, for a minute or two, but most appeared to be content to remain in tidy isolation in their cabins.

Hannah did not take well to such confinement. Perhaps it was in response to her years in the small quarters off Race Street. Perhaps it was that her heart, piqued by the summers she had spent growing up by the ocean, had always yearned for the vastness of the sea and she had simply failed to recognize the yearning. For on this voyage, Hannah seemed to go below deck to eat and sleep, and little else.

She drew the chair as far from the outer rail as possible. A large clipper ship, in shifting winds, would be scrambling with sailors, squirreling up ropes and hauling sails up or down. Canvas needed to be tied off and trimmed to the rails. So Hannah held close to the below-deck covers and closed her eyes to the ever warming tropical sun.

Then the silence was shattered by a crash. The sound came from only a few feet behind her, and Hannah tumbled from her chair in surprise. She spun around, half expecting to see a sailor crushed upon the deck, having fallen from a mast or its rigging.

But there was no man, just a splintered mass of rope and pulley and bar.

A sailor swung down from the deck from a lower mast. "You hurt, ma'am? Did you get nicked a'tall?"

Hannah, on her knees, felt her face and arms and frame. "No . . . I do not believe I did."

"But you took such a tumble. You sure that no harm is on you?"

She patted at herself again, then pushed to her feet. "No, I think all is well. I was simply surprised by the crash."

The sailor lifted the pulley, now split into two parts. "I might say that riding the decks be too dangerous for you, ma'am. Things like this happen. Why, if a man drops a small rope stay from up top, it could do some damage if you catch it right on top of your noggin."

Hannah nodded.

"A man gets knocked like that, and well, he ain't right from then on. No telling what might happen if it be a woman that gets knocked like that."

A hatch from the quarterdeck cover popped open, and a swarthy man clamored out, carrying two buckets. He stood, spit, and launched the vile-smelling material toward the ocean. Not all of it made it, and some splattered near where Hannah stood. The first sailor set into a very long curse and invective, questioning the morals, the manners, and the birthright of the second sailor. The two cursed at each other for a full minute, then stopped abruptly.

The first sailor bowed to Hannah. "Begging your pardon, ma'am. We ain't used to ladies being on board, I guess."

Hannah had heard the words before, perhaps not used quite as often in the same sentence. "I am not harmed. And I do not expect you to act differently because I am on deck."

The first sailor took a step forward. "I'm called Tinker–'cause I do a lot of tinkering, I imagine."

"And I am Hannah Keyes."

"Ma'am?"

Hannah waited for the question she knew would follow.

"I know this be most forward of me and all."

She waited.

"And me being just a mate on ship and all."

She waited.

Tinker looked at his feet, then at the billowing canvas overhead, then back to Hannah. "The rest of the mates say you be a doctor. They say that be the name you signed the manifest with. I say that you ain't 'cause you being a woman and all."

She smiled and sat down again. "I am a doctor." Her answer was calm and practiced because she had repeated it many times before.

"And menfolk come to you with ailments and all?"

"They do."

"And you do what doctors do?"

"Well, Tinker, I am not sure what all doctors do, but I treat all patients the same–men or women."

Tinker blushed red. "You know what I mean . . . doctors being well acquainted with all the parts and that."

Hannah tilted her head and smiled. "Yes, Tinker, I am acquainted with all the parts and all that."

Being direct, she had found, was the safest and most expedient answer.

"That be the truth?"

"Tinker, that be the truth indeed."

He offered an embarrassed smile.

"And if you ever run into a problem, you come see me. I have my medicine and tools with me. I could take care of you, if you want."

"Well, if something happens to me that the ship's mate can't tend to, then I'll be coming to you." He offered a wry smile. "That is, if you truly know all the parts and what they do."

She narrowed her eyes as a schoolteacher might at a naughty student. She knew indeed what he meant.

Then he winked and waved to her as he backed away.

Hannah watched him as he climbed the ship's rigging. In a moment, he was at the top of the center mast, where he waved again. She leaned back, closed her eyes to the sun, and let the hiss of the sea and the groan of the rope and canvas lull her to a peaceful nap.

Off the Coast of Argentina
July 1855

Hannah almost would have preferred taking the shorter route to California by heading across the jungles along the narrow strip of land that connected Mexico with the South American continent. Jamison Pike once traveled that very route and claimed that path was the shortest and most direct. But he also warned that the route was hazarded by bandits and thieves and all manner of tropical disease. Hannah carried crates and crates of supplies and medicines and could not imagine portaging them through dense forests, nor did she want to encounter any strange and untreatable malady.

So instead, she and the *Vancouver* would sail south, as far south as a ship could sail without encountering large ice floes. Then the ship would set sail west for a short time around the southern tip of South America, then head north. It was a long voyage. Yet Hannah took great comfort in that the ship was seldom more than a half day's sail from land. Being close to ports meant that the food was generally of good quality, and fresh water was readily abundant.

As they traveled farther south, the winds grew harsh and chilled. A fine mist followed them for a week, and the decks and rigging were coated with a thin veneer of ice. It was as if the entire ship was bejeweled, and it sparkled like a diamond in the afternoon light. Hannah bundled herself in a thick sea coat and a blanket about that and stood, under the eaves of the quarterdeck, and watched as the thin ribbon of the South American coast slipped past.

Sailors, she found out, thoroughly disliked days such as these. The rigging, greased with ice, became even more hazardous. The winds had been fair, and the canvas was allowed to remain set for nearly four days straight. But now a freshening of wind carried the threat of a squall. With full sails, the ship could be tossed hard to shoals or rocks. So the captain called out a furling of half the canvas.

Even Hannah could tell the reluctance in his voice.

A dozen men appeared at poles and ladders and began to climb, then spread out along the masts, furling the thick canvas and tying it off, slowing the ship as effectively as brakes and anchor.

Hannah faced toward the stern of the ship, squinting at the reflection of sunlight from the water.

Then came a scream, and a chorus of shouts and curses. Next a crumpling sound, as if a sack of wet flour had slammed into the wooden deck.

And then came another scream–long and shrill.

She spun about. No more than ten steps away from her was a man lying on the deck, arms waving feebly in the air as if searching out to gain a purchase. Hannah skittered across the icy deck. She slid the last few feet and wound up kneeling at the man's side. With great care, she turned the figure over.

It was Tinker.

His eyes were barely open. His breath came in shallow gasps. She looked down, and his right leg was twisted at a most awkward angle. She bent to him and saw the red stain crawling across the fabric of his trousers. Through a rent in the cloth, she saw the jagged sawtooth of a broken bone.

"Lie still, Tinker," she ordered. Pulling a scarf from her throat, she quickly wrapped it about his thigh and tightened it. He moaned.

"You still be knowing what parts be what?" he gasped.

"I do," she replied. Around her formed a grim-faced backdrop of sailors. A leg injury such as this was a most serious matter. A hobbling sailor was often a dead sailor.

Without looking Hannah barked out, "Get a stretcher for this man. Take him below to someplace with a good lantern . . . a couple of good lanterns!"

It took only a few moments to get Tinker flat on a long table in the officer's mess.

As Hannah was slicing off the trousers on that leg at midthigh, the ship's official doctor blustered in. Hannah smelled the strong hint of brandy about him. He reeled slightly, holding on to the rafter above more tightly than required.

"I be the doctor on this ship, I'll have you know," he offered, though Hannah paid him scant attention.

She straightened Tinker's leg, and he screamed again.

The ship's doctor, Sam Macalus, belched as he leaned forward. "No hope there. I'll get my bone saw, and we'll take her off at the knee."

Tinker heard and started wailing and thrashing about. "Don't take my leg!" he screamed. "Don't take my leg!"

Hannah looked up at Macalus and stared at him as hard as she could. "There'll be no taking legs off. Not while I am here."

Macalus banged his head into the bulkhead, swearing and jostling about, seeking out a foothold. "You ain't the doctor here. And yer a woman. Ain't right–a woman pretendin' to be a doctor."

Hannah felt as close to physical violence as she had ever felt. "Listen! I am not pretending. You're drunk. And I will not let you cut off his leg."

"You callin' me a drunk?"

"I am."

He glared at her. "Cuttin' off that leg be the easiest for everybody."

"Easiest for Mr. Tinker?"

"Listen, woman, you muddle about with a splintered bone and old Tinker might go plumb crazy from the pain. And even if you do–the wound will go bad, and then I got to cut it off before the blackness spreads. They teach you that at yer fancy medical school?"

Hannah peered closer at the wound. Though the bone had

splintered at midcalf, she thought it would piece back together. Flesh had been rent apart in a large gash. She assessed her options.

"See?" Sam Macalus said, leering. "You'll be cuttin' here as soon as me. No man puts a break like that back together."

Hannah called out to two nearby sailors, "You two there, get down in the hold and find one of my crates marked *Surgery*. Open it up, and bring a bottle of ether with you."

They both stared at her. It was obvious they could not read.

"Who here can read?" Hannah called out.

A very young sailor raised his hand.

"Then you go. The ether bottle is clearly marked *E-T-H-E-R*. Can you remember that?"

He nodded and set off at a run.

"And someone fetch my black bag from my cabin."

No one moved.

"Now!" she shouted, and two sailors set off in a panic.

Hannah closed her eyes, took a deep breath, then bent to Tinker's ear. "Tinker, are you a religious man?"

Through his shivers of pain, he shook his head no. "Ma'am, I ain't never had time for it."

Hannah placed her hand on his shoulder.

"That mean you ain't going to save the leg?" Tinker asked.

Her gentle laugh was reassuring. "No, Tinker, but I am going to pray for you first. Will you let me?"

"Go ahead," he gasped. "I ain't going nowhere particular at the moment."

She took his hand, surprised at the power of his grip. "Dear God," she began softly, "I am sure you have seen what happened here. Tinker is a good man, but he doesn't know you. I do. And I am asking you to guide my hands today. Heal Tinker's bone as I work. Use this to show your power. These men have never seen a miracle, and I pray that you will grant a miracle this day. Show these men your power and your truth."

Keeping her head bowed, she continued to hold his hand until voices interrupted her prayer.

"Here's the bottle."

"And here's your black bag."

Hannah snapped up. "Pull the lanterns close. Hand me a piece of cotton."

She had no time for precision. She sprinkled the cotton with the ether and placed it over Tinker's mouth. "Just breathe in, Tinker. This smells real sweet, but it'll take the pain away."

In a second, Tinker's eyes closed, and his head lolled to the side.

"Is he dead?" one sailor asked softly.

"No, just asleep. But come here and hold the cloth over his mouth–just like this."

And she took a scalpel, needle, and thread from her bag and bent to Tinker's leg and bone. She extracted several large splinters from the flesh, then positioned the leg just so and pulled from his ankle, drawing the bone together. She felt with her finger to make sure the break had lined up correctly. Satisfied, she aligned the open flesh back together and then threaded the needle. With the practiced skill of a woman who had done much embroidery, she stitched up the flesh and drew it tightly together.

Hannah looked up. "I forgot one thing. From that same crate are several tins marked *Carbolic Acid.* I need a pinch of it, dissolved in a cup of water." She addressed the young sailor. *"C-A-R-B-O-L-I-C A-C-I-D.* Can you remember?"

In less than two minutes, he was back.

She poured the liquid over the wound. "Now I need a half dozen straight stays–about this long," she said, indicating a length, "and several dozen lengths of thick canvas."

Within a half hour, she had fastened a tight splint about Tinker's leg.

"You can take the ether away," she finally ordered.

And within another few minutes, Tinker's eyes fluttered open.

Bending down, she said, "Your leg is in a splint. It won't hurt now, but it will in an hour or two. When the pain gets intense, call, and I will give you one of these laudanum pills."

He nodded, then reached for her. "Thanks," he whispered.

Hannah stood and said, "Now take him to a bed where he won't have to move his leg."

"Can he walk?" a sailor asked.

"Not for a long time," she answered.

Sam Macalus had watched the operation with veiled interest. "And he ain't ever goin' to walk. I'll be cuttin' that leg off soon enough. You mark my words."

Hannah faced him directly. "If God wants this healed, it will be healed."

And with that she turned and followed Tinker as they carried him to his bunk.

August 1855

"It pains me some, Miss Hannah, but I bet I'll soon be making my way up the ropes."

Tinker stood on the quarterdeck where Hannah sat in the sun, reading through a medical book.

"When you do, you must promise me that you'll be careful up there. I am sure that the leg may never be quite as strong as it once was."

He nodded to her and wiped his brow. As the ship neared the southern coast of California, the weather had turned sultry. The voyage had taken a few weeks longer than expected. They were forced to ride out a week-long gale in the port of Santiago in Chile, and ill winds dogged them for weeks afterward.

"It may not, but I can still walk. And that be the miracle."

Hannah shielded her eyes from the sun as she looked up at him. "It was God's miracle, you know."

Tinker leaned against the mast. "But, Miss Hannah, why would God do that for me? I ain't never really put much stock in him."

"Tinker, do you believe in him now?"

"Oh yes, I do. Ain't a man on this ship that didn't think I was a dead man when I fell. And now there ain't a man who don't know what God can do."

"Then that is why God used you that way."

"You think that be true?" Tinker said, brightening. "God used me?"

"I am certain he did," Hannah said. It was clear to her that God had used both Tinker and herself to bring an awareness to every sailor on the ship. Even Sam Macalus had attended one of Hannah's informal prayer and Bible meetings that she began soon after Tinker's accident. "He used both of us."

"But I only slipped. You did the fixing."

"Tinker, let me tell you a secret. When they laid you out on the table, and I looked at the wound, I should have let Sam do the cutting. I knew there was no chance I could fix what was broken."

Tinker appeared surprised. "That be true?"

"For breaks that severe, all the books I have ever read would recommend that the leg be taken off. Hard medicine is sometimes the best medicine."

"Then why did you do all that you did?"

The ship rolled in the wind and Tinker grabbed hold of the mast, shuffling on his bad leg. Hannah held tight to her chair. She would miss this constant motion.

"God told me."

"He did? Just like that? Came out and spoke to you?"

Hannah examined her hands, as if searching for an answer hidden there. "I don't know. I am new at this faith, too. But I knew, as soon as I heard you fall, that God had me here for just that reason. To show his power."

Tinker rubbed his chin. "Awful complicated, ain't it?"

Hannah laughed. "It may have been–but it worked on both of us, didn't it?"

A sailor standing at the stern of the vessel called out. "Tinker, get over here. Stop bothering Miss Hannah. You can talk to her tonight during the prayers."

Tinker shouted back that he would be there shortly.

Hannah had remarked on several occasions that the day Tinker first walked after the accident, virtually all cursing on the ship ceased. It was as if the sailors knew they were in the presence of a miracle and would not profane it with coarse language.

"Got to do my job, Miss Hannah." But as he started to leave, he turned back and said softly, "Miss Hannah, will there be a job at this hospital you're building for a man like me? I've been at sea too many years, and I believe I need to learn more about this God."

Hannah smiled. "Tinker, I think there will be."

"And I'll admit to any man that I ain't got the nerve up there I once had."

Hannah watched him walk away, a bit slower than a man might walk, and with a hint of a limp, but walking nonetheless.

FROM THE DIARY OF HANNAH COLLINS KEYES

SEPTEMBER 1855

I am on California soil!

It has been several months of great contrasts and surprises.

The weather is so idyllic, I wonder why any man would leave this coast. It is cool at night, pleasant at sunrise, and mild throughout the day. A breeze comes from the ocean, and the air always smells sweet and willing, unlike the fetid air of Philadelphia.

And the sights are nothing less than awe inspiring.

The sea changes from day to day, from hour to hour, but is always there, hushing against the shore. Clouds fill the sky and play catch with the sun. A lush, verdant strip of green foliage runs from the shore well inland. There is a scent of oranges and salt in the air.

And it has been so good to see old friends.

Gage was on the dock waiting. How good he looks! He is a little gray at the temples, a little more solid about the middle, but he has the same vitality and enthusiasm as I remembered. I was treated as visiting royalty. I believe most of the townsfolk came out that day, including the mayor, the city council, and even the lieutenant governor of the state.

I am glad Gage prepared them all for my arrival. This has been the first place where I have not encountered stares and incredulity and even hostility at being a woman who happens to be a doctor.

I believe they were all grateful for my presence. Monterey and its environs soon felt like home to me.

I brought Tinker ashore and told Gage he was the fourth employee of the hospital. I quickly set him attending to a hundred last-minute building details.

The hospital is perhaps the most beautiful I have ever seen. Situated on a rise, perhaps a half mile from the shore, the building is a long, two-story affair, with patients' quarters on the top floor. Large windows overlook the ocean and will provide a splendid view, improving a patient's recuperative powers and allowing the sea air to wash through each room. Doctors' quarters are below, and there are three large operating theaters–well lit and well ventilated. They are done in white tile so cleanliness will be easy to maintain.

To the side of the hospital, down a hillock, there is situated a modest cottage. It is nearly hidden by a grove of orange trees and overlooks a quiet sea pool. When I inquired as to the nature of the building, Gage told me with great delight that it was the home of the new head of the hospital. It took me several moments to realize that he meant me.

The home is so lovely. It is done in adobe, which is the Spanish style, and is a copy in miniature of Gage's massive residence on the far side of the harbor.

Within a day, under Gage's direction, everything I brought had been unloaded and organized. All my supplies were taken to the hospital and unpacked. Even my personal belongings were taken and placed in drawers and closets. Gage furnished the home, down to pillows, sheets, towels, and kitchenware.

In the first days, I have gotten the impression–mostly from Gage's maid and house manager–that I am somehow seen as Gage's intended.

Truly!

It was sad how he lost his beloved Nora, and I think I am seen as the second Mrs. Davis. "After all, you as a widow would know what it is like to be lonely," I have heard from more than one. Gage has not said a word about this, and I have searched his eyes for some confirmation, but he remains enigmatic.

His daughter Hope is the most beautiful child I have ever beheld. Like the rest of the village, I have fallen in love with her. She is bright and pretty and precocious and, from what I recall of Nora, her exact duplicate. But behind her gay eyes there is sadness–as if she is searching for something lost.

Does she see me as a new mother?

Such questions and quandaries.

But nothing can match the surprise and befuddlement of what I am about to describe:

I had been in Monterey only a week. I had begun to settle in, finding the grocer and baker and all the necessities of life. Folks had been to the hospital in a steady stream, all looking for an appointment to see me. Some matters of a serious nature I tended as needed. I did not want to leap into my new practice too soon after the voyage–and needed a few days' rest and acclimation to the surroundings.

Thus, I found myself at Gage's for dinner. It was a sumptuous repast and so unlike the bland and uninspired fare aboard ship.

Nearing the end of the dinner, Gage slapped his forehead and exclaimed that he had forgotten to pass on to me a letter in his possession. I asked who might have written to me here.

"Why, Jamison left it, of course," he said with no hint of explanation.

I immediately inquired as to the details.

"You missed him by two weeks," Gage added.

I expressed great shock at that fact.

"I thought you knew," Gage said. "He was on his way to the Sandwich Islands. He said he knew you left New York. He had taken the jungle route."

I am sure my shock was a surprise to Gage.

"You did not know he was heading west?" Gage asked.

I told him I knew so little of Jamison. Gage handed me the letter with an air of reluctance, as if he did not want me knowing what Jamison wrote. It was my first indication of any interest from Gage in that "man and woman" sense. I had the proper manners not to open the letter then and there–although I desired it–and I think Gage desired to know as well.

It was late that night when I found myself at home and alone. I slit the letter with an old scalpel. This is what Jamison wrote:

September 1855

My Dear Hannah,

I imagine you are a month behind me in reaching Monterey. I was told of your departure from New York by our friend Mr. Grossman. He informed me as to your discussion with him.

I took the jungle route, and I am quite gratified that you did not choose the same. A motley group of bandits set upon our little caravan. Two of our party were killed, and I barely escaped with my life. I do not write this to worry you, but to let you know that any delay going around the Strait of Magellan was well worth the extra miles and weeks.

I am on my way to the Sandwich Islands. The New York World *wants a series of articles on the island's royalty, who are supposed to be a most colorful family. Readers like such tales–exotic, flamboyant, with just a hint of intrigue and danger.*

So I am off to meet the Kamehamehas.

Then I am on to the land of China. From there I plan on returning home.

I have spent many hours thinking about what to write next and how to explain myself.

If you spoke to Mr. Grossman, and if he is telling the truth–and of that I am not totally certain–then you know that I have not been completely honest with you.

I can offer no defense of my actions other than the fact that you were married, and I thought it best if I stayed away. That separation was for my benefit, not yours. And when I heard that you were widowed, I continued to stay away. It was fear that kept me from you and fear that kept me telling you tales.

You might look at my life and imagine that I have no fears–fighting off bandits and Indians and the like.

I have no qualms about those dangers. They are physically real, and one is able to confront them face-to-face. A man wins and walks away. A man loses and lays dead. Either way, the solution and resolution are quite readily discernible.

But there is another whole genre of fears that immobilizes me.

It is the fear of that "something next to friendship."

It is not love, but something else altogether.

I think of you and the darkness nibbles at my heart, saying I have no right to be friends with a woman as noble and beautiful as you. The darkness takes hold of me and reduces me to such a loathing that I avoid such encounters even though my heart cries out for such.

I am botching this letter so, but I know that a second draft would be more muddled than the first.

Perhaps you will understand what I have said. I am not certain I do.

When I return, perhaps you will consent to see me. Perhaps then I may be able to explain fully.

I promise to return.

Yours,

Jamison Pike

He thinks of me as beautiful!

Hannah stared out at the dark flatness of the Pacific, where the moon glistened off the waves.

And if it is not friendship or love, then what must it be?

She carefully refolded the letter and tucked it into the pages of her Bible. Her hand remained on the closed cover until the church bell in the village chimed midnight.

CHAPTER TWENTY-ONE

Monterey, California
April 1856

FROM just beyond the window of her bedchamber there came a delicate, yet insistent fluttering. Hannah leaned up on her elbows on the bed. The sun barely cleared the mountains to the east, and light poured into the coastal valleys. She blinked several times. The fluttering, a feathery beating, continued.

She slipped out of bed and snatched her robe. It was not for the weather that she did so, for it was temperate this day–as all days had been since her arrival, she thought. She sought her robe for the sake of modesty and decorum. Most arrivals to California soon found the less restrictive manner of dress to be preferable to the high button necks and long sleeves of the East. But Hannah had not succumbed to the temptations. She wore the dresses that she traveled with from Philadelphia–proper dresses with high collars and tight sleeves.

She had been nearly shocked to find women wearing trousers, just like men wore, and riding horses, just like men did.

She smiled when she shook her head in outrage, knowing her reaction would be similar to Elizabeth Collins' response, had she seen a similar sight. Hannah wondered how often she had warned herself never to do what she had just done–behave exactly like her mother.

She drew the robe about her neck and chest, cinched it tight, and peeked out the window over a shrub.

The wind was from the sea and carried a hint of salt and the perfume of hibiscus bushes along the shore. The sky was bluer and clearer than the skies had ever been in Philadelphia, Hannah thought.

The fluttering continued and became more insistent.

Hannah pushed the branches of the shrub apart and peered in. Near the base a brown thrashing rattled the branches.

It was a little brown and red bird that had become ensnared in a length of fisherman's line. She hurried outside and stopped as she rounded the far side of the house.

Perhaps I have changed, she thought, *for back in Philadelphia, I would have died before I left the house in a robe.*

She bent to her knees and wrapped her hand about the tiny, frightened creature. She secured the twine to her finger and pulled, drawing the bird close to her face. Its eyes were frantic. The twine was tight about the one leg and wing.

"How did you manage to get so far and so tangled?" Hannah cooed as she carried it back inside. She found her old scalpel and carefully cut the twine. There was a slight tear in the skin of the foot, she saw, but what troubled her more was the odd tilt of the bird's wing. She gently touched it and tried to extend it. The bird fluttered again and chirped loudly as it turned, attempting to peck Hannah's finger.

She smoothed the small head and unconsciously began to rock back and forth, ever so slightly. The bird squirmed a bit but slowly grew calm and still.

I wonder if I can find a birdcage in town?

She rose and walked into her bedchamber.

If anyone would know, Tinker would.

With one hand, she emptied out all her stockings from a drawer in her dresser, spread a towel inside, carefully placed the bird on the towel, and gently closed the drawer, cooing all the while. The bird sat and watched with some interest. Hannah left the tiniest crack open for air. She peered down close and saw the bird's black eye blink twice, then close as if to take a nap.

And as Hannah hurriedly dressed, she found herself whistling.

"Another wee wild one?" Tinker said, laughing.

"I think its wing might be broken," Hannah said as she explained her need for a birdcage. "But it might only be bruised."

Tinker wiped his hands. He had just finished a repair on the hand pump for the hospital. "Miss Hannah," he said as he slipped the stained rag back into his trousers, "you got to stop thinking you can save everyone. A bird like that–well, nature should do the deciding–not you."

Hannah crossed her hands over her crisp white smock. "Tinker, it is what I do. Now, do you think you can find a birdcage for me? Or must I visit every merchant in town myself?"

Tinker held up his hands in surrender. "I'm going. I believe Bell's got one. How much will you allow me to spend on one?"

Hannah laughed. "More than you'd like, I am sure. Now go. I have rounds to do, and that bird wants its new home by lunch."

Tinker walked away, shaking his head.

FROM THE DIARY OF HANNAH COLLINS KEYES
APRIL 1856

My new rescue is happily bouncing about in the birdcage Tinker found at a decent price. He says the bird is a Williamson Thrush–and is native to England. How he got blown this far off course is anyone's guess.

I suspect that some might make the same inquiry about me. And if they did, what manner of answer could I provide?

It is April, and I am sitting outside looking at the ocean in my bare feet. My mother would be aghast at a woman without shoes in the middle of the day. Yet it is such a delicious feeling (though I feel a twinge of guilt).

I am set on two new nurses for the hospital. Neither has much training, but both are a compassionate sort. Perhaps that is the most necessary qualification for nursing anyone back to health. And with these two young women, this hospital that Gage has built is now fully staffed and equipped. There are the two other doctors I hired in addition to myself, and a small cadre of nurses and cooks and cleaners and groundskeepers and the like. There are folks who have traveled here from San Francisco for treatment–which is a testimony to our good works.

Monterey is a wonderful town, situated as it is along the calm bay and warm waters. There is a fair number of eccentrics here, but most seem to be of a gentle nature and spirit. Tinker, of all people, has been my ears and eyes into the community. He tells me the latest gossip (which I often tell him I do not wish to hear–but he rambles on regardless) and lets me know who might need a physician's call. There are many here who think going to a doctor is but one step from going to the coroner. We are doing our best to change that way of thought.

I will always be in Tinker's debt for one thing he has done: He has told the story of his fall and brokenness and recovery to nearly everyone who will stand still long enough to listen. That miracle–for it was not of my hand but of God's–has elevated my stature and respect more than any other thing that I could have imagined.

People now see me as a healer and are more willing to seek out my help–all because of Tinker's tale.

And I am also in his debt for the number of good citizens who have inquired about his faith and my faith. One grizzled prospector came to me, limping badly. He spit out his tobacco and said, "I heard what you did to that sailor." Then he pointed to his leg. "Can you do the same for me?"

There was no break but a lesion on his calf that I cut away, stitched, and cleaned. Within a week, the fellow was on his feet again.

That was not the miracle–it was that he accepted the gift of God's love and forgiveness while the surgery healed.

God's grace and timing are so wondrous.

Yet in all of this, I am still most unsettled at times. Yes, I know I am a child of God and not in risk of losing that faith. But . . .

I should be able to share my thoughts in my diary, for I know no one will read them. Yet I hesitate.

I met with Pastor Kenyon last week. He laughed and hugged me and thanked me for all the new converts who are streaming into his church. "Without you, I would be preaching to many empty pews."

He is wrong, of course, for he is a gifted pastor, and I have little credit in building his rolls.

However, something is missing in my heart. I often fret about my parents and have written them several letters with nary a single response as of yet. I ask for forgiveness, yet none is given. Will I ever find peace?

And then I often think of Robert and tears come. I know that I promised him more than I could give. Perhaps his rage was a result of my not giving enough. Perhaps I should not have been so hard-headed in my determination to become a doctor.

And as his mother claimed, would he still be alive if I had simply become a wife who remained at home?

Such thoughts often plague me in the middle of the night. I wake and listen to the waves and the wind and think how different my life has become from what I once imagined.

Back at the Destiny everything seemed simple and easy. Life would remain smooth and uncomplicated, I was sure. That dream remained a dream.

Pastor Kenyon told me that an individual's life and actions cannot and should not determine another's happiness or satisfaction, and it is foolish to hold the guilt that I hold. He says that if my parents are unhappy, that is because of their actions and choices, not mine. I nod and I understand what he means, but still my heart is torn.

How many people have suffered simply because I refused to abandon my dream?

Pastor Kenyon says I need to stop looking backward. He says I need to look forward. He says I am still a young woman and need to be aware of the rest of my life, not just what happened in the past.

He is a smart and tender man, but I am not certain I can do what he asks.

I know Gage has not orchestrated this, but I think Pastor Kenyon and the rest of the village would have me and Gage married by the end of the year. I have dined with Gage on numerous occasions–after all, he is the patron of the hospital. He is lonely at times. I see that in his eyes. He has stated as much as well.

But he has his daughter, and she is a rare delight. I might consider a relationship with Gage just to maintain my closeness with Hope. We play and take walks together, and sometimes I feel an emptiness inside myself.

The child I lost has never once left my thoughts. She is always there. Every day of every week of every year, the loss of my own daughter is there at the edge of my consciousness. What would the child have looked like if she had lived? How I wished I had seen her.

There is a pain in my heart like walking on splintered glass.

I have never mentioned this to another soul. The past is the past, they would say, and life is for the living. All that is true. Yet I wonder if this emptiness in my life will ever be filled.

Tinker and Gage and my work at the hospital have been a wonderful tonic, but I am still empty. I look to the Scriptures and they provide some comfort, but I am still lonely and lost.

And yet no one knows it, and I do my utmost to keep it hidden. It would not be right to complain and grow tearful in public. I must deal with these problems by myself.

Monterey, California
July 1856

Tinker shoved the handle of the operating table. Something had jammed in the gearing so the platform could neither raise nor lower.

Hannah had been forced to find a stool on which to stand as she operated. Now that the patient was upstairs recuperating, Hannah and Tinker were struggling with the balky equipment.

"I believe I heard you say that this brand was the best," Tinker complained as he pulled the gear.

"It is," Hannah insisted. "I paid a great premium for this model. They claimed it would operate for years with no problems."

Tinker rapped a lever with a small hammer. "They lied to you, Miss Hannah."

She sighed.

"But don't despair. I'll fix it. Just take a bit of time." He reached in and rapped it again.

Hannah leaned heavily against the wall and slowly slid to the floor. Tinker whacked at the machine a few more times, then looked over at Hannah. "You don't look good, Miss Hannah. Coming down with something?"

"No, I'm fine, Tinker. But thanks."

Scratching his nose, he stopped and stared at her.

She stared back with a wan smile. "What?" she asked.

Tinker shrugged. "I was just wondering."

"Wondering what?"

"I can't ask. It be too personal, I'm afraid."

Hannah sighed again. "Tinker, I am a doctor. There is not much 'personal' that I have not seen."

Laughing, he said, "It's not that kind of personal."

"Tinker," she asked, "is it a man and woman sort of personal?"

He nodded.

"Does it have to do with love?"

He nodded again.

"Are you in love? Is it that kind of personal?"

Tinker snorted a laugh. "Land sakes no, Miss Hannah. Me? No. That ain't it at all."

She sighed one more time. She often tired of drawing out information from reluctant men. As a doctor, she faced the task myriad times daily. *Men,* she thought, *have no business learning the language, for they use it so seldom.* Some of her patients went so far as to have a friend come in, complain of their ailment, and pass on the medicine or treatment required. Hannah could never understand why they could get more personal for another and not themselves, but such was the case.

"Tinker . . . just ask me the question. I am too tired today for parlor guessing games."

He reddened. "Well . . . I guess I wondered why you and Mr. Davis ain't married yet. Nearly everybody in Monterey thinks you're going to. Ain't he asked you yet? And land sakes, you ain't said no, have you, Miss Hannah?"

Not sure of whether to laugh or cry, Hannah just shook her head.

FROM THE DIARY OF HANNAH COLLINS KEYES

JULY 1856

How does one answer such a bold query as Tinker made today?

Should I have laughed? Should I have been offended?

I must forgive Tinker, for he is a simple man in many ways. (But then, are not all men simple in the ways of emotions?) He means well, for he truly is my friend.

But Gage has not asked, nor do I think he will.

It was just last night that we enjoyed a lovely dinner at his home. It is always open, and many friends drop by every night. I was the only one formally invited, but by the time Rosala had dinner on the table, there were twelve in attendance.

After all had left, Gage and I sat on the second-floor veranda. We stared at the vastness of the star-filled sky. The sea was so still that the heavens were doubled in reflection. A sliver of moon arched to the east.

I was not sure how it occurred, but Gage was nearly at my side.

"Beautiful night," he told me.

"Indeed. A bit of chill," I said.

Within a heartbeat, he had draped his arm over my shoulder and held me close.

"This will be warmer," he said.

And while he held me, I think we both expected something to occur, some revelation. This was the first time since my arrival that such a thing has happened–touching another man–other than in my medical practice, that is. (And that, for certain, does not count as the same thing.)

We stood there, with his arm about my shoulders, looking into the darkness for many minutes. Then I said that I must leave, for I had an early surgery set for the morning. He nodded and removed his arm.

It was no different than if a brother or cousin had his arm about my shoulder.

At least I think so.

Does Gage view it as different? If so, he has given me such little to draw on.

Men . . . how difficult they are to understand.

And then Tinker's query has me questioning matters. Am I too cold and reserved? Have I waited a long enough time? Should I even concern myself with such things . . . pleasures of the flesh, as my mother would sneer?

And if the entire village thinks we should be married, then is that a sign of some sort?

It is not what I would expect a sign from God to look like, but then so many things from God are not as I expected them.

How could I have imagined that I might find God because of poor Lawrence? (And I think I might have found Lawrence. I sent a letter to Eureka–in the northern part of the state. A sailor whom I treated claimed that he met a fellow by the same name. If it is, I will demand that he visit me. Regardless of the nature of his failings and sin, I still value his friendship. Perhaps out here he has turned from his vices.)

And as I read all this, I look to my past. My father, a cold and distant man, made colder and more distant by his weaknesses and failures, looms large in my thoughts. I have not once felt truly loved by him and see that as a reason for my own need to be loved. As I ponder such things, I wonder if I merely imagine Gage's interest in me. Am I merely seeking the approval of a man, since I never received such approval from my own father?

Or are such thoughts mere feminine muddling?

I do not know, but I will attempt, now, to be more deliberate with Gage. If he has such interests, I should be direct. After all, the years are passing, and it is a fallacy to think I grow more desirable.

And he does have a daughter who might call me *Mother*.

Would that fill the hole in my heart?

Such questions. I had hoped life would grow easier as I aged, but it surely does not.

Monterey, California
July 1856

Hannah selected a thinner dress made from cotton, with short sleeves and an open bodice.

I am not becoming less modest, she told herself as she looked in the mirror in her bedchamber. *But I am becoming a realist. The weather here is most temperate, and there is no need to be shielded from the cold. And this is still not an immodest dress.*

She stepped out into the golden afternoon.

It was not common for her to have a free afternoon, but the hospital was only half filled and Doctors Neuman and Ballantine would have matters well in hand.

And there is a time when authority must be practiced in order to develop further. It is time for them to assume the mantle of responsibility.

There was a narrow lane that led from Hannah's house to the main road that curved toward the water and Monterey. On a good day it was a pleasant fifteen-minute stroll, and it was a stroll Hannah took with great infrequency. Tinker handled most of her requirements, and the Chinese grocer delivered foodstuffs to her twice a week. Hannah would have claimed in her own defense that working in the hospital was so demanding that she had little time for shopping and such civilities. And the hospital did require much of her. But Hannah had another reason not to visit town often.

She knew the town's citizens expected her to marry Gage Davis, and that made Hannah nervous and hesitant to show her face.

But this morning was so beautiful, she thought, and her hospital tasks so light, that she decided she could no longer be forced into the life of a recluse just because a few people imagined they knew what was best for her.

And even if Gage would view me that way, I am so perplexed by this situation that I do not see the matter clearly anymore. It's time to venture out boldly and let God show me the life he wants me to lead.

She carried no bag, purse, or medical instrument and felt remarkably light and unfettered. The village spread about the harbor, streets and buildings fanning outward from the water like a spiderweb. The harbor bobbed with a profusion of vessels–some small fishing skiffs, some large three-masted schooners, and two steamships, each wearing a hat of smoke and steam. Longshoremen and teamsters hustled about, loading and unloading crates and cargo with jumbled shouts and calls. Hannah could hear the low moan of cattle and sheep. Many whaling ships made Monterey a port of call on their route from San Francisco to the Sandwich Islands. When she saw them, she could not help but think of Jamison, across the vast expanse of water, so very far away.

She skirted the harbor by two streets. As in most harbors, the closer the water, the less savory the atmosphere. She had heard that four or five shops, new within the last two months, had opened on Pacific Street. Hannah did not need new frocks, but it had been months since she had visited to see the current styles.

For nearly the entire morning, she took in one shop after another, chatting with the clerks, discovering new cuts and fabrics, discussing the changes to Monterey, talking about the hospital, dispensing medical advice, and gathering news in general.

"I have heard Tinker speak of a new restaurant called

McCormick's," Hannah said to Mrs. Carolyn Allen, the new proprietor of The Allen Rose Shoppe.

"I would not eat there unless you held a weapon to my head," she said haughtily.

Hannah was surprised, for Tinker had gone on and on about the merits of the food and atmosphere.

"I think it might be a meeting place for . . . well, for those manner of women," Mrs. Allen whispered, arching her brows in a nudge.

Hannah had not imagined Tinker to be that sort of man. Flustered, she said, "Well, then, Mrs. Allen, where might you suggest?"

Mrs. Allen took Hannah by the arm, steered her to the front door, and pointed down Pacific Street. "See the green awning down there? That is Forrester and Crumb. It is a delightful place. Reminds me of the tearooms back in Charleston. A lady would have no problems there dining alone."

Hannah thanked her.

"And you will give some thought to the green dress, will you not? It would look stunning with your hair."

"I promise I will, Mrs. Allen," Hannah replied. The dress had looked wonderful on her, she admitted to herself, and was quite striking with her hair. But it was more than Hannah had ever spent on a single outfit.

Hannah walked leisurely, enjoying the pleasant day. She peered in the window of a new notions shop and a store selling all manner of men's furnishings. A sign on a vacant storefront gave her great joy. It announced that a new bookseller would be taking possession of this space within a fortnight and would feature the latest works of current writers, such as Charles Dickens and Harriet Beecher Stowe, as well as all the latest magazines.

Hannah slipped in to a table overlooking the harbor at Forrester and Crumb. The air was fragrant with the heady scent of tea and oranges.

"Hannah?"

She turned around. "Gage," she replied brightly, then whispered, "what are you doing here? I thought this was a tearoom. Do men go to tearooms?"

Gage laughed. "Do you mind if I join you?"

"I would love to have the company."

"And men do go to tearooms–if they produce the same manner of delicious scones as this cook does. I haven't tasted anything like it since I left New York."

He looked about, then leaned over to Hannah. "You must promise to never tell Rosala, but I get homesick for New York food at times. Rosala is a wonderful cook, but when she attempted scones at my insistence, they tasted much like tortillas."

The two fell into guilty giggles.

After three plates of finger sandwiches and two full plates of scones, Hannah finally said, "Enough."

She never would have asked for a second or a third order of sandwiches–even though she may have wanted them and did eat most of them. It would have been unladylike to have done so.

"I am glad you have eaten your fill, Hannah. I have to say that you have looked a little drawn as of late. The hospital is too demanding."

She shook her head. "Not now. At first, yes, but not now. It is just that cooking and preparing meals for one is such a lonely business."

"Then why not take the cook I offered?"

Hannah stiffened a bit. "Oh, Gage. Must we discuss this again? I have no need for a servant. I am a single woman who can take care of herself. A servant would fade from boredom in my house."

"But a cook would do you good. Provide proper meals and all."

Hannah crossed her arms. "The matter is settled, Gage. No servants."

He shrugged in surrender. "Then come to my house more often for dinner. There is always a crowd, and I would love to have you join us."

"You are such a dear friend. Perhaps I will. I have been too sequestered as of late."

"You have been, Hannah," Gage said tenderly. "When I asked you to come to Monterey, it was not my desire to see you work so hard. You must enjoy life."

"I do, Gage. I do."

He shook his head. "Not nearly enough, Hannah. God desires us to be joyful and filled with laughter."

Hannah looked away. A minute passed.

Gage touched her hand. "What is it, Hannah? Did I say something in error? Why have you grown so silent?"

She faced him again, and there was a tear in her eye. "You know, Gage. You of all people know."

He stared at her. Then he nodded. "Let me guess. When you laugh you feel as if you are betraying Robert?"

She nodded and wiped her tear.

"It has been years, Hannah. No one can grieve for a lifetime. You must go on. You must seek out joy."

"I try, Gage. I do. But I think of Robert . . . and maybe even more of the child I lost–and then the joy evaporates. And I don't know what to do about it."

He squeezed her hand. "Maybe men are better at hiding things . . . and I do have Hope."

She sniffed loudly in reply.

They gazed at each other for a long moment.

"I don't know what words to say to you, Hannah. All I know is that God has touched my heart. The hurt isn't gone. Maybe it will never be gone. But he wants the living to go on living. I can weep no more for Nora. I will always love her. But I can shed no more tears."

Hannah lowered her head and hid her eyes.

"Maybe you should talk to Joshua. Remember how skilled he was at getting at the truth? Remember how crazed you made him in our late nights at the Destiny with your talk of Brook Farm and all those odd eccentrics?"

Hannah laughed through a sob. "Oh, I do. I do."

Gage hesitated, then embraced Hannah.

Hannah closed her eyes and wrapped her arms about him so very tight, drawing him as close to her as a man had ever been.

From a Letter to Hannah Keyes
Monterey, California
October 1856

My Dear Hannah,

I may have written books and scribbled a thousand words under pressure of a deadline, but none intimidate me as much as penning a simple letter to a friend.

How I wish I had made a copy of the last letter I sent, for I think I need to correct a dozen misconceptions.

I am penning this in a tiny restaurant on the docks of Hong Kong. While I am not the tallest man in America, here I am–other than for sailors and foreign merchants. Most everywhere I go, I attract a small army of curious children. It is odd being such a center of attention. I have found that my best work is when I can stand in the background and observe without being observed.

That will never happen here–and since I need to travel with an interpreter at all times, I will not disappear in this land.

While I could write a multitude of pages on this place and its oddities, I suspect that is not the type of letter you wish from me. And if you do want to read of my travels, you have only to find the New York World. *They will begin the series as soon as the pages reach them.*

When I left, I knew I was but a few weeks prior to your arrival.

Do not hate me, but I left, with purpose, before having to see you again.

I sat on Gage's veranda overlooking the ocean and played with sweet little Hope and realized I had no right to be there. I know he and I are friends, but I saw in his eyes a longing. And I believe that longing was for you, Hannah. And now having expressed the thought, I hate myself for it, for it is as if we are not considering your heart.

But I write of the world as I know it, and this is the truth.

Gage is searching. I know that he is. Hope needs a mother. And it is no good for you to be alone. Perhaps as you read this letter, you will have come to the same conclusion. Gage is a good man, Hannah. He will be a good husband. And Hope needs a loving female in her life (besides Rosala, that is).

Promise me that you will save a wedding dance for me, Hannah. You have my blessings.

Your friend,
Jamison

As Hannah read the letter she stood up and began to pace.

When she came to the last lines, her teeth ground together. She read Jamison's tight signature and, in a flash, crumpled the letter into a ball and hurled it across the room.

"You give me permission?" she yelled out loud.

She ran over to the crumpled letter, picked it up, and hurled it again.

"I have your *blessings* to marry Gage?"

Hannah stepped to the letter and threw it once more, her anger increasing, her face reddening.

"Jamison Pike! You are the most thickheaded man I have ever known!"

And then she threw the letter again, letting it stay crumpled on the floor.

"And I don't care if you ever come back!"

CHAPTER TWENTY-TWO

Monterey, California
January 1857

HANNAH took back every thought she had had about the permanent and constant warmth of Monterey. For the past month, since before Christmas, a fog had settled in about the land and with it brought wisps of bone-chilling wind. To Hannah it was every bit as cold as the worst blizzard in Philadelphia. Even a roaring fire did little to dissuade the dampness from clamping on one's bones and holding on like a famished dog.

Hannah walked about her house, wearing all the shawls she owned and several pairs of stockings, and kept her fireplace constantly stocked with cords of wood. It must have been amusing to others who were more acclimated–for while Hannah wore mittens, hats, and coats, others went about their business in shirtsleeves.

Hannah stopped going to town, for the sight of anyone without a coat and hat brought a new round of shivers to her frame.

"Is there a warmer place to live, Tinker?" she asked as he delivered another cord of wood to her house.

"Plenty. The Sandwich Isles. The lands of New Guinea. All throughout the Pacific. Why do you ask, Miss Hannah?"

"I keep praying that God will send me to such a temperate place, and all he brings is additional sheets of rain and fog. It is nice to know there are warmer climes than this."

"There be plenty warmer," he said, sweat coloring his shirt.

"Perhaps I shall pack my bags and depart on the high tide."

Tinker stood and arched his back and then bent, as he often did, to massage his leg where the break scarred his flesh.

"Does it hurt?"

"A minor irritation, Miss Hannah. And when the weather turns damp like this, I notice the twinge now and again. But no more than any ache and pain of a man my age, I must guess." He dumped another barrow full of split logs. "And you might be a touch serious about traveling to the warm?"

She tried to laugh. "No, I imagine I am not. Just wistful thinking."

He rubbed his chin. "I ain't one to be calling you on this, Miss Hannah, but things like praying for a warmer place–even in a jesting manner–well, I think that mightn't be the most prudent manner of praying."

Hannah tossed two more logs on the fire. "You're right, Tinker. I should not even speak lightly of such things."

He nodded. "I bet God has a way of hearing things that we sort of only half mean in our prayers. I hope he knows that you've been being playful is all."

"I am sure he does, Tinker. I am sure he does."

He dumped the final barrow of logs on the large pile. "That should hold you the season, Miss Hannah."

She arched her brows in surprise. "The season? They might not even last the week."

He laughed as he waved good-bye to her and trundled the barrow up the hill to the hospital.

When she arrived home that evening, after a full day of rounds and appointments at the hospital, there was a frayed and stained envelope on the table by the front door.

She seldom locked any door and most likely could not locate the key if asked. Tinker and Mr. Bell, to whose store letters were often delivered, might place personal correspondence to her in such a spot.

She laid her bag in the corner, where she always placed it–just in case it might need to be located quickly in an emergency. The envelope looked worn, as if it had traveled a long way on its journey to her.

As she saw the handwriting, her heart jumped.

It was a letter from Jamison.

Holding it in her hands for the longest time, Hannah debated whether or not to open it immediately or to let it lay unopened for the next few hours as an unsatisfying way to punish the man who wrote the letter.

Hannah walked into the kitchen for a moment, then returned and picked the envelope up again. She held it close to her face. The cancellation was from a place called *Lahaina.* The heavy brown paper envelope was creased and watermarked. She turned it over, and there was a dark blue circle of sealing wax–still intact.

Hannah looked about the room, as if attempting to see if she were under observation or not.

"Hannah, this is foolish," she said aloud. "He is not here to be punished. And you know you will open it eventually. Why waste the entire night playing cat and mouse with it? You should just open it."

And she did, slipping her finger under the flap. The wax broke in blue splinters and spilled into her cupped hand. Within the envelope there was a single sheet of coarse brown paper, lined heavily with Jamison's bold strokes.

The letter was dated only a month prior.

Dear Hannah,

I know you have not married Gage.

There was a ship's captain here who had just sailed from Monterey and claimed some friendship with Gage. That does not surprise me, for Gage appears to know everyone.

He claimed no wedding had taken place, nor did he view any obvious preparations in progress, or hear of any townsfolk gossiping about such an event.

I state these things for a reason.

I am here on the island of Maui in the small archipelago of the Sandwich Isles. It was a scheduled stop as part of my story on the island's royalty, since they are in residence here. I was planning on staying only a fortnight, but there is an element here that has bid me to remain longer.

There is some manner of illness or disease that is killing the natives. It is the children who seem to be most affected and suffer the longest and loudest. I have been on this soil for only a week and have been witness to a dozen funeral pyres. The wailing colors the air during the day.

I have no skill in this, and the native doctors are no better than charlatans and fools. Even the missionaries with some medical training are befuddled. Death is too much with us. And I have seen too much of death in my travels to ignore it. I know you have faith to deal with such matters, but I am not sure. Are we not to stop and help where and when we can?

And that is what I am doing.

I have no right to ask this of you.

But I will.

Can you sail to Maui as soon as you are in receipt of this letter?

If not, I have fear that this island will soon be devoid of children–and that all these islands will lose their future, indeed.

I have paid handsomely for this letter to be taken to you. The captain altered his itinerary from the port of Seattle to Monterey for this. Time is of the essence.

If you cannot attend to this, can you please send me books or equipment or written advice on how to deal with such a calamity?

Your friend,
Jamison Pike
Fodor's Tavern and Inn
The Port of Lahaina
The Island of Maui
The Sandwich Islands

Hannah stood as she read the letter and looked west, out over the vastness of the Pacific. Without evaluating the implications, she began to scratch out a list on the back of the envelope that carried Jamison's letter.

FROM THE DIARY OF HANNAH COLLINS KEYES
JANUARY 1857

Of course I should not undertake this journey. I know that even as I attend to the last-minute details of the journey. I have no ties to this island and these natives.

And Jamison . . . why, he all but married me off to Gage. I am certain he would have settled for any doctor to offer aid.

So then why do I go? Why have I set upon all provisioners and merchants and medical suppliers with a frenzy to locate precious supplies so I might make an early sailing at the beginning of the next month?

I have no true answer that stands under the cold clear light of logic.

Perhaps it is all Tinker's fault–but saying that even a playful prayer is answered by the Almighty seems a bit ludicrous. But, land sakes, how much of a coincidence is needed to see the hand of God in it? I ask for a warmer place, and that very day, after Tinker invokes God's listening, I receive a summons to just such a place that is in desperate need of my skills.

Is this how I uphold the promise of my life?

Perhaps it is.

When I explained all to Gage, I could see a misting revelation in his eyes. It was as if he had suddenly become aware that he and I would not be the pair as envisioned by the rest of Monterey. It is so curious. And I believe I felt it as well–and at the same instant. A look passed between us that indicated to me Gage is not who God would have me with. It was not an audible word from God. But it was certain and direct.

And I do not think it will be Jamison instead. I am most certain of that. It is my estimation that God may use me as I am–like the apostle Paul, who remained unmarried so he could serve with alacrity and dispatch wherever it was that God called.

If I were to be married–to anyone–then I would not be able to undertake this journey.

And Jamison, by the strokes of his last letter, all but admitted that he has not himself found belief in God.

So Gage hugged me as a brother and wished me well. He, of course, has done much more than that. He expedited supplies and found a fast ship and paid for much of it. He is such a generous person. After his loss, he has said, he sees no earthly reason to hoard his fortune. Rather, in giving it away he can best serve God.

And now I am told that the sailing will be within the next fortnight. Winds are favorable, and the sea is ready.

I am not sure I am ready, but I am going through this door God has opened. He has promised to take care of his children and that if we simply trust in him, he will lead us to our place of service.

And that is what I have done.

On Board the Alberta and Comstock
February 1857

There was no hesitation in Hannah at all as the ship plowed through warm winds. She stowed her gear and sought out the breeze and sun on the foredeck of the ship. She paid no attention to the looks of the crew, who saw her as a great oddity, or other passengers, who viewed her as addled by spending so much time in the open air.

Every slip upward of temperature brought a broader smile of relief to her face. She leaned back, feeling the sun dry out the dampness of her bones.

How could I have ever lived in Cambridge and Philadelphia? she wondered. *How could I ever face snow and sleet and harsh cold again?*

Beneath decks lay a dozen large containers, filled with the latest medicines and equipment. Hannah had no knowledge of tropical ailments and so spent the days at sea reading through a stack of medical books and journals tailored to that specific subject.

For what one book described as dengue fever, another would describe differently, offering a new name and a new cause and an entirely different treatment.

Hannah was a realist. There would be many diseases that had no cure or palliative treatment. Even a skilled doctor would often find frustration at the ravages of an illness. She knew she might find a situation she could not treat or solve. But in addition to being a realist, Hannah was practical and observant. If a patient lost fluids in any manner, Hannah would insist that the fluids be replenished through broth or tea. If a patient suffered high fever, Hannah would try immersion in cooling baths. If a patient suffered great chills, Hannah would warm and wrap a patient until the fit passed.

Hannah knew God desired that a body might knit itself back together–given care and time and tenderness. It was a doctor's duty to treat the patient as God would have that patient treated–with love and compassion.

Not all physicians saw her treatment as expeditious.

Some doctors tried to accelerate those same symptoms, helping the body do what it seemed to desire to do. So if a patient began to lose fluids, the doctors might prescribe further heating, to sweat more of the poisons out of the body. If a patient was hot, they would increase the heat to help drive out the impurities.

Some would practice bloodletting on every patient, expecting that the ill humors would be drawn off in the spilt blood. To Hannah, this was foolishness. As she watched patients being bled, she would observe they became weaker and weaker. Often death was the ultimate result.

She could never accommodate the two observations: If a patient lost much blood in an accident of some sort, that patient would always die, and if a weakened patient suffered under a bloodletting, then that patient often died as well.

Hannah was the sort of physician who searched for other reasons.

So as she read through the dense texts, she realized that no one treatise understood all the mechanics of every illness. She did not despair over that fact. She simply realized that she faced a great uncertainty and that if God would help her, she would be of use.

"How long till we arrive, Captain Killeen?" Hannah asked as she sipped her tea. Tea drinking was not the dainty activity it was on land. The cook brewed up a large pot of stiff tea, laced with honey. Then it was poured into deep cups, only filled halfway. A full cup might slosh and spill. A half full cup rarely did.

Captain Killeen shrugged as he scanned the horizon with his brass telescope. "The winds have been powerful in right directions. If they stay favorable, we be there in three days. They turn against us, the voyage lasts two weeks."

"Then I shall say a prayer for favorable winds," Hannah said. "I have prayed every day for good travel, and every day God has answered my prayers."

The captain smiled and lowered his telescope. "If God does your bidding as he has this voyage, then I shall commission you on every such journey. If we make landfall as I think we might, it will be the fastest traverse I have ever done."

Hannah held on to the railing as the ship pitched forward into the valley of a wave. "It is not me; it is the Almighty. I believe he wants these medicines on the island of Maui. And if he wants something, nothing that man or nature can do will deny him."

"You believe that?"

"The efficacy of prayer? I most certainly do, Captain. Without such support, we would all surely perish."

He stepped closer. "I heard what you did with that sailor on your voyage to California."

Hannah appeared surprised.

"Miss, there ain't that many sailors. Word travels most quickly."

"It must indeed," Hannah said, "for it occurred so long ago now."

"Sailors don't have much else to talk about, I imagine."

Both dipped as the ship clipped back up the swell of a large wave.

"So then it's true. That you healed him? That the flesh came together in a moment?"

Hannah laughed. "It's not quite that dramatic. But it was a miracle. Would you like me to tell you the story?"

"Would you, ma'am? I would be grateful."

"This evening then, at the general mess. I would be honored if I could address you and your crew."

The captain appeared to almost blush. "They would love to hear from you, ma'am . . . you being such an attractive woman and all."

"I am just a servant, Captain."

"That too," he said. "Until this evening, then."

As Hannah watched him hurry away, she was reminded again of the ever widening ripples of her life. A simple decision to follow God's urging continued to impact and change people's lives.

Perhaps this evening she might find a ready heart or two as well.

"Off the stern, Cap'n! There be land! That be Maui," the ship's lookout shouted from his perch on the main mast.

Hannah ran to the rail and squinted into the morning sun. There was a jagged green line at the horizon. They had passed the northernmost tip of the Sandwich Isles at the previous day's end. From the middle of the island there were several plumes of dark smoke.

"The smoke there, Captain, what might that be?" Hannah asked.

"Could be whalers rendering blubber. Could be funeral pyres as well. The land has a sickness. That be one reason we ain't spending more than a few days in harbor this time. We're setting your supplies off and sailing away."

Hannah nodded.

The island glistened like a green gem in a field of azure blue. There was a jagged mountain range at each end of the island, joined by a long flat plain of land between the heights. The northern mountain looked steeper and had great jagged folds, covered with a dense thickness of green, pocked with mists and clouds. The mountain to the south appeared to be taller and with a gentler incline. Clouds broke over the summit as a ship breaks through the water.

Hannah could do little but stare at this strange and foreign place.

Several sailors expressed great surprise when they learned of her destination and her stated goal. Word did travel fast, and the news of an epidemic would drive off ships and traders for months and even years.

Hannah watched as the village of Lahaina came into view. Ramshackle buildings clung to the waterfront, like the teeth of a jack-o'-lantern. Here and there were a few more substantial structures, one a two-story green-and-white building that appeared to be a house. Next to it was a small building built of dark, jumbled rock. And interspersed with familiar architecture were huts with stone bases and covered with the woven fronds of palms, appearing as if a strong wind might cause them to topple. From what Hannah could see, every building seemed to be a tavern, a brothel, or a restaurant.

The harbor held over twenty whaling ships. Captain Killeen said such a number was shocking–usually upward of a hundred whalers bobbed at anchor.

Because of so few ships, the village was curiously quiet as the *Alberta and Comstock* snugged in at the dock. The black smoke diluted the sunshine and cast a pall over the waterfront. Within no more than an hour, Hannah stood facing a pyramid of crates on the dock planking–every crate bearing her name, each marked with a red cross.

The captain appeared at the gangplank that hung between the ship and the dock. "This be the lot of it," he said as he stared at the crates.

"It is, Captain. Everything is accounted for."

"And you have your personal belongings from your cabin?"

Hannah nodded.

"Then, ma'am . . ."

Hannah touched his arm. "If you want to leave, you may. There is no need for you to stay longer than necessary."

"It ain't that we're in such a hurry. But the tide be running out now. If we wait, we'll be here for three days. And I ain't a praying person like you are. I believe, but don't God favor those who do the most talking?"

Hannah laughed in spite of the situation. "I have never heard it put quite that way, Captain Killeen. But God will protect whom he has chosen. I am in God's hands, and I am certain he will look after me."

The captain hesitated.

"Please, you must feel free in leaving me here. My friend will meet me. All will be well. God is indeed in control."

His hands were folded, and he nodded as if he did not truly believe her words. "If you are certain."

"I am."

"Then we will take our leave. May God bless you, then."

"And you, too, Captain Killeen. I will pray for you."

He smiled and then called out to his crew. "We'll sail on this tide. Make haste. Set the mainmast sails first. Undo the dock stays. We need to catch the afternoon winds."

And like a cat slipping from a warm perch by a window, the ship edged from the dock, sails and masts gently groaning. Hannah stayed where she stood, waving at the ship until she could see no longer the single face of any man.

Then she turned, held a length of her dress in one hand to keep it from snagging on the splintered dock, and set out to find Fodor's Inn.

"Jamison Pike?"

Hannah felt a combination of anger, frustration, and fear. "He is a guest with you. He has been for a month. Could you fetch him for me, please?"

The clerk behind the desk, a dark-skinned fellow–not Negro, but native of another land altogether–appeared most befuddled.

"Jamison Pike?" he repeated and scratched his chin. "Not sure 'bout dat name. Not sure he be here. Not sure I seen dat man. Not sure."

Hannah closed her eyes. She hoped she could hold her emotions in check. "Yes, Jamison Pike. I received a letter a month ago, mailed from this address. I am sure he is here–and if he had to move on, he would have left word for me. I am Hannah Keyes."

"Hannah? I hear a man talkin' 'bout woman he call Hannah."

"Yes, and who was this gentleman?"

"Be light man. White skin, dat man."

"Yes, that must be him. Where is he?"

The clerk shrugged. "Don' know. He don' tell me he go. He don' tell me he stay."

Hannah's form went limp. She was on the verge of tears. After such a long voyage to be dropped off in such a strange place with no one to greet her was almost more than she felt capable of bearing.

"You take drink? You wait. Dat man come back. I bet dat man come back."

She looked up. "Do you have tea? A cup of tea would be wonderful."

"We got dat. I get. You sit. You wait. Dat man come."

She took a floral-printed upholstered chair, the most comfortable one she had sat in for some time, and dragged it close to the front window of Fodor's. She watched a few ships ply the harbor and stared at the small green island across the water, no more than a few miles distant. All looked peaceful and calm. Yet there was a gray pall about the village, a mixture of smoke and something else altogether. To Hannah it was as if the warmth of the sun had been leached out before it reached earth.

Hannah was heartened that Fodor's was not as debauched as she feared. The building was two stories, with an overhanging porch running the entire perimeter of the second floor. The ceilings were high with great open floor-to-ceiling windows all about, allowing the fresh winds to circulate freely.

She took her tea, heavy and sweet with fresh cane squeezings, and sipped it with satisfaction. It was the first cup of tea she had had in weeks that she did not fear would be spilled by an angry sea. She sipped and felt the warmth spread out from her belly.

It had been a hard trip–fast, but hard, she told herself. She would allow a moment of rest to her limbs here in the afternoon sun. Her eyes grew heavy, and she held the cup in her lap, not worried that it might spill and stain yet one more dress.

Her eyelids fluttered closed.

"Hannah."

She blinked wide awake and spilled the remaining swallows of tea into her lap. That surprised her even more and she nearly jumped from the chair, spilling the cup and saucer to fragments on the floor. She jumped and turned to the voice.

"Hannah."

She stared at him. In the months since his letters, she had rehearsed this very moment a thousand times, trying to find the perfect greeting, the perfect response to a man she both disliked and loved as an old and dear friend.

Such a perfect response was never found, and she had decided, weeks ago, that she would say whatever her heart told her to say at that minute.

"Hello, Jamison," she said, taking in his face. "It is so . . . it is so nice to see you again."

Jamison appeared at once so very, very gladdened and so very apprehensive. "And you, too, Hannah. It is . . . nice to see you as well."

His eyes never left her face. He took only a half step toward her and without thinking, without hesitation, both found each other in a most welcoming and intimate embrace.

"I took the liberty of having the crates on the dock moved for you, Hannah," Jamison said. "The islanders are wonderful people, but they don't necessarily share our belief in personal property. If the crates stayed where they were . . . well, they wouldn't have been there much longer."

"I had no idea," Hannah said as she followed Jamison down the main street of the village. "I would not have left them if I thought it was unsafe."

"No matter. And one more thing–I will not have you staying at Fodor's."

She appeared puzzled. "It seemed very nice." Then she reddened a bit. "Or is it one of those places?"

Jamison turned to her and reddened even more. "Oh no, it's not that type of place. If it were I wouldn't stay there either. It's just that it can get very noisy and if a lot of sailors are in town, it can get very noisy far into the night."

"Thank you, Jamison."

"I thought first about securing you a room at the boarding school for women in town. They do have rooms, but then I had another thought altogether. I have taken another liberty for you, Hannah. I rented out an empty storefront. For your office. And on the second floor is a tidy apartment."

He stopped and pointed to a small two-story building done in clapboard and painted white. There was a large overhanging porch in the front that shaded the front windows and entrance. The banisters appeared recently painted, yet showed the wear from the salt and the sea.

She stopped at the front step as he fussed with the keys. "Jamison," she said softly.

"Yes?" he said as he faced her.

His face was, as she remembered from Harvard, not too long, with a strong jaw and high cheekbones–like a passionate New England farmer, if there was such a man. His dark hair, once as full as a horse's mane, had thinned a little. He wore it much shorter now. His eyes were still dark and penetrating. His body had gone a bit thicker but still possessed a hungry look about it.

He tilted his head. "Yes? You had a question?"

She smiled. "How did you know I was going to come? If I hadn't, all of this would have been a waste. How could you be so sure I would make the journey?"

He stepped toward her and placed the keys to the building in her hands. "I don't know why exactly." His eyes found hers again. "I'm really not certain, Hannah. I wish I had a better answer. But I . . . I just knew you would . . . somehow. I just did."

And with that he opened the door and ushered her in.

"How long has the sickness been here?" she asked.

Jamison stabbed a bit of pineapple with his fork. They sat at Fodor's having dinner. Jamison claimed that for food, it would be fine, but not for her permanent lodging.

"They tell me at least a season–about three months before I landed. So a total of a half year."

She chewed her fish, a most delicate white meat touched with a ginger sauce. "And no one knows the cause?"

"No. The local people have a shaman who claims it is because of the missionaries on the island and the fact that some of them have been baptized. But then, he's just protecting his power when he says that, isn't he?"

Hannah shrugged.

After dinner, and after her possessions had been stored away at her new residence, she insisted she was not tired and asked if Jamison might take her on a short tour of the environs. He was at first reluctant.

"You do remember me from the Destiny, don't you, Jamison? I am not a woman who is easily deterred."

He smiled. "I do recall that very well. Can you ride?"

"I haven't in years. But I do know how."

Jamison returned with two sorrels, each with saddles. He helped her onto her horse. Hannah giggled as he did, for he obviously had no idea of how to help and where to lift and how a lady might find or not find offense. She finally had to tell him.

"Take my hand, and help me lift."

He led the way, and for an hour they rode slowly along the shoreline. Just beyond the white sand was a thick fringe of palms. In some areas a thickness of cypress trees grew, and they had to skirt about the tangled roots by going inland. There was a profusion of birds with sharp, wondrous colors hastening past her eyes as they darted about. A half mile from shore the air grew heavy and humid and filled with the tang of decay.

"Is that scent always here?" she asked.

"I have smelled it before in other jungles. Things grow fast and die fast."

They reached a small natural harbor. Scattered about the clearing were several score of huts, some with thatches of palm fronds for roofs, some with slats of wood, perhaps made from the remnants of ships. A trio of long canoelike vessels lay on the sand, each with two long poles attached to a cigar-shaped float.

Jamison held them back at a rise about a quarter mile distant. "That's a native settlement," he said. "It's best not to go unless you are prepared to spend the day. They seem to take offense if you stop and want to leave within an hour or so."

"And the sickness is there as well?" Hannah asked as she swatted a fly on her arm.

"Yes. They lost ten children since I wrote you."

"Any adults?"

"A few. Mostly the older folks from what I can gather."

Jamison turned his horse and spurred it gently back the way they had just come. After riding in silence for a mile or two, Hannah looked over to Jamison.

"Jamison," she called out, "would you mind if we dismounted and walked awhile? I'm afraid that the years since I rode last are very obvious to certain muscles. A short break would be most appreciated."

Jamison jumped off and helped Hannah down. "Would you like to stop awhile? We're only an hour from town. And we have perhaps three hours of daylight left. We could rest."

The waves breaking on the shore seemed to be calling out to her. "Well, perhaps a short break. That water does seem most inviting."

Jamison tied the horses to a palm tree. "You're not going to do what you and your cousins did in Bay Head, are you?"

Hannah spun about, an angry flash in her eyes. "Did Gage tell everyone?"

Jamison retreated three steps. "Hannah, I did not mean . . . I mean . . . I thought . . ."

She narrowed her eyes, enjoying watching him wither. "Honestly. You men seem to be all alike."

Jamison appeared sheepish.

"And it has been years since that occurred. You remember that above all else?"

He nodded.

She shook her head. "Honestly," she repeated as she kicked off her shoes and headed toward the hush of the surf.

FROM THE DIARY OF HANNAH COLLINS KEYES
FEBRUARY 1857

Honestly!

When Jamison made that remark about our bathing at Bay Head, I was as close to striking another human being as I have ever been in my life. And if Gage were here, I would have. Jamison and Joshua were simply led astray by the man.

And now I am in the Sandwich Islands.

Such a terrifying beauty about this land. I have managed to take a short sail about the coast–at least the north coast–and there are mountain clefts so drawn and steep that no man could climb them. And each face of these terrible clefts is covered in the greenest down of vegetation. There are mists that circulate at treetop and hide the jungle floor from prying eyes. To the south, and to my great consternation, is a volcano. Jamison never once mentioned a volcano. The natives claim it has been silent for generations, yet I see smoke curl from the slashed top of the mountain. Jamison states that one can travel there and peer into the very molten guts of the earth.

I declined, quite sensibly.

My office has been swept and painted and sweetened with a flurry of flowers. There is an apartment above–four rooms with a balcony that overlooks the sea. It provides music for my sleep every night.

In my first few days on this island, I have already seen over thirty patients–so far none of them natives, unfortunately. Jamison insists that they will come eventually. If they do not, we will go to them. He says it may have something to do with being a woman. I suspect their shamans do not trust a woman for healing–even though it is women who perform most of the healing techniques in many cultures.

I will not wait long. If it is a simple matter to cure, and children are dying because of ignorance, that I will not tolerate. Yet I cannot simply barge into their villages and insist they see me. That is a most certain way not to be trusted.

And then . . .

I ask myself, what of Jamison?

He shared few intimacies when I first arrived. He was a gracious tour guide, and I do not remember him being so fearless. We once confronted a band of natives in the dense jungle north of here and they came upon us, shouting and brandishing clubs of some sort.

I must inform all that I was never so terrified in all my life. The men, half clothed, if at all, screamed and whooped all about. Yet Jamison remained calm. He stood up straight, pointed to one man who appeared to be the leader and called him over to him. All the while I was quaking behind a tree.

He gestured and called and acted out some manner of charade, then called me over to him. I was loathe to come, fearing these savages might simply do with me what they would. Jamison could not fight them off for certain.

He whispered to me a bizarre set of instructions. There is a spot on the forearm that is fleshy and yet without much sensation of pain. A good surgeon could insert a sharp needle through the area and the patient would scarce acknowledge it. He pulled a long pin from my hair and told me to do exactly that.

"I've seen it done, Hannah. I've seen it done in taverns to win a bet. I know you can easily find the spot."

I took hold of his arm and felt for a moment. Then with the savages in a circle about us, I plunged the pin straight through his arm till it came out the other side. Jamison stood there, motionless, and asked if any of them might want to try my powers. He was gesturing about with the pin still in his arm. The poor fellows went white, staring at me and jabbering, and fled like deer from a hunter.

"Your reputation as a shaman is now being spread," Jamison told me and then instructed me to remove the offending pin from his flesh. I bound up the wound with a strip torn from the hem of my dress. He applied the juice from a local tree–a tea tree, I believe–which he has learned has great healing properties.

He was willing to do all that to protect me.

Now I sit in the glow of a tropical sunset and spend much time pondering my future.

I know I once said I had ruled Jamison out of my future.

Now I am not so sure.

CHAPTER TWENTY-THREE

Lahaina, Maui, Sandwich Islands
April 1857

"IT is hard to believe that outside of this forest, the land is still bathed in sunlight," Hannah exclaimed. "I can no longer discern if it is still light outside or if the sun has slipped from the sky."

Jamison wiped his brow and nodded. "The trees and vines grow so thick and thatched that the ground stays perpetually moist," he explained.

To Hannah it was as if he were writing an article on the jungle. His words made the reality of their hike even more real.

"Even in a thunderstorm," he continued, "scant rain falls directly on this ground. The canopy above breaks the rain into a mist that simply fogs the air. That is why there are so many rainbows. And much of the rain finds the earth in rivulets that pour down the trunks of the palms. That's the reason the greens are so lush and pervasive. Even the moss appears to have moss growing on it."

She laughed, and her merriment hung in the humid air with a clarifying purity. "You sound as if you grew up here–you seem to be knowledgeable on so many subjects."

Jamison laughed. "Thank you, but I only claim a shallow pool of knowledge on many subjects. And I have spent some time in jungles–here, in the Central Americas, in Asia, some in Africa."

Hannah leaned against a towering palm and sipped water from a canteen. "I forget you have been everywhere and have seen everything."

"Not everywhere. Close, perhaps, but not everywhere." He slipped a long machete back into its sheaf and peered around the dim green cathedral of palms and ferns and vines.

Hannah walked behind him, carefully stepping on the moss-covered rocks and downed palm trunks. The humid warmth felt more encompassing and enveloping than a bath. Hannah would have liked to have been able to wear one of the native costumes–a simple throw of colored fabric bound about the frame with little or no encumbrances.

Instead she wore her thinnest and lightest frock and still felt the sweat simply pour from her body.

Hannah had asked Jamison to lead her to the headwaters of the stream that flowed down the mountain and through the native settlement near Lahaina. She could not tell him exactly what she wanted to find, nor did she know, save that she thought it might be important.

No native guide wanted to lead them, fearing that a woman venturing into the darkness would be upsetting to the gods.

Hannah understood their fears.

She lifted her skirt to her ankles to navigate a particularly large log. Halfway over, with one hand on her hem and one hand waving about to maintain balance, Hannah leaned too far in one direction and simply tumbled to the ground, twisting her body in an odd position to break her fall. As she rolled, her dress gathered about her knees, and she found herself in an awkward, almost compromising, position for a lady.

Jamison was at her side within a heartbeat. She appreciated that he had not stared at her bare legs, as would most men.

"Are you hurt? What happened? Can you walk?"

Hannah tried to smile through her embarrassment. "I am fine. Just a spill. This dress is too long for the jungle, I am afraid."

Jamison appeared to be thinking of a worthy response but held his tongue.

"Maybe I could sit for a moment and rest," she said as she stood. "My left ankle is a bit tentative."

From his pack Jamison quickly pulled out a length of stout canvas and laid it on a flatness of rock. "Here. This will be dry. Shall I try a fire for tea?"

"In this dampness? Nothing could burn here."

Smiling, Jamison drew a small tin from the pack with an odd wire contraption and a little pot. "A mixture of whale oil and paraffin. Burns even in a downpour. I found the tins in Burma, of all places. They use it on tiger hunts in the jungle."

"Well," she said happily, "some tea would be pleasant–even in this heat."

"Fight fire with fire, I say," Jamison replied as he set about boiling water.

Hannah watched him as he worked. She was not hurt from the fall, but she enjoyed the rest. Hiking through a rain forest was a hard, hot activity–one that could drain the energy from anyone.

I have been here for weeks, and this man surprises me every day.

She leaned back against a palm. She sniffed. Mixed in with the smell of ginger, the decay of flowers, and the rain was the comforting aroma of strong English tea.

And yet, for what we have shared in the past, he has remained cool and aloof. He keeps such a distance between himself and everyone.

Averting her eyes, he handed her a cup of tea. "I didn't bring sugar. I hope that unsweetened tea is acceptable."

"It is. I often drink it that way. Stronger somehow. More potent." And as she said those words, she turned away from him, feeling her cheeks redden.

He blushed too and pretended to look around into the dark greenness about them. After a long silence, he cleared his throat. "Have you found what you are looking for?"

Unsure of what question he was asking, Hannah became flustered.

"In the jungle, I mean," Jamison said quickly. "You said you were looking for something but were not sure of what."

She blinked several times. "No, not yet. I don't think I have. . . . Actually, I'm not sure. Nothing is what I expect. Like life."

"Truly?"

"All our talks at the Destiny–none of what I expected to occur, did. When we were young, I would have thought by now I would have children and live in a big house and have retired from medicine altogether. But look at me. Still in the thick of it. And alone."

"Like me," Jamison added and then turned away, as if revealing too much. He stood abruptly and brushed the leaves from his trousers. As he did, they both heard rustling and coarse crackling in the dense foliage to their left.

Jamison held his finger to his lips and drew a revolver from the holster at his waist. The scrabbling and snorting grew louder and louder until a boar the size of a large dog crashed into the opening.

Hannah screamed and leaped to her feet. Jamison raised the pistol and aimed at the wild pig. His finger tightened about the trigger, but he hesitated. The boar shuffled about, leaning to one side. Its eyes were clouded and vacant as it lifted its tusks into the air, sniffing wildly, its sides moving like fast bellows. The animal took a step forward, then stumbled again and fought to gain purchase, hooves clamoring in the moist dirt.

"Wait," Hannah hissed. "Don't fire."

Jamison nodded but kept his pistol raised and aimed.

The animal fell twice again and walked in a great wobbly circle about them. It must have caught their scent again, for it bellowed and pawed at the ground.

"It will charge, Hannah. I need to fire," Jamison whispered urgently.

She nodded and turned her face.

The pistol roared, and the humid air muffled the echo. Hannah opened her eyes to see the animal on its side, its legs moving as if slowed by some invisible force. They gradually grew still.

The silence felt deafening after the pistol shot. It was nearly a minute until either Hannah or Jamison spoke.

"That animal was sick, was it not?" she asked.

"Yes. Any wild boar would have been on us in a flash. This one was either very old or very sick."

Hannah stood above the animal. "It did not look old but dazed."

"Yes, there was a most vacant look in its eyes."

Hannah took a step closer, tentative, as if the creature might suddenly spring to life again. She looked back at Jamison. "Do the natives eat these beasts?"

Jamison nodded. "When they can catch them. They're hard to kill with just spears alone. Not many natives have rifles."

"Are there larger animals on the island? Wolves or tigers or such?"

"No."

"And these boars drink the same water as do the villagers?"

Jamison nodded again. "I don't see any other source for their water."

Hannah nudged the creature with her toe. "I think I have found what I was searching for."

Jamison turned to her with a most puzzled look on his face.

From the Diary of Hannah Collins Keyes
May 1857

I feel such a surge of power and relief and thanksgiving. When Jamison and I trekked into the dark jungles of this island, I had no idea of what I might find. I had no idea of what discovery I might search for.

That makes the discovery truly God's handiwork.

I pressured Jamison to guide me, and he did resist. The natives here truly saw my venturing into their *heauaus*–sacred grounds–as akin to defacing a church would look to me. But God's gentle urging was so insistent that I could no longer ignore it. He drew me to that darkness for a reason, and it was up to me to obey and discover.

When we returned, I insisted that Jamison talk with several of the native chieftains. He reported back to me that the boars were easier to catch this season, some even wandering close to the village at night as if drunk.

I have no standing with the local shamans and chieftains and had to do all such communication through Jamison and others. I told him to tell them that the boars were inflicted with some manner of evil spirit. No doubt it is some animal illness that is being passed on to anyone who eats their flesh. And roasted boar is a most often served dish in native celebrations. The reason children seem to be affected more than adults is perhaps due to their weaker constitutions. I wonder if the illness is tainting the water supply as well?

Now the shamans can claim it is their discovery and my being a woman will not taint the news.

After a few weeks, following our witnessing of the death of that one boar, the illness seems to have been stemmed–at least on this side of this island. There remains sickness and death, of course, but not the virulent, oppressive manner of the disease that had occurred only months prior.

And the medical supplies I have brought are still finding great usefulness. I have managed to treat several children suffering from wounds. If the child is younger than twelve years, it seems no one minds that a woman treats the illness or wound. Once past that age, the patient will no longer be comfortable under my care and will seek out the shaman.

I have treated several of the missionaries on the island–but again, only the women and younger children. There was one fellow, a pastor from a small church in the village of Wailuku–who fell from a horse, and the spiky leaf of a native plant pierced him in midthigh. And when brought to me in great pain, he refused to allow me to touch him.

He called out in a most vile manner, claiming that no woman would touch such parts of his body. I assured him that my virtue would not be compromised by the sight of a man's bloody thigh, but he would not be dissuaded. Ultimately, a doctor from a whaling ship removed the spike. Unfortunately, he did not even attempt to sew the wound together. And based on the appearances of this ship's doctor, I would not have trusted him with livestock, let alone a human life.

I promised to pray for him, and he all but snorted at my offer. I do not understand how a person who seems to have no human kindness can represent the love and grace of our God. I think the Almighty must be saddened by these people.

And when I tell others of my faith, as I try to do as often as possible on this island, are they seeing me in the same way as they see this man? I hope not, and I attempt to portray God's kindness and care through my actions.

Some patients behave so very well and others still see me as suspect–as if a woman cannot understand such complexities.

But such are the prejudices I still encounter. As I grow older, I react with less concern and anger and more with compassion and understanding.

June 1857

After the epidemic caused by the diseased boars had passed, Jamison had hurried to the town of Honolulu on another of the islands in the Sandwich chain. He had promised his editors a full report on all the complexities of the Royals, and that is where they resided.

The funeral for Kamehameha III, last son of Kamehameha the Great, had been held two years prior in January of 1855 with all the pomp and pageantry befitting the noblest of the islands' kings. On the following day, Alexander Liholiho, the adopted son of the former king, had taken the oath of office in his formal inauguration as Kamehameha IV. Shortly thereafter, he married Emma Naea Rooke, his childhood sweetheart, a beautiful and refined woman with royal blood, who had been educated by a private tutor at the Royal School and who spoke fluent English.

Honolulu was a growing town of some seventy-five thousand people. To Jamison, it resembled a New England seaport. The royals lived in the finest building in town, known as *Hale Alii,* House of the Chief. It was a large residence built of coral block and the site of many European-style soirees attended by foreign diplomats, missionaries, prominent merchants, and American military leaders.

It was at this royal palace where Jamison had been received by the king and queen. He had been invited for tea and had spent an hour visiting, talking mostly with Queen Emma, who was a most gracious hostess and generous with information about the life of the royal family.

While Jamison was gone, Hannah filled her time treating those who would come to see her. She also spent a great deal of time instructing several young native boys on the use of the equipment she brought and the effects of the medicines she carried. She knew she could impart only a little knowledge in so few weeks, but whatever they learned was more than they knew before Hannah came.

End of June 1857

"Jamison," Hannah asked, "do you know where Gage's wife was buried?"

Jamison glanced up from reading a month-old copy of the *Lama Hawaii,* the *Hawaiian Luminary,* the island's first newspaper.

He screwed up his face in puzzlement. "I believe it is up the coast a few miles. But I have never been there." It was obvious Jamison just now became aware of his oversight. "Why do you ask?"

Hannah sipped her tea. "I would like to go and pay my respects. It seems like a proper thing to do."

"Well, I am sure someone knows of the location. We could go today, unless you have other plans."

She shook her head no. "But, Jamison, you just returned from your trip. There is no urgency to the matter."

Jamison folded his paper. He and Hannah had taken their reunion breakfast on the front porch of Fodor's, enjoying the warmth and the whisper of a breeze from the ocean. There was a faint clicking of palm leaves as they bent and swayed.

"No. We can travel today. There is no telling when a ship will arrive. If you want to visit there, we should do so now. If a ship docks this afternoon, there may not be much time to pack."

Hannah nodded. They had not discussed specific plans, but Jamison indicated that he would be heading back to California and then New York and take passage on the first ship heading east. He did say that he hoped the first ship bound for California would dock soon.

"And you'll be going back to Monterey, won't you?" he had asked. "Now that the illness has been stopped? That is your plan, is it not?"

She nodded but had not fully considered all the implications of that decision. She had begun to feel part of the island and had adapted to its slow, gentle rhythms. No one seemed in a hurry here, since no one had any place to hurry to. Hannah observed that the only ones who hurried were the recent arrivals–missionaries mostly, and some business adventurers. They would scurry about, trying to keep up to some manner of internal deadline. But the natives ignored all that and moved about in a most languid way, getting things done, but on island time.

Hannah blinked several times and slipped back to the reality of her tea and Fodor's front porch. "Well, if you have nothing else planned for today," she said, her words hopeful.

"No, nothing else. I have pages and pages of notes from my trip to Honolulu that need to be fleshed out into my articles, but there is no ship. And if there is no deadline, I do not work efficiently. And I can always work them into a longer article on board ship and have them completed by the time I reach California."

"The grave is right up there," the caretaker said, pointing up through a narrow break in the dense hibiscus and bougainvillea.

Hannah bent and peered through the fragrant greenery. "And there's a path?"

"Almost. You keep walking uphill. Keep the ocean in view, and you will find it."

"It's as if he wanted it hidden," she said softly.

"Yes, ma'am. The ground about the grave is flat and tended. Mr. Davis wanted the approach to stay wild, so it would be an effort to find the site. He said all good things needed to be preceded by a struggle. He said to let the jungle claim all the land about the grave, except for the clearing. It's a beautiful view of the ocean from there. The trek is worth the effort. Very peaceful."

Hannah nodded. She looked again at her dress, full and almost to the ground. Once again she chided herself on being a slave to fashion. It would be so much easier to simply wear what the native women wore.

It took them nearly a half hour to shoulder their way through the dense and fragrant walk. Then they broke free into the clearing, no more than an acre square. The land was flat, green with grass, and calm. The vista to the west was filled with the blue of the Pacific and of the sky and heavens above. The palms at the end of the clearing arched upon themselves, as if pointing in green fingers toward God and heaven. All the jungle about the site seemed to swell and push against that opening, and yet the persistence of the grass appeared to keep the jungle at bay. There was a simple headstone, no more than a dozen feet from the edge of the cliff that tumbled down to the waves and rocks below. There was a cross off to one side.

Hannah, who was short of breath as they broke into this space, gasped again at the sacredness of it all. "It's like a church," she whispered.

Jamison nodded. "More like a church than most churches I have visited. More . . . spiritual all by itself."

They walked slowly to the grave. Hannah lowered her head and whispered prayers while Jamison stared at the carved dates and then to the wild vastness of the ocean beyond them.

After a moment, he cleared his throat. "It's so sad," he said.

Hannah looked at him for a moment. "Yes, but not really."

He turned his head, puzzled. "But it is. She died so young," he said. "All her life was ahead of her. And she left a daughter as well. That's not fair, and it's sad." At the end Jamison's voice went warbly and loud as if he had to increase his volume to decrease his emotions.

Surprised by Jamison's strong emotions because he so seldom raised his voice, Hannah replied, "It is not sad. She is in heaven. It was God's plan."

Jamison dismissed her comments with a short wave of his hand. "It's sad and it doesn't make sense."

Hannah placed her hand on his arm. "Jamison, a Christian cannot be a sundial believer and only count the sunny days. There is pain, but God has a purpose."

He pulled his arm away, not in anger, but with something else altogether. At that, Hannah was shocked. He walked to the very edge of the land, just a foot or two away from the edge.

"Jamison . . . ," she called out, and he did not turn.

Any other moment and she would have pursued him, pulling him back, offering him soothing words and explaining how God works in the world.

But as he walked away, she heard a voice saying, *"No."*

Perhaps it was the voice of God–she was not certain–but it was louder than the sound of the surf below. She took a step, then stopped, and at that moment, felt absolutely right in letting Jamison stare off into the west alone, without her whisperings, without her advice.

He knows the truth but cannot face the pain of life, she thought. *He cannot bear to see loss. He does not trust the fact that love can overcome the pain.*

And in sudden, overwhelming illumination, she saw Jamison for what he was, a scared child who never had experienced true love and would never risk loving someone until he knew that specific emotion would never hurt him. And Hannah knew there were no such guarantees offered by life.

She held back and watched him. Instead of seeking a cure, seeking to heal and to mend, she simply prayed for him–that God's love might be revealed to him. It would be the only love that could not fail him.

And she bowed her head and committed his life to God. She prayed she might be well used as God's servant.

After a few minutes she lifted her head. Jamison had turned and was watching her. His expression told her so little. While it was not anger, it was not love either. It was as if he had pledged to stay on his solitary path regardless of the pain that it caused, regardless of the grayness that it brought.

But then he hesitated and offered Hannah a most enigmatic smile, as if her prayers were welcome, even though he might consider them fruitless.

He walked to her and extended his hand. She reached out and took his hand in hers.

"We should head back, Hannah. The time is short, and I do not want to be trapped in that denseness after sunset."

Hand in hand, they walked toward the darkness of the jungle.

Two days later, Jamison called upon Hannah at her medical office. He was forced to wait nearly an hour as Hannah treated several sailors who had experienced symptoms of scurvy. Hannah had no medicine to treat the illness but exhorted them to consume as much fruit, especially lemons, as they could tolerate.

"The fruit has something in it that fights against scurvy," she said. "Take some with you when you sail."

Hannah smiled when she saw Jamison sitting on the rickety bench on the porch outside her office. "What a pleasant surprise," she said as she sat down next to him. She unbuttoned her cuffs and pushed her sleeves high up on her arms. She leaned back and extended her feet.

"You look comfortable," Jamison said.

"I am," Hannah replied. "I am done with my work today, and I have nothing planned. I shall laze in the shadows and watch the clouds slip by."

Laughing, Jamison replied, "Do you ever notice how quickly you have become an islander? It has only been a few months. You have taken to the island ways with great enthusiasm. I might be afraid you will stay here once I leave."

Hannah sat up and faced him directly. She thought she saw a hint of anxiety in his eyes. "Well, I just might do that. The weather here is such a pleasure. My skills are in demand. I am in the middle of teaching four young native boys all I know of medicine. Perhaps I will take you up on your suggestion and make this place my home."

His expression clearly showed his concern. "Are you serious?"

She stood and walked to the end of the porch. From there she could see the ocean, only a short walk from her office. "Perhaps. I'm not certain. I suspect I will be forced to decide when the first ship bound for California arrives."

Hannah was not certain why she said what she did. She had never truly considered staying on the island forever. While it was idyllic, it was still so very far from home. And she had the hospital in Monterey to consider. Yet that situation gave her no true concern. The staff was competent and could handle any possible situation that might arise.

A small catamaran slipped out of the harbor on its way south, with twelve native men stroking the seas with paddles.

"And what will you do when you get home, Jamison?" she asked without looking at him.

"Go back to New York. Write my second book. They paid me for it. It's the least I can do, I guess."

She nodded, still without turning about.

From out far into the ocean, she thought she saw the hint of a sail. It was the hard edge of canvas slipping by at the far western horizon.

That could only mean one thing–a large sailing vessel on its way to the island. Without thinking, she turned back to Jamison and sat next to him, closer than she had been.

"Let's take a picnic to Black Rock," she said. "One of the sailors said it is a most spectacular spot. I heard that the sugarcane workers cut a road through the jungle so that the entire journey can be made in less than an hour. Would you like that, Jamison?"

"Why, yes," he replied, surprised. "That would be very nice."

"Could you rent the horses?" Hannah asked, knowing the livery was several blocks inland and away from the sea. "I'll run to Fodor's and have them put a basket together for us."

Hannah scanned the horizon as she hurried to Fodor's. The sail did not reappear. Ships occasionally visited Lanai first and then made their way to the island of Maui. And it may have been a ship heading farther east.

Regardless, Hannah hurried. She was not certain the reason for her urgency. There was no small voice urging her on, no sudden awareness. But if these were to be their last few days on the island, she wanted them to be a pleasant memory.

As she hurried, she debated on changing her frock. She scanned the horizon and found no sail, so she turned back to her apartment and took the stairs two at a time. In no more than a minute, she found her lightest and thinnest dress, one that was made on the island by a local seamstress and was a curious combination of Eastern sensibilities and island comfort. She stood in front of a very small mirror, trying to assess the cut and the fit and the modesty of the garment. She tugged and pulled and decided it would have to do. At the last instant, she discarded her laced-up boots and slipped into a pair of sandals–again, a purchase she had made on the island.

She did not run toward the livery but nearly did.

Jamison met her halfway. He dismounted and tied the basket to his saddle. If he noticed her dress, he did not say, but she thought his eyes lingered upon it longer than what she would have considered normal.

He helped her mount her horse, and the two of them rode out of town, following the narrow, freshly cut road that led north. The road skirted the sea and was usually a full half mile inland. The distance would prevent a heavy storm and waves from washing out their efforts.

Birdcalls followed them as they rode, a symphony of chirps and caws and songs. Hannah thought their calls had been orchestrated by some master musician, so sweet was their sound.

Jamison rode ahead a bit, then called out and pointed, "There! There's Black Rock."

Black Rock, a lava formation from perhaps centuries ago, rose a hundred feet against the sea and formed a high parapet from which to view the western coast of the island. It was said that in the past, natives would perform magical ceremonies there, dancing about bonfires that sparked and crackled into the darkness.

Since the white men began to arrive, the rock was used less and less as a sacred place, and from what Jamison had discovered, had fallen from favor as a *heauau.*

"Perhaps their magic moved on," he told Hannah when he first recounted the stories.

Hannah laughed and replied, "Jamison, you are an educated man. Surely you do not suppose that such places can truly be magic, with powers of the dark. No man or place is more powerful than God."

Jamison tilted his head and said, "I would not be too sure, Hannah. There is much in the world that we do not know. Magic exists. It does. I have seen many things that defy explanation. Even for a Harvard man."

She would argue it no further, but when she stepped upon the black rock, glinting like a dark diamond, she felt a chill in her body. She dismissed it and told herself it was only because she knew that this rock was once burning, molten, and alive, pulsing and sliding, hissing into the sea.

Jamison found a small patch of grass at the top, near the far western edge of the rock, shaded from the sun by a thick stand of tall palmettos. He spread a stout canvas on the grass and placed the basket between the two of them.

"Shall we see what Fodor's has provided?" he asked, lifting the lid of the basket.

"I told them we wanted the best of what they had," Hannah explained. "I didn't think we had the time to be picky."

The basket had proven to be heavily laden with all manner of meat and biscuit and fruit and sweet. The two stared at the ocean as they ate and watched the surface of the water change every few minutes. It caught the late-afternoon sun and turned crimson. Then when a thickness of clouds scudded by, the water went gray and ominous. Hannah shouted when she saw the flukes of a pod of whales heading by.

At the end of their meal, dusk was only a few hours away. Hannah realized that if she were to say anything, it would have to be now. For if a ship did arrive, headed for America, then they both would assume their old lives.

Their time on the island held their past lives in abeyance and gave them both time to think about the future.

For Hannah these months were a time of gradual awareness and awakening. It was as if she had slowly become more comfortable in her own skin, and in her own frame. For all of her past, she was always in effort to please a parent, a gentleman friend, a husband–some external judge and jury. But here it was just herself, and she began to feel most comfortable with Hannah as she was, not as she was promised to be.

"Jamison, we may not be on this island much longer."

He looked at her. "And why is that? Are you now empowered by this magical place to tell the future? I told you there was magic in the world. Now you believe me?"

She tossed the end of a roll at him with a great laugh. "You do like to tease, don't you?"

"No. I just want to know how you know the time is up here."

Her eyes dropped. "I saw a sail on the horizon. That's when I told you to head to the livery. I wanted to have an afternoon with you–with no rush to pack and ready ourselves for departure."

"You did? A sail?"

She nodded. "I feel guilty now. I should have told you."

He reached over and touched her arm. "Do not worry yourself. I saw it, too. As I went to the livery."

"You did? Then why didn't you say something to me? I thought you were quite ready to leave."

"I am. But I wanted this afternoon as well–if indeed the ship does dock at Lahaina."

Hannah gazed at her old friend, knowing she would never truly understand him. He stared back, and for several moments they just looked at each other. Jamison's habit was to look away, even when speaking, as if embarrassed by his words or something else that only he knew and could not share. To simply stare into another's eyes was so atypical and so unusual that Hannah felt lost and swallowed up by his gaze.

As the years passed, Hannah knew that time with friends became more and more precious. And she became more and more bold.

She did not think but merely said the words that her heart gave rise to. "Have you ever been in love, Jamison?"

He did not move, though his eyes darted to the ground and then the sea and then the sky, as if trying to escape. He offered no answer.

"It's a simple question, Jamison. For a man who has made his life asking questions of others, is it that difficult to answer?"

He looked back at her. "But why such a question now?" he asked with a slight edge. "It is not a subject we have discussed before. What would the profit be in such a discussion?"

Hannah stood. She was almost angry and was not sure why. Once again she merely allowed her heart to speak and not her head.

"Jamison. You have sent me cryptic notes from around the world. Your words sounded as if you might be implying a desire for some manner of relationship with me. Then, in a most infuriating manner, you have me married off to Gage, as if I am some type of option to be handled. We have skirted about this subject before. Why not ask about love now? Is it something that you do not understand?" She gestured with her hands, an act that was most atypical for her.

"And now, over these long weeks and months on this island, with only the two of us, you act as if you cannot get any closer than an arm's length to me. You treat me as a stranger at your table, not as a friend of more than a decade's duration. I don't understand you, Jamison. I simply do not understand you. I ask of love . . . because . . . well, because I want to know. I think I may expect an answer. I think I deserve an answer."

Her own words, the strong emotion behind them, and her rapidly beating heart all surprised her. She walked away, stopping near the edge of the precipice.

He stood and followed her yet did not speak.

She spun about to face him. "And now you ask about the profit of such a discussion? How long do you think your life is, Jamison? How many years will you have to not love?"

He turned away as if slapped.

Hannah did not step toward him. "I understand you may not have seen love demonstrated in your family. That is sad, but do we not all have some manner of demon in our past–some manner of emotional tragedy that we can allow to mar us forever? Yet everyone has a choice in life. You have free will. God has given you that. Shall the example of your parents continue to cripple you? Don't you need to be free of that?"

His eyes flashed with anger; his fists clenched. "And what of you? You are not in the shadow of your parents? They use up your promise to regain their standing in the rich and cultured. And you go along with them. You spurned Joshua, who loved you so purely. You spurned everyone who did not have a guarantee of wealth and riches. Robert seemed a nice man and I am sorry that he is dead, but he was mean-spirited and manipulative and no one could understand why you said yes–except the fact that he promised you wealth."

Hannah's eyes widened. "That's not true."

"It is. And then you ask me why I cannot talk of love."

She stepped to him and faced him. The afternoon breeze flowed from water to land. It rose in a warm breath up Black Rock and fluttered Hannah's hair about her face. Her dress caught the breeze, and the skirt flapped about her legs, exposing her skin up to her knees at times.

"Jamison–you take that back–what you said of me. I have never let my heart be swayed by money."

He did not back down. "Perhaps now you have changed. But you made your interests most clear at the Destiny Café. A life of privilege is what you sought. Maybe I was insensitive when I wrote to you of Gage. Perhaps your heart is now different. But you cannot deny who you were back then. Not in front of me and your God. You cannot."

She glared at him, and their eyes locked. Her heart pounded. And then, with blinding realization, she recognized that what he had said–at least about her past–was true.

"And I stood there, in the background, at the Destiny Café, at Harvard, and beyond, and watched you live your life in pursuit of wealth and position. It broke my heart, but I knew I would never be wealthy."

"But you are rich now," she replied. "You have written a book. I bought a copy. Thousands of people bought copies."

"One would be surprised how little an author gets from a book. All manner of expenses are deducted from the price. And a reporter makes even less. I am rich in experiences perhaps, but I am no richer than . . . than Joshua."

She tried to find a word to say, but the proper words were not where she could find them.

"And yes, my parents were cold and bitter people who seldom smiled and even less seldom laughed. I do not blame them, for they did only what they could," he added.

Hannah could not speak nor move. Jamison's eyes shone with a pleading and a passion that Hannah had never seen there before.

"I watched you marry. I watched the only woman I have ever loved marry someone else. And when I return and find myself near to penniless, how can I step back into your life? How do I know you have changed?"

"But you visited me in Philadelphia. You saw how sparse my life was. I had nothing then."

"But you wanted more. I could tell that in your eyes. When you showed me where you lived, your eyes were begging me not to judge you by the less-than-perfect furniture and unadorned walls. You were as uncomfortable as a cat in a roomful of dogs."

She stared at him, then glanced away. She knew he was right.

"And I loved you with all my heart, Hannah, and I could never tell you. How could I? How could I compete? How could I ever hope to give you what you needed? How could I ever promise enough? My promises would be empty."

She looked up at him. "You loved me?" Her words were soft as a prayer.

"Yes, I loved you. From that first day I saw you I loved you. And when I see other women, I see your face. You think I am alone because I have cold-spirited parents? That is no reason at all. I am alone because I love you."

"You love me?"

As if in great pain, he extended his hand to her.

She raised her hand to meet his.

"I love you more than the sun and the stars and the very air I breathe. Do you not realize how horribly difficult it is to be near you and not carry you off in a great passionate embrace? Do you not know how tempted I was to blurt out my true feelings every moment of every day? My heart has not known rest since I first saw you, Hannah. It is not your fault that I suffer such torment–it is the fault of my own heart."

Her eyes arched as in preparation for tears.

"Do not cry, Hannah," he pleaded. "I will never want to make you cry. You must not cry."

She shook her head. "I'm sorry," she whispered. "I never knew."

And then, as if being pulled close by a slow-moving current, the two of them opened their arms and found each other in a long embrace, an embrace that had waited years and years for fulfillment.

And they remained that way–silent, together, locked arm in arm, as the sun gradually edged to the western sea and the crimson and gold of the sunset colored all about them.

❦

A letter waited for Jamison when the two of them returned to Fodor's. There had been a ship on the horizon, and it now lay docked in Lahaina. The letter was marked *Urgent.* Jamison tore it open and quickly read the contents. He offered the most puzzled expression as he handed the letter to Hannah. She looked up at him.

"You need to read this," he said. The sheet of paper had the letterhead of the *New York World.*

Dear Jamison,

We trust that all goes well. We hope this letter finds you. As a writer, you are nothing but a frustration to me–always at some odd corner of the world. But, as much as I hate to admit it, our readers find your articles so captivating. And what captivates, sells. And what sells makes me happy.

Jamison, I want you to make me happy.

I want you to make me very happy.

You have promised me a long series on the king and queen of the islands there. Be sure to play up any human sacrifices or women in scanty attire and any manner of sensational facts. Be creative if you would. Your readers expect to be outraged and titillated by your journeys.

I am telling you nothing new.

After you have completed that assignment, I have one more waiting for you. Since you are already halfway there, I would like you to continue west and voyage to New Zealand. I have heard that the Maori are on the warpath, and there is nothing our readers love more than a good battle between settlers and some savage tribe.

I know that the journey is long–and as a result I am combining your advance on this story with a future book contract. I know I am being ludicrously generous, but I am not in a position to bargain. I must make you say yes. The offer is for twenty thousand dollars.

No, I have not taken leave of my senses.

But I must have the New Zealand piece by the end of the year. I am told that the Globe *and the* Examiner *have men en route as I write this. You will beat them, and we will have an exclusive.*

You must say yes. If our friendship means anything to you, you must say yes.

Reply to our office in San Francisco at once. The ship that carries this letter will carry you to New Zealand as well.

Yours truly,
Dexter R. Rikler
Editor-in-Chief
The New York World

Hannah looked up at Jamison.

"That is more money than I have made in ten years. How can I turn that down?"

And at that moment Hannah saw something in his eyes and knew she would have to say good-bye one more time.

And she prayed in that moment that somehow, in some way, God would find Jamison's heart. For if he did not, their good-bye would be more final than Hannah thought she could bear.

CHAPTER TWENTY-FOUR

Lahaina, Maui, Sandwich Islands
First of July 1857

JAMISON looked as if he had not slept. His eyes appeared hollow, and his chin was marked with dark stubble.

"Jamison," Hannah said softly as she came upon him on the veranda of Fodor's, "is there anything the matter?"

He jumped at the sound of her voice.

"I'm sorry," she said as she slipped into the seat across from him, "I did not mean to startle you in any way."

He greeted her with a weary smile and extended his hand to her. She took it and felt the gentle squeeze of his fingers. She smiled back.

"Do you want coffee?" he asked. "I'll call for a new pot."

She nodded. Examining his eyes, she said, "You haven't slept, have you?"

He shook his head. "How do you think that might be possible? At long last I hold the woman I love, and she holds me back, and then, in the space of less than an hour, I am offered more money than I have ever been offered to leave her side. Do you think that sleep will come easily after being presented such a dilemma?"

Hannah touched his hand to her cheek. "So, you do love me? Yesterday was not some tropical mirage?"

His expression traveled quickly from amusement to great pain in the span of a few heartbeats. "Yes, I love you. My saying it was not an illusion, Hannah, though I should ask the same question of you. Was your response overlooking the ocean an act of pity, or could you learn to love me as well?"

She knew that his question was genuine and not simply an attempt to elicit an "I love you" in response to his own. "Do you want me to be truly honest, Jamison?"

With an expression of great trepidation, he nodded.

"I . . . I think I love you as well."

He appeared very puzzled and anxious.

"I want to be honest," she continued. "Now that I am at the age I am, I think I owe it to you and myself to be honest. And I owe it to God as well. No more pretending to be what I am not. And no more wanting what I do not need nor desire."

"And your answer then was . . . a qualified perhaps?"

Hannah took both his hands and faced him. "That is not what I mean, Jamison. It simply means that my heart is not as far as your heart. When you held me last night, I felt such a sense of peace and security–such as I have never known. I felt so protected in your arms, like a kitten by its mother."

"But not love?"

"Jamison, love is not that simple nor fast."

"But can you see such a thing occurring? Will it happen, or am I deluding myself?"

"You are not deluding yourself," she said gently. "I will not ask a man who has waited for all these years to be patient–but I can say with all my heart that I am more in love with you than I have been with any man in my life. There is a gulf between us . . . and that is one of faith. But I will pray every day that the gulf be bridged. Every day, Jamison."

"And that is the truth?" Jamison looked most incredulous.

"It is, Jamison. Allow me to grow accustomed to this knowledge of our hearts. For up until yesterday, we were best of friends. And now it is something else altogether, is it not?"

He smiled.

"You are such a sweet man, Jamison, such a sweet, wonderful man."

She saw the glint of a tear in his eye, something she had never seen in a man before–an ability to be tender.

She let her heart move her body. Leaning forward, she placed her lips gently on his. They stayed there for a long moment. Then she leaned back.

Jamison appeared stunned.

"Perhaps I am closer to loving you than I imagined," she whispered, then kissed him again with even greater earnestness and passion.

Jamison no longer merely appeared stunned. He *was* stunned. For Hannah to do what she had just done, in full view of passersby on Front Street, was a great public statement.

A breeze washed in off the ocean and the letter from the *New York World* fluttered on the table as if it were a wounded bird.

"But what do I do with this?" Jamison finally asked, with his words clearly outlined in great anguish.

❧

For the rest of the morning Hannah listened as Jamison discussed what course he might follow. The amount of advance money was so large as to render an objective decision difficult. Hannah found it hard to be objective. If Jamison replied positively, he would be nearly wealthy but gone for up to two years. With such an advance, he could return to Monterey, if he chose, build a house, furnish it, start his own newspaper, and have funds left over.

From a large map that he carried with him, Jamison showed Hannah where New Zealand was located and the possible routes one could take to voyage there. And then, once braving those risks, Jamison might find himself in further dangers, if the native peoples were truly warlike, as the editor's letter hinted.

Yet the advance hung there, like a great golden treasure, promising Jamison security and freedom upon his return.

He debated himself, arguing with great passion for both going and staying. Hannah alternated between resignation and dismay.

A waiter brought yet one more cup of coffee to the table. Jamison stirred in sugar, took a sip, then said softly, "There is no right answer. There is no way to decide this."

He reached into his pocket and took out a twenty-dollar gold piece. Without hesitating, he flipped it high into the air. As it rose, he said to Hannah, "Call heads or tails." He caught the coin and slapped it to his wrist.

"Surely you are not serious," she said. "You will not let such a decision be decided by a simple act of fate, will you?"

"Yes, I will, for I cannot decide. I could stay, ignore the money, be with you. I could go, take the money, return to you a wealthy man. How do I choose? What would Solomon do?"

Hannah appeared frantic.

"What do you say, Hannah? Heads or tails?"

"Don't make me decide like this. There must be a better way."

"There is not. Heads or tails?" Jamison insisted.

I am between the devil and the deep blue sea, she thought. *If he stays, will he become despondent over the loss of such a sum? If he goes, will I lose him?*

"Tails," she finally said.

He lifted his hand and neither smiled nor frowned.

"Well?" Her voice was nearer to pleading than any other emotion.

"I will return to you. That much I promise."

Later that day, after Jamison stumbled off to sleep, Hannah found the captain of the *Pride of Wisconsin* leaning against the rail at Fodor's. He did not appear totally sober, yet he did not have that flailing, incoherent style that marked many sailors their first few days back on shore.

"You are Captain Fox?"

He raised himself from the rail, yanked his coat together, arranged his shoulders, and then wiped his lips with the back of his sleeve.

"That I am, miss. And you are?"

His none-too-subtle leer was not lost on Hannah.

"I am Dr. Keyes."

Captain Fox looked both pleased and confused. "A doctor, you say? Well, be 'bout my time for a full examination, don't you think?"

It was not a line Hannah had never heard before. She slipped a scalpel from her bag in a very practiced move. "Yes, and you will allow me to do whatever surgery I deem necessary?" she said, as sweetly menacing as she could.

He gulped and retreated back a full step. "Well, that is . . . I am not feelin' at all poorly, ma'am."

Hannah placed the scalpel back into her bag and smiled. "Now that we understand each other . . . I have a small favor to ask."

"Sort of depends on the favor, don't it?"

"You will head to New Zealand after you depart from here?"

He nodded.

"And you will depart at week's end?"

He nodded again. "No true rush I imagine, but best be goin' while the winds are favorable, ma'am. But why be this any of your concern?" He brightened. "You be bookin' passage?"

She smiled again and patted her bag. "No. However, a friend of mine will be."

"And?"

She pulled out five gold pieces from a velvet pouch. She handed him one of the coins. "Wait a fortnight until you sail. If you do, I will pay you the rest then."

He bit the coin and carefully examined the dent his tooth made. "You be serious 'bout this, ma'am?"

"I am."

"And the reason be?"

She shook her head. "There is no need for you to know. Will you delay the sailing a fortnight?"

He grinned, showing several gaps in his teeth. "Ma'am, I could get one of my crew to kill someone for this much gold. Stayin' a fortnight will be no problem. No problem a'tall."

As she walked away, he called out after her, "You sure you don't want nobody killed?"

She laughed and turned away.

If he is going to leave me for a year, I want these next two weeks. I want to know if his promise is real.

The two weeks before the *Pride of Wisconsin* sailed seemed to evaporate as quickly as rain on a hot day. Hannah would have gladly paid an additional five gold pieces to hold Jamison nearby for another two weeks. But their good-byes would eventually have to be said.

"You could come with me," Jamison said as they walked hand in hand along the empty shore. "I'm sure there is room on the ship for another passenger."

Hannah squeezed his hand. She did not tell him that she had seriously considered doing just that and had actually approached Captain Fox to ask about the same matter. There was an extra cabin, private and larger than most, that was available.

Even as she discussed costs and the rest of the details of such a voyage, Hannah knew she would not go. To spend so long with a man who was not her husband would no doubt lead to great temptations for both of them.

In these last two weeks, Hannah would admit later, her willpower had been severely tested. What might occur over more than a year was not difficult to assess.

"I wish I could," Hannah replied. "But you know, and have known, that I must return to Monterey. I have promised Gage that I will stay at the hospital for five years. And now I have been gone for nearly six months. It is time for me to return."

He stopped, and she turned to him. The moon was over his shoulder, hanging like a golden lantern above the hushed waters of the Auau Channel. The breeze bore steadily from the east and augured well for a quick sail. The palms above them clattered softly, and from the forest and jungle beyond came the call of the nighttime hunters, owls, and ravens. There was a strong scent of pineapple and ginger in the air.

Hannah looked up at Jamison and smiled. He placed his arms about her and drew her closer. She willingly fell against him, wrapping her arms about him as tightly as she could hold.

"Come with me," he whispered.

"I can't," she whispered back. "But you must know there is nothing more I desire than to be with you."

The last two weeks had been the most idyllic of Hannah's entire life. Hannah and Jamison would take a leisurely breakfast together. She would return to her office to see patients, and Jamison would retire to his room to write. They would join for lunch and spend the rest of each day in each other's company.

The nights were Hannah's favorite. The heat of the day would be replaced with delicious warmth, and a cooling breeze would often slip off the ocean, tinted with salt, the seasoning scent of greater journeys. She and Jamison would simply walk along the shore, one evening to the north, the next to the south.

And as they walked, they would tell stories of their lives. They had known each other for so long but never truly knew each other. Hannah could often scarce believe the tales that Jamison told, but he swore each was true.

And she would tell him of patients she had treated and people she had met.

It was as if each fulfilled the other. Hannah knew people, Jamison knew places, and together they formed a more perfect union. Yet Hannah knew that this union was so fragile–and might one day be dissolved if Jamison never found his peace with God.

And as they walked back to Lahaina and back to their respective rooms, Jamison would find a secluded spot to stop for a longer interlude. He would turn and embrace her with great tenderness and reverence. She would hold him as well, finding great solace and peace in his arms. And then they would walk slowly until they reached their homes.

Often Hannah was so jangled by the experiences and emotions that sleep would elude her for hours.

If Jamison felt the same troubles, he did not share it with her.

And on this night, the night before Jamison was to sail, Hannah had one last question that she knew she had to ask.

Jamison led her by the hand to a hillock of sea grass. He bent it down, forming a soft cushion, and sat, then extended his hand to Hannah.

The moon was reflected a thousand times on each wave crest in the ocean, and the light sparkled off the palm branches above them.

He placed his arm about her and pulled her close. She snuggled into his chest and placed her hand over his heart. She could feel the steady beat and the warmth of his body against hers. Placing his hand under her chin, he lifted her face to his and gently kissed her. In that moment, when the world and the ocean and the air itself all but disappeared, Hannah sat back and drew a great breath as if to clear her senses.

"I do not desire to leave you, Hannah," Jamison said, breaking the silence.

She nodded. "I know. I do not desire for you to depart either. But the world is not a perfect place, and our desires are not always met."

"I don't like this," he admitted. "To finally hold you and then to let you go."

Hannah sat back and smoothed her hair. Several long tendrils had slipped from place. "Jamison, I must ask you to promise me one more thing as we face our good-byes."

"Anything, sweet Hannah. Anything in the world."

She looked out to the dark sea. "I think this will be difficult for you."

He bent to her and turned her face to his. "More difficult than leaving you?"

"Perhaps." She looked away again, attempting to compose her thoughts. "Jamison . . . ," she said, then hesitated again.

"Ask me, Hannah. Do not keep me in suspense. If the question is not posed now, then I shall have months and months to agonize over the nature of your request."

She turned back to him and took his hands in hers. She held them very tightly. She felt the roughness of his skin, the powerful muscles, even in his hands. She drew them up to her lips and kissed them both. "Two weeks have never slipped by faster."

"For me as well."

"And these evenings are such a delicious time. I cannot recall ever feeling such passion in my heart. You must know that."

He nodded and smiled.

"But there is something else that I need to say. Something that has nudged my heart and thoughts since you first held me in your arms. And this time, rather than hints and nudges, I must be as blunt as a cold winter shower."

Jamison did not respond. She looked in his eyes and felt certain that he knew what question she was ready to pose.

"You do not believe in God, do you, Jamison?"

He looked at her for the longest moment without speaking. His expression was not of anger or disappointment but more of resignation. His lips moved as if he was about to speak, then he stopped and, dropping her hands, stood and walked three steps toward the ocean.

Hannah hesitated a moment, then stood and walked to his side. "I'm sorry," she whispered, and took his hand. He let her hold his hand tightly in hers. "But I could not let this pass unspoken between us. You know I am a child of God. You know what that means, Jamison. You listened to Joshua as much as I did. You know what I can and cannot do. The passion in my heart these last two weeks is tempered by that gulf between us."

He did not look at her.

"I hold on to my faith in God to keep me alive. Do you?"

He did not answer but shook his head no.

"There is a gulf," she all but whispered.

Neither spoke. A cloud covered the face of the moon, and their faces plunged into almost absolute darkness. In that darkness, Hannah placed her hand on his forearm and turned to him. "You will leave tomorrow. You must promise me only one thing."

"And that is?" His voice was a teary whisper.

"You must promise that you will search for the truth. Search for it away from me and away from the temptation of saying that you have found God to please me. Search for his truth. Approach his truth as a child, Jamison. You are an intuitive reporter. You sense rather than know. I want you to do the same with God. Ask him the same questions. I will not be with you to see your weakness. No one will. There will be no shame, and I know that you hesitate, for you think all who know you will think you have grown weak. That is not what will happen. Search for the truth, Jamison. I am not asking you to change for me. I am simply asking you to promise to search. Will you promise me that? Will you do that much for me?"

"You ask a great deal."

"You do love me?"

"More than my own life," he answered.

"Then promise you will continue to search. I am not asking for you to change now–simply to go on looking. Will you promise me that, Jamison?"

The clouds slipped away and she saw his face, streaked with tears.

"I promise, Hannah. I promise." And his arms wrapped about her in a great encompassing embrace that lasted until the moon once again was hidden by the clouds.

From the Diary of Hannah Collins Keyes

Lahaina, Maui

July 1857

I do not know how I endured his departure. I saw so little as my world was a mass of tears and sobs. His ship pushed off and gently, almost imperceptibly, slipped away from the dock. I cried until I could no longer see the sails at the horizon.

I am certain that onlookers thought me deranged, but he has found something in my heart that no man else had discovered. I do love him so, and I will pray every day that he holds to his promise of last night.

I still feel his arms, hear his voice, see his face. I could have died then, and I would be a woman who had known total contentment.

There are still no ships heading back directly to either Monterey or San Francisco. Some head to Seattle and some to Mexico, and both destinations would require then another voyage. Perhaps it has been God's way to keep me here. As I write and plan, I believe I will stay on this island for another several months. The young men that I am instructing have asked me to do so, as well as several of the local businessmen. They realize that having men trained will be of great benefit to the community. As I look over a very accelerated course of studies, I may extend my stay as needed.

FROM THE DIARY OF HANNAH COLLINS KEYES
ON BOARD THE MONTEREY ZEPHYR
NOVEMBER 1857

I cannot truly believe I am leaving such a paradise. But as I write these words, the islands are but a sliver of green at the far western horizon. I am heading back to Monterey, back to the hospital, and back to my real life.

I have left all the medical supplies and books and medicine with my four young students. Only two of them are educated in reading, so the books will provide them instruction after I am gone. Of course, they are not qualified doctors, but they are much more skilled than most. I am sure they will be able to save lives.

They tell me it is their dream now to come back to America and to study. Perhaps they will one day do just that.

In the weeks following Jamison's departure, I could not recall ever feeling so leaden and colorless and invisible. It was as if joy suddenly bloomed after a long drought and then was snatched from me again by an evil windstorm. I trudged about, not seeing, not caring, not tasting.

But no one can be so gray and be a believer at the same time. God does not desire any of his children to be without joy.

I decided I would make use of my time and threw myself into my teaching.

And I wrote a long letter to my mother and father, which I am carrying with me. I have apologized to them for the last time, and I seek their forgiveness, though I will not grovel for it. I have sent along a bank draft, which is most of my money on earth. It means so little to me. It will be enough for them to find housing and live comfortably for the rest of their lives–should they choose to spend it wisely.

I will have an income from the hospital upon my return and that will be sufficient. What Jamison said about me that day was true, painfully so. I did desire wealth. I did seek out the comfort of riches. And now I realize that wealth is all but a vapor and will disappear in an instant.

I am returning home, to be a doctor. And I believe that is the true promise of my life.

From a Letter from Jamison Pike, dated February 1858
Sent from Auckland, New Zealand
Forwarded and received in Monterey, California
September 1858

My Dearest Hannah,

I have never thought I could be this far away and still be on this noble globe. This island is so very, very, very far away. I trust this letter will find you well. The man I have entrusted it to has pledged on his Holy Bible that he will hand deliver it to you in great haste.

I have found the story that I seek. The battles between the native people and the settlers here are fierce and without comparison to anything I have seen in my travels. Yet I am certain to maintain my safe distance and merely act as an observer of this struggle.

The land here is fiercely beautiful. Within these two small islands there are such divergent climes that one has a tropical rain forest and the other glaciers and fjords. In between lie volcanoes and hot springs and lakes that reek of sulfur and brimstone. Parts of the land appear much like I would think hell itself appears–filled with stench and steam and molten mud pits, bubbling and oozing from fires deep within the earth. There are the oddest of birds and animals here, such as I have never encountered, and caves filled with millions of glowworms.

The settlers fight with the land, trying to tame it; all the while the Maori struggle against them. Darts and arrows appear out of nowhere, streaking across the sky, often finding their flesh amidst screams of surprise, pain, and terror.

It is a story that needs to be told. And it appears that I am the first–and only– journalist from America who has set foot on these lands.

This journey has all the makings of a fantastic novel on a grand scale.

Yet despite all the grandness and all the strangeness and all the wondrous sights I have beheld, I can see only you in my dreams. I think back to those nights on the shore, holding you close, tasting your sweet lips, feeling your heart beat next to mine–and when those visions present themselves to me, I am overtaken. It is all I can do to keep from swooning over the passion I feel for you.

Hannah, I miss you and I love you and I will return to you as soon as I am able.

And I vow that my promise to you will be broken by neither man nor nature.

I will return. I promise you that.

All my love,

Jamison

Hannah read the letter a hundred times that first day and a dozen times every day after, and she slipped the paper into her Bible so she might never forget to pray for his safety.

FROM THE DIARY OF HANNAH COLLINS KEYES
MONTEREY, CALIFORNIA
NOVEMBER 1858

Life in this village goes on.

There is talk of Gage standing for the governor's position in the next election. He would be such a sound choice. As he ages, he matures and becomes more gentle and compassionate. It is an honor to call him an old friend.

Monterey grows as does all the state. The gold, they tell me, has been all but picked clean. There are some still mining, but so many of the forty-niners–as they called themselves due to the year they left–are now settling to be farmers or fishermen or shopkeepers.

I have seen Joshua! It is remarkable. We have been only days apart and yet neither of us had been able to bridge the gap. I have not beheld a happier man. He is surrounded by a giggling brood of five children. His wife–an oriental woman named Quen-li–is so graceful and gracious. I attended a church service and found his preaching to be more powerful than I remembered. His church, in Bakersfield, is home to nearly five hundred souls. (His hair is thinning, however, and his wife must be quite the cook, for he has taken on some extra girth.)

When we met he embraced me in a great hug and actually spun me around in the air. His soul must be filled with joy.

The only pain I feel is that I have gone for months without a word from Jamison. I pray for his safety every day and for his salvation twice as often. I know God will call him as his child. I know it.

Monterey, California
December 1858

The sharp rap on her door was so unexpected that Hannah jumped from her chair by the fire. Most guests simply stuck their head inside and called out her name. A knock meant that the visitor was a stranger.

As soon as Hannah opened the door, she knew the man was a sailor. His skin was burnished to a dark brown, his clothing smelled of salt and fish and canvas. He wore a bandanna about his neck as only a sailor can do.

"You be Hannah Keyes?" he asked. There was a tension in his voice.

"I am. And you are?"

"I be Gregory Longstreth. I'm a sailor . . . a captain. Well, I was, at any rate. I come at the request of a man named Jamison Pike."

Her heart leaped into her throat and thudded wildly. "Jamison? Is he safe? Come in, please come in."

He stepped inside. "I've a letter here," he said as he reached into his coat pocket and extracted a nearly threadbare envelope, tattered and torn in some spots. "I can't read, but he described you right well."

The letter was dated nearly five months prior.

My Dearest Hannah,

I have but a few minutes to write this. Our ship is trapped, and there are natives gathering at the shore. The captain says they will attack at nightfall–when the spirits of victory are most intense.

There is magic in the world, Hannah. There is. But I now believe with all my heart that God is greater.

I have held to my promise.

And now I will promise you once again. I will return to you. I will fight through all the demons of hell to once again hold you in my arms. I will continue to draw breath until my eyes once again gaze on your most lovely countenance. Without you I am as empty as the dark.

Promise me, Hannah, that you will wait for me. Promise me that your arms will be open for me when I return.

And until I do, listen for my voice on the wind. With every breeze you will hear the trees' branches and leaves calling your name and declaring my love to you. My heart will be carried by the clouds. Look up to the sky, and I will be there, Hannah.

Promise me you will wait.
Promise me your heart, my sweetest Hannah–my love, my life.
Always,
Jamison

Hannah's vision was lost to tears as she finished the letter. The words, done in thick pencil, were faint and almost illegible, but Hannah felt them as much as read them.

She sat back in a chair and looked up to the stranger before her. "What happened? Where is Jamison?"

Gregory averted his eyes. "Me ship was jammed on a reef in the Whitsunday Islands. And before we knew it, a band of the demon Maori set upon us. It be nightfall when they began, whooping their calls of the devil upon us. The ship, she took fire. And as she began to spark, Jamison thrust the letter at me and said God told him to pass it to me, for I would be home before him. He made me promise on the sainted soul of me mother that I would get this to you. And now I done it, and my job be through." He turned to the door as if to leave.

"Wait!" Hannah cried, clutching his sleeve. "What happened? Where is Jamison?"

He turned and looked away again. "Ma'am, I don't know. They be on us with fire and knives, and all hell descended on that poor ship. I got off on a skiff and paddled for my life. I turned and watched and me poor boat burned to the waterline. I took refuge in a small tuft of an island. When dawn came, I looked about, but all I seen was charred remains and the dead stacked on the beach. Them Maori took their heads clean off. The sand was as red as a scarlet robe, ma'am."

Hannah felt a sob in her chest. "And Jamison?"

"I looked, ma'am. I didn't find him. Maybe he took off and made it away. Maybe the sea got him." The sailor tipped at his hat. "I did what I promised, ma'am. I got that letter to you. And it be a promise kept."

Hannah did not hear the door shut, nor see the sunset, nor the sunrise. All she saw was Jamison's face before her eyes, lost in an ocean of tears.

From the Diary of Hannah Collins Keyes
January 1859

I do not know how I endured these last two weeks, so great was my pain. I actually called upon God to take me as well. He did not.

I have done little else save ponder my life. I shout at God and demand an explanation as to why he has taken something so precious from me. And to my greatest surprise, his answer fills my heart.

If Jamison is gone, he is with Jesus. And if that be true, and my heart says it is, then I am happy–for I will see him again in paradise.

The sudden, searing, and horrible pain is being replaced by God's peace in my heart. I do not understand it, but I accept it. If God had not planned for Jamison to return to me, then it is God's perfect and just plan. I will be sad forever–or at least that part of my heart will be sad forever.

But I will be content with God's plan.

I will, for I am his child.

Hannah finished writing. She laid her pen down on her desk. Rising, she took a single rose from a vase by the window. Carrying it gently in her hand, she walked down the path to the sea below. She stood at the edge of a large flat rock and stared out to the west, to where Jamison might be. She bowed her head and prayed. When she was finished, she looked to the heavens, then tossed the rose into the water.

The water accepted the flower, and within a heartbeat, the waves took it from her and carried it away on the cold, gray surface.

Hannah stared at the west until her tears stopped. Then she turned and began to slowly walk uphill, away from the ocean, and back to her home.

Epilogue

I have debated for weeks and weeks and weeks, and I am no more certain this is the proper ending than when I began the debate.

If I add a single additional word to the previous story, does all tension and worry evaporate like a mist in summer? If I write that single word, then the reader knows, in that instant, that I did not perish in the warm waters of New Zealand.

So be it.

My disappearance is how Hannah's story ended, and another story began.

In all her pain, Hannah's faith was resolute. She faced every day since the last we were together with joy and grace and the calm that only faith in God can produce.

Now the next year in her life would be so very, very different.

And I sit here, with pen in hand, ready to tell the final tale.

It will be the most difficult.

It will be my own.

Jamison Pike
Monterey Bay
The State of California
December 1861